8/31

BILLIONAIRE'S
BABY OF
REDEMPTION

BILLIONAIRE'S BABY OF REDEMPTION

MICHELLE SMART

MILLS & BOON

First published in Great Britain 2018
by Mills & Boon, an imprint of HarperCollins*Publishers*
1 London Bridge Street, London, SE1 9GF

Large Print edition 2019

© 2018 Michelle Smart

ISBN: 978-0-263-08193-0

MIX
Paper from
responsible sources
FSC® C007454

This book is produced from independently certified
FSC™ paper to ensure responsible forest management.
For more information visit www.harpercollins.co.uk/green.

Printed and bound in Great Britain
by CPI Group (UK) Ltd, Croydon, CR0 4YY

This book is for Jennifer Hayward,
Pippa Roscoe and Nic Caws,
who all made the writing of
Javier and Sophie's story an utter joy. xxx

CHAPTER ONE

JAVIER CASILLAS KEPT his eyes fixed on the wide corridor ahead of him, jaw clenched, feet working automatically. He could feel the eyes upon him; had felt them all evening in the private box he shared with his twin. He'd steeled himself for it. His wildly infamous parentage meant the media spotlight was something he'd learned to endure but the past two months had magnified that spotlight by a thousand.

He would give them exactly what he had always given them. Nothing.

He had not allowed a flicker of emotion to pass his face throughout the performance.

Inside, the rage had built. He'd watched Freya, the woman he'd intended to marry, put on the performance of her life, listened to the rapturous applause, and all he had wanted to do was go home and beat the hell out of his punching bag.

Tonight was the culmination of a long-standing dream between Javier and his twin brother,

Luis. A decade ago they'd finally had the funds to purchase the crumbling Madrid theatre and ballet school their prima ballerina mother had spent her childhood learning to dance at, buying the ballet company with it. They'd renamed it Compania de Ballet de Casillas in her memory and set about turning it into one of the most eminent ballet companies in Europe. They'd then bought another parcel of land close to it and built on it a brand-new state-of-the-art theatre and ballet school. Tonight was its grand opening. The world's media was out in force, but instead of focussing on the theatre and ballet company and celebrating Clara Casillas's memory, their focus was on Javier and his ex-fiancée.

The whole damn world knew she'd left him for his oldest friend.

What the whole world did not yet know was that Benjamin Guillem had stolen her in a sick game of revenge and that Freya had been happy to be stolen.

They were welcome to each other. Freya meant nothing to Javier. She never had.

The corridor he walked through on his way to the aftershow party forked. About to turn left with the group he was with, which included members of the Spanish royal family, Javier felt a hand settle on his shoulder and steer him firmly in the other direction.

No one other than his twin would have dared touch him in such a manner.

'What's the matter?' Javier asked, staring at his brother with suspicion as they walked.

'I wanted to talk to you alone,' Luis replied.

There was something in his brother's tone that lifted the hairs on the nape of his neck.

Tension had simmered between them since his twin's foolhardy trip to the Caribbean. How Luis thought that marrying Benjamin's sister would restore their reputations was still, well over a month on, beyond Javier's comprehension. Although wildly different from him in both looks and personality, his brother usually had excellent judgement. His opinion was the only one Javier ever thought worthy of consideration.

Fortunately his brother had seen sense at the last minute and returned to Madrid as a single man but things had not been right between them since.

Luis was his only constant. It had been the two of them, facing the world and everything it could throw at them, together, since they had shared the same womb.

Luis waited until they were out of anyone's earshot before turning to him. 'You knew we were ripping Benjamin off all those years ago, didn't you?'

The rage that had simmered in Javier all evening blazed at the mention of his nemesis's name.

Seven years ago the Casillas brothers had invited Benjamin to invest in a project they were undertaking in Paris, the creation of a skyscraper that became known as Tour Mont Blanc. They had invited his investment only because the seller of the land, to whom they had paid a significant deposit, suddenly told them they had until midnight to pay the balance or he would sell to another interested buyer. They didn't have the cash. Benjamin did.

'We didn't rip him off,' Javier reminded him icily. 'He was the fool who signed the contract without reading it.'

'And you should have warned him the terms had changed as you'd said you would. You didn't forget, did you?'

Javier might be many things but a liar was not one of them.

Luis had been the one to invite Benjamin onto the project. His investment was worth twenty per cent of the land fee. In the rush of sealing the deal Luis had told Benjamin it meant twenty per cent of the profits. Their lawyer, who drew up the contract in record time, had been the one to point out that the Casillas brothers would be doing all the work and that Benjamin's profit share should be only five per cent, a point Javier had agreed with.

The contract had been changed accordingly. Javier had emailed it to Benjamin expecting him to read the damn thing and negotiate if the new terms were not to his liking.

'I knew it.' Luis took a deep breath. 'All these years and I've told myself that it had been an oversight on your part when I should have accepted the truth that you never forget. In thirty-five years you have never forgotten anything or failed to do something you promised.'

'I never promised to email him.' Javier never made promises he didn't intend to keep. People could say what they liked about him—and frequently did, although never to his face—but he was a man of his word.

'Not an actual promise,' Luis conceded. 'But

look me in the eye and tell me it wasn't a deliberate act on your part.'

Luis had asked him to give Benjamin a heads-up about the changes in terms when Javier emailed the contract. At no point had Javier agreed to this request and Luis should be thankful for it. Benjamin's failure to read the contract before signing it had made the Casillas brothers richer to the tune of two hundred and twenty-five million euros. Benjamin had still made an excellent profit—*profit*—of seventy-five million and all he'd had to do for that substantial sum was transfer some funds. That he'd had the nerve to sue them over it was beyond the pale. That Benjamin had refused to accept the court's judgement when the judge had thrown the case out, and then stolen Javier's fiancée from him, was despicable.

And the world thought *he* was the bad man in all this?

Blind, prejudiced fools, the lot of them. He knew what they all thought. The world looked at his face and saw his murderer father.

'For what reason would it have been deliberate?' he asked coldly.

'That is for your conscience to decide. All I

know for sure is that Benjamin was our friend. I have defended you and I have fought your corner—'

'*Our* corner,' Javier corrected, his limited patience right at the point of snapping.

Now his own *twin* was questioning his motives?

What happened to the loyalty that had always bound them together?

'I assume this burst of conscience from you is connected to that damned woman.'

He'd had a sense of foreboding in the pit of his stomach since spotting Chloe Guillem, Benjamin's sister, in the audience that night.

Chloe had betrayed them as greatly as her brother had; had aided and abetted his plot to steal Freya and was, unquestionably, the cause of all the tension that had hung between Javier and Luis since Luis's return from the Caribbean.

A darkness rarely seen on his brother's face suddenly appeared, and before Javier had time to blink, Luis had grabbed him by the collar of his shirt. 'If you ever speak about Chloe in that way again then you and I are finished. Do you hear me? Finished.'

'If you're still defending her to me then I would

say we're already finished, *brother*.' He spat the last word directly into Luis's face.

Javier knew in his bones that something had happened between Luis and Chloe. Luis had always had a roving eye for the ladies but never had Javier had cause to suspect a shift in his brother's loyalty from it.

If Luis wanted to be with that bitch after what she had done to him then Luis could get the hell out of his life. Loyalty counted for everything and if Luis had lost sight of that then he was no brother to him.

Eyeball to eyeball, they glowered at each other, the venom seeping between them thick enough to taste.

Then Luis released his hold and stepped back.

Javier stared at the man he had shared a womb with, had shared a bedroom with, had fought with, had protected, had been protected by, had grieved with, the other side of the coin that was the Casillas twins, and watched him take backwards strides until he turned his back on him.

Breathing heavily, his hands clenched into fists, his hardening heart thumping, Javier watched Luis collide with a petite blonde woman in his haste to get away from him.

In all their thirty-five years neither of them had ever turned their back on the other.

It would be the first and last time Luis walked away from him.

In the periphery of his vision he saw the woman his treacherous brother had bumped into come towards him, but with his gaze on Luis's retreating back, it was only when she stood a few feet from him that her features came into focus.

Javier stared at the face he had last seen two months before when he had shown her to the door of his house.

Big pale blue eyes stared back, apprehension shining out of them.

The rage inside him ratcheted up another notch. Any higher and there was real danger he would combust.

This was a face he had never wanted to see close-up again.

'You should be at the aftershow party,' he snapped.

Sophie Johnson was part of Compania de Ballet de Casillas's *corps de ballet* and had a contractual obligation to attend the aftershow party.

Colour flamed the pretty heart-shaped face,

a pained crease forming in her brow. 'I quit the company two months ago.'

His heart thumped to hear that surprisingly sultry voice again.

Sophie had the sweet looks of an innocent but a voice that evoked thoughts of dark red satin sheets and dim lighting.

She had quit the company…?

He had hardly looked at the stage during the performance.

'Then what the hell are you doing here?'

But he knew. The pressing weight in his already tightly crushed chest told him the answer. He did not want to listen to it.

Her throat moved.

He'd kissed that throat…

'I need to talk to you.'

'Now is the worst time to speak to me.' And she was the last person he wished to see or speak to. Not now, when he could feel the fabric of his life dissolving around him.

He stepped past her and nodded a dismissal. 'Excuse me.'

He'd taken no more than two paces when she said, 'It's important.'

His heart began to thrum wildly, every nerve

ending standing on edge. Memories of their brief interlude surfaced in a wave, memories he'd not allowed himself to think of since showing her out of his home.

Pinching the bridge of his nose, he half turned to her and inhaled deeply.

'No,' he told her harshly. 'This is not a conversation we are going to have now. Go home.'

'But—'

'I said *no.*'

The vehemence in Javier's gravelly tone made Sophie recoil.

She watched him stride down the long corridor, clenching her jaw so tightly it stopped the threatening tears from splashing over her cheeks.

She had shed enough tears these past two months.

She staggered on shaking legs to the nearest chair and sank down into it.

Covering her mouth, she forced deep breaths into her choking airway and drew on all the ballet training that had been instilled in her since early childhood to stop her frame collapsing.

A glamorous couple strolled past her, hand in hand, the woman giving Sophie a sideways glance.

She tried to give the smile that normally came automatically whenever she met another person's eye but could barely move her cheek muscles.

She had once thought herself in love with Javier. *Fool!*

The stories about him being a cold-hearted bastard had all proven themselves to be true.

That she had ignored them, convinced that his was a soul in torment and that his reputation was not formed from a heart set in stone, was her own fault.

Sophie had taken one look at Javier when he'd paid a visit to the ballet company almost a year ago and felt her heart move and all the breath leave her body in a rush.

It had been a visceral reaction unlike anything she had experienced before.

Unlike the sculpted men of the ballet world, Javier was a bone crusher of a man, enormously tall and broad with a presence that made everyone look twice. He wasn't handsome in the traditional sense, his nose too wide and with a bend to it, his light brown eyes too hooded and with a permanent look of suspicion etched in them to ever be considered a pin-up, but he had a magnetism that turned those flaws into something mesmerising.

He had mesmerised her in more ways than one. Always attuned to others' emotions, the pain she had sensed in Javier had reached deep into her.

She had spent months longing for a glimpse of him. The times she did—and they were rare times, his involvement with the day-to-day running of the ballet company minimal—her heart would soar. She had known it was a crush that would go nowhere. Javier Casillas was the co-owner of her ballet company, a property magnate with a net worth she could scarcely comprehend, an arrogant, aloof figure who conjured fear and admiration in equal measure. He would never look twice at her.

But he did look twice at Freya.

Freya was her oldest and closest friend, the reason for Sophie being in Madrid dancing for the company that had made Freya a star. Freya was beautiful. Freya was a dancer with the world at her pointe shoes, a dancer who stole the heart of everyone who watched her perform.

Sophie had never shared her feelings for Javier with Freya. It had been too personal and unlikely to share with anyone.

Javier's marriage proposal and Freya's acceptance of it had devastated her.

For months she had sat on her despondency, determined to support her oldest friend even if she did have grave misgivings about their forthcoming loveless marriage that had nothing to do with her own breaking heart. She even gamely agreed to be their bridesmaid.

Then, the week before they were due to exchange their vows, Freya had run off with Benjamin Guillem, leaving Javier for dust. A media frenzy had ensued.

Sophie had been trying to do a good deed when she'd gone to Javier's home. She'd been packing Freya's stuff for her from the flat they shared and had come across a copy of Freya and Javier's prenuptial agreement and a file of other pertinent legal documents. Freya didn't want them, so, not knowing what else to do, Sophie had decided the best thing would be to let Javier decide. She was pretty sure he wouldn't want the documents to reach the public domain.

The day after Freya and Benjamin married, Sophie had braced herself and set off for Javier's home.

His house was a secluded villa that more resembled a palace than a home. She'd had to speak into a camera before the electric gates had slowly opened and admitted her into his domain.

She remembered walking the long driveway, sick to her stomach with pain for him. He might not have loved Freya but he must be shattered that she had left him for his oldest friend and in such a public fashion too.

The whole world knew about it and had put the blame squarely on Javier's shoulders without knowing even a basic fact—even she didn't know a fact about it, Freya's only communication being the one asking her to pack her belongings together—and was seeming to revel in portraying him as a monster in disguise. Sophie's heart had twisted to hear the vile rumours about him.

Expecting a member of his household staff to open the front door for her, she had been surprised to find it opened by Javier himself.

What followed had been even more unexpected.

That was when she'd understood his ruthless reputation had been based on truth.

If he'd even given her a single thought since, he would have known she'd left his ballet company, left Madrid and returned to England. In the vain hope he would seek her out she had left her forwarding address on the company files.

He could have found her without any effort if he had wanted to.

He hadn't even noticed her absence from the stage that night.

She'd used those two months of silence to come to terms with the reality of her situation and get herself in an emotional place where she could face Javier again.

She would seek him out again tomorrow; seek him every single day until he was willing to have the conversation they so desperately needed to have.

Only when she was certain she could get back to her feet without her legs crumpling did she stand up, inhaling deeply.

Concentrating on putting one foot in front of the other, Sophie headed back the way she had come. The theatre's wide corridors were almost deserted now.

When she reached the top of the ornate red-carpeted stairs that led down into the foyer, her heart skipped to see Javier striding up to her, his long legs taking the steps two at a time.

She held tightly onto the gold railing and stared at the emotionless, menacing face fixed on her.

When he reached the top, he inclined his head

for her to follow him, leading her to a secluded section of the corridor.

He stopped walking and gazed down at her, breathing heavily through his nose.

'Why now?' He ran a hand through his hair. 'Why did you choose tonight of all nights to tell me? Why not approach me in private?'

She kept her gaze steady on him. 'Because after the way you treated me, I didn't trust you would agree to see or speak to me.'

He had gone from blazing passion to ice-cold in the whisper of a second.

He had escorted her out of his home.

His face twisted. 'You are carrying my child?'

How she kept her composure to answer him without bursting into tears she would never know. 'Yes. We're going to have a baby.'

CHAPTER TWO

HOT DARKNESS FILLED Javier's head, swimming like a blood-red fog through him.

He'd known the moment Sophie had come into focus why she was there but his already overwhelmed brain had fought to deny it.

He was going to be a father.

But the mother wasn't the perfect woman he had sought to bear his children but this waif-like creature who had ignited something in him that should never have been allowed to breathe.

He wanted children. He and his treacherous brother had adopted their mother's surname the moment they could legally dump their father's and he wanted to carry that name on to the next generation.

He'd waited his entire adult life for the perfect woman to come along and bear him those children.

Freya had been that woman. Beautiful, coldly perfect Freya, who would have given him beautiful, perfect children and who had not elicited the smallest glimmer of desire in him and shown no desire for him either. Perfection in all ways.

Javier knew the danger of passion. His orphaned state was living proof of those dangers.

The dangerous blood that had swirled in his father lived in his own veins too. It pumped hot and strong inside him, a living thing he was reminded of every time he looked in a mirror.

He should never have allowed Sophie, this warm-blooded, sensitive creature, to come anywhere within his orbit.

She sighed and pulled a business card from the small black bag she carried. She held it out to him with those tiny fingers that had caused such mayhem to his skin when she had touched him.

'This is the hotel I'm staying at,' she said quietly. 'Take the time to process what's happening and then come and find me when you're ready to talk.'

'What is there to talk about?' he asked roughly, not taking the card, not willing to risk touching her in any way.

He knew what he had to do. There was no point in wasting air discussing what was a foregone conclusion.

He'd walked away from her with his head reeling and the weight of the world crashing down on him. He'd intended to work all the stress out and bring himself to a point where he could trust himself to have this difficult conversation without exploding.

He'd got as far as his car when the implications had really hit him and he'd known that to leave her there would make him as big a monster as the world believed him to be.

'We're having a baby, Javier. I would say there's a lot to talk about.'

'Not for me there isn't. If you're carrying my child then there's only one thing that needs to be decided on and that's the date of our wedding.'

She blinked. 'You are willing to marry me?'

'My child will bear my name and if you want any kind of financial support from me then you will agree to it.'

Sophie was naïve. Damn her, she'd been a virgin, a fact she had neglected to mention when they'd been ripping each other's clothes off.

If she had any illusions about him or their future relationship let her have them dispelled now. If she didn't already know what kind of a man he was—and his failure to seek her out in any form these past few months must have given her some clue—then let her know now.

She would never know it but he was doing her a kindness.

To his surprise, a small smile curved her pretty lips. 'You don't have to threaten me. I want us to marry.'

That took him aback. 'You do?'

Her throat moved as she nodded.

He laughed, a guttural sound that grated to his own ears. For all her naivety and surface sweetness, Sophie was already making the financial calculations of how being his wife would significantly improve her bank account.

But there was no returning laugh from Sophie. Her eyes did not flicker or leave his face. 'Our child is innocent. It did not choose to be conceived. It deserves to know and be wanted by both its parents.'

He made no attempt to hide his cynicism. 'If that is true then why wait so long to tell me? You must have known for weeks.'

He was no pregnancy expert but he had studied biology at school and knew the ways a woman's body worked.

'I knew within a week,' she said steadily. 'I

could feel changes happening inside me. I took the test the day after my period was due, so I have known for certain for six weeks. Technically I'm ten weeks pregnant as the due date is taken from the date of my last period. I waited before telling you because I needed my head to be in the right place before I faced you again.'

'Did you have to research the best ways to leverage cash from the situation?' he mocked brutally. He had never met a woman who didn't have cash signs ringing in her eyes.

Having more money than he could spend in a thousand lifetimes was good for many things but leverage was its greatest gift. He'd used his wealth to buy Freya and she, the coldly perfect prima ballerina that she was, had been happy to be purchased. It was what had made her so ideal for him. 'Is that why you have set your path on marriage to me?'

But, again, there was no flicker in Sophie's pale blue eyes. 'I want nothing but what is best for our child.'

From the corner of his eye he saw two security guards approach. They would be making a sweep of the theatre before locking up for the night; the aftershow party taking place in a basement conference room.

If there was one thing Javier despised it was people knowing his business. His family had been fodder for the world's consumption since before his birth.

He might still be trying to process that he was going to be a father but already he knew that he would do whatever it took to protect his child.

Rubbing his jaw, he took a deep breath. 'Whatever you say your motives are, our unborn child is the only thing that matters.'

'Yes,' she interjected softly.

'It is late. This is something that needs to be discussed when we have fresh minds. I have had an incredibly difficult day.' She couldn't begin to understand how difficult it had been. 'My driver will take you to your hotel. Get some sleep. You look tired.'

That made her eyes flicker.

'I'll have you brought to me in the morning,' he continued, now walking back to the stairs. He kept his eyes focussed straight ahead of him, no longer wishing to look at the woman who had just detonated a bomb into his already turbulent life.

The bomb was of his own making, he accepted

grimly. He was the damn fool who had failed to use a condom for the first and only time in his life.

He was the fool who'd invited her into his home.

Their baby was the consequence of that fool-hardiness and, as Sophie had already pointed out, an innocent in all of this.

She remained silent as she kept pace beside him, silent all the way down the stairs and through the foyer. Only when they reached the exit door did she turn to him and say, 'What time will your driver collect me in the morning?'

'Arrange that with him.' He stepped out into the warm night air and strode to his waiting driver.

'Take Miss Johnson to her hotel,' he said, then, without a word of goodbye or a second glance at her, set off for his home.

He could feel Sophie's gaze upon him but kept his sight fixed ahead, increasing his pace.

As he power-walked the three miles to his home, the memories he'd spent two months suppressing came back to him with crystal clarity.

He'd woken that fateful day to the news Freya and Benjamin had married and a barrage of hate mail. Someone had leaked his personal email address online and keyboard warriors had had an excellent time aiming their poisoned ire at him. So angry had he been that he'd dismissed his household staff for the day.

His rage was best kept private. It was safer that way. For everyone.

And then his intercom had rung and he'd looked through the monitor to see Sophie standing there, a thick folder in her arms, which, she had claimed over the intercom, contained private documents of his.

He'd recognised her immediately. Freya's dance colleague and flatmate. The wallflower who had never met his eye on the few occasions he'd been in her presence. If anyone had inside information on Freya and Benjamin's treachery that he could use to his advantage it would be her.

It had been a baking summer's day. She'd been dressed in a thin pale grey shirt dress, her long light blonde hair tied in a loose plait. When she'd removed enormous sunglasses to speak to him and fixed huge pale blue eyes on him, he'd seen compassion shining from them.

Not once in his adult life had he stared anyone in the eye and not seen a glimmer of fear shine back at him. Grown men, titans of industry and power brokers would shake his hand with a nervous laugh; glamorous, self-confident women would give him the come-to-bed eyes with excitement-laced fear.

This young English woman, a petite ballerina with the appearance of a waif, had turned up at his home and displayed not an ounce of fright.

The rage that had been bubbling so furiously inside him had suddenly reduced.

She had given him the sweetest, most sympathetic smile he'd ever been on the receiving end of. 'How are you holding up?' she'd asked softly.

In the week since Benjamin had stolen Freya from him, Sophie was the first person to have asked him that. The most he'd received from his twin had been a stoical slap to the shoulder.

He'd invited her in, made her a coffee, led her to the dining room, sat beside her at the huge table with the documents between them and quizzed her.

When she'd professed her innocence in the matter of Freya and Benjamin, he'd been surprised to find he believed her.

This belief had disconcerted him.

She had disconcerted him with those non-judgemental eyes and her subtle yet obvious compassion.

He'd found himself trying to get a rise out of her, asking if she'd read the documents, making it sound like an accusation.

She'd been unfazed and unabashed. She'd nodded and said, 'Yes, I read through them with Freya. I won't be sharing them with anyone, so don't worry.'

'You won't share the details with the media?' he'd asked cynically.

'If I wanted to share anything with them I would have done so by now. They've been camped outside my apartment block all week.'

Something had crept into his veins at that, something he'd never felt before.

That this petite young thing should be harassed with no one there to protect her had set the anger boiling again.

Of course, he knew her waif-like frame belied a physical strength all ballerinas had but that didn't change what his eyes saw when he looked at her.

Dios, he'd been unable to tear his eyes from her. He had never seen such naturally pink rosebud lips before...

A new kind of tension had sparked to life.

Sophie's eyes had kept flickering to him, then

darting away, pretty colour flushing across her pretty cheeks.

She really was incredibly pretty. How had he not noticed it before…?

He'd found himself leaning closer to her, catching a whiff of a light, floral perfume that had delighted his senses.

'Speaking with the media would boost your profile,' he'd pointed out.

A burst of antipathy had glittered in her eyes. 'I don't care. I'm not going to add to the frenzy and make things worse for you.'

Again, he'd found himself believing her but also curious…

Worse for *him*?

She didn't even know him.

Professional dancers spent their lives fighting to get to the top and when you were as driven as that any advantage for name recognition would be snatched upon. His own mother had been shameless in her quest for media attention.

Sophie had ducked her head and refused to answer questions even when it would have seen her face plastered over the tabloids as a bit player in the biggest scandal Spain—indeed, most of Europe—had had for years.

What was her agenda? Everyone had one, so what was hers? Why go out of her way for him?

He'd leaned even closer and dropped his voice to a murmur. 'Why are you here?'

The colour already staining her cheeks had darkened, the pale blue eyes darkening with it. It had been the most beguiling sight.

She had cleared her throat, the pink rosebud lips opening and closing as if she were trying to get out words that did not want to be revealed.

It was sheer impulse that had led him to kiss those lips.

What happened next had been utter madness.

Javier increased his pace and inhaled the Madrid autumn night air deeply to counteract the blood thickening all over again at the vivid memories.

She had kissed him back.

And then he had hauled her out of her chair and into his arms.

For a few brief moments all his torment and anger had been dispelled and forgotten.

Sophie's kisses had been the sweetest he had ever tasted and instantly addictive.

Desire like nothing he had ever experienced

had pulsed through him. Heady, hungry and utterly consuming.

He tried to throw the memories off him now, not wanting to remember any more, disgusted with himself for the manner in which he'd used her hot, willing body.

That was his only saving grace, he thought grimly.

Sophie had been utterly willing.

There had been nothing one-sided about it.

In that moment, the madness had lived in both of them.

He'd spread her flat on his dining table, drinking in her hot, sweet kisses as he'd plunged into her that first time. He'd felt the resistance of her body and known in an instant what it had meant.

Her eyes had widened.

He would have pulled out there and then if she hadn't then smiled at him, put her hands to his face and kissed him so deeply that he had lost all sense of himself.

But as soon as it was over the only thing he'd been able to taste was revulsion, at himself for his actions and at Sophie for throwing away her virginity in such a seedy way and on a man such as him.

But mostly at himself.

They hadn't used any protection.

He hadn't used any protection.

He'd needed her gone before he said or did something he regretted.

He felt no pride in remembering how he'd coldly walked to his front door and held it open for her.

She would never know it but he'd been saving her from herself.

And now she was pregnant. Sweet, sweet Sophie was pregnant with his child.

Damn it all to hell.

Javier had experienced only one day worse than this. The day his father had murdered his mother.

Sophie waited until the driver opened her door before stepping out in front of the imposing Tuscan-style villa that was Javier's home.

The first time she had been there she had been filled with so many emotions she had hardly taken anything in other than its titanic size.

Now there was an array of sights and smells filling her senses. She'd noticed that increase in her perceptions during the first week of her pregnancy. It was like discovering secrets of the world, an unexpected symptom that warmed her.

She needed all the warmth she could get.

She'd lain in her hotel bed telling herself over and over that she was doing the right thing. Not telling Javier about the pregnancy had never been on the cards. He was the father. He deserved to know and deserved to be involved if that was what he wanted.

She was glad for their child's sake that he did want to be and that he'd come to the decision of marriage so quickly. For once, it hadn't been the anguish she always felt at the thought of disappointing her adoptive parents, good, loving, decent people who believed strongly in the sanctity of marriage, but for her child. Her child deserved nothing less.

Sophie often thought of her biological father. Had he ever known of her conception? Had he been party to the decision to abandon her? Or had he spent twenty-four years unaware he had a daughter out there, being raised by people who were strangers to him?

These were just some of the many questions that had haunted her life. She had long stopped seeking answers for them—they all led to dead ends—but had never stopped wondering. She would wonder about the man and woman who had given her life for ever.

Her child would not. Whatever happened between Sophie and Javier, her child would know who both its parents were.

Stepping onto the marble stairs that led to a wrap-around porch, Sophie followed the driver, who had insisted on taking her suitcase, to the front door.

Everything about Javier's home looked so much richer and more palatial than her first and last visit. Private and secluded from the bustle of Madrid's busy streets, it screamed opulence. This was the kind of house any self-regarding billionaire would be proud to call home.

Marble pillars flagged the wide oak door that opened before the driver could raise his hand to knock.

Javier stood there, casually dressed in an olive-green shirt unbuttoned at the neck and black jeans that showcased the muscularity of his thighs. Thick stubble covered his jawline. His hooded light brown eyes met hers for the briefest of moments before he nodded his thanks at the driver and dismissed him.

'Refreshments are being made for us,' he said as he led her through the grand reception room twice as high as a normal room and adorned with ancient Egyptian relics, including a bust of a sphinx almost as large as Javier himself.

The first time she had been there she had been too overawed at being invited in by the man she had mooned over for so long to pay much attention to anything, but now she was determined to keep an analytical head and pay attention to everything.

'Is it okay to leave my suitcase in here?' she asked.

He stopped and turned, a frown creasing his forehead, fleshy, sensuous lips pulling together. 'Why have you brought your suitcase with you?'

'I checked out of my hotel.'

Now his eyes narrowed. 'I hope you are not expecting to move in today.'

'I've checked out of the hotel because my reason for staying in it is done—you know about the baby. I'll fly back to England when we've finished discussing everything and set a game plan out.'

Disconcerted, Javier ran his fingers through

his hair. He could read nothing but honesty in Sophie's wide gaze and he didn't trust it an inch.

The dreamless sleep he had hoped for had proven fruitless. He doubted he'd had more than an hour of solid sleep.

Sophie was pregnant with his child. The puffiness of her eyes was proof she must have found sleep as elusive as he had, but where his stomach was knotted with thorny barbs she had a calm serenity about her.

She'd had a head start on getting her head around being a parent, he reminded himself grimly. She'd known for certain for six whole weeks and had kept it to herself when she should have told him immediately.

Dios, his head felt ready to combust. All these betrayals, it was like a sickness. Benjamin's refusal to accept his own negligence and then stealing Freya from him had been only the start, culminating in the disaster that had been the night before, the night when he and his twin celebrated their mother's memory with a world determined to remember her torrid death rather than her magnificent life, now tainted for ever. Luis, his own twin, had betrayed it and had betrayed him so greatly it felt as if he'd been sucker-punched.

The business they had built from nothing would have to be split, the brotherhood that had driven his life rent apart with one gross act of disloyalty.

And he was going to be a father. He was going to marry a woman so far removed from his ideal of what a suitable wife for himself should be that she could be from Venus.

'Let us discuss our game plan now,' he said icily, leading her through to one of his four living rooms, his least favourite for relaxing. He would never allow himself to relax again around Sophie. It was too dangerous, especially for her.

Initially he'd planned for their meeting to take place in the dining room but when he'd stepped into it a powerful memory of making love to her on that table had sent a thrill of desire racing through him, so, with a click of his fingers, he'd ordered the documents to be moved.

He indicated the sofas arranged in a square around a coffee table. 'Take a seat.'

She obeyed his command by sitting gracefully and crossing her legs.

He wished she hadn't. Until that moment he had refused to pay any attention to her attire but now his eyes focussed on the athletic but decidedly feminine figure clad in fashionably ripped jeans and an oversized thin sweater that fell off the shoulder. She'd left her long blonde hair loose.

A member of his staff entered the room carrying the refreshments he'd ordered and he was glad of the diversion.

He waited until the drinks and pastries had been laid out before seating himself opposite Sophie and pouring himself a coffee. 'Help yourself.'

Again, she obeyed. Soon she had a palmier on a plate on her lap and was sipping a glass of fresh orange juice.

He allowed himself a slight breath of relief. So far she was displaying all the signs of obedience. Things would be much easier if she were to fall in with his plans without questioning them. He knew little about Sophie but the impression he'd formed before he'd stupidly made love to her had been of a shy woman who had little in the way of spine or gumption.

He'd climbed out of his bed that morning knowing he needed to learn something concrete about the woman he was going to marry, so he had woken the ballet company's human resources manager, ordering her to email Sophie's employment file to him. It had been a quick but illuminating read. Sophie had been educated at the same ballet school as Freya, worked for a provincial English ballet company upon her graduation, then followed Freya to Madrid. She'd had no starring roles in any ballet production of note and was described in the file as warm but shy.

It had been illuminating in that it had confirmed his prior thoughts about her.

She was probably so relieved he'd agreed to marry her that she would now agree to anything to keep him onside.

Perfect.

He downed his black coffee and poured another, then waited until she had bitten a delicate amount of pastry before saying, 'Those documents on the table are for you to read through. They're the prenuptial agreement you'll need to sign before we can marry.'

Her eyes remained on his face as she chewed slowly. When she swallowed, a flicker of pink tongue popped to the side of her mouth to lick a stray crumb.

Javier inhaled deeply and forced his attention back to the documents she now leaned forward to pick up, only to be confronted by a glimpse of cleavage as her sweater dipped.

He clenched his hands into fists and commanded his loins to stay neutral.

Sophie was only a woman. There was nothing special about her, nothing that should make his loins twitch and his veins heat. He would not allow the memories of their one time together to trick his body.

She leaned back and casually flicked through the documents he'd woken his lawyer at six a.m. to produce, right after he'd called the human resources manager.

After a few minutes of silence she put the file back on the coffee table and stared at him. 'This is the same contract you signed with Freya.'

'With a few modifications.' Namely the section on children being in the future at a time of his wife's choosing. That was an issue now taken out of both their hands. 'Everything about how our marriage is to proceed is laid out in black and white. There will be no ambiguity and no need for us to argue about any issues at any point in the future because they are all set out in this. You will see that you are also generously provided for.' He would treat her fairly and well. She would be his wife and the mother of his child and he would respect her for both those roles.

Something undefinable sparked in her eyes. 'Your provisions are generous but the rest of it… I'm not signing this.'

He fixed her with the stare that had been known to make an entire conference room of business people freeze. 'If you want me to marry you, you will.'

She shook her head slowly. 'No.'

No. A simple one-syllable word rarely uttered in his earshot and even more rarely directly at him.

He leaned forward and rested his elbows on his thighs. 'Then let me explain it like this. If you won't sign the contract I will not marry you and I will take custody of our child. If you want to be a mother to it then you will sign. Otherwise you can leave right now and stop wasting my time.'

CHAPTER THREE

SOPHIE STARED INTO the light brown eyes fixed on hers with such hooded cruelty and experienced an unexpected wave of compassion for him.

She didn't want to feel anything for Javier, but right then, how could she not, even when she knew it was her compassion towards him that had got them to this point?

This was a man who had lived through the worst thing a child could live through: the murder of his mother at the hands of his father. Judged and feared by the world, was it any wonder he hit back at it by encasing his heart in steel? She had felt his pain from the first moment she had set eyes on him and fallen under his spell.

He folded his arms across his chest, his stare menacing. 'Well?'

Her heart thundering painfully beneath her ribs, Sophie got to her feet.

Not giving herself time to reflect on what she was doing, she walked around the coffee table and stood before him. Javier was such a tall man and she so short that they were the same height with him seated.

She put her hand to his and locked her fingers around his wrist, feeling him jolt with surprise at her forwardness. His surprise was to her advantage, enabling her to pull his arm free from across his chest and place his hand on her belly.

She tried not to shiver as the heat of his hand permeated through the fabric of her sweater and sent shocks of sensation travelling through her bloodstream.

She had to ignore it.

She should wish she had ignored it two months ago but that would mean wishing her unborn child away and she would never do that.

He tried to pull his hand away but she refused to let go, holding it tightly to her abdomen, grateful for the first time for the physical strength all the ballet training she had endured through her life had given her.

'I know you can't feel it yet but, under your hand, our child is growing inside me,' she said quietly. 'It is over an inch long and has eyes and ears and a mouth. Its fingernails are beginning to grow and it can already bend its arms and legs.

You can't feel it but *I* can. My body's changing because of this little kumquat, and our little kumquat is wholly dependent on me. As it grows, it will learn the sound of my voice. If you are by my side it will learn your voice too and when it's born it will recognise both of us. It is innocent of everything and needs us both, so I beg you, please, do not use our child as a weapon to threaten me with. I won't sign that contract because I disagree profoundly with the reasons behind it and I disagree with every one of the clauses you have in it. If we are going to marry then it should be a real marriage.'

Not the cold business arrangement he had made with Freya. That was a marriage Sophie could never tolerate for either herself or her child.

Javier wrenched his hand from her hold, his movement so sudden that Sophie stepped back in shock, straight into the coffee table. She would have toppled backwards onto it if his reflexes hadn't kicked in and the hand he had just snatched from her hadn't flown forward to grip onto her elbow and pull her to him.

She gazed into the eyes holding her with such loathing, greatly aware of the heavy thuds of her heart and the melting of her insides as his tangy scent crept into her senses.

His chest rose and fell at speed, his tanned throat moving, his lips pulling together, nostrils flaring.

For the wildest moment Sophie felt a compulsion to take the one step forward needed to become flush with him.

How could she still react to him like this? He had made love to her, then escorted her out of his home moments later as if she were the carrier of a disease. He had made no effort to contact her when he knew there was a danger he had impregnated her. He'd cared so little that he hadn't noticed that she wasn't on the stage at the theatre opening, had not cared to discover she had left his ballet company.

She should not react like this to him but she would not lie that a part of her wasn't glad she still felt this desire for him. If she was going to get her way and forge a proper marriage with him then they needed a glue to keep them together other than their child.

Javier did not scare her. He probably should. He was a ruthless, coldly arrogant, wildly rich control freak. He'd threatened her with the removal of their child.

But he *was* human. She had experienced his human side, glimpsed the pain in his eyes and knew in her heart that his own heart wasn't so far gone in the dark that his humanity could not be reached.

She would never love him, not now she knew the depths of his cruelty, but, whether they married or not, their unborn child meant they would always be in the other's life.

Javier stared into pale blue eyes with a thousand emotions churning through him. Where had this woman with her calm, compassionate logic that could neuter his arguments come from?

And why the hell was his body straining towards her…?

Disgusted with himself, he released his hold on her elbow, got to his feet and strode away from her.

'I do not want a real marriage,' he told her as he paced. 'What you are asking for is impossible. I like my solitude.'

'We both need to make sacrifices. Speaking on a personal level, you are the last man I would wish to commit my life to but this is not about you or me, this is about our child, who deserves the best life can give. It deserves to be raised with a mother and father who are united. If you're worried that I'm after your money then I am happy to sign an agreement that protects your wealth if we divorce.'

He pounced on her words. 'You are already thinking that far ahead!'

He'd known she couldn't be as self-sacrificing as she was making herself out to be, her words all a script designed to make him feel like a bastard for wanting to protect her from the dangers he posed.

Dios, how could she be so naïve? There was a reason he had reached the age of thirty-five without a single long-term relationship to his name. For a woman proving herself to be far more intuitive than he had credited, she should surely be able to see it.

'If we both enter marriage with open minds we can make it work for our child, I truly believe that,' she replied, following him with her eyes. 'But I am not stupid. The odds are against us and we should work together to protect our child against every eventuality. I will be glad to sign a contract that states that should we divorce the only thing I get from you is a home of my own here in Madrid so we can share custody of our child. I don't want a war with you, Javier, and I absolutely do not want our child to be a casualty of it either. I would have thought you of all people could appreciate that.'

For a moment he stopped pacing to stare at her, stunned.

No one—*no one*—ever alluded to his parents, not to his face.

His parents' marriage had been fodder for the press long before his mother's death. His father, Yuri Abramova, had been a ballet dancer from Moscow from the days of the USSR and had defected to New York in the seventies. Clara had been a Spanish prima ballerina, much younger than her famous husband, whose own fame had soared with her talent until she had eclipsed him in all ways. Their marriage had been volatile and filled with infidelities and jealousy on both sides. Lovers had popped up like cockroaches to sell their stories to an eager press who had known stories of the most famous marriage in the ballet world always sold out its print run.

In the midst of all this toxicity had been two boys who had both suffered but who had got through it by sticking together and protecting the other.

If someone had told the young Javier that his twin, his only confidant, would one day betray him for a woman he would have laughed in their face.

But now their brotherhood was dead, as dead as the mother Javier had worshipped but who had always preferred Luis and as dead as the father who had worshipped Javier and hated Luis.

His entire past was gone. The grandparents who had raised him and Luis after their mother's death and father's incarceration had died within a year of each other a decade ago. Louise Guillem, his mother's closest friend, who had been like an aunt to them, had died seven years ago. Benjamin, Louise's son and Javier and Luis's oldest playmate, was alive and kicking but effectively dead to him.

They were all gone and yet…

Inside this woman who stared unblinkingly back at him, life grew. A child. His child.

An unexpected stab of guilt plunged into his guts.

Sophie was right. Their child was innocent, just as he and Luis had been innocent. His child deserved more than to be used as a weapon before it had grown bigger than his thumb.

Staring hard at the mother of his child, he could see in her eyes that already she loved it enough to fight for its best interests in any way she could. As a child he would have given anything to have been on the receiving end of that kind of love from his own mother.

Was that how Sophie had found the nerve to allude to his childhood and not flinch? How else could she look at him and not recoil in fear at the man who stood before her?

But she hadn't been scared when she had turned up at his door with the same documents he'd had remade early that morning in her name...

Coldly perfect Freya had never displayed any overt fear for him either, but that had been understandable because coldly perfect Freya had never shown any emotions other than on the stage when she came alive in her dance.

Why wasn't Sophie scared of him?

He dragged his fingers down his face and contemplated her some more before nodding slowly. '*Bueno*. I do not know what your expectations of a real marriage are...'

'One that doesn't give the husband a licence to take a mistress for a start,' she interjected drily.

He gaped at this unexpected glimpse of humour. 'You expect fidelity?'

He'd had the clause put in that he could take a mistress if he chose as a black-and-white warning that he was committing to a marriage only on paper. Freya hadn't blinked an eye at it.

'My only expectation is that we both try to make things work.' She expelled a long breath of air and sat back on the sofa. Taking hold of her glass, she gave him a rueful smile. 'All we can do is our best. To be faithful, to be honest, to just…try.'

How could he argue with that? he thought, anger mixing with incredulity.

Sophie had flipped everything on its head and made it all sound so easy.

Did she not see that she was asking the impossible? Javier had no idea if he was capable of fidelity; he'd never had a relationship run long enough for him to find out.

But honesty he could do. He was always honest.

'Do not expect the impossible,' he warned her darkly. 'You know the kind of marriage I had envisaged for myself. I like solitude. I always have and always will. I suspect your idea of a real marriage differs greatly from mine.'

She shrugged. 'The contract makes clear the kind of marriage you want, my refusal to sign it makes clear it's not the marriage I want. We'll both have to make compromises. I'm willing to try if you are.'

For the first time in his adult life Javier found himself in the uncomfortable position of having to bend to someone else's will. With Luis there had been much compromise in the way they ran their business but they had been so in tune with each other's thoughts it had never been an issue. Besides, Luis was his twin. It was a different scenario.

Sophie was only…

The mother of his unborn child.

Damn her, being so reasonable, leaving him little room to manoeuvre.

The thought of sharing his daily life with another person made his skin crawl. The thought of sharing it with this woman made his chest tighten and his stomach cramp.

He made sure her attention was fixed on him before giving a sharp nod. '*Bueno.* We will try it your way, but I warn you now, keep your ex-

pectations realistic. I live my life to please myself. This is my home and it is run to suit me. I
will make accommodations for our child when
it is born, but if you want to enter a marriage
where the small details of our lives are not already agreed on then you must live with the consequences when you find the reality not to your
liking.'

For the third time in as many months, Sophie
approached Javier's front door. This would be
her last approach as a visitor. When she stepped
through it this time, she would be staying.

This beautiful villa was going to be her home.

This was the best course of action, she told
herself firmly, for what had to be the hundredth
time.

The past fortnight had passed in a whirl of ac-
tivity, Sophie busy packing and making arrangements for her new life. She had lived and worked
in Madrid for eighteen months but it had never
been permanent and she'd lived a minimal life
there, always intending to return to England for
good when her ballet career was over. Now, embracing that the rest of her life would be spent in

Madrid whatever happened in her marriage, she was moving her entire life over.

She had no idea what Javier had been doing since their short meeting where they had thrashed out an agreement that suited neither of them but was best for their child.

She would give their marriage her best shot and she would force him to give it his best too. He had agreed to try. She had to hold onto that even if his actions since she'd returned to England had been less than positive.

He'd politely declined her offer to go to the hospital with her for the first scan, claiming he was too busy, so she had gone with her mother.

Her mother, bless her gentle heart, had been enthralled with the image on the screen. Her father had spent an age staring at the grainy picture she had given him of it. It had broken Sophie's heart to tell the loving couple who had adopted her at eighteen months that their grandchild would be raised in Spain, but she had been able to offset their disappointment by promising lots of visits. She knew it had comforted them to know she would be marrying, although it had been another disappointment to them that they wouldn't meet the groom before the wedding day.

Her poor parents. They'd masked their disappointment at her unplanned pregnancy well but she'd seen the pained glances they'd exchanged before embracing her and offering their full support.

Her parents had both been virgins on their wedding day. Sophie had never expected to stay a virgin until her own but she had been waiting for the thunderbolt they had both told her about, that certainty that she had found 'the one', the man she would spend the rest of her life with. She would never willingly disappoint them with anything less.

Javier was the only man she had looked at and felt her heart and pulses soar.

She had emailed the scan to him but received no response, either positive or negative. His next message to her had been to confirm the date of their wedding, written in the style of a business memo.

The man who had threatened to take full custody of their child if Sophie didn't comply with his demands had so far shown zero interest in it.

She would force an interest. By the time their child was born in six months, she was determined Javier would be as excited for its arrival as she was. She didn't expect miracles. She doubted he would be a hands-on father—the thought of that towering inferno of a man changing a nappy evoked hysterical laughter in her—but for their child's sake she wanted Javier to reach a place where he could open his heart and love it.

She had to believe he was capable of love. She had to.

To be fair to him, he hadn't abandoned her completely. She'd arrived back in the UK to find a chauffeured car waiting for her at the airport, the driver informing her she had him at her disposal until her return to Madrid. When they had settled on the date for her to move in with him, Javier had insisted on sending his private jet to England to collect her. He'd also arranged for a company to collect and transport all her belongings. They should have beaten her here, her stuff all ready for her to unpack in the house she very much hoped would soon feel like home.

Her heart thudded painfully as she took the heavy knocker in her hand, not yet ready to simply walk into this mansion as if she belonged there. She had barely moved it when the door opened.

A thin man in a sober suit greeted her with a

nod. 'Miss Johnson, please, come in,' he said in impeccable English. 'I am Julio, Mr Casillas's butler. I run the household staff.'

Sophie tried to stop her eyes popping out of her head.

Javier had a butler? Wow.

On her previous two visits she had seen only one member of staff and had thought little of it. But now she did think about it and realised there was no way a house of these proportions and of such magnificence could be maintained by only one person.

'How many staff are there?' she asked curiously.

'Nine. Three of us live in. Can I get you any refreshment?'

'I ate on the flight over, thank you.'

He smiled. 'Then shall I show you to your room so you can get comfortable?'

'Is Javier not here?'

'Mr Casillas is in a meeting. He will be back this evening.'

She forced a smile to hide the pierce of disappointment.

Javier hadn't said he would be at home to meet her. She had made an assumption that he would want to greet her and make her feel welcome because that was what decent men did for the women carrying their child.

She had a feeling this was a deliberate act on Javier's behalf, a throwing down of the gauntlet, a reminder that this marriage was not how he wanted it and he would not have his space encroached.

'Then show me to my room,' she said with artificial brightness. 'Has my stuff arrived yet?'

'It was delivered last night,' he confirmed, leading the way up the grand staircase that spread like wings at the top for the two long sections of the house. He turned right and strode down the wide landing lined with *chaises longues* and cabinets filled with ancient artefacts until he reached the furthest door at the end and opened it for her.

Sophie stepped inside and immediately sucked a breath in.

The room was beautiful.

'I hope you don't mind but we took the liberty of unpacking for you,' Julio said. 'If you are not happy with where your possessions have been put then we will put them where you think more suitable.'

She grinned, her sense of humour tickled at the

butler's gravity. 'I'm sure wherever they've been put will be fine and if it's not then I can move them myself.'

'As you wish but please remember we are here to serve. Whatever you require, it is our job to provide it.'

Slowly she gazed around the fabulous room with its three high, wide windows overlooking Javier's beautiful garden, the furthest revealing a glimpse of a swimming pool. She opened a door to find a bathroom bigger than her childhood bedroom, another that revealed a dressing room as large as the living room of the flat she had shared with Freya.

Everything was so soft and clean and feminine...

Narrowing her eyes, she stared harder and walked back into the bathroom.

There was not a single masculine product to be found.

As casually as she could manage, she turned her attention back to the butler, who now stood formally by the bedroom door. 'Where's Javier's room?'

'At the end of the west wing. Would you like me to show you around the rest of the house?'

It placed a great strain on all her facial muscles to pull a smile to her face but she managed it. 'No, thank you, Julio. I'm sure you have work you need to be getting on with. I'm happy to explore on my own.'

'If you are sure?'

'I'm sure.'

After asking once again if she required anything and giving instructions on how to contact the staff for when she did, he left the room, closing the door quietly behind him.

When she was alone, the smile on Sophie's face dropped and she folded her arms protectively around her belly.

So much for them creating a real marriage. Javier had stuck her as far away from him as he could get her.

CHAPTER FOUR

JAVIER SENSED SOPHIE'S presence the moment he stepped through the front door.

There was nothing of her in his eyeline, everything in the same spotless order it was always in, but he could feel her there nonetheless, as if she had arrived and imprinted herself on the walls. If he closed his eyes he could smell her perfume.

All day there had been a tight feeling of impending doom playing in his guts that had distracted his thoughts from the important meeting he'd been holding with his lawyer.

Separating his business interests from Luis's was proving to be much harder than he'd anticipated, almost as hard as wrapping his head around the fact he would be sharing his home with the Englishwoman who carried his child.

In the two weeks since he'd seen her he'd carried on as normal. Apart from booking their wedding, that was.

He'd lodged all the necessary paperwork and

arranged for the officiant to marry them here in his home. The ceremony itself would be short and without any fanfare.

In six days' time he would be a married man.

Losing his single status meant nothing to him. He'd always known he would marry when he found the right woman to breed with and continue the Casillas line. Freya had been that right woman, not Sophie. Freya, who would have recoiled at a 'proper' marriage as much as he did.

Not the seemingly sweet, compassionate blonde woman who appeared to have a spine made of much sturdier stuff than he had initially credited her with.

He had never thought about Freya in his private time. Yet Sophie…

She was all he could think about, and as hard as he tried to push her from his thoughts, the harder she pushed back, those wide pale blue eyes staring straight into his whenever he closed his eyes.

She had refused to sign a contract that would have given her an abundance of money each month.

How could anyone be that selfless? It was not possible. Surely it had to be an act?

If it wasn't, if Sophie really was as sweet and

giving as she portrayed herself to be, then she would be fragile with it. Sweet things broke easily.

He did not want to break her but she had to understand that he could. The contract he'd wanted her to sign would have protected her as much as him. A person knew where they were with a contract. You signed it and abided by it, something Benjamin had failed to understand when he'd accused Javier and Luis of defrauding him. Benjamin had signed that contract. Javier could not be held responsible for his failure to read it.

Without a detailed contract to knit their marriage together, they would have to forge their own path. Sophie spoke of compromise but that was a meaningless word in itself if both parties looked at compromise with different markers.

He would not allow her to get close to him. Whether she liked it or not, their marriage would never be real in the sense she wanted it to mean.

He looked at his watch and decided to take a shower before dinner and give himself a few minutes of solitude before he had to face her. He would be undisturbed, his staff knowing not to seek him out. Julio ran his household with military precision. Everyone knew their job and did it well.

Treading heavily up the stairs, he loosened his tie from round his neck. He opened his bedroom door, went to step inside and came to an abrupt halt.

Sophie was sitting on the ottoman at the end of his bed, her hand frozen on a stocking she was halfway through rolling up her bare leg.

After a moment's pause she turned to him and smiled. Only the stain of colour on her cheeks betrayed any nerves or fear she might have. 'Good evening, Javier. Have you had a nice day?'

A swell of rage punched through him, which he did not bother to disguise. Propping himself against the doorway, he growled, 'What are you doing in here?'

A small crease formed in her brow. 'It's moving-in day. You sent your private jet to collect me, remember?'

'What are you doing in my bedroom?' he clarified through gritted teeth.

The crease deepened. 'Getting ready for dinner. As it's our first night I thought I would make an effort.' Then she smiled brightly. 'I'm afraid there was a mistake and my stuff had been put in a room on the east wing. I could see how busy your staff were, so I moved it over myself. It didn't take long. I found some empty space in your dressing room to put my clothes in; don't worry, I didn't touch any of your stuff. I'll find space for my books and other bits and pieces to-morrow.'

He had to inhale three times before he could be certain of speaking without hurling obsceni-ties. 'There was no mistake.'

'Yes, there was.'

'No mistake. My staff put you in the room I designated for your use.'

'Oh, I do apologise for the confusion. I didn't mean your staff had made a mistake in where they put me. I meant *you* had made a mistake.' Then, dropping her eyes from his gaze, she rolled the stocking up over her knee and to her thigh, then patted the lacy top of it to keep it in place. 'I've never worn hold-ups before,' she added con-versationally. 'I normally wear tights but they've started getting a little tight around my belly and I'm not ready for maternity wear yet. I hope they don't fall down.'

Her nonchalance, her *nerve*, were astounding.

Javier gritted his teeth even tighter and cursed

himself for allowing his eyes to take in the milky-white thigh now encased in black lace.

Sexy lingerie had never done anything for him and he could not believe his blood was pumping harder to see it on her.

But, *Dios*, she was sitting on his antique ottoman, her cherubic looks and hair reminiscent of an angel, her blood-red dress, modestly cut though it was, reminiscent of a vampire. His grinding teeth were taken with the compulsion to sink into the milky flesh still exposed over the top of the lacy hold-ups…

He clenched his hands into fists.

This stopped right now. Whatever game Sophie was playing ended here. She had tempted him once, dressed only as a waif, had driven him to a place he had never gone before and which he had regretted the moment it was over.

Healthy desire was good. Sex was good. Choosing the right person to have sex with was what made it good, a person you desired on a physical level, who made your loins tighten but with whom your heart kept its normal beat. A woman you could walk away from and never have to think about or consider again. A woman with whom wearing a condom was at the forefront of your mind, not a cursed afterthought when it was all over.

'This is my bedroom,' he said tightly. 'My private space. You have been given your own bedroom for your own private space.'

'Your house is big enough for us to both host individual parties without disturbing the other, so I would say there's plenty of space to escape to if we get on each other's nerves.'

'Do not be flippant,' he snarled.

Sophie got to her feet and smoothed the red dress she had donned because it was her only decent dress that still fitted properly with her growing breasts, praying he didn't notice the tremors in her hands and that he couldn't see the beats of her frantically beating heart.

Why did he have to walk in when she'd been putting the hold-ups on? Julio had told her Javier was expected home at seven p.m. but he had arrived back half an hour early. She'd wanted to be ready for him, be sitting on the light grey sofa that backed along the far wall, fully dressed.

She still didn't know how she'd found the nerve to move her stuff over to his bedroom. She had sat alone for almost an hour mulling over her options on how best to proceed. Should she stay in her designated room at the furthest point from his and hope that at some point in the future she would be allowed to join him in it? Or should she fight from the start for the marriage she wanted and which he had promised to try for?

The latter had won and now she had to brazen it out.

Standing as tall as her five-foot-nothing frame would allow, she stared up at his towering six-foot-plus form. 'I know you and Freya were only going to share a bed one night a week but that is not something I can contemplate. That is not a marriage.'

She remembered feeling sick to read that contract when it had been designed with Freya in mind, the flash of jealousy that had wracked Sophie to imagine her best friend in the arms of the man she had developed such strong feelings for. To see it replicated in her own contract had filled her with despair.

'I am aware you work long hours and travel a lot for your business, so the evenings are often going to be the only times we share together,' she continued. 'How can we form any kind of bond if we're in separate wings of your house?'

'If it's sex you require then I can accommodate that without you moving into my personal space.' His eyes flashed dangerously as he finally crossed the threshold of the huge, luxurious bedroom and kicked the door shut behind him. Walking towards her in slow, long strides, like a big cat stalking towards its prey, he put his hands to the buckle of his belt. 'If it is relief you are after then take your dress off and I will satisfy it for you.'

'Sex is a part of it,' she answered, refusing to be intimidated by this power play instinct told her was designed to frighten her, 'but I'm talking about intimacy.'

He stopped a foot away from her, his face contorted. 'I do not *do* intimacy.'

'But that's what a real marriage entails. If you won't share a bedroom with me then it proves you're not willing to try like you promised you would and, if that is the case, I might as well have our baby in England, where I will get the support I need—'

'You dare threaten me?' he cut through her, his incredulity obvious.

'I would *never* threaten you,' she said, horrified he would think her capable of such a thing.

'You just threatened to return to England with our baby.'

'Only until it's born.' She sat back on the ottoman and threaded her fingers through her hair as she tried to explain her thoughts without getting so emotional that the tears started falling.

Javier was so ice-like that it felt as if she were trying to get through to a sculpture.

'I haven't made this move for my sake but for our child's. If I was thinking only of my own interests I would have stayed in England and had my parents' support throughout the pregnancy. I don't expect miracles, but if you won't share a bed with me when that's the most basic part of a marriage then what's the point? I made it very clear that I want a real marriage and this for me is it. Sharing a bed. Getting to know each other, and getting to a point that when our child is born we're comfortable together and united. That's my red line. I need you to prove your commitment. Either we share a bed or we forget about marriage because it will be far more damaging for our child to be born in an unhappy home than be born to two separate but content homes. Our child can still have your name because I know that's important for you. I'll be happy to live in

Madrid after the birth so we can share custody. You can still be a father even if you won't be a husband.'

Javier listened to Sophie speak knowing she'd outmanoeuvred him again with her damned reasonableness.

She was giving him a way out of their marriage and if he had any sense he would take it.

'Do you know what my experience of a real marriage is?' he asked harshly, sitting on the edge of the bed so she was only a blur in the corner of his eye. 'My parents.'

He heard her suck an intake of breath. 'I know that to call your childhood hard would be an understatement but I don't want our baby to suffer for it. I'm not asking you to commit emotionally to me, Javier. I am asking you to commit emotionally to our child.'

He thought of the scan she'd emailed to him the week before. He'd stared at it for so long his eyes had blurred.

Their baby. Their innocent baby, who had no idea what kind of a father it had been burdened with.

He'd been prepared to leave the raising of any

child he had with Freya in her hands. Sophie, he suspected, would want him to be involved.

Sophie, who wanted him to share a bed with her every night. To share a space.

Dios, he hadn't shared personal space since he and Luis had left their grandparents' home when they'd turned eighteen to set out on their own, determined even at that young age to earn themselves a fortune. They had rented a small two-bedroom apartment and for the first time in his life Javier had found himself with a room to call his own. The freedom had been like learning to breathe for the first time.

He thought hard before rolling his neck and taking a sharp breath. '*Bueno*. You win. We will try it your way and share a bedroom but only here in this house. I have made it very clear what my own red lines are. I need my solitude. I am a loner and I will never change. I dislike company. When I travel on business, you will not be invited to accompany me, so don't waste your time thinking of arguments for why you should. I have no need for a confidante, so do not expect me to pour my heart out to you. If I wish to go out for an evening on my own do not expect me to take you with me. If I tell you I need space then I expect you to respect that.'

'I will respect all of that,' she promised.

'Good.' He nodded tightly and got to his feet. 'Excuse me but I need to shower before dinner.'

He strode to the bathroom before she could object, needing to get away from Sophie and that floral fragrance she wore that had already permeated the walls of his bedroom.

She might have inveigled herself into it but he was damned if he would let her get a foot in any other aspect of his life.

He could manage nights with her, he reasoned. After all, night-time was for sleeping.

He would dine out more frequently, he decided. Work even longer hours than he already did, hit his personal gym with more vigour, exhaust himself so greatly that when he did rest his head beside hers he would not care that Sophie and her sinfully tempting body lay there. He would simply fall asleep.

'Is Luis going to be your best man?' Sophie asked when she could bear the silence no more.

They'd finished their first course of cured meats and accompaniments and were now eating their main course. They'd been sitting in the dining room for half an hour and Javier had hardly exchanged a word with her. Her every attempt at conversation had been met with monosyllabic answers and grunts.

To make the tension in her stomach even worse, this was the very table he had made love to her on.

It felt so long ago now it could have been a different life but being in here with him brought back memories and feelings that had been smothered under the weight of the fear she had carried with her since, from the horrifying realisation they had failed to use protection to the terrifying realisation she was pregnant with his child.

His lips tightened but he didn't look up from his phone, which he was typing on with his left hand while working his fork absently between his food and his mouth with the other. 'No.'

His own twin wasn't going to be his best man? 'Who is, then?'

'I'm not having one.'

'Why not?'

'I have no need for one. We do not need guests. Our wedding ceremony will be quick and serve a function.'

Not need guests? What kind of a wedding would it be without them?

'I've already invited my parents.'

'Un-invite them.'

Sophie put her fork down, folded her arms across her chest and stared at him for so long that eventually he noticed and flickered his eyes at her.

'I am not getting married without my parents,' she told him flatly. 'It wouldn't be fair. They've already booked their flights.'

His jaw clenched. 'Have you told them they can stay here?'

Do I look stupid? she wanted to retort, settling instead on 'They're booked in a hotel.'

He stared at her for so long tumbleweed could have crossed the huge dining room twice. 'Have you invited anyone else without consulting me?'

'I didn't realise I needed permission to invite my parents to our wedding.'

'Consultation is not the same as permission.'

'I quite agree, which is why I think it's outrageous you've decided we should have no guests at all without any consultation with me.'

She did not drop her stare. Respect worked both ways and he needed to learn that.

A pulse throbbed in his temple.

Javier, she realised, was so tightly wound that to pull him any tighter would make him snap.

It didn't scare her. Javier needed to snap. It could not be healthy keeping everything bottled inside him all the time.

'I am very close to my parents,' she told him in a gentler tone when he made no effort to respond. 'It would break their hearts if I married without them.'

His lips pulled together before he finally inclined his head.

'*Bueno*, your parents can come.'

She bit back the words of thanks she wanted to say. Gratitude on this would make her look weaker than he already thought her to be.

The sooner Javier came to regard her as his equal, the better.

She had a feeling that with the exception of his brother, he rarely saw anyone as equal to him. Freya had gained his respect, she thought with a pang that felt suspiciously like jealousy, but then Freya was the female version of Javier; single-minded and driven.

If Sophie could cut through Freya's walls then she could at least chip away at Javier's.

By the time their child was born she would have chipped away at enough of it that he could be the loving father their child needed and deserved.

Taking her cutlery back in her hand, she cut a bite of the delicious pork fillet and added some of the red pepper and chorizo sauce.

Eighteen months in Madrid had given Sophie a great appreciation of its culture but its food had been something she'd limited herself with, her ballet diet too strict for her to dare eat out much. It had been safer to prepare all her own tried and tested meals and ignore the tantalising aromas that had greeted her whenever she'd stepped onto Madrid's bustling streets. She had missed out on so much but what surprised her was how little she had missed dancing since she'd quit.

She'd been so ashamed of what she'd done with Javier that she had left the company the next day. By the time she'd taken the pregnancy test she'd known she would never dance professionally again. Without the drive of constant performances and tours to keep her in top condition and with the tiredness that had drained her in the early weeks of pregnancy, her exercise regime had gone from seven intense hours a day minimum to hardly anything. And she didn't miss it at all. She found it liberating in a way she'd never anticipated. She could eat the wonderful salt-baked new potatoes that made her taste buds tingle in delight without an ounce of guilt.

The magical food Javier's chef had created deserved to be appreciated much more than Javier currently was appreciating it, his attention again back on his phone.

'Is Luis coming to the wedding?' she asked before popping the fork into her mouth.

Start as she meant to go on, she reminded herself. This was *their* wedding. She'd been happy to leave the arrangements in Javier's hands but she would not exchange her vows blind to everything.

He didn't look up. 'No.'

'Is he too busy?'

His shoulders rose and his nostrils flared before he answered. 'Luis and I are finished, as brothers and business partners, and if you would stop asking me inane questions I could respond to this email my lawyer has sent me about it.'

The Casillas brothers were finished? Had she really heard that correctly?

The tightness of his features proved she had not misheard.

'What's happened?' she asked quietly. She would not allow his bad temper to push her into silence. Sophie had dealt with temperamental dancers and choreographers her entire life and had long ago stopped being silenced by anger.

Anger always went hand in hand with pain, something she had learned at the age of nine when her paternal grandmother had died. It was the only time her father had ever lashed out. A normal Sunday dinner in the weeks after the funeral became a memory of a plate full of food smashing into the wall, her father offended by the lack of seasoning, ranting, face red and furious, shouting obscenities Sophie had never heard before. Her mother had watched in silence, then had gone to him and taken him in her arms.

The howl of pain her father had given as he'd collapsed into her mother's arms was a sound Sophie would remember for the rest of her life.

Javier's sharp eyes suddenly found hers again 'Luis's engagement to Chloe Guillem was announced a week ago. Is that explanation enough?'

'Benjamin's *sister*?' Not just Benjamin's sister but a costume maker employed by Compania de Ballet de Casillas.

He nodded and took a drink of his water.

'Didn't you say she'd been involved in Benjamin stealing Freya away from you?' She was sure he had, right before they had made love on this table. He had made her coffee and asked her the questions she'd guessed had been playing on his mind for a week. She'd been sad for him that she couldn't answer them but, in truth, she'd been as surprised as he'd been by what Freya had done.

Freya didn't love Javier but she'd been desperate for the money marrying him would have given her, which she had planned to spend on an expensive experimental treatment for her mother, who had a rare neurological disease. The treatment wouldn't have saved her life but there was a chance it would extend and improve the quality of it.

'Chloe conspired with her brother to make Luis and myself late for the gala, which enabled Benjamin to pounce and steal Freya away to his chateau in France.'

'And Luis is now engaged to her? How does that work?'

His eyes glittered with menace. 'My brother's loyalty has transferred to the Guillems. I'm surprised you haven't read about it. The press have loved reporting that latest twist in the saga.'

'I've been avoiding the news since I went home to England,' she admitted. 'That doorstepping left a very unpleasant taste in my mouth.'

Javier stared at her, suddenly remembering the strange protective feeling that had raced through him when she'd spoken of the press harassment. And with it came the memory of how his eyes had been unable to do anything but drink her in.

He could keep his eyes fixed to his phone as much as he liked but every nerve ending in his body was aware of the woman seated opposite him and every muscle remembered with painful intensity the sensation of being burrowed deep inside her.

'Luis is a traitor,' he answered flatly, speaking aloud the fury coiling like a viper inside him for the first time.

It was not the press Sophie needed protecting from, it was him.

Sophie needed to know who she was marrying.

'I have protected him since childhood and carried him through the business and he repays me by defending and choosing to marry the woman who conspired with her brother to destroy us. He is dead to me and I would thank you not to mention his name in my presence again.'

Her eyes widened, whether at his tone or his words he did not know or care.

When it came to his brother, there would be no compromise.

Luis could rot in hell.

CHAPTER FIVE

SOPHIE LAY IN Javier's huge bed fighting to keep her eyes open. She must have lain there for an hour waiting for him, thrills of different shades racing through her: terror, excitement, nausea, until eventually they all melded into one that tasted of disappointment.

When she had climbed into the bed, she had thought he would soon follow. They'd finished their first meal together with him telling her to go up and make use of the bathroom before he joined her. She'd thought he was being considerate and giving her a little privacy. She didn't need to tell him she'd never brushed her teeth around a man before or taken a shower near one. He would know.

She sighed.

It was only her first day there. She had to remember that. Javier had huge adjustments to make, fundamental ones that, she suspected, went far deeper than her own.

Building a bond would not happen overnight. It would take time. He was not a man who trusted easily and he was having to cope with a heck of a lot; the humiliation of Freya leaving him for Benjamin, Sophie being pregnant with his child, marrying her and now the destruction of his relationship with his twin.

She wished she had known about that. It would have made her think twice about asking about Luis.

She sighed again, the sigh turning into a wide yawn. Her eyes were getting really heavy. Much longer and she'd be asleep.

Pregnancy had brought about many changes in her: weight gain, the sudden appearance of breasts, the softening of muscles that had always been hard, but the tiredness had been the biggest challenge. Usually she had bagfuls of energy. In the early weeks she'd found herself nodding off so frequently she'd done an Internet search asking if narcolepsy was a pregnancy side effect. The tiredness had got better in recent weeks but she wasn't back to her normal energy levels yet. She'd had a full and busy day, physically and emotionally, and now her body craved nothing but sleep.

Five more minutes.

She would try to stay awake for five more minutes...

Javier stood at his bedroom doorway and breathed deeply.

The air felt different. The only illumination, which came from the dim bedside light on Sophie's side, the side he usually slept, felt softer.

Treading onto the carpet, he felt the thick ply beneath his bare feet in a way he'd never felt it before.

How could the bedroom he'd slept in for five years feel so *different*?

There was no movement from the mound burrowed under his bedsheets.

She'd fallen asleep, just as he'd hoped.

To be sure, he went to her side and peered down. If she was awake he would ask her to move over to the other side.

The sheets swaddled her, her pretty face peeking out, locks of blonde hair spread in different directions over the pillow.

She breathed deeply, the serene sleep of an innocent, oblivious to him staring so intently at her, unaware of his hand hovering closer…

He shoved his hand into his pocket, turned on his heel and, his heart thundering, went into the bathroom, locking the door behind him.

He'd been seconds from stroking her face.

The hour he'd spent pounding his punching bag and running on his treadmill had done nothing to dent his awareness of her.

Her mere presence at the dining table had dragged what should have been a relatively simple email exchange with his lawyer over the entire meal, Sophie snatching his attention even when she wasn't pulling him into conversation.

He'd felt the blood pumping through his veins in a way he had never felt it before, still there, racing through him, alive, with every beat of his heart.

His awareness of the waif-like ballerina was becoming torturous.

Dios, awareness of a beautiful woman was one thing, a healthy thing, but this was something else entirely, as if something with its own heartbeat had infected his blood.

The thought of climbing into bed with Sophie

with all this awareness simmering in him had been unthinkable.

He cursed under his breath.

When they made love, he needed to approach it as he always did, from a place of detachment, make it the mechanical exercise sex had always been for him.

'Detached' was not a word to describe how he felt with Sophie under his roof.

Sex with her had not been a mechanical exercise.

It had been mind-blowing. He had carried the feelings it had brought about in him for weeks after, even when he'd refused to allow Sophie herself into his thoughts.

It was only because she'd caught him at such a low point, he reasoned grimly as he brushed his teeth. It had been the perfect storm. An empty house. A beautiful woman with a sympathetic ear and compassionate eyes. What man wouldn't have reacted in such a manner in that situation and with a woman who had melted at his first touch?

Those feelings had gone eventually, and the feeling of new life in his blood would disappear eventually too.

What else could he do to speed up the detachment? He'd worked out, taken a cold shower in the basement changing room he'd had installed next to his gym, and it had done nothing.

He stripped off his clothes with the exception of his boxers. He always slept nude but tonight that would not be an option, not until he'd got a grip of all these...*feelings*.

He cursed again.

Feelings were dangerous. Especially for him.

Sophie opened her eyes.

Something had woken her.

Then she heard faint sound coming from the bathroom and her heart began to pound.

Javier was in there.

He had finally deigned to join her.

Yawning, she groped for her phone to check the time, blinked and looked again.

She'd been alone in this bed for two hours.

In her heart she knew he'd intentionally waited all this time. He *wanted* her to be asleep.

For the first time it occurred to her that the reason Javier didn't want to share a bed with her was nothing to do with his craving for solitude but because he simply did not fancy her. She'd been nothing but a convenient, willing release for him with huge unintended consequences.

The bathroom door opened. She squeezed her eyes back shut and held her breath.

She sensed rather than heard him tread to the bed.

There was only the slightest of dips as he climbed into it, then settled himself down with his back to her, keeping a distance that could only be breached deliberately. A moment later the room plunged into darkness.

How long she waited for him to do or say something she could not guess. Time lost its meaning in the dark.

There was no movement from him as the time dragged on. No sound either. Nothing. It was like lying beside an empty vessel.

While she had tried hard to stop herself assuming anything about what the night would bring, she'd been unable to stop herself making the fatal assumption that he would hold her in his arms and, at the very least, touch her stomach holding their growing child within its secure confines.

'Goodnight, Javier,' she whispered in the darkness.

There was no answer.

* * *

The following five days passed in a flash. It was a passage Sophie would remember as being a time of blurring nothing.

She spent the days themselves wandering around Javier's villa and gardens, familiarising herself with everything, trying her hardest to feel comfortable within the spacious halls and learn more about the man she was soon to marry. This was her home, she constantly reminded herself. She should not feel like an unwanted trespasser.

The only things she learned about the man himself were that he had a penchant for ancient artefacts and no need for mirrors. In this villa that contained eleven bedrooms and twelve bathrooms, the reflective surfaces were confined to internal glass walls and doors, and shaving mirrors. The only bedroom with a full-length mirror was the one she'd been initially designated.

Things would be easier to manage and cope with if Javier didn't continue to keep her at arm's length. He left for work early and on three of the evenings failed to make it home in time for dinner, leaving her to dine alone. He would make a point of saying hello to her when he arrived back but would then disappear, joining her in the bedroom when, she knew, he hoped she would be asleep.

He made no effort to touch her. Sophie would find herself lying wide awake in the darkness psyching herself to turn over and put a hand to the cold shoulder facing her.

She didn't think he slept either. He was just too still.

If she had more confidence she would say something but every time she opened her mouth her throat would close. She didn't know the words to say without making herself sound like a needy nymphomaniac.

He was doing as she'd asked and sharing a bed with her. If he didn't desire her she couldn't force it.

Or was it something else? It hadn't been just the contract he'd wanted her to sign that stated they would share a bed only one night of the week, but the contract he'd drawn up for Freya too.

Could it be simply that Javier had no interest in sex?

The conception of their child proved the lie in that, not just its conception but the way it had been conceived. Sophie had been a virgin but she had also spent her life in the hotbed of the ballet world, where passions always ran high. She knew passion when she saw it and in Javier's arms she had felt it, had tasted it in his kisses.

Whatever lay behind his reluctance to touch her and however many times she told herself that it was early days and to give it time, Sophie's hopes of creating a bond with him were fading.

The arrival of her parents brought some happiness into her heart and she spent the day before her wedding with them, plastering a smile to her face, keeping up the pretence that everything was fine and that this was a marriage she was entering with high expectations that it would last.

Luckily, Sophie was a pro at convincing her parents that everything was rosy. Their love and pride had given her the focus to get through ballet school and work like a Trojan to succeed in the ballet world. Her first concrete memory was of her mother clapping her hands in delight to see four-year-old Sophie perform in her first ballet recital. Her pride had filled Sophie's heart and been the kick-start to the rest of her life.

Through dance she could make the woman who

had given her a home and showered her with love beam with happiness.

The nights when she would lie awake yearning for the path her heart wanted would be put aside when the morning came. She would fix the image of her parents in her head and drag herself out of bed to start another day.

On that last day as a single woman, she was enjoying a meal out with them when her phone rang.

She would have been less surprised if it had been the Spanish prime minister calling.

The restaurant being too loud to hear, Sophie excused herself and went outside to call Javier back.

'Where are you?' he asked, picking up on the first ring.

'In a tapas bar with my parents,' she answered, surprised to hear what could be interpreted as brusque concern in his voice.

'Where?'

She named the street and district. 'Do you want to join us?'

'No. Why didn't you use my driver?'

'I didn't know I could. I took a taxi. Why do you sound so cross?'

'I'm not cross.' He sounded affronted at the mere thought. 'When will you be back?'

'Tomorrow. I've checked into my parents' hotel. They've brought the wedding dress over, so it makes sense for me to stay with them.'

'I should have been consulted on this.'

'It was only decided today. I was going to call you later to tell you.' She looked at her watch. It was eight thirty.

'*Tell* me?' he said dangerously.

Sophie rolled her eyes at his double standards. 'Considering you do as you please with no consultation with me, you're hardly in a position to moan when I do the same.'

The line went silent until he said tightly, 'So this was punishment for me working hard?'

A wave of weariness washed over her and she took a seat on a nearby bench. 'No, Javier, it wasn't a punishment. You haven't been home earlier than nine o'clock these past three nights. I didn't want to disturb you while you were working. I was trying to be considerate.'

Another lengthy pause. 'Next time, disturb me or message me.'

'Okay. But if you want me to account for my movements, it's only fair if you do the same.'

A grunt played into her ear before he said, 'Message me the details of the hotel. I'll send my driver to collect you in the morning.'

'Not too early,' she interjected. 'My mum says it's bad luck for us to see each other before the ceremony.'

The grunt he gave this time had a tinge of impatience to it. 'He will collect you at eleven. Enjoy your evening.'

'What are...?'

But she never got to ask him what his own plans for the evening were because the line had gone dead.

Sophie put her phone to her chest and closed her eyes, the beginning of a smile forming on her lips.

It had never occurred to her that Javier would come home at a decent time and that he would be worried to find her missing. She'd thought the only thing he would feel was relief to have the place to himself.

Her legs felt much lighter when she walked back into the restaurant. Her chest felt lighter too.

Javier had worried about her, and even if his concern had been because she was the vessel that carried his child, it still meant that, in his own way, he was beginning to care.

Javier splashed the remnants of shaving foam off his face, then turned his back on the small mirror and patted his face dry as he walked into the empty bedroom.

He could not believe how heavy his limbs had become. His chest felt as if a lead weight were compressing it.

He dressed methodically, underwear, white shirt, charcoal trousers, navy silk tie, then sat on the unmade bed to put on the hand-stitched shoes he'd had buffed and polished.

He'd expected to sleep well without Sophie lying beside him and catch up on all the sleep her presence had denied him this past week.

He could curse. With or without her fragrant body beside him, sleep had become a foe.

The one good thing was he'd been able to reclaim his usual side of the bed but that had turned into a bad thing because the sheets hadn't been stripped and so he'd spent the night inhaling her perfume that clung to her pillow. Chucking the pillow on the floor and using his own had done nothing to help because by then her scent had crept into his senses and stuck there. He'd still been able to smell her when he woke after a few snatched hours.

At least he hadn't felt compelled to lie like a statue all night. He could spread his limbs out, roll over, all the usual things a person did in the comfort of their bed without having to worry about accidentally finding a part of himself brushing against Sophie's silky skin.

Dressed, he went back in the bathroom to tame his hair. Usually he made quick work of it, never meeting his own eye.

Today, he dipped his fingers into the pot of wax and stared hard at the reflection he despised but which his father had delighted in.

His father would stand beside him at a mirror and smile with satisfaction at the similarities.

'You are my son,' he would purr in the Slavic accent Javier had come to detest.

If Javier had more closely resembled his mother as Luis had done, would his father still have purred? Or would he have despised him as he had despised Luis?

His father's love of him had been superficial at best, a form of narcissism, its value worthless. It hadn't stopped his father beating Luis, even in the younger years when Javier would cry and beg him to stop. His tears had only made his father hit harder.

He had trained himself not to cry, to hold the emotion in and concentrate his energy on keeping his troublemaking twin out of the escapades that always evoked their father's wrath, his punishments delivered with a gleam that had made Javier sure he enjoyed dispensing them.

And his, Javier's face was the face his father had delighted in looking at, Javier the son he'd felt the affinity with, the child he'd believed was *just like him*.

How could Sophie look at that face and not recoil? Was she so blind she couldn't see the danger in it?

There was a knock on his bedroom door.

'Come in,' he called out brusquely.

Julio appeared. 'The officiant has entered the grounds.'

Javier nodded and worked the wax into his hair. 'And Michael?' he asked, referring to his driver.

'At Sophie… Miss Johnson's hotel.'

He gave his reflection one last look.

It was time to get married.

* * *

Sophie thanked whoever or whatever had looked out for her since her birth for her parents. Their excitement on this, her wedding day, was infectious and did much to curb the nerves chewing in her belly.

As Javier's driver pulled up outside the villa, her mother practically squealed with excitement. 'This is your *home*?'

Unable to speak, Sophie nodded.

The excited chatter between her parents fell to awed silence when they entered the house. Julio and one of the maids greeted them with smiles that didn't quite meet their eyes. If anything, their smiles could be interpreted as sympathetic, which sent alarm bells ringing in her.

Her father holding her arm tightly, they followed Julio through the house, aglow with autumn sunshine pouring through the beautiful intricate skylights, until they reached the orangery.

The orangery was one of Sophie's favourite rooms and she'd been delighted when Javier had suggested they marry in it. More a giant conservatory than anything else, when its doors and windows were open the most wonderful scents from the garden filled it.

She'd not allowed her expectations of what the orangery would be transformed into for this day run away with her but neither had she allowed herself to think about stepping into it and wanting to burst into tears.

The only difference in the orangery was that an oak desk had been placed in the centre with a handful of chairs facing it, presumably for her parents and their witnesses, Julio and his partner, to sit on.

There were no flowers, no balloons, nothing to indicate what an important event this was.

She took it all in slowly with a heart that wanted to smash out of her chest.

If she'd realised that there was to be no effort whatsoever she would never have worn this dress. She would have worn a pair of jeans and trainers.

A quick and functional ceremony was one thing but this...

This was humiliating.

She felt like an imposter, she realised with a wrench. The wrong bride.

Freya, whom in a fit of guilt Sophie had messaged that morning confessing her pregnancy and warning of their marriage, knowing when the press discovered it they would start hounding her and Benjamin all again, was supposed to have stood there.

The man who waited for her, his back currently turned to her—no change there—as he spoke to the rotund officiant, would never have made the choice to marry Sophie if it weren't for the baby.

She wouldn't want to marry him if it were not for the baby either, she reminded herself. Her body still yearned for him but her pounding heart would never yearn for him again. Her heart had learned its lesson, and thank God it had because this would have broken it.

The only effort he'd made was to don a suit. An ordinary suit. The kind of suit he wore every day for work.

And then he turned around and his eyes met hers.

The pounding of her heart became a thrum that vibrated through to her bones.

Javier's mouth had run dry.

He stared at Sophie, hardly able to believe what his eyes were showing him.

He'd never imagined she would wear a traditional wedding dress.

He'd never imagined she could look so beautiful or that his heart would thump so hard the beats could be heard by anyone who listened.

White lace skimmed across her collarbones, forming long fitted sleeves to her wrists, the long lace-wrapped silk dress itself hugging her figure like a caress.

She didn't look pregnant. She looked like a curvaceous nymph and as ravishing a sight as he had ever seen.

He inhaled deeply as he tried to get his thoughts in order.

But she had blown him away.

Pale blue eyes shone back at him.

Suddenly he realised why they were shining. They brimmed full of unshed tears.

That knowledge brought him back to his senses.

He inhaled deeply again, this time fighting anger.

Sophie had no reason to be upset. He'd explicitly told her the ceremony would be quick and functional. She'd chosen not to listen.

But then he watched her demeanour change. Her shoulders lifted and her neck elongated as she raised her chin and said, 'Are we going to do this?'

He stared at her for a further brief moment before nodding.

Yes. It was time to marry this blindingly beautiful woman and give the full protection of his name and wealth to the growing life inside her.

They stood side by side in front of the officiant and, as the quick and functional ceremony began, the weight that had been compressing in his chest since he'd awoken sank lower into him.

For the first time since he'd cut Luis from his life he felt his absence.

He'd never thought he would marry without his brother beside him.

And he'd never thought he would marry with a maelstrom of feelings erupting in him strong enough to knock him off his feet.

He almost choked his vows out.

By contrast, Sophie's Spanish was flawless and her sultry voice carried clearly. He pressed his palms against his thighs to prevent them reaching for her until it was time to exchange rings.

She held her hand out to him.

He took a deep breath and took it into his own.

Her hand was delicate. The nails on the elegant

fingers were smooth and polished, the skin soft and dewy.

This time he was not quick enough to shake the stab of guilt away before it could plunge into him.

Sophie had made a huge effort for this occasion. Her actions had shown him more clearly than any words could that this was a commitment she took seriously.

He slid the ring onto her finger knowing she deserved so much more than the man she was pledging herself to.

Then it was her turn to put the ring on his finger.

His father had never worn a wedding ring. For that reason alone, Javier would wear one.

She took his hand gently in hers and then, her eyes gazing right into his, pushed the cold metal over his knuckle.

Its weight hit him like a physical mark to his person.

He stared down at it.

Where for thirty-five years there had been nothing, a gold band now lay.

Her fingers tightened around his.

Suddenly he became aware of expectant eyes upon him. The officiant's, Sophie's parents'…

And Sophie herself. Except hers weren't expectant, they were pleading.

He could read everything contained in those pale blue eyes that shone beautifully under the bright sun filtering through the glass roof.

For my parents' sake, please kiss me, her eyes beseeched.

Kiss her?

She should be pleading with him to never touch her again.

The weight pressing down inside him increased, making it hard for him to draw breath.

He had to kiss her.

A kiss to seal their marriage and spare her humiliation was the least she deserved from him.

Tightening his fingers around hers as hers were clasped around his, he placed his other hand lightly against her waist and lowered his face to hers.

There was not a sound to be heard. Only the thrashing of his heart.

Holding his breath, he pressed his lips to her mouth.

The thrashing turned into a heavy thud.

The floor he stood upon began to sink beneath him and he had to dig deeply all the way from his toes to keep himself grounded and not sink with it, not give in to the nerve endings all straining to her.

He counted to five, then pulled away.

Then he made the mistake of looking at her.

That beautiful face, cheeks slashed with colour, eyes wide...

He forced air into his lungs.

Her perfume fell in with it.

He shuddered and, gritting his teeth, turned back to the officiant.

He had done his duty. Now it was time to sign the document that would confirm them legally as husband and wife.

CHAPTER SIX

SOPHIE EMBRACED HER father tightly, holding onto the wonderful feeling of safety that engulfed her for the last time.

This was a different goodbye from all the others they'd shared. Before, there had always been the knowledge that Sophie would return, not necessarily to her parents' home but to England, somewhere close enough that their lives would entwine again.

Living in Madrid as she intended to do for at least the next eighteen years, that would not be possible.

Then she embraced her mother and squeezed her even harder.

Without these dear, loving people taking her into their hearts and their home, who knew how her life would have turned out? She owed them everything.

And then they were gone, bursting with happiness for their only child, their blinkers well and truly switched on, seeing exactly what they wanted to see, as they had always done and as Sophie had always enabled.

They had watched her perform hundreds of times, blissfully unaware that her heart had yearned to be elsewhere.

Now they had seen her marry a fabulously wealthy man, seen the home she would raise their grandchild in, and that had been enough for them to leave with contented hearts.

If either thought it strange that neither had had the nerve to embrace their new son-in-law, their faces hadn't shown it.

Sophie turned her head.

Javier was leaning against his giant sphinx artefact, his arms loosely crossed over his stomach. He'd removed his jacket and tie during the horrendously awkward meal they'd shared with her parents. The meal hadn't been pre-planned. He'd snapped his fingers and ordered it to be done after they'd exchanged their vows and before Sophie had had the humiliation of telling her parents the celebrations they expected were not happening. A bottle of champagne had been produced, the first alcoholic drink served since

Sophie had moved in. Javier had stuck to the same sparkling grape juice that she'd consumed.

Sophie thought hard, trying to remember if he'd drunk alcohol in front of her at all, but came up blank. Was he being considerate of her pregnant state?

Somehow she could not believe that to be the reason. Javier would not make a concession like that when he barely knew what the word 'concession' meant and refused point-blank to learn it.

But he had arranged the meal and raised a toast to his bride, all for her parents' benefit.

Maybe he did have a conscience in that steel heart of his.

She sighed. 'I'm going to have a bath and go to bed.'

He nodded but made no verbal answer.

She wished she could read him but he was impossible to interpret. She had never known anyone so capable of keeping their thoughts and emotions hidden.

Did he even have emotions? That was something she was beginning to doubt.

But she thought she'd seen something in his eyes when he'd given her that fleeting kiss right after they'd exchanged their wedding rings.

He hadn't touched her since, not even an accidental brush of his arm to hers.

She ran the bath and added a good dollop of scented bubble bath to it, watching the foam develop in the swirling water, determined not to cry.

When it had filled sufficiently, she walked back through the bedroom to the dressing room and armed herself with a pair of pyjamas, her oldest, most comfortable pair. Javier wouldn't care that they were as sexy as a clown's outfit. She'd worn her prettiest nightdresses all week and he hadn't even cared to look at her in them.

She was about to step back into the bathroom when a vibrating sound caught her attention and a quick look found her phone on the bedroom table. A member of the staff must have put it there. She'd forgotten all about it, not having used it since at the hotel with her parents that morning.

She turned it on to find three returned messages from Freya.

She read the first.

What? Sophie, you CANNOT marry Javier. He will eat you alive. Come to France. We'll take care of you and the baby.

The second:

Call me.

Then the third—the one she'd heard vibrate a moment ago.

It's never too late. Please, Sophie, for your baby's sake, take your passport and run. If you cannot escape then just say the word and we will rescue you.

Sophie read the messages with unfamiliar anger swelling inside her.
She fired a message back.

I don't need rescuing. Javier is the father of my child. I've married him.

Less than a minute later came the reply.

You don't know what he's capable of. He destroyed Benjamin and they'd been friends since they were babies. His own twin has disowned him. He is unfit to be a father. He's dangerous. He will destroy you and your baby. Let us help you.

'You look worried.'

Sophie screamed and jumped.

She had no idea how a man as large as Javier could tread so quietly that she hadn't heard him enter the bedroom.

She backed against the wall and pressed the phone to her chest, an automatic action, which caused him to narrow his eyes.

'Something I should know about?' he asked when the only sound coming from her was ragged breaths.

She wanted to smile and say there was nothing wrong but knew her scarlet cheeks would betray the lie.

He treaded slowly towards her with his hand extended. 'Give me the phone.'

She shook her head and whispered, 'You don't need to see this.'

He really did not need to see those messages.

'I will be the judge of that.'

He stood before her, the expression in his eyes clearly stating she would be going nowhere until she gave him her phone.

She dropped it into his hand, her heart dropping to her feet with it. If she didn't let him read them it would fester in him. He might make assumptions that were even worse.

They needed to build trust between them, which meant openness and honesty.

But she wished he wouldn't read them.

By no stretch of the imagination could Javier be described as an angel but those were messages no one should have to read about themselves.

He scrolled through them, emotionless.

After an age had passed he looked back at her, a pulse throbbing in his temples. 'Do you believe yourself to be in danger from me?'

She didn't have to think twice about her answer. 'No.'

He was dangerous, that she did believe. Javier was a man you crossed at your peril. Cross him and he would strike back twice as hard with all the force at his disposal.

His chest rose as he breathed deeply. 'Maybe you should believe it.'

'And maybe you should trust that if I thought you were a danger to me or our child I would never have exchanged vows with you. I would have kept our baby a secret from you.'

Silence stretched between them and with it a tension, there in the air they breathed, thickening as it wrapped its tentacles around them.

The intensity of his stare upon her, the swirling shapes forming and darkening the light of his eyes...

She had never seen it before. Not even when he'd leaned in to kiss her...

Low in her belly a heat began to grow. It spread into her veins and down into her bones, then pulsed to cover her skin with warm, darting tingles.

His breathing deepened visibly but still he didn't speak, his jaw clenched too tightly for words.

The ache she carried with her intensified and suddenly Sophie knew, as she knew he would never hurt her, that he would never make the first move to touch her. She didn't know why but she knew it to be true.

If she wanted their marriage to be a true one and not a piece of paper she had to be the one to instigate it.

Gathering all her courage, she slowly turned her back to him and tried to breathe through the thuds of her heart. 'Could you undo my dress for me, please?'

There was a long pause.

'Please? I can't reach.'

She closed her eyes and held her breath.

The hairs on the nape of her neck lifted and her skin warmed as he stepped to her.

At the first touch of his fingers to her spine the breath she'd been holding escaped.

Javier fought to keep his mind detached from what his fingers were doing.

He found the top button, a tiny, delicate creation, and, careful not to touch her milky skin, undid it.

Then he unbuttoned the one below and the one below that, not allowing even a breath of air into his lungs as he worked.

When he reached the final button at the base of her spine, he stepped back and cleared his throat. 'You're done.'

Was that *his* voice sounding so thick?

'Thank you,' she murmured.

About to make his excuses and leave the room, she turned back around and faced him.

Her eyes were a darker shade of blue than he had ever seen.

The lump that he'd only just cleared from his throat returned.

Her eyes not leaving his, she took the top of one lace sleeve between her fingers and slowly slid it down her arm, then did the same with the other.

When both arms were free, she pulled the dress down to her waist, pinched a hidden zipper at the side and pulled that down too, then let the dress fall to her feet.

Javier tried to force his feet to move, to leave this room and all the danger charging in the electricity Sophie was creating, but they refused to obey.

And now she straightened, those beautiful eyes still on him, not a single word uttered from the rosebud lips, wearing only a lacy white bra and matching knickers, and the most incredible high, lace-covered white shoes.

His mouth ran dry.

Suddenly he no longer fought his feet to move. Now he was fighting his heart's erratic rhythm and his fingers' itchy determination to touch the silky white skin.

Hermosa. That was what Sophie was. Beautiful.

He'd noticed the changes their child was making to her body earlier but seeing it like this now, in the flesh, sucked all the air from him.

In a little under three months her athletic femininity had softened. The small breasts his hands had covered so thrillingly had grown, the flat stomach now softly rounded, her narrow hips wider. She was like a flower coming into bloom and there was not a single part of him that did not ache to see it.

Still looking at him with that open yet endearingly shy expression, she raised a hand to her hair and pulled a long pin out of it. She cast the pin aside as the blonde tresses fell down.

Heavy beats sounded around the room like a drum was playing in it.

And then he realised the beats were coming from inside him, from the rapid tattoo of his heart.

The bra was the next item to be removed.

Now he could hear his breaths too as he forced air in and out through his nose.

Her bare breasts jutted out, ripe, beautiful and more tempting than the apple in the Garden of Eden.

Then she put her hands to the band of her knickers and down they went too. When she stepped out of them, she stepped out of the shoes, naked from head to toe, every trembling part exquisite.

Her shoulders rose as she took a long breath, then put one foot in front of the other to stand close enough that the scented heat of her skin landed like a heady punch to his senses.

She placed a hand on his shoulder. Raising herself onto her tiptoes, she grazed the lightest of kisses to his mouth, then pulled back enough to stare into his eyes, a plea resonating from hers.

As if she had willed it—there was no conscious thought from himself in the action—his hand reached forward to rest on her hip. With no conscious thought from himself, his fingers kneaded into the warm satin skin.

All week he'd resisted the walking temptation that was Sophie, the consequences of their one coupling there in every step and every breath she took.

The detachment he'd been waiting for before making love to her had never felt so far away.

But his need for her had never been so great.

Dios, his skin burned through his shirt under the gentle weight of her hand on his shoulder.

He snatched at her hand and covered it tightly. 'Do not expect more than I can give you, *carina*.' He had to drag the warning from his tongue but he had to make her understand.

If any other woman had offered herself to him like this he would already have taken her but this was no ordinary woman and it wasn't just because she carried his child.

Sophie was like no one he'd ever known before.

Her face drew closer to his. Her lips parted, brushing against his like a sigh. The sweetness of her breath mingled with his as she whispered, 'I want no more than you can give.'

His heavy heart lightened although the beats continued to thump against his ribs.

The relief when Javier returned the pressure of her lips was so immense Sophie could have wept.

She'd never known she possessed the courage she'd found to strip completely naked for him. Nudity was nothing to a ballerina but this was different.

This was her opening herself to him and the very real danger of his rejection but she had known she had to keep going, known that Javier had the strength of mind and the willpower to lie beside her every night for the rest of their lives without making a move on her, and now she understood why.

He did not trust her to take him at his word that their marriage could never be about emotions.

In his own way he was trying to protect her.

She did not need protecting. Once, she'd had

romantic dreams and ideals about this man but her eyes had been opened. To fall for him would be to have her heart broken.

But her desire for him had never dimmed. This was the man she had taken one look at and felt something inside her move as it had never moved before. Javier had awoken something in her. When he'd made love to her, that awakening had become a life force that refused to go back to sleep.

She didn't want it to go back to sleep. She wanted this. All of this.

When the hand holding her hip slid round her waist and splayed on her back, the little control she had was lost. Suddenly it was Javier setting the pace, kissing her, sweeping his tongue into her mouth and filling her with his dark taste, holding her so securely that when her knees weakened at this wonderful assault on her senses there was no danger of her falling.

Such wonderful, heady kisses, deepening, tongues entwined, lips moving in a dance of their own creation, sensation fizzing through her all the way to the fingertips of her arms that looped around his neck.

Her mind closed to everything but Javier.

She shivered to feel his fingers spear her hair and then his mouth caressed over her cheek and dipped down to her neck, the stubble on his jaw rubbing against flesh she'd never known could be so sensitive.

And then she was lifted off her feet, her stomach swooping with the unexpected motion, and carried effortlessly to the bed she'd been losing hope would ever be used for anything but sleeping.

He laid her down with a gentleness that belied his strength and knelt beside her, upright, magnificent. Beautiful.

Nostrils flaring, he gazed down at her through his hooded eyes, deftly unbuttoned his shirt and threw it onto the floor.

Her heart expanded as she drank in the rugged hardness of his torso. Javier was the epitome of masculine. Whorls of dark hair covered his darkly tanned, muscular chest and thickened over the flat plane of his abdomen where his strong hands were pulling apart his belt.

Her own abdomen contracted and filled with fresh heat that burned like molten liquid inside her.

There was such sensuality to his movements

and such arrogant confidence too as, his eyes not leaving hers, he pushed his trousers down and revealed the erection she'd touched and had buried deep inside her but had never looked at.

Everything inside her seemed to melt into a puddle.

With a sigh that seemed to come from her very soul, Sophie watched him rid himself of the last of his clothing and then he was as naked as she, but dark where she was light, hard where she was soft...

Those whirling eyes were devouring her in the same way hers devoured him, sweeping over every inch of her naked form.

For years Sophie had worked hard sculpting her body to be the best it could be. It had never been enough. She had never been the best.

Pregnancy had liberated her in so many ways, more than she could ever have expected, and now, for the first time in her life, under the weight of Javier's sensuous stare, she felt beautiful.

She felt like a woman.

It came to her then that she'd been waiting her entire life to feel this way but then the thought was swept away before it had fully formed as he leaned down and set her mouth on fire with his kisses all over again.

She closed her eyes and embraced it, wrapped her arms around his neck to embrace him.

And then he made his way down her body to kiss her in places even fellow dancers' eyes had never seen.

Over her swollen, sensitive breasts, kneading them, caressing them, so close to her he would be able to see and hear the jagged beats of her heart. Over her thickened stomach, a circle around her belly button, his tongue and mouth leaving trails of fire in their wake. He kissed and touched her everywhere with such expert precision that when he parted her legs to bury his face into her pubis her eyes flew open and, chest shuddering, she was pulled back to reality.

Sophie stared at the ceiling, a feeling rushing through her that she was part of a game that involved painting by numbers.

She was in danger of losing her mind but from Javier there was no sound other than his lips against her flesh.

The thought dissolved when his tongue flickered against her most feminine nub and then she did lose her mind.

Squeezing her eyes back shut, she submitted to the pleasure he was evoking in her, submitted to the pulses thickening and swelling deep inside her and let go, letting him take her high into a land where nothing but white light shone.

Only once the sensations had abated did he move back up her body and position himself between her legs.

Again came the distant thought that this was painting by numbers for him.

There was no danger of Javier losing his control.

He was going through the motions.

He had given her pleasure and now it was his turn.

But, again, the thoughts were pushed away as he covered her with his glorious body and drove himself deep inside her, filling her so completely that she was helpless to stop the cry that flew from her mouth at the sudden drive of pleasure.

Javier adjusted himself so his elbows lay by her shoulders and began to move, concentrating hard as he thrust deeply into her.

He had to keep his concentration.

Otherwise…

A black void beckoned him. It was a void

falsely dressed in sunlight, a trick, a mirage, a promise of...something beautiful but which was a lie. It was a void with razor-sharp teeth hidden beneath its seductive exterior.

He *had* to concentrate.

He wanted Sophie to have the pleasure. All of it belonged to her. He would take his too but his would be the release of sex. He would not allow it to be anything more. He could not.

And so he gritted his teeth and kept his head exactly where he needed it to be and let Sophie's reactions guide him.

Dios, she was so hot and tight around him...

Do not let go.

Hold on. Keep your head. Close your senses to the woman lying beneath you. This was only normal pleasure, nothing special. It meant nothing.

Nothing at all.

His resolve teetered when her fingers burrowed into his hair and he found her wide-eyed stare, full of wonder, piercing straight through him.

He shifted his position slightly and upped the pace, then screwed his eyes tightly shut and banished the sight of her open-mouthed sighs from his retinas.

But he couldn't banish the sighs from his ears.

They deepened, becoming moans. The hand tracing marks up and down his back tightened around him, the fingers burrowed in his hair grabbing as she crushed herself to him, limbs wrapped tightly around him as if she were melding herself to become a part of him.

He felt her climax as powerfully as if it belonged to him. It gripped him and pulled at him, winding him tighter and tighter...

The sensations were...

Incredible.

Dios, this was like nothing he had ever felt before, stronger and deeper than even their first time together.

He was starting to float, the void right there before him, ready to swallow him into its dangerous depths...

Right before he could fall into it, sanity found its way to him. Clenching his jaw so tightly that only the slightest extra pressure would see it snap, Javier turned his face from Sophie and forced his eyes open.

His gaze burning a hole in the wall, his attention wrenched far from the woman coming undone in his arms, he accepted the rush of his own, determinedly unremarkable release.

It was over.

When he was certain Sophie had taken all the pleasure she could, he let out a breath and rolled off her onto his back.

He swallowed hard, his gaze now fixed on the ceiling, and braced himself for her to say something.

For a long period of time the only sounds in his bedroom were their breaths, both ragged.

There was light movement beside him, the shifting of air...

He turned his head to see her slip into the bathroom.

She locked the door behind her.

CHAPTER SEVEN

SOPHIE SOAKED IN the bath she'd rerun for herself until the water went cold and her toes had turned into prunes.

She did not want to go back into the bedroom and face Javier's cold shoulder.

What they had shared had been wonderful. It had also been awful.

His distance had made it awful.

Where she should be bathing in a heady glow at all the wonderful sensations and feelings that had erupted in her, all she wanted was to crawl under a rock and bawl her eyes out.

Javier had committed himself with his body but the part that really mattered, the heartfelt connection she hadn't realised she craved until it had been denied her, had not been there and that had been deliberate, she was certain of it.

She did not deny that he'd been generous in his attention to her. In that respect it had been glorious but she could savour none of it because it all felt tainted.

Would he have held back so absolutely from Freya…?

She pulled at her hair and stifled a scream.

Comparing herself would do her no favours. Freya was incomparable. She always had been.

After she'd brushed her teeth and pulled her old, comfortable pyjamas on, Sophie felt better in herself, better enough to deal with the silence that would be waiting for her in the bedroom.

She rubbed her stomach and made a promise to their child that she would not admit defeat. They'd been married only half a day!

She was expecting too much from him.

She was suffering a severe case of reality trumping expectations when she should be rejoicing that she'd broken enough of his barriers for him to share their bed as it should be shared, not whinging that he hadn't stared deep into her eyes and declared his undying love.

Whoa!

Her hand was on the door as that thought went through her head.

She walked back to the small shaving mirror and stared at her reflection sternly.

Stop thinking, she told it. *You knew the man you were committing to was an emotionless control freak, so stop being surprised when he acts like an emotionless control freak and don't give even a passing thought to love. It's not going to happen. Javier's incapable of love and you're not stupid enough to fall for the man who threw you out of his home after taking your virginity and then forgot all about you.*

Rolling her shoulders, Sophie tucked her hair behind her ears and walked back into the bedroom.

Her resolution almost faltered to find the bedside light still on and Javier lying in bed, an arm crooked on the pillow above his head, the sheets pulled up to his waist.

His eyes were open.

He didn't say anything, just watched her pad to the bed.

She was glad of her pyjamas. It meant he couldn't see her shaking knees.

She climbed onto the bed and crossed her legs, facing him.

It warmed her that his returning stare was curious rather than hostile or indifferent.

A bubble of laughter flew up her throat that

she only just managed to stop from escaping, but it wasn't the laughter of amusement, only the laughter of sadness.

She guessed he'd prepared himself for histrionics from her.

Did her calmness relieve or disappoint him?

She pulled at a loose thread at the ankle of her pyjama bottoms and, in as casual a tone as she could muster, asked, 'What happened with Benjamin to make him hate you so much?'

His features darkened, just as she'd known they would.

This was a conversation they needed to have. Why not have it now, when they were both awake and alone?

Better to talk than lie in silence with only her thoughts.

'That is none of your business.'

She'd expected the brusqueness of his reply. 'I'm your wife. Like it or not, that means your business is now my business.'

He laughed mirthlessly. 'That didn't take long.'

'What didn't?'

'For you to assert your wifely rights.'

'It's going to come out, you know that, surely? The world knows you and Luis took out an injunction on Benjamin and sooner or later some journalist or other will find the details and publish them.'

'Nothing can be published. The injunction prevents it.'

'It can in America. Do you want me to hear it from the press or from yourself? Or shall I ask Freya?'

'You are to have nothing to do with her.'

'Javier...' She sighed at his bullishness. 'Freya's the reason I'm asking you this. You read the messages she sent me. Whatever she believes you did, she hates you for it. Whatever went wrong between you and Benjamin, I would rather hear your side first before anyone else's.'

'My *side*?' he asked in that all too familiar dangerous tone.

'It will be different from theirs because you will see things from your own perspective. I reached out to her today because Freya's my oldest friend and I didn't want her to learn about our marriage from anyone but me. She's found happiness with Benjamin and I am very happy for them but my loyalty now belongs to you.'

'That does not say much about your loyalty if it is so easily transferred.'

'Freya has had my loyalty and friendship since we were eleven years old. She will always be my best friend but I did not take our vows lightly. You're my husband. You're the father of my child. That means everything and if your vows meant anything then you have to start trusting me. I'm not your enemy, Javier.'

Trust her? As if he would trust anyone ever again.

But there was something in the softness in those pale blue eyes and the soothing melodiousness of her voice that made Javier wish...

In that softly thickening belly lay his child.

He had observed Sophie with her parents that day and seen the bond she had with them. She had given up the support she would undoubtedly have received from them throughout the pregnancy and birth to be with him. She had signed the iron contract he'd drawn up that stated exactly what she'd suggested: that in the event of them divorcing she would be entitled to a home in Madrid and that they would share custody of any children they had.

She had read it thoroughly in front of him, asked for a pen and signed it. She hadn't argued any of it. She had signed it knowing she would get nothing else from him.

He'd been testing her. He'd been prepared to give her much more but she hadn't asked.

Damn Freya to hell for trying to poison her against him. He had been straight down the line with Freya and she repaid him like this?

He had to give Sophie credit for not simply calling Freya and demanding the details.

If she was prepared to hear him out then he could meet her halfway.

'Benjamin thinks Luis and I owe him two hundred and twenty-five million euros in profit from the Tour Mont Blanc project,' he said heavily. 'When a judge threw his case out of court, he refused to accept it. He stole Freya from me in revenge.'

'Why did he refuse to accept it?'

'He won't accept responsibility for his own actions. He didn't read the contract. If he had read it he would have seen his share of the profit had been changed from twenty per cent to five per cent. That was on the advice of our lawyer.'

She didn't say anything for the longest time. 'They say money is the root of all evil and it really is.'

'They are wrong. Evil is the root of all evil.' His father had been evil. He'd been charming when he'd wanted to be but his malevolence had never been far from the surface.

'But you were friends with Benjamin since you were babies. All those years and all those memories thrown away for cash.' She shrugged and gave a sad smile.

'Sentimentality does not pay the bills,' he told her roughly.

His and Luis's friendship with Benjamin had been foisted on them by their mothers. The two women had deliberately conceived their children at the same time so they could raise them together. Benjamin's mother had been Javier's mother's personal costume maker; mother and son accompanying them on all Clara's tours around the world, the boys expected to get along and play together.

'I get that,' Sophie said with a sigh, 'but...'

'If you show weakness in life then people learn they can walk all over you.'

'But he was your friend. Why didn't he read the contract? Didn't he know the terms had been changed?'

'You would have to ask him that.'

'I'm asking you. You're the one who took the injunction out.'

'We took it because he'd become emotional and unpredictable and would not listen to reason. He threatened to destroy us.'

He remembered clearly Benjamin's shouted threats that had ricocheted like a bullet in the courtroom and the rage on his face.

Javier and Luis had filed the injunction immediately, both certain Benjamin's threats would be acted on and that the consequences would be disastrous for them.

If the world believed the Casillas brothers could rip off their closest friend, who would ever trust them in business again?

Sophie winced and drew her knees up to her chest, wrapping her arms around them. 'Where did all his anger come from? Please, don't think I'm not listening, I'm just trying to understand. Freya had no fears about marrying you even though you have a fearsome reputation and I'm trying to understand why her opinion towards you has shifted so completely.'

'Benjamin has poisoned her towards me.' And if he and Luis hadn't slapped the injunction to stop him talking about the soured business deal he would have poisoned the world against them too. Benjamin's actions in stealing Freya had almost succeeded in doing that for him but they had ridden the storm of malicious press as a united force, right until Luis had turned his back on thirty-five years of brotherhood to be with Benjamin's sister.

Chloe Guillem had stolen Luis's loyalty in a way her brother had never been able to do.

The destruction of the friendship lay not at the feet of the Casillas brothers. They hadn't put a gun to Benjamin's forehead and made him sign. He'd had five hours to read the contract and get back to them if the terms were not to his liking and, sure, it had been argued in court, by Benjamin, that they had known he'd been preoccupied that day but, as Javier had counter-argued, that meant Benjamin should have given the contract to his lawyer to read for him. That was what lawyers were for.

'Freya knows her own mind,' Sophie stated with certainty. 'She never listens to gossip.'

'If you think so much of her opinion then why are you still here?' he bit back.

'She's just being protective.'

'Why? Does she not think you know *your* own mind?'

'No, it's just the nature of our friendship. We've looked out for each other since ballet school.'

Grabbing at the change of direction in a conversation that was making his brain burn and his skin feel as if it had needles poking in it, Javier sat up. 'You two are an unlikely friendship.'

Freya was cold and driven; Sophie warm and open.

She tightened her hold around her knees. 'I know, but the differences weren't so pronounced when we were kids. She was amazingly talented, even back then, and it was obvious to everyone that she was a dancer who would set the world alight but when we first met she was incredibly shy and insecure. She comes across as cold but that's because she had to be to get through school. She was really badly bullied, especially that first term.'

'Were you a part of it?'

But he knew the answer to that before she shook her head in denial.

He doubted Sophie was capable of bullying a dormouse.

'God no. I just felt sorry for her. She was this

scared little thing, away from home for the first time, from a poor background when everyone else came from families with money. She was admitted on a full scholarship, which was incredibly rare—I mean, I only got in because my parents paid the fees.'

'Your family has money?' Her parents didn't have the moneyed air about them that most rich people had.

'Not as much as most of the other girls had but my parents would have lived in a shed if it meant me going to ballet school. Luckily it didn't come to that,' she added, rubbing her chin on her knee.

'You weren't scared, being away from home yourself?'

'I'd already built a resilience. Freya had to build hers. She had the talent—my God, did she have the talent—but it was a tough time for her. The other girls hated her. It was jealousy, pure and simple.'

'You were not jealous yourself?'

'I was definitely envious but not jealous.'

'Is there a difference?' Javier remembered his mother once telling him sharply to stop being jealous of Luis and Benjamin's friendship when she'd caught him sitting on his own, scowling as he'd watched them plot ways to put itching powder in the *corps de ballet* costumes.

She hadn't understood that he was watching over Luis, ready to step in if things went too far.

Benjamin had brought Luis's worst instincts out in him. They'd egged each other on in their troublemaking, leaving Javier to cover for their messes as best he could, terrified his father would hear and mete out punishment.

Their father had needed little excuse to punish Luis.

Had Javier been jealous of Luis and Benjamin's friendship as his mother had accused?

No, he assured himself. He'd been looking out for his brother.

Every mark their father had made on Luis's body Javier had felt as if it had been delivered on his own skin.

'Sure there's a difference,' she answered with a rueful smile. 'I would have loved to dance as well as Freya did but I would never hate her for it. I felt so sorry for her and the way those mean girls treated her that I wanted to protect her. I became her shadow. The poor thing couldn't get rid of me.'

'You weren't worried they would turn their cruelty on you?'

'It didn't cross my mind and I wouldn't have cared if they did. I could never sit back and watch someone suffer if it was in my power to help them.'

'What are you, some kind of saint?'

Her answering laugh was as mocking as his words. 'Hardly.'

Maybe not a saint, he thought, gazing at her, noting for the first time that she had not met his eyes once since getting on the bed, but there was an inherent goodness about his new wife.

His heart thumped loudly against his ribcage as the strangest impulse to gather this beautiful, compassionate creature into his arms filled him.

He closed his eyes and breathed deeply, willing the impulse away, not knowing where it had come from, just knowing that nothing good could come from it, not for her, pampered and cosseted all her life as she had been.

It was easy to be a good person, he thought scathingly, when you'd known nothing but love and indulgence in your life.

What troubles had his wife had? Not being

the best dancer in the school was the extent of it and that wasn't something that had bothered her, strange though the concept of a professional dancer happy to settle for being less than the best was to him. Even their unplanned baby she considered to be a blessing.

The harsh, cruel realities of the world had never touched Sophie on a personal level. She had only ever observed it, had no concept of what it was like to feel it and live it.

He quite understood why Freya had felt compelled to warn her of him. Look at her, sitting there, not caring of the danger she was in just to share a bed with him.

She wanted to know why Freya and Benjamin hated him so much? He would tell her. Let her eyes be opened by the truth.

'Benjamin hates us because we approached him for the investment in the Tour Mont Blanc project on the day his mother's cancer was diagnosed as terminal.'

Now her eyes did rise to meet his.

'He doesn't just believe we ripped him off but believes we took advantage of him,' he added for good measure.

'And did you?' she asked with a whisper.

'We did not rip him off.' Of that he was vehement.

'What about taking advantage of him? Did you?'

'Not deliberately. We'd paid the seller of the land a huge deposit. He then came to us and gave us twenty hours to pay the remainder or he would sell to another interested buyer. We didn't have the ready cash for it, so we asked Benjamin if he wanted to invest. Neither Luis nor myself were aware that Benjamin had just received that diagnosis. He'd been minutes from calling us with the news. His mother had been best friends with our mother.'

Their friendship had seen the two women raise their children as family. When Javier and Luis's mother had been killed, Louise Guillem had been the one to break the news to them. Afterwards, she had taken them under her wing as much as she could.

Javier had felt little in the way of emotion since his mother's death but when he'd carried Louise's coffin he'd felt the weight in his heart as on his shoulder.

'He signed the contract that same day?' she asked.

'Yes.'

'Thinking he would receive twenty per cent of the profit?'

'Yes. I didn't know he hadn't read it until after it was signed.'

'You didn't warn him?'

'Why should I have done? I thought he would read it or get his lawyer to.'

'That's cold.'

'Just starting to realise that, are you?' he mocked. Let her see the truth because so far she'd seemed determined to keep herself blind. 'Business is business. He didn't have to say yes to the investment.'

'So you did take advantage of him.'

'Not initially and not deliberately. When I realised he hadn't read the contract my feelings on the matter were simple; it was his own fault. It was business, not personal.'

'But Benjamin doesn't see it like that,' she supposed, rightly. 'And I would guess that he wouldn't have entertained the idea of doing any business that day if it hadn't been you and your brother doing the asking.'

'Maybe he wouldn't have but he did. Do not forget, Benjamin made seventy-five million euros in profit on that investment. He has been handsomely rewarded.'

'But not as handsomely rewarded as he'd thought he would be.'

'If he'd read the contract he would have seen the terms had been changed. If he'd been unhappy about that he could have negotiated.'

'If you didn't warn him the terms had changed he didn't know to read it. He trusted you.'

The stab in his guts at this truth hit him hard.

He refused to let it take hold, just as he'd resisted it for seven years.

He allowed no room for sentimentality in his life, never mind his business, and he would not allow Sophie's soft chastisement to breach that.

Throwing the covers off, Javier climbed out of bed and grabbed his boxer shorts off the floor. 'Trust should not have come into it. Not with business. I would never sign a contract without reading it first, no matter who presented it to me.'

'You were not in his shoes. Couldn't you have made an allowance on this occasion? For his state of mind about his mother? Torn the contract up and renegotiated?'

'No one made allowances for me after my father killed my mother.'

Even under the dim hue of the bedside light he saw her face drain of colour.

Good. She needed to wake up to the truth.

He was his father's son, his father's favourite, his father's mirror image inside *and* out.

Shaking his trousers out first, he pulled them up. 'Luis and I had to fight to get the business world to take us seriously, to get credit, to get investment...we've had to fight for everything. We live with the legacy of our mother's death every day of our lives and if that has made me cold and ruthless then so be it. It's called survival, something you with your unicorn-and-rainbow-filled childhood know nothing about. I warned you of the man I am, so go ahead, judge me and condemn me, but understand your condemnation means nothing to me.'

Turning his back on Sophie's white, shocked face, he stormed out of the bedroom and headed down to the basement, to his gym, intent on nothing more than pounding the crap out of his punching bag.

Dios, everything inside him felt as if it were being ripped in a hundred different directions by vicious hands.

She had wanted the truth and he'd given it to her.

He'd warned her before they married. He'd kept his distance since she'd moved in. He'd arranged their wedding to be as sparse as it could be. He'd made love to her with a detachment that had been brutal but none of it had been enough.

Sophie saw the world through eyes set to a different filter from his own.

Listening to her relate how she'd willingly put herself in the bullies' firing line to protect and support Freya and stop her feeling alone had hit a strong nerve in him.

She touched him in ways that were dangerous and Freya had been completely right that she needed protecting from him.

He was his father's son!

He'd wanted her to see him for who he truly was, see the monster that lived inside him, never have her rest her hands on him and look at him with those eyes in the way she had again.

He never again wanted to look into her eyes and feel as if she were reaching down into his soul…

He sensed rather than heard movement behind him.

Lowering his hands from the punching bag he'd been battering, he turned.

Sophie was standing in the doorway, a glass of water in her hand and an apprehensive look on her face.

CHAPTER EIGHT

IN THAT MOMENT, standing in the doorway of Javier's gym, Sophie glimpsed the anger and pain resonating from his eyes and knew she had made the right decision to come to him.

For the second time in one night she had found courage she'd never known she possessed.

His revelations about his treatment of Benjamin had shocked her to her core but not, she suspected, for the reasons he'd wanted her to be shocked.

There had been fleeting remorse when she had questioned him about the contract. Only fleeting, but she had seen it.

Javier wanted her to hate him, she'd realised as she'd sat frozen on the empty bed.

He hated himself.

When he'd looked at her and made the cutting comment about his father killing his mother...

It had been a veiled warning to her that had

suddenly made sense of everything: his distance, his solitary life, his brusqueness...

Javier had built the steel heart to protect himself, believing he was protecting others from himself.

Was it coincidence that he didn't drink?

His father had been a violent alcoholic whose drunken outbursts and hair-trigger temper had seen an early, ignominious end to his dance career.

By contrast, his mother's career had soared. Today, over twenty years after her death, she was still regarded as one the most dazzling ballerinas to have graced the world's stages.

Clara Casillas's dazzling star had been snuffed out when her husband had locked her in her dressing room after she'd performed in *Romeo & Juliet* and strangled her with his bare hands. Javier and his twin had been thirteen.

What kind of life had they had with a father like that, even before he'd so cruelly taken their mother's life?

It twisted her heart to imagine the cruelty Javier had been on the receiving end of and witness to.

His heart had been so damaged that he'd remorselessly used his oldest friend to his own advantage and cut his own twin from his life.

If she had any sense she would cut and run, flee from this beautiful villa and keep running as far as she could from him.

But how could she do that and live with her conscience?

Javier was trying to protect her from himself. That in itself proved the father of her child was not irredeemable.

Buried deep inside him was a good man fighting to get out.

And here, in his private gym, he'd been fighting his demons with a punching bag, his bare torso glistening with perspiration, evidence of the exertion he'd used.

He would never use her or any other person as his punching bag. That was a certainty she felt right in her marrow.

She was not ready to wave the white flag.

She stepped over to him.

'I thought you might be thirsty,' she said softly, holding the glass out.

His throat moved.

The fleshy lips pulled into a tight line before

he took the glass from her and, his eyes holding hers, drank the water in four huge swallows.

The knuckles holding the glass were red.

'Shouldn't you wear boxing gloves?'

His shoulders rose in a shrug, the light brown eyes still not moving from hers.

She longed to touch him. She longed to gather this great bear of a man into her arms and caress all the demons out of him. To make love to him with his eyes holding hers. To free him.

She settled on removing the glass from his hand, putting it on the ledge beside her and taking hold of his hand to gently rub the raw knuckles.

The tension coming from his unresponsive fingers made her want to cry.

She sighed. 'I'm sorry for pushing things but, Javier, please, try not to see me as your enemy or as some fragile creature who needs protecting from you. I'm tougher than you think and you're not going to scare me away. It's not going to be easy but we *can* make our marriage work but only if you meet me halfway. I'll stop pushing for more than you can give if you stop pushing me away at every turn. How does that sound?'

The hand she held flexed imperceptibly. Slowly,

as if they were being wound by an old unused lever, his fingers closed around hers before his other hand buried into her hair and he brought his forehead down to rest against hers.

His features were taut as his eyes bore into hers. 'I am afraid I will hurt you.'

The raw honesty in his voice punctured her heart.

Sophie swallowed back all the emotions racing up her throat and rested her palm against his cheek. 'The only way you can hurt me is if you don't give us the chance our child deserves.'

That was who she was fighting for. Their innocent child.

'That is not the kind of hurt I am talking about.'

'I know.' She brushed her lips to his. 'And I know you will never hurt me or our baby in the way you mean.'

'How can you be so certain?'

'Because I would feel it.'

'Feelings cannot be trusted.'

'Sometimes feelings are all we can trust.'

The fingers gripping her hair tightened as he breathed in deeply.

It would take no effort to hurt this woman, Javier thought. No effort at all.

How could she trust he wouldn't abuse his disproportionate strength and power against her as his father had done, first to his brother, who he had revelled in abusing with the form of corporal punishment he'd malevolently deemed to be necessary and corrective, and then on that fateful night when he had used his strength as a weapon to take his mother's life?

Where did Sophie's trust come from? She must know it would take little effort for him to do serious damage to her.

It would be as easy as breaking a butterfly's wings.

Could those eyes staring so trustingly into his read the train of his thoughts?

It felt as if every organ in his body clenched, the strength enough to send a wave of nausea racing through him.

Why had the fates brought this woman of all women into his life? What cruelty had set them on this path together?

How could she put her life and trust in nothing more than a feeling?

He could not begin to comprehend it, nor comprehend why his heart hammered with such strength or why he was bringing his mouth to hers to taste those rosebud lips and the sweetness of her kisses again.

Dios, this had to stop.

Breaking the kiss, he took her face in his hands.

'I will try to meet you halfway,' he said roughly, 'but I promise nothing. I can't make promises when I don't know if I can keep them.'

'I wouldn't want to hear them if they were lies.'

'That is one promise I *can* make. I will never lie to you.'

'And I will never lie to you.'

His lips found hers again as if they had a will of their own.

Her lips returned the kiss as if she were taking the air she needed to breathe from them.

Everything about her was so soft. Her skin, her hair, her heart...

Soft, pliable and being entrusted into his large, brutal hands.

'How long are you going to be away for?' Sophie asked, making sure to keep her tone neutral.

She did not want Javier to know how much she dreaded the thought of him going away.

In the two weeks since they'd been married, it would be the first time they had slept apart.

He looked up from his phone. 'Five nights if it all goes well.'

Her spirits sank even lower.

Five nights?

When he'd casually mentioned that he'd be going on a business trip to Cape Town for a few days, she'd thought he meant two or three.

His case was already packed and in the car.

She supposed she should be grateful that he'd stayed to eat breakfast with her before leaving.

Although he hadn't said so in words, she was aware the exclusive apartment complex he intended to build in the South African city was the first development he would be undertaking without his brother.

The pressure he was under must be horrendous.

She'd deliberately held herself back from asking too many questions about it.

They had reached an understanding on their wedding night. She was not to push too hard. He was to stop pushing her away with so much force.

So far it was, tentatively, working.

She put no pressure on him and asked nothing of him.

He ate most evening meals with her. Sometimes he even put his phone down and talked to her.

He no longer slept with his back to her.

That was the best and worst aspect of it all. Now that the genie of sex had been let out of its bottle they made love every night.

She wished they could make love more. During the long, boring days when she whiled her time away swimming either in the outdoor pool when the weather was sunny or in the indoor pool when it was a bit too chilly for her, or exploring Madrid's streets as she'd never had a chance to do before when she'd spent six days a week in a dance studio, she found her thoughts continually drifting to him.

She'd made a promise not to push him for more than he could give but as the days passed she found she wanted so much more. Sometimes the urge to call him, just to hear his voice, would overwhelm her.

And although their lovemaking was regular and frequent that magic ingredient she kept hoping for never came through. The connection she craved still wasn't there.

Javier was still holding back.

He was always considerate; on that she could not fault him. He never took his release before she found hers.

When they were done, she would lie with her head pressed against his chest, her hand in his. On paper, he was ticking all the boxes, painting in all the numbers.

She wanted more. More passion, more spontaneity, wanted to feel that he desired *her*, that he wasn't going through the expected motions with the woman he'd been forced into marrying because she carried his child. When their lovemaking was over, she longed to drape her limbs all over him, mesh herself to his skin and relish the scent of their sex that lingered in the air, but always held herself back from doing any of these things.

Javier reached for his coffee and surprised her by continuing the conversation. 'I've been thinking...'

'Oh?'

'While I'm away, you should start organising the baby's nursery.'

'Really?' she asked dubiously.

'You said only last night that you're bored.'

He'd listened to her?

It had been a passing comment made after yet another day of doing nothing useful. She might not miss dance but she missed being active and having a purpose in her life. She hadn't expected Javier to take her comment seriously.

'Don't you want to have any input with the nursery?' she asked.

'No. I'll get my PA to sort a credit card out for you today. Spend whatever you like on it—there will be no limit. It will be yours to keep.' His eyes narrowed as he contemplated her. 'I also think it's time we sorted out an allowance for you.'

'I don't need one.' If she needed money there was a petty-cash drawer in Javier's home office filled with an ever-replenishing stack of euro notes that she helped herself to at his insistence, always leaving a note of how much she'd taken and what it was for. 'It's not as if I have any bills to pay.'

'Everyone needs money to call their own. You shouldn't have to feel that you need my permission to spend money.'

'I don't feel that,' she protested.

His gaze was critical. '*Carina*, you're my wife and carrying my child. Your clothes are tight on you.'

He'd noticed?

'You will have an allowance,' he said in the tone she'd learned not to bother arguing with.

'While I'm away, I want you to go shopping and spoil yourself. If you have the time, arrange the nursery. Julio will have the names of decorators who can paint it out in whatever colour and style you want.'

'I can do it however I want?' she clarified.

His gaze was serious. 'This is your home. You need to start treating it as such.'

Everything inside her swelled so big and so quickly it felt as if she could burst.

She had never dreamed Javier would say those words to her.

'Which room shall we put the nursery in?' she asked, trying not to beam her joy at this break-through with him.

'There's a pair of adjoining rooms on the east wing...'

'The east wing? But that'll be too far from us.'

'The nanny will have the adjoining room.'

'What nanny?'

'The nanny *you're* going to employ.' He gave a smile that showed he thought he was being a good guy. A smile from Javier was such a rare occurrence that it momentarily startled her away from what he'd just said.

She remembered reading the clause in the old

contract that had mentioned wraparound care for any child, presumably because he expected her to go back to work.

Sophie wouldn't care if she never danced again. The thought of putting her pointe shoes on and performing made her feel all tight inside.

'We're not having a nanny,' she told him flatly, her brief moment of joy gone.

'Of course we are.'

'We are not. I'm not letting someone else raise my child.'

'A nanny would not raise it. A nanny would do the mundane chores.'

Now she was to use the tone that meant he could argue with her but she would not bend. 'This is our child and I'm not palming it off on a stranger.'

His face darkened. 'You are prepared to care for it 24/7?'

'It's called being a parent.'

'What about work? How are you going to return to dance with a baby? Do you expect to pirouette with it strapped to your back?'

'I'm not going back to the ballet.'

He stared at her as if she'd just announced

an intention to fly a car to the moon. 'Why on earth not?'

'I don't want to.'

Not want to? Javier had never heard such words from a ballerina's mouth. His own mother had returned to the stage four months after giving birth to twins. To be a professional dancer meant a life of dedication and single-mindedness. His father had driven himself to alcoholic despair when the work had dried up, admittedly because of his drunken rages and violence against fellow dancers and choreographers. Javier didn't know a single ballet dancer who had quit before the age of thirty-five, most usually only doing so reluctantly when their bodies failed them, all the injuries sustained through their careers finally taking their toll.

Sophie was twenty-four. She hadn't even reached her peak.

'But you're a dancer.'

'And now I'm going to be a mother.'

'You can be both.' He shook his head, trying to comprehend this woman he was beginning to suspect he would never understand. '*Carina*, you're young. You're in excellent health. There is no reason for you not to be able to continue to dance.'

'I don't want to,' she repeated with an obstinacy he'd never seen before. 'I'm done with dance. It's not as if I was particularly good at it.'

'What are you talking about?'

'I only got into ballet school because my parents paid the full fees.'

'Did you not have to audition?'

'Well...yes, but my parents still had to pay. I'm not saying I'm a bad dancer but I'm never going to be the best. I only got the job with your ballet company because Freya put a good word in for me.'

'Rubbish.'

'It isn't rubbish...'

'Compania de Ballet de Casillas does not employ second-rate dancers. I should know; it's my company. You think anyone would dare go above my wishes for only the best to be employed?'

She gaped, a crease forming in her brow. Then she tucked a lock of hair behind her ear and grimaced. 'It doesn't matter.'

'It does. You're a dancer. You're an excellent dancer. It's in your blood.'

'It isn't,' she insisted. 'I love the ballet but...

I'd been thinking of quitting before I joined your company. I think I would have done if Freya hadn't needed me here. She was having a hard time, really struggling with being so far from her mum—you know how ill she is—and I wanted to support her. Just be there when she needed a shoulder to cry on.'

'You were already thinking of quitting?'

She nodded, a wistful look on her face. 'I love the ballet, I really do, but dancing was never... My heart was never in it. It was not what I wanted to do in my life.'

'What did you want to do?'

'I wanted to be a vet.'

'A *vet*?'

His wife, a professional ballerina, who'd dedicated her life to dance had never wanted to do it. She'd wanted to be a vet.

He could hardly wrap his brain around the notion.

He thought back to their wedding night and her comment that her parents would have lived in a shed if it had meant Sophie getting into ballet school. At the time he'd treated it like a throwaway comment but now it began to resonate...

Had Sophie spent her life working for a dream that wasn't her own?

What kind of a person did *that*?

The answer stared back at him. His wife. The only person in the world who he suspected was capable of such self-sacrifice.

Before he could question her further his phone buzzed. Catching the time on it, Javier blinked and hauled himself to his feet. 'I have to go. We'll finish this conversation when I get home.'

Downing the last of his coffee, he contemplated Sophie one last time.

It suddenly came to him that he wouldn't see her for another five days.

'Call me if you need anything.'

She nodded but the easy smile that was usually never far from her lips didn't appear.

Was she angry at him for giving his opinion on her career?

He didn't have time to worry about that now. He had a flight slot to fill.

Taking hold of his briefcase, he walked to the dining-room door.

'Have a safe trip,' she called to his retreating back. 'Please call or message to let me know you've got there safely.'

He took one last look at her.

'I will,' he promised.

Now she did smile but nowhere near enough for it to reach her sad eyes.

As his driver steered them out of the electric gates, Javier put his head back and closed his eyes with a sigh.

Leaving his home had never felt like a wrench before.

Whoever had coined the term 'retail therapy' could not know how right they had been.

Sophie had prevented herself bursting into tears at Javier's leaving by a thread.

He wouldn't have wanted to see her cry. It would probably have repelled him.

She didn't understand why his leaving left her feeling so heavy and wretched. They were hardly in the throes of a traditional honeymoon period. They hadn't even *had* a honeymoon!

An hour after he'd left, his PA had turned up at the villa with a credit card for her.

By what magic or trickery Javier had made it happen so quickly she could not begin to guess but it had lifted the weight off her considerably and brought a genuine smile to her face.

He'd thought of her. He'd flexed his muscles for *her* and made the impossible happen. For her.

The minute Michael, his driver, had got back from the airport she'd coerced him into taking her shopping.

She had an unlimited credit card, a nursery to fill and prepare, and a new dressing room of clothes for herself to get. Javier's observation that her clothes were getting tight had been correct. Only four months pregnant, she wasn't yet large enough for maternity wear but clothing she could breathe in easily would be welcome.

So she'd hit the shopping district she remembered exploring once with Freya, when neither of them had had the funds to do more than window-shop: Salamanca.

From there she had shopped until her feet ached, stopping only for a light lunch in a pretty little café along the Calle de Serrano.

Now she sat in the back of Javier's car, imagining the furniture she would have in their child's nursery, exhausted but happier than she had felt in months.

Javier had gone away but he had left with them in as good a state as they could be. Their marriage wasn't perfect but for the first time she really felt they were making headway.

He'd told her to treat his house as her home.

The car stopped for the electric gates to open and welcome them home.

Resting her head to the window, she noticed a tiny black bundle on the kerb.

She squinted her eyes to peer closer.

The tiny bundle made the tiniest of movements.

'Stop!' Sophie screeched before Michael could start the car again.

Unclipping her seat belt, she opened the passenger door, jumped out and hurried to see what she hoped with all her heart she was wrong about.

She wasn't wrong. The tiny black bundle was a puppy.

She crouched down next to it and put a tentative hand to its neck.

It opened its eyes and whimpered.

That was when she saw the blood and burst into tears.

CHAPTER NINE

JAVIER CLIMBED THE stairs and followed the scent of fresh paint to the room next to his.

He stepped inside it and stared around in wonder, his heart fit to burst.

'What do you think?'

He turned to find Sophie behind him, dressed in a black jersey dress that fell to her knees and covered the belly and breasts that both seemed to have grown in his absence. It would not be long, he guessed, before she would be obviously pregnant.

She looked more beautiful than ever. His bursting heart managed to expand some more.

For the longest time neither of them spoke.

Five days away from her...

He had never thought time could drag so much.

He'd expected to be relieved to have a bed to himself again.

He had not expected to find the nights so empty without her.

'You did this?' he asked.

The walls had been painted the palest yellow and covered with a hand-painted mural of white clouds and colourful smiling teddy bears.

She smiled, a wide, sweet grin that pierced straight into his chest. 'I hired a local artist to do it. I discovered her at a plaza near Calle de Serrano and offered her an obscene amount of your cash for her to drop all her other commissions and do it immediately.' Then the smile dimmed a little. 'I was hoping to warn you before you saw the room.'

'Warn me that you've turned the room next to ours into a nursery rather than the room on the east wing that I said should be used?'

She nodded and rubbed her belly. 'Even if we do agree on getting a nanny, I know there is no way I'd be able to sleep if I thought my baby was crying in a room too far away for me to hear.'

He'd thought of that too, in his time away.

He wanted Sophie to accept him for how he was. It worked both ways. He had to accept her for how she was too. He'd known from the start that she was different from everyone else who traversed his life.

She might not be the perfect wife he had wanted

for himself but she would be the perfect mother for their child.

Sophie would protect and love their child in a way that would make it hardly aware of its father's remoteness.

'I need you to understand that if you won't have a nanny then you have to be prepared to do it all yourself,' he warned her. 'I'm not going to be one of those modern hands-on fathers. I am not designed that way and I work too-long hours.'

The light in her eyes dimmed a little more. 'Being hands-on would be good for you.'

'I doubt that and I doubt it would be good for the baby. I'll pay for any help you need but I won't be doing any of the work myself.'

Seeing she was prepared to argue, he cut her off. '*Carina*, we have months until the baby comes. I've had five very long days in the company of sharks and now I want nothing but to go for a swim and have some dinner.'

Her brows drew together. 'Did the trip not go well?'

Her obvious concern sliced through him. 'It was successful. The deal was signed.'

But the negotiations had been a lot tougher than he'd anticipated.

The Casillas brothers had always negotiated together. It had not felt right without Luis there, as if he were negotiating with an arm tied behind his back and a leg missing.

Luis had always been the counterpoint to him, charming the people who mattered, willing to play the game when Javier would rather cut his toes off than schmooze.

This time he'd had to play the role of good cop and bad cop in one.

He had managed it though.

His successful negotiations had been the proof he needed that he didn't need his brother in his life in any capacity.

'Will you have to spend a lot of time in South Africa when the development starts?'

'Yes. There will be occasions when I'm away for weeks at a time.'

He only just managed to cut himself off from suggesting that she accompany him on some of the trips.

The light in her eyes dimmed into nothing. Her lips drew tighter but then she hugged her arms around her chest and took a step back. 'I have something to show you.'

'What?'

'I have to show you, not tell you.'

He stared at her quizzically, then shrugged. 'Go on, then.'

He followed her down the stairs. As they walked, she kept up a light chatter about the nursery. 'I've also hired a local carpenter to make some bespoke furniture for it but he can't start working on it for a few weeks yet.'

'He had some scruples, did he?' he asked drily, wondering why she suddenly seemed so nervous.

She laughed but it sounded forced. 'I discovered that not everyone can be bought.'

You can't, he thought. In a world where money ruled he had married perhaps the only person on it who could not be paid for.

His thoughts turned to a blank when he stepped through the door Sophie opened that led into the smallest of his huge living rooms.

Lying on his solid oak floor, which he had treated twice a year to keep it in immaculate condition, fast asleep on a plastic oval bed heaped with blankets that dwarfed its tiny size, was a dog.

'What the hell is that?'

As he spoke, the dog opened its eyes and clambered to its feet.

'A puppy.'

He glared at her. 'I can see that. I meant what the hell is it doing in my house?'

'*Our* house.' The dog had padded to her feet and was scratching at her knee. She scooped it up and held it protectively in her arms. 'You said I should treat it as my home.'

'That does not give you licence to buy a dog.'

'I didn't buy it. I found it by—'

'You've brought a stray dog into my house?' he interrupted. 'What's wrong with you? Who knows what diseases it has?'

'*He* has no disease. I found him bleeding outside the gates of the house and took him to the vet. He was covered in puncture wounds, so we think he was mauled by another dog. The vet treated his wounds. Other than being terrified and in pain from the mauling, there's nothing wrong with him.'

'Why hasn't he been returned to his owner?'

'He isn't microchipped and no one's claimed him. It's likely he's been abandoned.'

He knew her intentions immediately. 'No.'

'Yes.'

'No. We are *not* having a dog.'

'We're not, *I* am. If the owner doesn't declare

him or herself by the end of next week Frodo will
be registered as mine.'

'Frodo?'

'He looks like a Frodo. He already answers to
it.' Putting her nose down to the black rug in her
arms' nose, she said, in word-perfect Spanish,
'You already know your name, don't you, Frodo?'

'Since when do you speak Spanish?' he asked
in amazement.

'I've lived here for almost two years.'

'You've never spoken it before.'

'I made my wedding vows in Spanish. Besides,
I haven't needed to with you,' she said, revert-
ing back to her native language. 'Your English
is much better than my Spanish. I speak Spanish with the staff.'

Realising he'd been distracted from the conversation at hand, he steered it back. 'He's not staying. We are not having a dog. You have enough
to cope with.'

She could not argue with that logic.

Turned out she could.

'The baby's not due for five months. That's
plenty of time to train it before the kumquat's
born. He's only a puppy. The vet thinks he's
about three months old.'

'What do you know about training a dog?'

'I grew up with dogs. And cats and guinea pigs and stick insects. I told you before you left for Cape Town that I always wanted to be a vet.'

Dios, the infuriating woman had an answer for everything.

But he would not be swayed.

'No. This is not a house for a dog. Think of the mess it will create. I have antiques and artefacts worth millions.' In the corner of this room alone stood a statue of ancient Greek heritage. 'It can stay until next Friday to recover from its injuries. If the owner does not come forward it will go to a dog rescue and be adopted.'

His word final, he strolled out of the living room, intent on finding Julio and demanding to know why none of his staff had seen fit to warn him of his wife's doings.

'How can you be so *cruel*?'

He took a deep breath and turned back around.

His heart wrenched.

Sophie's eyes were bright with unshed tears, her chin wobbling. The puppy nuzzled into her hand. 'This is a poor, defenceless puppy who's been abandoned by its owner and now you want me to abandon it too. Well, I'm sorry but I can't.

Look at the poor little thing. You think a stupid artefact is worth more than a *life*? If he doesn't stay then I don't stay.'

He stared at her with disbelief. 'I thought you didn't make threats.'

'I'm not making a threat. I'm telling you how it is. I will not abandon him. He needs me.'

'He does not need you. He needs a family, agreed, but it does not need to be this one.'

'It *does*!' She took a long inhalation, seeming to suck the tears back before they could fall. 'He's just settling in and now you want him to be uprooted all over again? What do you think that would do to him after everything he's been through? This house is *enormous*. We can compromise, we can put one of the living rooms aside for his use—this one would be perfect—and clear it of your precious artefacts so he can't damage anything, but if you won't compromise then I shall pack my things now because I am *not* giving him up.'

His incredulity grew. 'I don't understand you. I keep thinking it isn't possible for you to have such a soft heart but then you threaten our marriage over a *dog*.'

She adjusted her hold on the ball of fluff. 'You

don't understand me because you think my life has been nothing but unicorns and rainbows. You have no idea...'

'Are you telling me it hasn't been?' he demanded. 'You, with your talk of a house filled with animals, parents who love and support you... You have been raised with everything a child could desire.'

Everything he'd been denied as he'd been dragged around the world with a mother who'd barely tolerated him, never home long enough between tours for them to entertain a pet, a volatile father who'd idolised him but been so cruel to his twin.

Sophie could have no comprehension of his life and what he and his brother had lived through.

'Not everything, no,' she said tremulously, her face contorting. 'If you had read the documents I couriered to you for our wedding you would know I'm adopted. I was abandoned as a baby.'

His disbelief turned into shock.

He hadn't read the documents. He'd trusted they were in order and got his PA to send them to the officiant.

His brain began to burn as he suddenly wished he had read through them rather than tossing them to one side as if they meant nothing when what they had represented was the woman standing in front of him only just holding herself together over a dog.

He swallowed his lump-ridden throat. 'You were abandoned?'

She nodded, her throat moving as she stepped back to sit on the hand-stitched Italian leather sofa, cuddling the puppy on her lap.

If she hadn't just dropped her bombshell he would have demanded she move the dog far away from his extremely expensive sofa.

'Don't think I'm playing for sympathy here,' she said. 'I would never play the victim card because I'm not a victim. I've been incredibly lucky and you're right, compared to yours, my childhood was unicorns and rainbows and I'm lucky that my parents—the people who adopted me—are all I can remember, but you said you don't understand me and maybe it's time you did.'

'How old were you?'

She drew her lips in and swallowed before answering. 'I was hours old when I was found. I'd been left outside a church in a village on the south coast of Devon. The vicar's wife found me—she'd come to lock the church for the night. I was lucky that she heard my cries because it was too dark for her to see me. I was put in the care of social services and fostered until my parents adopted me when I was eighteen months old.'

He swore, the burn in his brain at boiling point. 'How old were you when you learned this?'

Her hands stroked the dog's ears. 'I've always known. My parents never kept it a secret from me. My mum had cervical cancer in her early twenties and had to have a hysterectomy, so they couldn't have children of their own. They always said I was their miracle from God, delivered to them at His house.' She met his eyes and smiled. 'They're wrong—they're *my* miracle. When I think of all the couples out there that could have adopted me, I was given to a couple who loved me more than any child could possibly be loved.'

His legs becoming too shaky to support his weight, Javier staggered onto the armchair across from her. 'I'm sorry. I wish you had told me all this.'

'There's nothing to be sorry for. It's not something I talk about much because it's not something I remember. My life as I know it began on the day of my adoption and it's been a wonderful life.'

Abandoned at her first breath and that was a wonderful life?

'Did they ever find your birth mother?'

'No. It was assumed she was a young teenager but she could have been anyone. No one came forward, no one was admitted to hospital with evident signs of recently giving birth, those who had given birth that day were all accounted for... She vanished. She could be anyone. My natural father could be anyone.'

'Do you wonder about them?'

'All the time.' Her smile saddened. 'I can't look at a new face without scanning it for a resemblance but I know I'll never find them. I pray my birth mother's alive and well.'

'You forgive her?'

'Whatever her reasons for giving me up, she must have been terrified and in so much pain.'

She meant it. He could see that clearly.

Sophie had forgiven the woman who abandoned her.

'How do you do it?' he asked starkly. 'How do you forgive? How can you open your heart so much when the people who should have loved and cared for you abandoned you as they did?'

'Because I was found.' She stared straight at

him. 'I will never know the reasons and I accept that. But I was found and I was saved—my cries were heard. I've known that all my life and all my life I've sworn that I will never ignore any living soul's cries for help.' She pressed a kiss to the puppy's head, her eyes not leaving Javier's face. 'This little thing is as innocent and as helpless as I was and I will not abandon it.'

'No.' He sighed heavily.

Everything about Sophie made sense now.

He'd known she was different from the very start. He'd seen that goodness and compassion shining out of her, the reverse lens of himself.

Where his heart had contracted into a shell, hers had expanded to embrace anyone who needed it.

But she was tough too. Her heart was as soft as a sweetened sponge but her spine was made of steel.

He did not doubt that she would take that abandoned dog and walk away from him if he refused to let it stay.

'No,' he repeated. 'I understand. The dog can stay. You can give it the love it needs.'

I can give you the love you need too, if only you would let me.

The thought popped into her head before Sophie could take it back but this time she did not push it away.

She rubbed the soft ears of the sweet, loving thing in her arms and wished she could hold Javier in the same way.

There was no point denying her feelings towards him any more. She loved him. She'd always loved him.

The heart was incapable of listening to reason and her heart had attached itself to Javier the first time she'd set eyes on him.

Whether he was capable of returning her love, she didn't know and told herself it didn't matter. His eyes had shone to see their child's nursery. He was developing feelings for their unborn child, she was sure of it. He'd agreed that Frodo could stay, so there was something akin to compassion inside him.

But Javier was far more damaged than the affectionate puppy in her arms.

Javier was reading the story he'd had emailed from a reporter who worked for an English newspaper when the landline on his office desk rang.

He pressed the button. He'd told his PA not to put any calls through unless it was his wife.

'I have Dante Moncada on line one,' she told him. 'He says it's important.'

He sighed. Dante Moncada was a Sicilian technology magnate who'd inherited a one-hundred-acre plot of land in a prime location off Florence that he had no use for and wanted to sell. Javier and Luis had been in talks about buying it from him. Nothing had been signed. It had been very early days in the talks when Javier and Luis had gone their separate ways.

Javier had held off doing anything about the deal while the lawyers set about severing the Casillas brothers' business, an issue that almost two months on was dragging interminably. Luis had communicated via their lawyers that he wanted to meet. Javier had refused. He never wanted to set eyes on his brother again.

His anger at Luis's treachery had not lessened in the slightest but he wanted a clean break for them.

He might despise the man he had loved and protected his entire life but he would not do anything to gain an advantage in the severance. The lawyers would ensure everything was split equally. That had been his firm belief until Dante had called him the week before to inform him that

Luis had made a private offer for the land and asking if Javier would like to counter it.

His brother's latest display of treachery had speared him but he had hardened himself.

If his brother could be so disloyal as to hitch himself to the bitch who had worked to destroy him then Javier should not be surprised that Luis was going behind his back to steal business by targeting the clients they had cultivated together.

Two could play that game. And Javier would win.

'Yes,' he had informed the Sicilian. 'I would like to counter it. How much has he offered?'

Dante had given him the figure. Javier had increased it. He'd been waiting for a response ever since.

'Put him through,' he said now.

'Javier!' came the thickly accented voice.

'Dante. What can I do for you? Have you called to say you will accept my offer?'

'I'm coming to Madrid tomorrow for a few days of business. I've bought an apartment in your city, so I'm going to throw a party to celebrate. Come. We can discuss business then.'

His heart sank. Dante's parties were as legendary as his party-loving brother's.

He estimated this was Dante's tenth property purchase. The man would not be happy until he had property in every city in Europe.

'Will Luis be there?' he asked, stalling while he tried to think of an excuse.

Javier loathed parties. He despised watching people lose their inhibitions through alcohol, becoming worse versions of themselves. It was why he never drank. His father had been volatile enough without the alcohol he had come to depend on. He would never risk doing the same. He'd attended his brother's parties only so he could keep an eye on him and stop him doing stupid things, like swimming drunk.

He would not go to any function his brother attended.

'He's not answering my calls, so…'

The unspoken implication did not go over his head. If Luis was incommunicado then the land was Javier's for the taking.

'What's the address?'

Dante gave it to him, then finished by saying, 'Bring your wife. Everyone's dying to meet her.'

He would rather swim with sharks with a gashed knee pouring blood than take Sophie to that Lothario's party.

Giving a non-committal grunt, he ended the call and rubbed his temples.

He had a headache forming.

He put a call through to his PA for a coffee and painkillers, then turned his attention back to the computer screen.

Right then he had more important things to think about.

It had taken him weeks to find the information he'd sought. He could have passed the job on to one of his employees to oversee on his behalf but this was something he'd needed to find himself.

The reporter he'd paid to trawl through the archives of an English paper from Devon had finally come up trumps.

Before him was a copy of a report dated over twenty-four years ago, published before the Internet had been the go-to place for news reports.

Sophie's story had been front-page news. The news report gave all the details she'd skimmed over and omitted.

She'd omitted to mention, for example, that she'd been so severely dehydrated the doctors hadn't thought she would survive the night.

When she'd been found, she'd been swaddled

in a pink blanket and left in an old box that had once contained crisps.

She hadn't been left on the church's steps where she would be easily found, she'd been left in the shrubbery.

It had been a miracle that she'd been found.

And she prayed for the woman who'd abandoned her and hoped she was alive and well?

Javier had no such compassion. He hoped, with every fibre of his being, that the woman who'd abandoned his wife to die had lived a short and painful life.

But there was no way of knowing. Sophie had been right that her birth mother would never be found.

That was something else he'd dug into these past few weeks. The police investigation had been extremely thorough, he'd had to admit. They had left no stone unturned.

Everyone had been of the opinion that it had been a young teenage girl who'd been terrified to discover she was pregnant.

Why Javier had been so determined to delve into that period of Sophie's life when, by her own admittance, she had always accepted it as a fact of her life, he did not know, but it had been

like a compulsion in him, a need to learn everything about her, to dig deep into her psyche and
discover how someone who'd been left to die on
her first day of life could contain such a beautiful, pure heart.

How could she live with him and his cold,
vengeful heart without being repulsed?

How could she bear for him to even touch her?

CHAPTER TEN

'WHAT ARE YOU READING?'

Sophie, sitting cross-legged on the bed with a pillow and laptop on her lap, looked up and smiled to see Javier in the doorway. She'd been so engrossed she hadn't heard him get back from work.

'I'm looking at veterinary nurse courses for after the baby's born,' she said, turning the laptop around to show him. 'I'm trying to work out if it's feasible.'

He strolled over to perch next to her. 'To train as a vet nurse?'

She nodded. The days she spent with Frodo had reignited her love of animals and her old dream of working with them.

His brow furrowed. 'Why would you do that?'

'I thought you were supportive of me working. All that talk about nannies—'

'I didn't mean it like that,' he cut in. 'I meant why would you want to be a vet *nurse*?'

'Do you think it would be too much?' she asked anxiously. 'From what I've read, I'll be able to do most of the studying from home—'

'No,' he interrupted again with rising exasperation. 'Why train to be a vet *nurse* when you've always wanted to be a *vet*?'

'It takes years to train to be a vet. Besides, I haven't got the qualifications.'

'Then get them.'

She blinked a number of times. The educational options that had been available at her ballet school had not included those that gave an entry into veterinary school. She would have to go back to basics. 'Just like that?'

'Why not?'

'Javier, it will take me years to get the necessary qualifications *if* I can get them...'

'Why would you not get them? You're not stupid. If you can be a professional ballerina when your heart wasn't in it then there is no reason whatsoever that you can't achieve the qualifications needed to train as a vet.'

'But then I'll have to spend years studying at university. I have to think of our child and—'

'Stop making excuses,' he snapped. He pulled the laptop off her and deleted the link she'd been reading before closing the lid. 'You've always wanted to be a vet, so stop making excuses and for once in your life start putting yourself first. If it takes ten years for you to do it then so what? It took Luis and me almost that long to start earning serious money from Casillas Ventures but we never entertained the idea of giving up and you shouldn't either. This is your dream, *carina*, so grab it.'

She stared at him, her heart blooming at his logic and defence of her dreams.

'Wouldn't it bother you?' she asked eventually.

'Should it matter if it did?' he countered.

'You're my husband. Of course your opinion and feelings matter.'

'More than your own? Is that not what you did before? Put your dreams to one side because you thought more of your parents' feelings than your own?'

'It wasn't exactly like that,' she murmured, embarrassed.

He raised a disbelieving brow.

'Okay, maybe it was a little,' she conceded. 'They loved watching me dance. It meant so much to them, so what else could I have done? They gave me so much. They gave me a home and a family. They gave me love.'

'Did you think if you went against their wishes they would withdraw that love?' he asked with an astuteness that stunned her.

Javier displayed such indifference to her that it was a shock to realise he actually paid attention to everything she said. And everything she didn't.

She sighed and pulled at her hair. 'I don't know. I remember worrying about that when I was little and fully comprehended what being adopted meant. They chose to bring me into their lives, so there was always that dread that they could then choose to give me back.' She'd forgotten that long-ago irrational fear, an unintended consequence of her parents' complete honesty about her beginnings. 'I think…it was this pregnancy that showed me their love for me was truly unconditional.'

'How?'

She shrugged ruefully. 'I was afraid to tell them. They're very spiritual. They believe greatly in marriage coming before children and I was afraid they would think less of me.'

'Did you think they would reject you?'

'Not on a rational level but it was there in the back of my mind, yes. I hadn't even realised how scared I was to tell them until they practically squashed me with their hugs.'

'Are they the reason you were a virgin when we conceived our baby?'

It was the first time this had been acknowledged out loud between them.

Sophie met his steady gaze and gave a tiny nod.

He extended a hand as if to reach for her belly, then changed his mind before he could touch it and got to his feet. He rolled his neck. 'It is time you thought of your own needs rather than always thinking of others. Our child will be much happier for having a fulfilled mother than one who settled for second best. If you want to be a vet then be a vet. Better to try and fail than never have the guts to try in the—' He cut himself off, now looking at the floor-length navy-blue dress hanging on the dressing-room door. 'Have you been shopping?'

Disconcerted by the sudden change of subject, she took a moment to remember.

'I popped out this afternoon. I meant to put it away but got distracted with all the vet nurse stuff.'

She moved the pillow off her lap and scrambled off the bed to get the dress.

Frodo, who had taken to following her like a shadow and been dozing by the bed, woke and jumped up in an attempt to grab hold of it but she whipped it out of his way and took it into the dressing room.

Javier followed her and rested his hand on the doorway.

She waited for him to make a comment on the puppy being in their bedroom, which he had effectively banned and she had effectively ignored if he wasn't in, but instead he asked, 'What's the dress for?'

'The party.'

'What party?'

'Dante Moncado's party tomorrow night.'

He was silent for a beat before asking, 'How do you know about that?'

'The invitation was hand-delivered this morning. It was addressed to both of us, so I opened it. I've put it on your dressing table.'

He took hold of it and read it silently. Then he put it back down and rubbed his face. 'We've been invited for business purposes. You won't enjoy it, *carina*.'

'How do you know that?'

'You're pregnant.'

'Yes, pregnant. Not dead.'

'It will be full of rich, posturing idiots. I'll go on my own, conduct our business and come back.'

Her heart thumped, the warm fuzzy feelings generated by Javier's brusque insistence that she should follow her dreams squashed back to nothing. 'Do you know, you haven't taken me anywhere since we married. Are you ashamed of me?'

'What a ridiculous thing to say. And I have taken you out.' He'd taken her to a business dinner where partners had been invited.

'A business dinner doesn't count. You haven't taken me out—out socially.'

'This is a party I've been invited to for the sole purpose of business, not for social reasons.'

'But it's an actual party. It says so on the invite. And my name's on the invite too. I want to go.'

'I didn't realise you were a party person,' he said stiffly.

'You never asked and we haven't been invited to any...' She narrowed her eyes, suspicions rising. 'Unless you didn't tell me about them.'

He stared back.

It took such a long time for him to answer that her suspicions became a certainty.

He had turned invitations down without mentioning anything about them to her.

'I never go to parties,' he eventually said in the same stiff voice. 'I don't drink. Who wants to watch people get drunk and make fools of themselves?'

'I do.' She hated that her voice sounded so forlorn and made an effort to strengthen it. 'If you won't take me then I really will think you're ashamed of me.'

Would he have these qualms about taking Freya with him? Sophie wondered.

He'd probably only said all that stuff about her becoming a vet so she would be occupied and out of his hair for the next ten years, she thought bitterly.

It hadn't crossed her mind that he wouldn't want to go to the party. She was well aware that her husband was not one of life's great socialisers but had assumed he would be willing to attend a party being hosted only twenty minutes from their home. Since his return from Cape Town he'd taken to giving her prior warning of meetings and functions he had planned that would take place outside normal office hours. It was a gesture that had given her hope. Slowly their marriage had been starting to feel like a real one. His attitude now put her right back to square one.

He had nothing booked in for tomorrow night.

All she could think was that he didn't want to show his second-choice wife to his peers.

So proud had he been of having Freya tied to him that he'd thrown a huge party to celebrate their engagement.

He hadn't invited a single guest to their wedding. They hadn't had a single guest to their home since they'd married.

'I am *not* ashamed of you.' He groped at his hair.

'Then prove it and take me,' she challenged. 'We don't have to stay for long. You can conduct your business and I can meet some new people and then we can come back.'

Even Frodo, sitting at her feet, looked at Javier expectantly.

Javier noticed. 'What about the dog? We can't take him to a party or give him free rein alone in the house, and you won't put him in a crate.'

Sensing victory, Sophie smiled and opened

the bedroom door. Marsela, the youngest of the household staff and a live-in one to boot, had been cleaning the spare bedrooms a short while earlier. She called for her.

A moment later, Marsela appeared.

Frodo spotted her and bounded over, his tail wagging happily.

'Have you got any plans tomorrow night?' Sophie asked.

'No. I have a date with a box set.'

'Any chance you could dog-sit Frodo while you watch it?'

Marsela's eyes lit up. 'I would love to.'

'Thank you!' Turning back to Javier, Sophie fixed him with a stare. 'So, are we going?'

His face like thunder, he gave a sharp nod, turned on his heel and stormed from the room.

She let him go, her heart battering manically against her ribs.

She could take no joy in her victory, however widely she pasted her smile.

Forcing his hand into taking her made it a hollow one.

Javier stepped out of the door his driver held open for him, then extended a hand to Sophie.

She took hold of it with a smile of thanks and, careful of her dress, climbed out.

Then she straightened, carefully smoothed her hair, which she'd styled into loose curls, and said, 'I think this is the part where we go in.'

He breathed deeply and gave a nod. 'Prepare yourself. Everyone will be watching you.'

'I'll be fine,' she said with a brittleness to her tone he'd never heard before.

He would learn soon enough if she was right.

She certainly looked the part.

When she'd appeared from the dressing room, it had taken everything he had to stop his mouth gaping open like a simpleton.

The light had shone behind her, making her glow like an angel.

Her floor-length dress, navy-blue mesh lace, low cut at the top to skim her ever-growing cleavage and puffing out at the hips, fitted her as well as if it had been made bespoke for her.

A more perfect vision of glowing beauty he had never seen.

The thought of lecherous eyes soaking in her beauty for their own delectation had made him feel like a thousand bugs were crawling over his skin.

He'd wanted to pull that dress off and make love to her so thoroughly that his scent would be marked in her, a warning to all others to not even look let alone touch.

It had been a fearsome thought that had him clenching his hands into fists and walking out of the bedroom before he could act on it.

They had not exchanged a solitary word on the drive over.

Resting a hand lightly to her back, he led her through the old, exclusive apartment building, where a concierge escorted them to the elevator that would take them to Dante's new penthouse.

The huge, open-plan space the party was being hosted in was already filled with guests.

The buzz of chatter increased in volume and excitement as Javier guided Sophie through the throng, his eyes seeking Dante, already keen to get this over with and get the hell out.

They could stare and gossip about him as much as they liked but his wife was not a piece of meat to be studied and gaped at.

He'd turned down four parties on their behalf since they'd married. Never minding his loathing of large gatherings, he'd had no intention of putting Sophie in the firing line of the inquisitive eyes he was always subjected to at these things. Now all he could do was get through his business as quickly as he could and get her out of there.

Swiping them a glass of fruit juice each from a passing waiter, Javier was taking his first sip when Dante approached, the easy smile so reminiscent of Luis's smile on his face.

'I knew you'd come,' he said smugly, before introducing himself to Sophie and putting his hands on her bare shoulders to kiss her cheeks in turn.

Javier clenched his jaw and forced himself to breathe, turning his mind away from the impulse to punch Dante in the face.

Get a grip of yourself. He's only greeting her the way he greets everyone; the way all polite society people greet each other.

His fingers still itched to punch him though.

Dante called his date over. She was a statuesque model, famed as the elite designers' clothes horse of choice.

Her eyes fixed on Javier with a gleam he recognised, part fear, part curiosity, part desire.

He only just managed to stop his face twisting with disgust.

The woman was beautiful, that could not be

denied, but she did not hold a candle to Sophie. No one did. No one could.

Dante turned to the woman. 'Lola, look after Sophie while I steal her husband away. We have business to discuss.'

If Sophie was bothered about being palmed off, she didn't show it. She smiled at Javier and gave an almost imperceptible wink.

'I'm afraid I have disappointing news,' Dante said as he led him into his private office. 'The sale's off—temporarily.'

'Oh?'

Dante opened a cabinet and pulled out a bottle of Scotch and two glasses. 'An illegitimate heir has come out of the woodwork. Her lawyers say she has a claim to the inheritance and therefore a claim to the land.'

'And does she?'

Dante's eyes glittered menacingly. 'I will make sure she doesn't.'

Javier shrugged. He couldn't care less about Dante's problems. All he cared about was taking his wife home.

'Drink?'

Javier raised his palm and shook his head.

'Oh, yes, I forgot you don't drink. That was always Luis's forte. And speaking of Luis, I'm surprised you're not in the Caribbean with him. Or are the rumours that you two have ended more than your business relationship true?'

Javier did not dignify that with a response.

His private business was no one else's concern. Dante might be comfortable sharing personal confidences; that did not mean Javier had to follow suit.

'When do you anticipate solving the problem with the illegitimate heir?' he asked, putting the conversation back on the business footing it should have stayed on.

'A few weeks. Maybe a month. I'll call you when it's done. I should warn you though, Luis has asked that I give him the opportunity to make another counter-offer.'

'Whatever he offers, I will top it,' Javier said flatly.

Dante raised his glass and grinned. 'I do love a bidding war.' He knocked back the Scotch, grimaced and poured himself another. 'My money would be on you winning.'

Despite himself, Javier's curiosity got the better of him. 'Why?'

Luis might be the more easy-going of the Casillas brothers but when it came to business he was as razor sharp as Javier. It was what had made them such a good team.

'When I saw him the other week he was all loved-up.' His grimace that time had nothing to do with the drink. 'His heart's not with the business, it's with his new wife…'

'He's not married yet,' Javier interjected.

Dante's surprise appeared genuine. 'You don't know? Luis and Chloe married yesterday. They released a statement about it this morning.'

Sophie stared around at the crowd of beautifully dressed people all so comfortable in their wealth and standing in society and felt as she'd done on her wedding day: like an imposter.

She had been so looking forward to this party, had been determined to ignore Javier's grumpiness about it and embrace something new in this new life of hers, something they could share together.

Lola, the cat-eyed supermodel, had abandoned her after a few minutes of not-in-the-slightest-bit-subtle questioning that Sophie had stonewalled with non-committal answers all delivered with a smile so as not to hurt her feelings.

But, honestly, did Lola really expect her to share confidences about her husband with a complete stranger?

She wished she could have a glass of the free-flowing champagne but she hadn't touched a drop of alcohol in her pregnancy and was not about to start now.

Sliding her phone out of her clutch bag, she messaged Marsela to check on Frodo, pretending not to see the inquisitive stares still being directed at her from all corners.

She missed her little shadow. He was such a playful comfort to her during the days when she felt Javier's absence like a hole in her heart. She didn't have a clue what breed he was, some kind of small poodle cross. The vet had suggested a DNA test on him but she'd decided not to. Whatever Frodo was, he was hers and she loved him. He responded to her love in a way she wished so badly that Javier would.

Javier hadn't even bothered to comment on her appearance. She'd made such an effort for him, desperately wanting him to be proud to have her on his arm, but he'd looked her up and down and left the room.

A slap on the face would have been kinder.

'You look lost.'

The man who'd approached her, who could only be described as a silver fox, smiled.

She smiled back at the friendly face that matched the unmistakable English voice. 'Not lost. Just soaking up the atmosphere.'

'Javier abandoned you, has he?' he said, his words and tone implying he and Javier were acquaintances.

They wouldn't be friends. Javier did not have friends.

'He's talking with Dante.'

'Were you not invited to join them?'

She pulled a face. 'It's about business, something I know nothing about.'

'Ah, yes, you're a ballerina. I remember watching you perform in *The Sleeping Beauty.*'

'Did you?' she asked dubiously. She had been a part of the *corps de ballet* and utterly inconspicuous in her costume.

He suddenly looked sheepish. 'My wife—she's Spanish—dragged me along to it. I only know you were in it because she told me on the drive over here. Dante told everyone that Javier would be bringing his new wife. You're the star attraction, you know.'

'Am I?'

'But of course. He's been hiding you away for months. We all wanted to see you for ourselves and make sure that it wasn't a vicious rumour that he'd snared another young English ballerina as his bride—' He cut himself off and winced. 'My apologies. That was callous of me.'

'No, it's fine.' She adopted nonchalance. There was no point in making a fuss over what everyone was thinking. Javier's engagement to Freya had been announced with huge fanfare. His marriage to Sophie had not even had an official press release. 'I'm the second-choice young English ballerina bride.'

'Maybe second choice but I would hazard a guess that you're not second best.' His eyes dipped to her belly. 'Because I can see the other rumour is true too...unless this is where you tell me you're not pregnant but had an extra helping of cheesecake.'

Sophie burst into laughter. 'Yes, I'm pregnant and the great thing about it is I can have as much cheesecake as I like.'

'You won't find any at this party if Dante's girlfriend organised the catering.' He guffawed. 'Let's see if we can find some food that isn't just fit for rabbits. We might find my wife somewhere too. I think she's abandoned me.'

Glad of the friendly company, Sophie was about to follow him when she spotted Dante in a corner, chatting with a group of people.

If his meeting with Javier was done with…

She craned her neck, then craned some more.

Where was Javier?

Javier steamed down the dark streets, his hands rammed in his trouser pockets, dodging the evening revellers spilling onto the pavements from the bars and clubs.

His blood raced with rage. Pure, undiluted, unfiltered rage.

He had finished his meeting with Dante with his brain burning to learn Luis had married.

The faint hope he'd unknowingly held onto that his brother would come to his senses and end things with Chloe had been stamped out.

He had married her.

Prepared to grab Sophie and insist they leave immediately, he had been confronted with her talking to a handsome man he vaguely recognised.

Not just talking to him either, he thought

grimly, remembering the laughter that had shone on her face.

She'd been enjoying the man's company so much that she'd been oblivious to her husband standing only ten feet away watching them.

In that moment he'd had a choice.

Either he could go to them, lift the man flirting so shamelessly with his wife into the air and hurl him out of a window or he could leave.

He'd left without looking back.

His phone vibrated in his pocket, the third time it had rung.

He pulled it out and, not looking at it, turned it off.

Right then he did not want to see or speak to anyone.

He did not trust himself.

Right then the urge to inflict the pain coursing through his veins on someone else was too strong to risk, that much self-awareness he did have.

He walked for miles, detouring through pavements he hadn't trod on since he was a teenager and his and Luis's only means of transport had been their legs.

Thirteen years old they'd been when Madrid had suddenly become their home. To escape the grandparents who'd been little more than strangers to them, they had explored the new streets they lived on, a tight unit, protecting each other as they had always done.

In every corner lay a memory.

Eventually he could put it off no longer.

He slowed his pace as he walked the long driveway to his home and climbed the marble steps.

Before he could open the door, it swung open.

Standing there, her face white with fury, was Sophie.

CHAPTER ELEVEN

SOPHIE DIDN'T KNOW whether to throw her arms around Javier in her relief or push him down the steps.

She'd searched everywhere in that huge apartment for him, refusing to believe he would have left without her.

She'd only confronted the truth when she'd gone outside to look and Michael, his driver, who'd been waiting for them, had gently told her Javier had chosen to walk home.

That had been three hours ago.

The realisation that he'd abandoned her with a roomful of strangers had knocked all the wind out of her.

She'd been too shocked to be angry.

Then the time had passed while she'd waited for him to come home and the anger had built.

That anger had been giving way to concern when she had spotted him in the CCTV camera feed she'd sat herself in front of.

Now she didn't know how she felt, just that she was so full of contrary emotions that she would either cry or scream.

He stared back at her, his features taut, a pulse throbbing on his jaw, hands rammed in his pockets, breathing heavily.

He was the one to break the oppressive silence.

'You need to step out of my way.'

She shook her head. 'No.'

'Sophie, at this moment I do not trust myself to be anywhere near you. Get out of my way.'

Holding her ground, she folded her arms across her chest. 'No.'

He swore loudly.

'I'm not moving until you tell me why you left me at the party without a—'

'You didn't look as if you'd care,' he spat back, suddenly springing to life to brush past her and enter the house.

She pushed the door shut and turned in time to see him storm up the stairs.

Barefooted, holding the skirt of her dress up, she pursued him.

She might be pregnant but she was still quick and she reached the bedroom door before he could slam it shut and lock her out.

'Sophie, you need to leave,' he told her tightly as he held the door frame, his knuckles white, refusing her admittance. 'Sleep in another room tonight. We will talk in the morning when I am not so angry.'

'When *you're* not so angry? I'm the only one who should be angry. You abandoned me.'

He winced at her choice of word.

Good. So he damned well should wince.

'I told Michael I was walking home. I knew he would get you back safely.'

'You *left* me there. You humiliated me in front of all those people who were already laughing at me.'

'If you felt humiliated you did a fine job of hiding it. You looked like you were having a damned good time without me. Now, I need you to go.'

'I am not going anywhere. You're not shutting me out, Javier. Why did you leave? Tell me!'

'It was either leave or throw your boyfriend out of the window. Would you have preferred I do that?'

'What are you talking about?'

'I saw you, *carina*. With that man. Laughing with him.'

She suddenly remembered the Englishman

she'd briefly chatted with, the only bright spot of her entire night. 'My God, were you jealous? Is that what this is all about?'

'Right now, I do not know anything other than that I cannot trust myself to be in the same room as you and you need to get the hell out of my sight until I am calm.'

Struggling for air, her heart thumping, Sophie took a step back, saw Javier loosen his hold on the frame of the door and, before he could close it, used the advantage of surprise to push past him and into the bedroom.

'Get out!' he howled.

'No, I will not! You're behaving like an idiot. All I was doing was talking. Or is that illegal now? Do I need your permission to talk to a man? Or maybe you would like to cover me in a bin bag when I leave the house? And what do you even care?' she continued, her voice getting louder as she gathered momentum, all her bottled-up feelings rising like poison inside her. 'I'm just a possession to you, aren't I? The second-best wife, not as good as your first choice, not as *perfect*, not good enough to be taken out in public with pride because I'm only a second-rate ballerina, not as pretty—'

'That's enough!'

His roar echoed through the walls as he lunged for her, taking hold of her biceps and leaning down to her, his breath hot on her face. 'Don't you ever put yourself down again, do you hear me? You are worth a million Freyas. Don't you see that? You are the most incredible, special person I have ever met in my life and it scares the *hell* out of me that one day I might hurt you. I felt *nothing* for Freya and she felt nothing for me and that was safe. You do not make me feel safe. You make me feel things I should never feel and the thought of anyone hurting a hair on your beautiful head makes me want to rip heads off bodies and that's what I've been fighting against since you walked into my life because I know the biggest danger to you is *me*.'

If a heart could burst then hers just did.

'Oh, Javier,' she whispered, a tear spilling down her cheek as she put a trembling hand to his face and gazed helplessly at the eyes that swirled with more emotion than she could have ever hoped to see in them. 'You are not your father.'

Javier stared at the beautiful, open face that haunted his every waking and sleeping moment and suddenly he was lost.

Pushing her against the wall, he kissed her with every ounce of feeling contained inside him.

Her lips parted to welcome him and then they were clinging together, her arms tight around his neck as he fed on her kisses like a condemned man taking his one last meal.

A desperation he had never felt before overcame him, a need to touch and be touched, and it hit him like a fever in his brain, the blood that had sprung to life all that time ago for this beautiful, incredible woman awake and crashing through his body, refusing to be denied or ignored any longer.

He lifted her into his arms and cradled her in them, gazing into her eyes as he carried her to the bed, marvelling with wonder at the colours and emotions he saw in their depths.

How had he never seen them before?

And she stared back with equal intensity.

Laying her on the bed, he put his palm to her cheek and caressed the satin skin his fingers always yearned to touch.

And then he kissed her again.

And then he was drowning.

Working as one as they devoured each other with their mouths, they stripped their clothes off, throwing them without a care for where they landed, the need to be naked in each other's arms too strong to care for anything but this moment, this here, this now.

Because whatever fever had him in its grip, it was in Sophie too, there in the hunger of her kisses and the urgency of her touch.

He wanted to feel every part of her, to give this woman who sang to his heart all the passion and love that had broken free from its casing for her.

He opened his ears to her sighs and let them seep into his senses and then he opened *all* his senses to her.

He was helpless to do anything else.

And she opened her senses to him.

Her fingers traced lightly over his chest, exploring him, her mouth following, her nose brushing over his skin to breathe him in, touching him in a way he had never been touched before.

Every breath of her mouth to his flesh seeped deep inside him to the bones that lay beneath.

He brushed his lips over every part of her too. He inhaled the scent of her skin so deeply that it became a part of him. He kissed her breasts and felt their weight in his hands. He ran his fingers over her belly, a distant part of him awed at what lay inside it but only a distant part because this moment was not about their child, this moment was for her, for him, for them.

When he inhaled the musky heat between her legs, he almost lost himself entirely.

How had he blocked it out so well before and for so long?

It was a scent he would remember for the rest of his life.

If he could love any woman it would be this one, he thought dimly, pressing a kiss to her hip before pushing himself back up to stare into the pale blue eyes once more.

Sophie gazed into the eyes staring at her with such hunger and felt every part of her expand and contract.

She pressed a hand to his face. He rubbed his cheek against it and kissed her palm. And then he kissed her mouth with such possessiveness that her heart bloomed.

Every part of her bloomed.

Her skin was alive from the flames of his touch, everything heated, scorched, her veins lava…and that was lava reflecting back at her in the depth of his stare and she realised that for the first time she was staring right into the heart of this man she loved so much.

The sense of detachment that had always been there…gone.

This was Javier as she had dreamed, touching her and making love to her as if she were the most revered thing in his life, holding her so close their skin could become one and their hearts unite.

His eyes stayed open, boring into her when he entered and…

Oh, the *sensation* that erupted within her…

This was everything. *Everything.*

Javier had no recall of entering her; found himself buried deep inside Sophie with her arms locked around him and his hands resting against her cheeks.

The expression reflecting back at him as he made love to her, the wonder, the tenderness…

The void he'd fought against for so long welcomed him into its depths.

He submitted to it.

Javier woke with a start, opening his eyes to the darkness.

Sophie was draped over him, the delicious

weight of her thigh hooked over his, her arm locked around his waist.

His heart pounded, his guts felt as if he'd been punched and for a moment it was as if he'd forgotten how to breathe.

What the hell had he done?

He'd lost all control of himself.

With Sophie.

He pinched the bridge of his nose and fought to inhale.

His movement must have disturbed her for she shifted, pressing herself closer to him; as if it was even possible for her to get any closer.

She could. She did.

He didn't know if she was fully awake when her lips brushed against his neck and she rolled on top of him, her cheek pressed to his, her silky hair falling softly onto his face, or if she was in the midst of a dream.

It felt as if *he* were in a dream of his own when she sank onto his hardness, a dream that had him holding her tightly, possessively, while deep in the back of his mind came the thought that if anything happened to this woman he would want to die.

*** * * *

Sophie stretched a leg out and smiled before she'd even opened her eyes.

This was the start of a new day that would mark the beginning of her new life.

This was the day that marked the true start of her marriage.

The breakthrough she had so longed for had finally been reached. Javier had opened himself up to her and then he had made love to her. Truly made love to her, with his heart and his mind as well as his body.

She still wasn't foolish enough to believe it would be plain sailing from here on in, but what they had found together under these sheets and the connection that embraced them tightly together...

She opened her eyes and her heart sank as if it had a weight attached to it to find the empty space between them.

Javier had moved to the edge of the bed, his back to her.

It wasn't his mesmerising face she was greeted with after the best night of her life but his cold shoulder.

She blew a puff of air out and told herself to put a curb on her imagination.

He'd rolled over? He'd probably been uncomfortable. He probably hadn't even done it consciously.

But that was a huge distance. To reach him she would have to stretch a hand out...

Before she had the chance to do so, he suddenly pushed the sheets off and climbed out of bed.

He strolled to the bathroom and shut the door without looking at her.

Disturbed but telling herself she was being silly, trying her hardest not to make a big deal out of something she didn't even know what, Sophie hurried to the dressing room and threw on an oversized T-shirt and a pair of leggings.

She needed to act normal.

Before she could leave the bedroom, he appeared from the bathroom, a towel around his waist.

'Good morning,' she said brightly.

She was answered with a grunt.

'I'm going to check on Frodo. Do you want a coffee?'

'I'll get one when I come down.'

'Okay... Is everything all right?'

He cast her a quick glance. 'Why wouldn't it be?'

She shrugged, not knowing how to answer, and backed out of the room.

Frodo was asleep at the bottom of the stairs. He woke up at her footsteps and wagged his tail excitedly to see her.

At least someone was happy to see her, she thought unhappily, scooping him up.

Javier was being…well, he was being exactly how he always was first thing in the morning: moody and distant.

He wasn't a morning person.

She'd try to add an extra sugar to his coffee to sweeten him up, she decided, brushing away the anxiety now gnawing in her belly.

She found Marsela laying out the breakfast stuff in the dining room and thanked her for looking after Frodo. 'I'll sort some money out for you when I go back up to get changed,' she promised.

Marsela looked positively affronted. 'I don't want your money. It was my pleasure to look after him.'

On impulse, Sophie planted a kiss to the sweet Spanish woman's cheek, the exact moment Javier came into the dining room.

Marsela hurried out.

He took a seat at the table and swiped at his phone. 'You are too familiar with the staff,' he said, not looking at her.

'Am I?'

'Yes.'

She sat opposite him and put Frodo down at her feet. 'Marsela's my age. I like her. If I want to be friends with her then I shall.'

His jaw clenched but he said nothing further.

Breakfast was brought in and placed between them.

'I was thinking of taking Frodo for a walk in the park later. Do you want to come?'

'I'm going to the office.'

She tried to cover her disappointment. 'On a Saturday?'

'I have much to organise before my trip to Cape Town.'

'That's not for another week,' she pointed out.

'I'm looking to bring it forward.'

'Any reason?'

'To get things moving quicker.'

'We've got the scan on Wednesday,' she reminded him. He hadn't promised he would be there, only promised that he would try. She had wanted to push it but had held back.

If this had been a conversation held an hour ago she would have pushed it, secure in the cocoon of passion they had created together.

'If I can come then I will come,' he answered shortly.

She was bewildered at the change in him.

The cold, emotionless man was back with a vengeance.

He drank his coffee and got to his feet.

'You're going to the office now?'

'Yes. I'll let you know if I'm not going to make it back for dinner.'

Stunned and hurt at the indifference being displayed, she watched him walk out before suddenly calling out to him. 'Javier.'

'What?'

She almost recoiled to see the coldness in his eyes.

'Last night…' But she couldn't say anything more. Her throat had closed up.

'What about it?'

She shook her head. 'Nothing.'

He left without saying goodbye.

* * *

Sophie was grateful to have Frodo as a distraction. Although still small, he was unrecognisable as the damaged puppy she had found on the kerb. Playful and loving, he had a marvellous time playing in the park with the other dogs and Sophie soon found other owners to talk with. For the first time, a complete stranger asked her if she was pregnant.

The thickening around her waist was turning into a small but recognisable swell, more pronounced on her petite frame than it would otherwise be. She was barely halfway through the pregnancy. There was still a long way to go.

But she had experienced flutterings in recent weeks, real, unmistakable signs that the baby inside her was growing strongly, that it was a *baby* in there.

On the short walk back to the house, she bought a newspaper from a vendor she passed. Javier would laugh at her for absorbing the news the old-fashioned way but she much preferred to read it in paper format than through a screen.

Reading the paper would be another good distraction. She no longer had to avoid the news, the Javier-Freya-Benjamin saga relegated to history.

Except it wasn't.

Her insides twisted with pain for her husband.

Page nine contained a half-page story on the marriage of Luis Casillas and Chloe Guillem.

CHAPTER TWELVE

JAVIER ARRIVED BACK LATE. It was too much to expect Sophie to be asleep but still he hoped.

He worked out for an hour in his gym to increase his chances and showered in the adjoining wet room.

The hurt he'd seen in her eyes had cut him in two.

Last night had been a terrible mistake and it was down to him to put their marriage on the footing it had originally been, for Sophie's sake even if she had trouble understanding it.

One day she would thank him for it.

It was with no surprise that he found her sitting on the bed, not even pretending to read or be doing anything that indicated she hadn't been waiting up for him.

She was still dressed.

He should be relieved. He'd half expected to find her dressed in lingerie, intent on seducing him.

Thuds of dread battered in him.

'How was your walk?' he asked, needing to cut through the strange, tense atmosphere he'd walked into.

'Fun.' She gave a half-smile. 'How was your day?'

'Long.'

'You're tired?'

'Exhausted.' Yet still wired. Electricity charged through the room but the buzz he felt on his skin was different from the usual charge he felt when with her and which he always tried valiantly to ignore.

'Javier... Have you seen the newspaper reports?'

'About Luis getting married?'

She nodded. 'You have seen them, then.'

'Dante mentioned it last night.'

There was sympathy in her narrowed stare he did not want to see.

'Why didn't you tell me?'

'Why would I have done?'

He hated the flash of hurt that rang back in her eyes.

'Because I'm your wife.'

'It isn't important.'

'What isn't? Luis getting married or that I'm your wife?'

His jaw clenched in the way that told Sophie he wouldn't answer.

He really was shutting her out.

'Did you rearrange your trip to Cape Town?'

He jerked a nod.

'And?'

'I leave on Tuesday.'

The swirl of nausea in her stomach was so powerful Sophie almost vomited from it.

She swallowed a number of times before saying, 'You're not coming to the scan, then?'

'No.'

Breathing deeply, she put her head in her hands before looking back at him. 'Was that deliberate?'

His jaw clenched again.

'We made love last night,' she whispered.

The pulse on his jaw throbbed.

'We *did*,' she stated in a stronger voice, in case he was inclined to deny it.

She would not have him deny it.

'We made love and it was wonderful. You said things to me I never thought I would hear. I thought we'd turned a corner. Was I wrong? Because today you have treated me like I mean nothing to you and I need to know if it's a case of you pushing me away because you're struggling with your feelings for me and have been trying to process them or if it's because you have *no* feelings for me.'

His breaths had become heavy. 'My feelings for you are…complicated.'

That wasn't a denial of feelings, she thought, experiencing a tiny surge of encouragement. 'How?'

'Last night… I could have hurt you.'

'But you didn't. You made love to me.'

He grabbed the back of his neck, the lips that had kissed her with such tenderness and passion pulling together. 'There is something inside me that's dangerous.'

'You said that last night.'

'And it's true. It has always been in me. I spend my life fighting it.'

'Has it beaten you before?'

His eyes found hers. 'Yes.'

'Who?'

'Some boys. When I was fourteen. They followed me and Luis home from school and made some comment about our mother. It was a bad day as it would have been our mother's birthday. I beat the crap out of them. One of them was hospitalised with a concussion.'

'Anyone else?'

'No.' His eyes gleamed with malice. 'I have wanted to though.'

'But you haven't.'

'Only because I keep tight control over it. I keep emotion out of my life. Last night should never have happened. My emotions got the better of me. It will not happen again.'

'Emotions aren't dangerous.'

'They are for me.' The malice vanished. 'Every time I look in a mirror I see the truth. I am my father's son and my father was ruled by emotions.'

'But you are not your father. You look a little like him…'

'I am his double.'

She shrugged. 'Not that I can see. But even if you are, you can't help who or what you look like. I haven't got the faintest idea who I look like or whose blood runs in my veins.'

'Then you have no legacy to live up to or break free from.'

'I have nothing to hide behind.'

His hooded stare narrowed. 'What do you mean by that?'

She swallowed again before summoning her

courage to say, 'I think you're using your father as an excuse to keep me at a distance.'

The rage that flashed in his eyes almost made her wish she'd kept her mouth shut.

'My father killed my mother,' Javier snarled.

Dios, how could she think that? As if he would ever use the bastard who had given him life as an excuse for *anything*.

'He put his hands around her throat and strangled her until she had no breath left in her. I spent my childhood trying to protect Luis from the worst of himself because my father despised him and needed no excuse to beat him—he threatened to throw him into a pool and let him drown once and he damned well meant it. My father loved only one person—me, but only because I looked so much like him. The genetic pool favoured me to him. He would rub my hair and tell me I was just like him.'

Every time his father had done that Javier had cringed inside but also, to his eternal shame, thrilled in it.

He'd thrilled at being loved by the man who'd caused such terror to his brother.

He'd hated his father with every fibre of his being.

But he had loved him too.

What had scared him the most was that his father's assertions were right. That Javier *was* just like him, on the inside as well as on the surface.

'He recognised something in me and my mother saw it too,' he continued. 'I *know* she did and if you looked closely enough you would see it too.'

He drew long breaths in as he stared at the woman he would give his last breath to protect.

She blinked rapidly, her chin wobbling, throat moving.

'I have looked closely,' she whispered. 'I don't see it.'

'Then you are a blind fool and I will not endanger you or our child by allowing what occurred between us last night to happen again.'

'Meaning that you intend to keep me at a distance?'

'Meaning our marriage will continue as we first set out.'

She rubbed her eyes with both hands and took a deep breath before fixing pain-filled eyes on him. 'I was afraid you would say that. I've spent the day thinking about what it would mean and trying to work out if it's something I can live with and I'm sorry but I can't. Not any more. I've tried. I think you have too. But it's not enough.'

'What are you saying?'

'That we need to admit defeat and call it a day.'

He reared back. 'You want to leave me?'

'No.' Her throat moved again. 'I don't want to but I know I have to. I don't care what you say, I don't believe for a minute that you would ever hurt me, but if you don't believe that and you keep holding me at a distance I think there is a very real chance you will destroy me.'

He didn't understand. She could be speaking in tongues for all he comprehended.

She must have read what he was thinking on his face for she laughed as tears suddenly rained like a waterfall down her face. 'And you say *I'm* the blind fool? I *love* you, Javier. I love you so much that it's killing me inside.'

'How can you love me?' he asked, disbelieving...not *wanting* to believe. 'I've treated you like dirt.'

'Not all the time.' She pushed the tears away with the palms of her hands. 'I always understood your actions were deliberate. I'm not a fool, whatever you believe. But you listen. You compromise when you can. You've been supportive...

so supportive. I cannot tell you how much that has meant to me, the way you tried to convince me not to give up dance when the baby's born, then when you understood my dream was to be a vet and your belief and encouragement that I could do it… You said I need to put myself first and you're right, I do. Me and the baby.'

She rubbed her face one last time and climbed off the bed.

Somehow, despite her tears, there was a dignity about her.

'I can't keep putting my dreams on hold for other people. My wonderful parents who rescued me, Freya… I regret none of it but now I know things have to change. *I* have to change. I refuse to put my whole life and heart on hold for you. I deserve better than to spend my life pining for you to fall in love with me when you won't give your feelings a chance. Our child deserves better too. I thought that given time you would at least fall in love with our baby but I don't see how that can happen when you won't allow it and that breaks my heart. I understand if you can't love me, but to deliberately withhold your love from our child…?'

As she spoke, the tears stopped falling and she

grew in stature. But anger was coming through too, a whole gauntlet of emotions showing on her.

'That's cruel and it's weak. Too scared to love a helpless baby?'

'I am not scared,' he disputed, furious at the accusation and her twisting of things. 'I am trying to protect you both!'

'Oh, yes, you are.' The tears had gone completely now, her face as hard as he had ever seen it. 'You are scared to love, Javier Casillas. It's not me or the baby you're protecting, it's yourself, and not because you're too damaged but because you're too scared to let us in.'

She practically danced into the dressing room, reappearing moments later with a large suitcase in her hands.

'You planned this?' His anger had risen so hard inside him he could choke on it. 'You already knew you were going to leave?'

'No. I hadn't planned to leave but I knew there was a good possibility of it.'

'Where are you going to go?' he demanded to know. 'It's the middle of the night!'

'I'll check into a hotel.'

'It's the middle of the night,' he repeated through gritted teeth.

She put the case down and opened the door. 'And why's that? That will be because you spent the entire day avoiding me. You should be grateful—with me gone, you won't have to hide from your own home any more. You can have a lovely time roaming your lovely *empty* house, which perfectly matches your empty life.'

'I was not—'

'Will you cut the crap?' she suddenly screamed, hair whipping around her shoulders as she turned wild eyes on him. 'As soon as anyone gets close to you, you push them away. You're already pushing our baby away and it's not even born! You brought your trip to Cape Town forward to avoid going to the scan with me and seeing your own child for yourself! If you won't let it into your heart and give it the love it deserves then it's better if you stay on the periphery of our lives and let me love it for the both of us.'

'You had better not be threatening to take my baby from me,' he warned. 'You will not deny me access to it.'

'Says the man who wanted to shove it in the east wing far away from us so you wouldn't be disturbed by its cries?'

'We signed a contract!' If Sophie wanted to

leave then good riddance but she would not take his child from him.

'I don't care! Our baby is *not* a possession, it's a living being who needs love and security, not a father too scared to let anyone into his heart, who screws over his best friend and cuts his own brother out of his life rather than admit to his mistakes and admit that he needs them. Because, guess what? You need your brother.'

'Do not bring Luis into this,' he roared. 'He's the disloyal one who walked away from everything we built together, not me.'

'Do you think he threw away your relationship and business on a whim?' she asked scathingly, throwing her hands in the air. 'At least he's not scared to open his heart, and he's lived through everything you have. He *loves* Chloe and if you had any concept of what real love is you would understand that and stop condemning him and accusing him of disloyalty. The world is not against you, Javier, whatever you think, and if the day comes when you see that too and are willing to open your heart to be a real father to our child and understand that you are not, I repeat *not*, your father, come and find me and you can have all the access you want.'

Extending the handhold for the case to wheel it beside her, she left the room without a backwards glance.

'Get back here,' he hollered down the corridor, loud enough to wake the live-in staff in their self-contained flats in the basement. 'We are not done yet.'

'Oh, yes, we are.' Sophie would not look back. She didn't dare.

Already the outburst that had exploded out of her from nowhere was fading and she could feel her legs weakening as her resolve faltered.

She must not let it falter.

'If you leave you will never come back. The next time you see me will be in a courtroom.'

She did not answer.

Her throat no longer worked.

Frodo was at the bottom of the stairs, sitting up and looking at her. For once his tail didn't wag to see her.

From upstairs a door slammed.

She squeezed her eyes shut, took the longest breath of her life, then messaged for a cab.

In the living room that had been cleared of all Javier's precious artefacts, she gathered Frodo's stuff together, put his lead on him and took him outside and down the long driveway.

The electric gate opened when she reached the bottom.

The cab pulled up.

Holding her dog tightly on her lap, she took one last look at the house she had hoped so hard would be her home.

And then the tears flowed freely.

The meeting was not going well. The government official Javier had brought in to look over the blueprint of the development plans before it was officially submitted was being deliberately obtuse and obstructive.

The lead architect, a rising star in Daniele Pellegrini's architectural empire, was looking everywhere but at Javier, clearly afraid to meet his eyes.

And so he should be scared. This was his fault and Javier would make damned sure Daniele knew it.

Aside from himself, five people sat in this meeting room. Incompetent fools, the lot of them. If they couldn't produce the blueprints to an earlier deadline without cutting corners they should never have agreed to do so.

His phone buzzed.

He snatched it off the table without looking at it, instead glaring at the people around the table. 'I shall take this call and when I get back I expect to be given solutions, not additional problems. Understood?'

He strode from the meeting room without waiting for an answer.

A few minutes alone-time would do him good. Hopefully it would purge his need to bang heads together.

He'd wanted to bang a lot of heads these past few days. His punching bag had had almost forty-eight hours of continual pounding.

He should have brought it to Cape Town with him.

His phone had stopped buzzing. He swiped it and saw his accountant's name flash up.

He was about to call him back when his phone buzzed again, this time a message alert.

This time, the name that flashed on his screen was not his accountant but his wife.

Heat rushed to his head.

Javier had not seen or heard from Sophie in four days.

He was damned if he would open it. From now on, all contact between them would be done through their lawyers.

As soon as he got back to Madrid, he would call his lawyer and get the ball rolling, couldn't think why he hadn't already done so.

That damned black mist had blinded him.

Damn her, they had signed a contract agreeing joint custody in the event that they split up, something *she* had insisted on. And now she wanted to break it. Not him, *her*, the woman who had professed her love for him in one breath, then thrown unfounded accusations at him with the next.

Clearly her declaration of love had been a lie, although for what purpose he could not begin to imagine.

He had been honest with her from the start. He had bent over backwards to find compromise and protect her and their child.

Sophie was not taking their child from him. He would never be a hands-on father but he would be a father and he would not allow her to deny him that.

In his mind, he would be a father who would

share an evening meal and impart authority and wisdom. He would be a father to look up to.

He would not allow himself to get close enough to be a father who was feared.

About to shove his phone in his pocket, he instead found himself swiping the message.

There was no text. Only a video attachment.

Rubbing violently at his scalp, he stared at the screen in his hand, then, again working of its own volition, his thumb pressed to open it.

He blinked hard, not quite recognising what he was seeing, his heart hammering in his throat, wonder increasing as the golden frames rotating in front of him suddenly became clear.

Little hands were curled in balls at the sides of a round head where eyes, nose and a mouth were clearly delineated, the lips slightly parted as if his tiny baby was snoring gently in its cocoon. A short neck, then a round belly moving up and down, tiny wiggling feet that ended with ten long toes…

Something hot stabbed the backs of his eyes and he blinked a number of times, inhaling deeply, fighting for air.

In his mind flashed the acute pain that had shone in Sophie's eyes when she had realised he'd deliberately arranged things so he would miss the scan.

Had she sent this as a rebuke?

A taunt?

He pinched the bridge of his nose and pulled shuddering breaths into his lungs.

He felt winded.

Sophie did not do taunts.

He dragged more air into his lungs.

It was only a scan. Only an image.

He needed to pull himself together.

He had a meeting to finish.

Five pale faces sat in silence on his return.

He took his seat and rubbed his hair.

All the anger he'd carried with him since Sophie had left had gone.

Now there was nothing but an acute pain clenching in his guts.

He'd taken his anger out on these people, he realised with a stab of guilt.

He'd been behaving in the exact manner he despised.

Instilling healthy fear was one thing—as a rule he didn't need to do anything but raise an eyebrow to achieve that—but acting like a pig-headed toddler having a tantrum was quite another.

'I owe you all an apology,' he said heavily. 'I realise I pushed for the plans to be completed early and that you have all worked your backsides off to achieve this.'

He lifted the landline phone and pressed the button that put him through to his PA, who had accompanied him on the trip. 'Can you arrange for refreshments to be brought in for us from Giglis?' Giglis was a deli a few streets away. 'Ask for enough to feed a dozen people, and make sure to buy some for yourself.'

Turning back to the startled faces before him, he got back to his feet. 'Food will be with you shortly. Eat, then take the rest of the day off. Get back together tomorrow to find solutions to the problems when heads are clear. When everything is ironed out, let me know and we can video conference. I'm going home.'

He didn't need to be there.

Sophie had called him out correctly that he avoided his home when she was there.

She was gone now. He didn't need to avoid it any more.

'What are you doing?' Javier asked when he walked into his dressing room and found

Marsela rifling through the clothes Sophie had left behind.

She spun around to face him, the colour draining from her face.

He guessed she hadn't received the message he would be returning early.

She stammered an apology, which turned into a garble. Eventually he was able to gather that Sophie had asked her to pack the possessions she hadn't had the time to take with her and forward them to England.

He held his palms up and backed out of the room. 'Carry on. Use our usual courier for it.'

This was good. Excellent in fact. His room, his home, were all becoming his own again. No more opening his bathroom cabinet to find ladies' toiletries in there, no more walking down his stairs avoiding tripping over a dog, no more clock-watching in the office knowing Sophie was at home waiting for him to return.

The nursery door was open.

He'd blanked it from his mind since Sophie had left but as he passed it something inside caught his eye.

A large white wardrobe, dresser and crib had

been delivered in his absence, all placed against a wall ready to be set in their new places.

Swallowing a huge lump that had formed in his throat, Javier was about to call for Marsela to explain where the items had come from when he suddenly remembered Sophie telling him she'd employed a local carpenter to craft the baby's furniture by hand.

That had been right before she had introduced him to Frodo.

Right before she had told him about her beginnings and he'd feared his heart would splinter.

On the wall beside the tall wardrobe rested a full-length mirror with an edging crafted in the same design as the other bespoke items of furniture.

He dragged his feet to it and stared at his reflection.

From as far back as he could remember everyone had always said how much like his father he was and how much like their mother Luis was. That resemblance had always been something Javier had hated. After their father had killed their mother, he had actively avoided mirrors. Who wanted to see the face of a murderer? Such was his loathing that when he did come across one he would squint his eyes to turn his appearance into a blur.

Sophie didn't see the face he saw or that others saw.

He narrowed his eyes and peered closer.

What did she see?

How was she able to penetrate the surface to find a part of himself even he didn't know was there?

He thought hard, remembering the day she had first come to him with the legal documents that would have tied him to Freya. He remembered the soft compassion that had rung out at him when he'd looked into her eyes.

No one had ever looked at him like that.

No one had ever looked at him the way Sophie did.

She looked for the good in everyone.

She'd ignored all the stories about him, ignored his warnings and all the evidence of his cruel nature and given her heart to him.

Why?

How could she trust her feelings the way she did and trust that the light would break through when all he ever saw was darkness?

But he had seen light with Sophie. Moments of

joy when his guard had dropped enough to allow the light to filter through the dark.

How could she put her heart and life in the hands of a man with the potential for such violence…?

His heart made a sudden thump.

The night of Dante's party…

The green-eyed monster had reared its head straight after his discovery that Luis had married. He'd been so full of angry emotion but he hadn't lashed out. Even at that awful, low point he hadn't raised a hand to her; he'd swallowed all that angry passion and made love to her instead, real love, not a mechanical act of going through the motions.

He hadn't raised a hand to the man he'd thought was flirting with her either, and why had that been? Not just because even in his rage he'd known on a fundamental level that to strike out would be wrong, but because he'd known Sophie would be horrified and that his actions would hurt her.

Sophie could not bear to see another's pain. It would have hurt her as much as his father's beatings of his twin had hurt him.

And he could not bear to see her pain.

He would never lay a finger on her, just as he'd been unable to lay a finger on Luis when they had had that terrible row.

Javier was not his father.

He could never hurt someone he loved.

CHAPTER THIRTEEN

Night settled in Madrid.

Javier sat on the floor of the nursery his wife had created for their unborn child, unable to move. His reflection shone back at him, lit by the light of the growing moon that cast shadows that loomed ominously over him.

Time became nothing.

The weight that had compressed in him on his wedding day had become a leaden pit that crushed all his organs.

Thoughts and memories he'd never allowed freedom to roam in his head had rebelled and now crowded in on him.

The ache in his guts was far beyond mere nausea.

And still he didn't move.

Not until the sun made its first peak on the horizon to start its ascent and clear the darkness did he break out of his stupor.

Sophie was *his* sun.

Without her, his life would remain cold and barren.

Without her, he would never feel the warmth she shone on his skin.

Without her, he was nothing.

He needed to go to her.

But first, there were things he needed to do. Wrongs he needed to right.

He needed to cleanse his conscience.

Breathing heavily, he groped for his phone.

He dialled from memory the number he had deleted from his contacts months ago.

The sleepy voice answered after three rings. 'Javier?'

His throat had become so tight it was an effort to speak. 'Hello, Luis.'

Javier took a deep breath, then rang the bell of the sea-fronted villa along the Mediterranean coast, less than thirty kilometres from Spain's border with France.

He was expected. The bell still echoed when the door was opened and a member of the household staff admitted him into the spacious, modern home.

Footsteps sounded in the distance, hurried, nearing towards him.

Then the gangly form of Chloe Guillem…no, Chloe Casillas appeared.

'You're early,' she said stiffly, making no pretence at pleasantries.

He did not blame her.

'I apologise,' Javier replied carefully. 'The drive was quicker than I anticipated.'

She scowled but then her face softened as Luis appeared from a side door.

The look on her face was all Javier needed to know that she loved his brother.

And now he too looked at his twin, struck by the changes he saw before him.

His perennial tan had deepened, his hair lightened by the sun…

But these were only surface changes.

His brother radiated happiness…but also wariness and curiosity.

There was none of the malice Javier had expected to see and which he knew he deserved.

'I'm going to leave you two to it,' Chloe said, planting a kiss on Luis's lips, then adding a whisper Javier knew he was meant to hear. 'Call me when he's gone.'

'Not my biggest fan?' Javier asked wryly when it was just him and his brother alone for the first time in months.

Luis ran a hand through his hair and pulled a face.

'I don't suppose I can blame her,' Javier said heavily.

Luis stared at him for a long time, eyes narrowed. Then he gave a sharp nod, the beginnings of a smile hovering on his lips. 'Let's get the pleasantries over with, shall we? Then we can talk.'

After a quick tour of the house Luis and Chloe had moved into only days earlier, both having developed a love of beach life from their time in the Caribbean, they moved outside to sit on the wall that overlooked Luis's private beach. Stilted small talk had been the extent of their conversation up to this point, catching up with each other's lives, both learning for the first time that they were going to be uncles as well as fathers.

'When do I get to meet Sophie?' Luis asked. 'I

know I must have done when she danced for us but, to be honest, I don't remember her.'

Javier swallowed. 'I don't know. She's in England. She's…left me.'

'Oh.'

'It's my fault. All my fault. Everything is my fault.'

Luis's silence gave voice to his thoughts on that.

'Did you speak to Benjamin?' Javier asked, breaking it.

He had tried calling him a number of times but his messages had gone unanswered. In the end he had called Luis again and asked if he would speak on his behalf and arrange a meeting for them.

Luis nodded. 'He is expecting you this evening.'

'Thank you.'

More silence fell, broken only by the waves crashing onto the shore.

'Why did you do it?' Luis asked quietly.

He'd been waiting for this. 'Rip Benjamin off?'

'Yes. Was it deliberate? Did you deliberately fail to warn him of the change in terms?'

They both knew the answer but Javier knew his brother needed to hear it from him.

And he needed to say it too. 'Yes.'

Luis nodded thoughtfully, his gaze fixed out on the sea. 'And did you know the night we signed the contract with Benjamin that he thought he'd signed it under the original terms?'

Javier closed his eyes.

'Yes,' he admitted heavily. 'He mentioned the percentage before I left. I knew then that he hadn't read it. I didn't see fit to warn him or correct his mistake or give him the chance to renegotiate because I was a stone-cold bastard who didn't care that he was suffering over his mother. I had no empathy. I was…dead inside.'

He'd been dead for so long that he hadn't noticed Sophie bringing him back to life until it was too late.

'The only person I cared about was you and I harboured a resentment towards Benjamin for the closeness you had. A part of me had always resented him. I see that now.'

It was an admission that left his veins cold.

'You were jealous?'

'I resented that you could have fun with him.'

'You were too busy trying to keep me out of trouble for fun.' Luis's own voice had the same heaviness to it. 'I regret letting you bear that weight.'

They both exhaled at the same time. Luis gave a grunt-like laugh, then said, 'What do you feel now?'

'Sick with myself. I shut down after our mother died. I was afraid I was like our father and that if I let emotion in I would become him. Instead I became a monster in a different form.'

Another long silence fell between them.

Javier knew Luis was thinking the same as he, of their childhood, two boys who'd shared a womb before being born into a world where the only option had been to survive by sticking together and protecting each other.

Eventually Luis said, 'Our parents screwed with our heads long before our father did what he did. But it doesn't have to define us.'

Javier thought of Sophie, again, the woman who had no idea who her real parents were, where she came from or why she'd been abandoned. She had never allowed that beginning to define her or close her heart off.

'Does Chloe make you happy?' he asked.

'More than I ever dreamed possible.'

'Good. You deserve happiness.'

Luis looked at him. 'So do you.'

He shrugged. 'I think it might be too late for me. I pushed her too far this time. I think she has let go.'

In his heart he knew she would never keep their child from him. But as for their marriage…

That he did not know how to fix.

'Talk to her. She might surprise you.'

'Sophie has never done anything but surprise me.'

Much later, Luis showed him to the door, promises made to get together very soon and work out a plan for their future.

'Good luck with Benjamin,' his brother said as he embraced him.

'Thank you. And thank you for getting him to agree to see me.'

'No problem. I'm just grateful to have you back in my life. I've missed you.'

'Did you approach Dante with the offer for the land deliberately?' Javier suddenly remembered to ask.

Luis gave his first genuine smile, the cheeky grin Javier had grown up looking at. 'I had to flush you out somehow.'

'How high would you have gone?'

'As high as was needed for you to come to your senses and talk to me. I never would have guessed a woman would have done that for me.'

He managed a returning smile. 'Neither would I.'

Sophie concentrated hard on the document she was reading at her parents' kitchen table, wishing she'd asked for the English version rather than the Spanish. She wouldn't have to keep looking words up for their meanings. But it was necessary doing it like this.

Once the baby was born she would return to Spain. It was going to be her home. If she wanted to be a vet there she would have to become fluent in all aspects of the language.

There was a rap on the front door.

Getting to her feet with a sigh, she closed the living-room door and went to answer it.

The top half of the front door was frosted glass. Through it she could see her visitor was a person of immense height and width...

Her heart thumped, then set off at a canter.

Keeping a tight grip on the door handle, she tried to breathe.

You're being ridiculous. It isn't him. It couldn't be him.

Javier had sent her only one message since she'd left him and that had consisted of two words— Thank you—after she'd emailed the scan.

It had taken him two days to write those two words.

She had read those two words so many times her eyes had blurred.

From that, nothing. No call, no message. Every letter dropped through the post in the eight days she'd been in England and every ping of an email had brought a thud of dread in her, fear that this would be the moment she received a legal notice of his intention to fight for custody.

It had taken every effort to keep her resolve and ignore the plaintive voice in her head pleading with her to apologise.

She mustn't.

Their marriage was over. All she could do was pray Javier came to his senses and realised he had it in him to be a real father to their child. Freya's phone call three nights ago had given her cause to hope. Now she had to hope this unexpected visit was the start of that journey and not the first blood of a nasty legal battle.

She counted to five, fixed a smile to her face and opened the door.

The smile would not sustain itself.

The moment she stared into the light brown eyes she'd missed more than she had thought possible everything swelled inside her and it took every ounce of effort not to burst into tears.

The features she had soaked into her memory bank were taut, his jaw clenched in that, oh, so familiar way.

She couldn't tear her gaze from his eyes. She had never seen that expression in them before. Such…softness…

'Hello, *carina*,' he said in a tone she'd never heard before either. It contained the same softness as his eyes. 'I apologise for turning up unannounced. May I come in?'

It seemed to take for ever before she could get her throat to work. 'Yes, of course.'

Her legs as she led him inside felt drugged. Her head felt drugged too, as if a thick fog had been injected into it.

So dazed was she at Javier's unexpected appearance that she'd forgotten Frodo was in the living room until she opened the door and he went bouncing round the room, his tail wagging as he then ran circles around Javier.

He gave a grunt-like laugh and picked the puppy up, Frodo immediately licking his cheek with frantic excitement.

'He's grown,' Javier said, carrying Frodo to a seat at the dining table and sitting him on his lap. Then he stared at Sophie, his eyes drifting down to her ripening belly. 'And so have you.'

Stunned at the welcome Frodo had given the man who had rarely paid him any attention, equally stunned at the fuss the man in question was making of him, Sophie could only nod vaguely. Her bump seemed to have exploded these past few days.

'Can I get you a drink?'

'No. Thank you.' He grimaced. 'Please, sit down. We need to talk.'

She took the seat next to him but backed it away to create distance and bunched her hands together on her lap, desperate to contain the tremors in them.

'How have you been?' he asked.

Miserable. Scared. Heartsick. 'I'm good. Baby's good. She's learned how to kick.'

'You can feel it?'

She nodded. 'She's very active, especially at night. I think she's asleep now though.'

'*She?*' His eyes widened. 'We are having a girl?'

'I didn't ask but the scan was so clear it was obvious. The nurse confirmed it for me.'

His features tightened. 'I'm sorry I wasn't there.'

'So am I.' She felt no malice towards him, only a deep sadness.

Her anger had barely lasted longer than the walk down the driveway from his home, its residue long put to bed.

'Freya tells me you've seen Benjamin.' That was what her old friend had called to tell her; their first real conversation since Freya had left Javier for Benjamin. Or, as Sophie now knew, since Freya had been *kidnapped* by Benjamin.

Kidnapped or not, Freya had been delirious with happiness. She had also been astounded at the contrition Javier had shown when he had turned up at their chateau.

Hearing his name had been a stab to Sophie's heart.

The next stab had come from Freya's demand to know what magic she had woven to make the ice-cold Javier Casillas admit to his faults and ask, in all sincerity, for forgiveness.

It was hearing this that had given Sophie the kernel of hope about Javier and their child.

But she had refused to let that hope gain traction.

The pain at the recognition that Javier would never change, would never love her, would always push her and the baby away…that pain had lanced her like no pain she had ever felt before. She could not put herself through that again.

He blew out a long puff of air and put Frodo on the floor.

Then he straightened in his seat and looked at her. 'I needed to apologise to him. I behaved… I can make all the excuses in the world but it doesn't change the fact that I did rip him off and for that there is no excuse. It was me. No one else.'

'How did he take your apology?'

'He refused to take the money back from me but he had the grace to listen. I hope one day he can forgive me.'

'I hope that too,' she said softly. 'I'm glad you accept what you did and that you had the guts to apologise. It couldn't have been easy for you. What made you do it?'

'Apologise?'

She nodded.

'You did.' He rubbed a hand through his hair. 'You've done something to me.'

'What?'

'You've…infected me. The way you see the world. What you lived through, your abandonment. That could have made you bitter and cold like me but you turned it into a force for good. You refuse to see the bad; you turn it over and see the sunny side.

'You and I… I've been doing a lot of thinking…' He rubbed his hair again. 'I have treated you very badly. I cannot tell you how sick I am with myself. I thought my behaviour was justified because I was trying to protect you but I see the truth now and the truth is that you were right—the only person I was protecting was myself.'

He closed his eyes. 'I shut myself off from emotions so long ago it is hard for me to be any other way. I do not know how to love. I've never been taught how to love a person in the way they should be loved. I want to try but…' His throat moved and now he fixed desolate eyes on her.

'I need your help. I want to love our child…that scan you sent to me, it made my heart hurt. It hasn't stopped hurting since. I know what I need to do but I don't know how. Please, *carina*, help me.'

Stunned, her own heart aching with pain at this admission she knew must have cost him everything to make, Sophie squeezed her balled hands even tighter to stop them from touching him.

'Of course I will help you,' she whispered.

How could she not? This was what she had demanded from him when she had walked out of his home: when he was ready to be a father to come and find her.

He was ready.

He had come and found her.

Whatever her feelings for this man, he was her daughter's father and she would do whatever it took for them to forge a close and loving relationship.

He blew out a heavy breath. 'In the back of my mind, I keep thinking, what if I'm like my parents?'

Now she did reach for him, unballing her hand to rest it on his arm. 'You are not your father.'

His eyes narrowed with intensity. 'I know. You

have shown me that. I do not fear hurting our child any more but I do fear...'

'Fear what?' she asked gently, moving her hand down his arm to wrap her fingers around his.

He squeezed. 'My mother never liked me. She never abused me the way my father abused Luis but she was never warm to me. My parents each had their favourite and we both suffered in different ways for it. What if I don't like our child?'

'You will. You will like her and you will love her.'

'How can you be so sure?' he asked, his expression haunted.

'That pain you feel in your heart? That's your heart opening itself up for you to love her. Your love for her is already in you. When she's born and you develop a bond with her, that love will grow, I promise. And I will help you. She'll have to live full-time with me in the early months as I'm hoping to feed her myself, but that won't stop you being with her. You can see her as much as you like and stay with us for as long as you like. My door will always be open to you.'

Javier stared into the only eyes in the world that had ever looked at him and seen the man he could be and not the steel façade he'd built to protect himself.

'Will you not come home to me, *carina*?'

Her silence before answering went on so long that the beats of his heart turned into the chimes of doom.

'I can't,' she whispered. 'I'll return to Madrid once the baby's born and I'll live there with her like we planned but I can't live in your home again.'

His throat closed so tightly he had to swallow numerous times before he could say, 'I thought you wanted us to be a real family.'

'I did.' Gently removing her hand from his, she put it back on her lap. She stared down at it, no longer looking at him. 'I'm happy that you want to be a real father. I swear on everything I love that I will help you however I can to love our daughter and be the best father you can be but I can't move back in with you.'

'You said you love me.'

'That's why I can't move back in.'

He stared in disbelief at the bowed head but it wasn't until he saw a tear drop onto her lap that it suddenly became clear to him.

Shifting forward, he gently took her cheeks in

his hands and raised her face to look at him. 'Do you still love me?'

Her lips and chin wobbled as more tears sprang out of eyes that had turned red. She jerked the smallest of nods.

Her voice was so low he had to strain everything to hear her. 'I have loved you for so long that I can't remember when I didn't but it isn't enough, not when you can't love me back. I can't put myself through that again. It would destroy me.'

'I am the biggest fool in the world,' he murmured, bringing his nose to rest against hers, his heart pounding as hard as it had ever pounded. 'I let you walk out of my life when you are the best thing to have ever happened to me. The single best thing. You told me once that your parents regard you as their miracle from God. You are *my* miracle, *carina*. You are an angel sent to save me from myself and I love you so much that it isn't just my heart that hurts, it is all of me. I ache from missing you. I pushed you away so many times that I wouldn't blame you if you didn't believe me but, *mi amor*, I have loved you from that first time I looked in your eyes. You have brought light into the darkness of my life—

you *are* my light. I am sorry beyond words for the pain I have caused you and I swear, on everything I love, that if you give me—*us*—another chance I will be a better man. I will be the husband and lover you deserve. I swear it. I love you, Sophie, with my whole life.'

Her tears had soaked his hands, drenched them with the misery and pain he had caused.

He would give his life to take that pain from her.

'How can you be so sure?' she whispered.

'Because I feel it.' Finally, he allowed himself to smile. 'A wise woman once told me that sometimes feelings are all we can trust.'

An arm suddenly hooked around his neck. She pressed her forehead to his and stared so deeply into his eyes that he felt the beam from it touch his soul.

And from that look, his soul flew up to his mouth and spilled out everything contained in it. 'I want to make love to you, to touch you, to taste you, to sleep with you locked in my arms every night for the rest of my life. You look at me and I feel I could walk on water. I want to fight the wolves that would harm you and I would give my life to keep you safe.

'Trust me with your heart, *mi amor*,' he begged. 'Trust it to me and I will keep it safe for the rest of my life.'

Her eyes continued to bore into him, searching, searching, searching until he was stripped of everything but the essence of who he was...

And then she smiled.

It was a smile of such pure, radiating joy that the last of the darkness that had lived in him his whole life was pushed out for ever.

When her lips found his and crushed him with her kisses he hauled her tightly into his arms, this angel sent to save his soul and warm his heart.

'I love you, Javier,' she whispered as she trailed kisses over his face. 'I love you more than I thought it was possible to love someone. I want to spend the rest of my life locked in your arms. I want to fight the wolves that would do you harm. I want to kiss you until all the pain in your heart has gone.'

'You have already done that, *mi amor*.'

Just having her in his arms like this and hearing her sweet words of love made his heart feel reborn.

And, as her lips found his and the passion between them reignited, Javier's last conscious thought before he carried her upstairs and made love to her was that this was the start of their new life.

With Sophie he had found his heart and his soul.

Four months later...

The midwife took his daughter from his beautiful, tired wife's chest and held her out to him.

Javier stared at the tiny form with the surprisingly long, kicking legs and allowed her to be placed in his arms.

Terrified of dropping her, it took him long moments before he dared to breathe.

He soaked in every millimetre of the delicate face, the creases, the rosebud lips that had parted in a wail when she had entered this world minutes before, stared with awe at the soft bundle of dark hair on the crown of her head, marvelled at the sharp little nails on the little fingers that had a tight grasp of his thumb...

His heart expanded. It bloomed...

And he fell madly in love.

EPILOGUE

'I CAN SEE IT!' called Sophie's daughter, Fiona, a sturdy six-year-old who was sporting an outstanding front gap in her mouth, her top two front teeth having both fallen out on the same day and absolutely *not* with any help from Fiona. None at all.

Fiona was pointing at the nearing island, her little feet tapping with excitement.

'I see too!' her brother squealed.

'No, you can't,' scoffed Christopher, Freya and Benjamin's son, rightly pointing out that three-year-old Roberto was lying his head off as there was no way he could see over the railing to Marietta Island.

The three families were heading for their annual summer break on Luis and Chloe's Caribbean island, a tradition amongst them since Luis had insisted they all go five years ago, to thrash out the past once and for all and put it to bed for good.

There had been no thrashing out. Whether it

had been the magic of the sun or whether it had been because Benjamin had come to understand Javier's contrition was genuine—a donation of the exact amount Javier had ripped him off by had been made to a charity of Benjamin's choice in Benjamin's name; two hundred and twenty-five million euros, plus interest—but before Sophie had known what was happening she'd witnessed her gruff husband slapping Benjamin on the back, the two men laughing uproariously.

She still wasn't quite sure if she'd imagined that. She loved her husband dearly but he still wasn't one for seeing the funny side of life. He was getting better though. Three children were teaching him that.

And there he was, emerging from the sun lounge, baby Raul in his arms.

Her heart lifted to see him as it always did and as she knew it always would.

Seven years of marriage and she had never once regretted her decision to give him that second chance.

It hadn't been easy but then she had never thought it would be. The damage done to her husband had been too deep and too ingrained to be erased overnight. She had learned when to give him space and as the years had passed he'd needed less and less of it. In return, he had been nothing but supportive over her studies. She'd got the qualifications needed to study as a vet but by then she'd had Fiona and was expecting Roberto, had added to their menagerie of animals with two more dogs and come to the conclusion that it was caring for the animals themselves that she loved to do and so, with Javier's support and backing, had opened an animal rescue centre instead. She employed Marsela to manage it for her.

She grinned at him.

He grinned back and held Raul out to her. 'One clean baby.'

She grinned again. 'See, I told you we didn't need to bring the nanny along.'

He grunted but there was a sparkle in his eye. 'You never said I would be taking on her chores.'

'I can see Thomas!' Fiona suddenly bellowed, now waving her arms frantically at her cousin, Luis and Chloe's eldest son born only weeks after her—which, naturally, meant Fiona was always in charge when the cousins were together—who was waving back with equal intensity. Running up behind Thomas were the four-year-old twins Gregory and Georgina, lagging behind their brother because they were punching each other every few steps.

The yacht's captain brought the vessel to anchor next to Luis's, which matched theirs for size—something incredibly important to both men, she and Chloe liked to snigger about—and then Freya appeared clutching her belly and looking a little green with morning sickness, Benjamin, who had no interest in yachts, preferring his growing collection of classic cars, supporting her, and they all followed the excited children onto the golden sand.

That night, wrapped in Javier's arms on a beach chair, watching her children and their cousins wading under the moonlight, Sophie sighed with contentment.

Sometimes it felt as if her heart could explode with happiness.

* * * * *

LET'S TALK

For exclusive extracts, competitions
and special offers, find us online:

facebook.com/millsandboon

@millsandboonuk

@millsandboon

Or get in touch on 0844 844 1351*

For all the latest titles coming soon,
visit millsandboon.co.uk/nextmonth

EDWARD WILSON

The Darkling Spy

ARCADIA BOOKS

Arcadia Books Ltd
15–16 Nassau Street
London W1W 7AB

www.arcadiabooks.co.uk

First published by Arcadia Books 2010

ISBN 978-1-906413-64-4

Typeset in Minion by MacGuru Ltd
Printed and bound in the UK by CPI Mackays, Chatham ME5 8TD

Arcadia Books gratefully acknowledges the financial support of Arts Council England.

Arcadia Books supports English PEN, the fellowship of writers who work together to
promote literature and its understanding. English PEN upholds writers' freedoms in
Britain and around the world, challenging political and cultural limits on free expression.
To find out more, visit www.englishpen.org or contact
English PEN, 6–8 Amwell Street, London EC1R 1UQ

Arcadia Books distributors are as follows:

in the UK and elsewhere in Europe:
Turnaround Publishers Services
Unit 3, Olympia Trading Estate
Coburg Road
London N22 6TZ

in the US and Canada:
Independent Publishers Group
814 N. Franklin Street
Chicago, IL 60610

in Australia:
The Scribo Group Pty Ltd
18 Rodborough Road
Frenchs Forest 2086

in New Zealand:
Addenda
PO Box 78224
Grey Lynn
Auckland

in South Africa:
Jacana Media (Pty) Ltd
PO Box 291784,
Melville 2109
Johannesburg

Arcadia Books is the *Sunday Times* Small Publisher of the Year 2002/03

For Frank and Joe, my brothers.

From Stettin in the Baltic to Trieste in the Adriatic,
an iron curtain has descended across the Continent.

Winston Churchill

... nor love, nor light
Nor certitude, nor peace, nor help for pain;
And we are here as on a darkling plain
Swept with confused alarms of struggle and fright,
Where ignorant armies clash by night.

'Dover Beach'
Matthew Arnold

Please allow me to introduce myself
I'm a man of wealth and taste ...

'Sympathy for the Devil'
The Rolling Stones

Berlin, Soviet Sector: 17 August 1956. They were going to put Brecht into a hole on the very edge of the cemetery. The grave was wedged in a corner overlooked by two high brick walls at right angles. The awkward position made it difficult for the diplomatic delegations to get near, but Catesby pushed his way through because he had a job to do.

The funeral was bigger than the *Volkspolizei* had expected. More than a million people had thronged the streets outside the walls of the Dorotheenstadt Cemetery. But Catesby was an accredited diplomat, so he was inside the walls. His official title was Cultural Attaché for Film and Broadcasting. He even had an office at the British Embassy in Bonn. But the CultAt post wasn't his real job. It was his 'legend', his diplomatic cover. Dip cover gave dip immunity. It meant that if you got caught, they couldn't prosecute you, they could only throw you out. They called it being PNG'd, declared persona non grata. It usually happened in places like Moscow or Warsaw, but one Brit had been PNG'd from Washington. It was ugly when it happened between allies.

Catesby knew he had to write a report and that he ought to take some photos, but he wasn't in the mood for spying. He felt sweaty wearing a black suit in the still August heat. And he felt sordid being a spy at Bertolt Brecht's funeral. Catesby admired the dead playwright, but it was an admiration he had to keep to himself. Brecht's politics weren't too popular with his bosses back in London – and even less popular in Washington. Catesby looked around at the mourners and realised that the US Embassy hadn't sent a representative. Not surprising for the funeral of a man who said that setting up a bank was a bigger crime than robbing one.

Catesby felt out of place standing with the diplomatic delegations. He felt like a black-market spiv who had crashed the party to pimp and sell dodgy jewellery. Well, spies were spivs. They weren't gents, not like the real dips. Catesby would have preferred a career as a diplomat, but he didn't think the Foreign Office would have him. He knew they wouldn't.

Catesby had pushed his way to the front so he could clearly see the main mourners. He was only ten feet away from Brecht's widow, Helene Weigel. He remembered Weigel playing Mother Courage. The character reminded Catesby of his own mother, and her desperate struggle for bourgeois respectability. And yet, if it hadn't been for his mother, Catesby wouldn't be carrying a black diplomatic passport and making good wages. He certainly wouldn't have gone to university. He would have left school at fifteen and become a 'decky learner' on a Lowestoft trawler or, at best, a fitter in a shipyard like his Uncle Jack.

Catesby put on a solemn face and folded his hands in front of him. The pall-bearers were carrying the coffin through the crowd. They had finally succeeded in getting the coffin to the grave where they lowered it on to wooden trestles. There wasn't a vicar or anyone religious, but there was a man in his fifties who seemed to be directing the practical side of things. The pall-bearers were joined by four hefty younger men who passed webbing straps under the coffin. It soon became obvious that a man who had devoted his life to theatre was being buried without any theatre at all.

As the body was lowered into the grave, Catesby tried to identify the family and close friends who lined up to toss handfuls of soil on to the coffin. The mourners were led by Weigel and a daughter from Brecht's first marriage; who were followed by the children from his second marriage. Catesby also managed to identify two of Brecht's girlfriends, who seemed on perfectly good terms with Helene Weigel. Catesby envied them all. They could be what they were. They could even flaunt it.

HUMINT, Human Intelligence, was an important part of Catesby's job: it meant watching people. The day before the funeral Catesby had spent twelve hours going through photograph files. Catesby had a trick to help remember which names belonged to which faces. He created animal familiars based on their looks: Friederun the Ferret, Helmut the Hare, Renate Rabbit, Walter Vole and so on. The faces in the files were a *Who's Who* of anyone who was anyone in the East Bloc. Sometimes the faces visited Catesby in his dreams, but not as humans. The previous night Catesby's world had transformed into a woodland where Pigling Bland and the Flopsy Bunnies were trying to kidnap the Fierce Bad Rabbit. Catesby suddenly woke up and remembered something. That's what they were trying to do to Kit

Fournier. He wondered when they were going to call him back to London. If the usual crowd didn't get Fournier and break him, they'd give him a bash.

Catesby had kitted himself for the funeral with a pinhole covert surveillance camera. He needed to take pictures for updating the photo files or for adding new faces. The tiny camera lens was located in his lapel buttonhole and he operated the shutter by pressing on his belt buckle. Catesby thought that, since it was a funeral, he would spend a lot of time with his hands solemnly folded in front of him. He thought that touching his belt buckle would look less obvious than scratching or having a hand in his pocket. But after a few snaps, he became aware that a female Swedish diplomat was looking at him in an odd way. Catesby avoided eye contact – God only knows what the woman was thinking. He quickly removed his hands from his midriff. The Swede continued staring and tightened her mouth.

Catesby watched as the last of Brecht's inner circle approached the grave. The sandy soil of Berlin was so light that it trickled through the fingers of each mourner. The thin soil reminded Catesby of Operation Stopwatch. Together with the CIA they had dug a thousand-yard-long tunnel into East Berlin to tap the telephone lines leading to Soviet Military Headquarters. Catesby had been to the tunnel to help the technical staff decipher the German telephone engineering manual they were using to differentiate various cables. The beige sandy soil had reminded Catesby of the sand cliffs at Covehithe in his native Suffolk. He rubbed the fine sand between his fingertips and said, 'It's all going to fall into the sea, you know – just like Covehithe.'

The technicians ignored his comment, but less than a year later Soviet troops burst through the roof and the monitoring staff had to run for their lives. The tunnel had been betrayed.

As the last mourner walked away from Brecht's grave, the delegations began to disperse and mix with one another. Catesby watched the UK Ambassador shake hands with Helene Weigel, who was elegantly composed and at ease. Walter Ulbricht, the leader of the East German government, was already walking towards his ZIL limousine.

Catesby could see the Ambassador talking to the security officer, a lumpy retired Glaswegian cop. Presumably, the Ambassador wanted to make a quick getaway and was wondering how they were going to get the Humbers through the crowd. The cars and their drivers had been requisitioned from British Military Headquarters to ferry them from Templehof Airport. Catesby reckoned they were stuck for a long time. The East Berlin Vopos who could have cleared a way with their lumpy Volga patrol cars had disappeared.

On the other side of the cemetery wall various groups had begun to sing Brecht-Weill songs. The funeral had turned into celebration. A woman with a deep voice was singing the Alabama song in a broad Berliner accent.

Oh, moon of Alabama
We now must say goodbye
We've lost our good old mama
And must have whisky, oh, you know why.

Catesby wouldn't have minded a drink himself: standing around at these things could be awfully boring. Suddenly, there was a voice next to him.

'I think I know you from somewhere, London perhaps.'

The speaker was obviously German, but spoke English with an American accent. He was a short balding man who looked about sixty. He was exactly the sort of nondescript person who passes unnoticed in a crowd or even alone – the ideal spy. Catesby recognised the face from one of the files – and from somewhere else too – but the man's name fluttered around the edge of his consciousness like an elusive butterfly.

Catesby smiled and said, 'I think we have met, but I've a terrible memory for names. I do apologise.'

'Please don't apologise. I can't remember your name either, but I'm sure we have met.'

Catesby turned to face the balding German so he could get a good photo through the buttonhole lens, then he tapped the shutter release under his belt.

The German smiled and said, 'Cheese.'

Catesby could see the Ambassador gesturing to him over the heads of the crowd. He gestured back, then said to the German, 'Unfortunately, it looks like we're about to leave. I wish we had more time to talk …'

'Maybe we'll meet again – and have a drink.'

'I hope we do,' said Catesby, but the inconspicuous man was already gone.

On the other side of the wall, the husky voiced *Berlinerin* was now singing another Brecht-Weill song:

Und der Haifisch ... and the shark has teeth
And wears them in his face.
And MacHeath has a knife
But it's a knife that no one sees.

It was nearly midnight when Catesby got back to the embassy in Bonn. The first thing he did was to remove the film from his miniature camera and pop it into the diplomatic bag, 'priority air'. He tagged the film envelope with a 'SECRET/Delicate Source' label and the address code that meant it would be taken by a Signal Corps motorcycle courier from the Foreign Office straight to the SIS lab above the car pool garage in Vauxhall. Catesby asked the night clerk in the embassy mailroom to sign a bag receipt, he left nothing to chance. He then went upstairs to the registry where a clerk named Sidney briefly looked up from *Sporting Life*. 'Doing overtime again, sir?'

'Yes.'

'I hope they pay you enough, Mr Catesby.'

'I get by.'

Catesby suspected that he was the only member of the diplomatic staff with whom the clerks and drivers dared banter. Sometimes he felt they were mocking him. They saw through him. They knew he wasn't a member of the officer class. He had had the same problem in the army.

'You want those photo ledgers again, sir, don't you?'

'How did you know?'

'Because they seem to be the only things you ever take out.'

'You're on to me.'

Sidney winked meaningfully, then walked into the vault to retrieve the ledgers. The FO and SIS still called document files 'ledgers' – as if they were books in a Victorian counting house. As he waited for Catesby to sign the classified document receipt, Sidney asked, 'How's Ipswich Town going to do this season?'

'They're going to win the league.'

'You think so, sir?'

'We'll see, Sidney.' Catesby picked up the photo-files.

When Catesby got to his office, he put the photo-files on his desk, turned out all the lights and locked the door behind him. He then sat in his chair, closed his eyes and listened to the night. It was a counter-surveillance trick that he often used. Sometimes he would sit in a darkened office for an hour at a time – or more if he fell asleep. On a few occasions he had heard furtive footsteps in a corridor – and once, he was sure that someone had stopped to listen at his door. But it had never got as far as keys in the lock. He wondered what he would do if he ever caught anyone snooping. Would he wrestle the intruder to the ground and shout for help? Or would he reach for the revolver in his desk drawer?

Catesby yawned and turned on the desk light. He sometimes wondered if he were going mad. Paranoia was an occupational illness – especially among the Americans. He listened to the night again. The only sounds were the whistles of trains and the horns of Rhine barges. Catesby sat perfectly still because he didn't want to frighten away the butterfly that was flittering through his brain. Suddenly, the butterfly settled on a bare branch that was London, 1949. Catesby closed his eyes and strained to put a name to the bald German's face; then suddenly said aloud: 'Gerhard Eisler.'

The interrogation had taken place in 1949 at a safe house in Oakley Street in Chelsea. Catesby was still new in the service and had been called in as an interpreter translator. In the end, his help hadn't been needed because Eisler spoke excellent English. The safe house had been damp and freezing. The only heating was a single-bar electric fire in the sitting room where the interrogation was taking place. Catesby was exiled to the kitchen where he made cups of tea without taking off his coat or gloves. He could hear muffled voices coming from the next room, but couldn't make out the words. From time to time Eisler laughed – he seemed a lot happier than the guys from D Branch and SIS. Finally, the kitchen door opened and Catesby was invited to join the group. Eisler must have guessed Catesby's role for he looked at him and spoke German for the first time:

'Herauf, herab und quer und krumm,
Mein Schüler an der Nase herum.'

The D Branch man, an ex-policeman named Skardon, turned to Catesby. 'What was that?'

'It's from Goethe's *Faust*. It means he's been leading his students a merry dance: "Up, down, sideways and bent …"'

'That's what we thought.' Skardon turned to a technician who was packing up an Ampex 200 tape recorder. 'Tell the goons he's ready to go.'

Five minutes later, Catesby was alone in the flat with Skardon and Henry Bone, the Head of R5 Counterintelligence. Bone was a former Olympic yachtsman who had a laconic and deceptively languid manner that clearly annoyed Skardon.

After an awkward silence, Bone turned to Catesby. 'Sorry, we had to keep you in the kitchen. We didn't want the subject to know you were one of our chaps instead of just an interpreter. What do you think of him?'

'He speaks with a slight Saxon accent – and seems sardonic and self-confident.'

'In any case,' said Bone, 'we're going to have to let him go.'

At the time, Catesby had no idea why the interrogation had taken place or what the 'subject' had done wrong.

Skardon rubbed his hands together. 'Bloody cold in here.'

Bone smiled wanly at Skardon. 'You're not happy, Jim.'

'Letting this bird go is a big mistake.'

Bone winked at Catesby. 'Jim doesn't like our man in Washington – you see it's all our man's idea.'

Skardon suddenly snapped, 'I think we should end this discussion now.'

Catesby had long passed the point where he wanted to sleep. Sometimes staying awake sharpened the senses and made you aware of things you missed before. Oakley Street safe house was now playing through his mind more clearly than ever. There were two factors that set Catesby's nerves on edge. The first was that 'our man in Washington', who had ordered Eisler's release, had been PNG'd by the Americans two years later. This was the only time since the British Army burned down the White House in 1814 that a British diplomat had been declared persona non grata by the Americans. The same diplomat-spy was still the centre of an ongoing espionage scandal that had set MI5 against SIS and SIS against itself. Catesby would love to read the files, but the relevant ledgers were UK EYES ALPHA with bells on.

The other factor that bothered Catesby was why Eisler had singled him out to make contact. It wasn't just social. Catesby cast his memory back over Oakley Street. Memory is like a clandestine tape-recording that you keep rewinding to search for more clues. Each replay ought to reveal something you missed before. But Catesby couldn't find a thing that would have led Eisler to make contact. It must be something else. He finally opened the photo-file and looked at the MI5 report that was stapled on the page next to Eisler's photo.

```
Born Leipzig, 1897. Decorated for bravery in World War
One. Prominent member of Communist Party in 1920s.
Reportedly made trip to China in 1920s where he was
known as 'The Executioner'. Alleged to be covert leader
of Communist Party in America during Word War Two.
Centre of 1949 diplomatic incident between UK and US
when he stowed away on a Polish ship from New York.
Removed from ship and arrested in Southampton by British
customs, but then allowed to proceed to East Germany
by UK authorities. Currently head of East German state
radio.
```

Catesby knew the Americans had been outrageous over Eisler. At least during the war, they had comported themselves like house-guests even if they found the plumbing awkward and the beds too small. But by '49 they realised they were kings of the world. When the Americans heard that Eisler was on a Polish ship docked in South-ampton, they virtually kidnapped him. The CIA Head of Station and a US consul boarded the ship with an extradition warrant to be served by a local magistrate and two police constables. But it turned out to be quite a scene. Two consuls from the Polish Embassy were already on board and protested that Eisler was under the protection of the Polish government. There was a brief shouting match, but the Americans shouted louder and in slightly better English. Eventu-ally, the magistrates took the US side and ordered the cops to arrest Eisler – who surprised everyone by fighting back like a demon. The plump little German managed to take out one constable with a knee to the groin and sent another's helmet spinning into the Solent. He was finally subdued with a truncheon blow and taken into custody. And then, Catesby remembered, there had been a big row in the House of Commons too.

Catesby locked his office door and walked downstairs to the embassy library. It held nothing confidential, but public documents often reveal more secrets than the most protected EYES ALPHA ledgers. You just needed to know where to look. Catesby had to stand on a chair to reach the *Hansard* for 1949. He carried the heavy red volume to a reading desk and paged through the Parliamentary proceedings for May until he found the Eisler debate.

Mr Gallacher: Then I will ask another question, Mr Speaker. Is the Home Secretary aware that it is a tragic situation when Ministers who claim to be socialists are responsible for such a shocking and shameless affair as the treatment of this anti-Nazi refugee? Is there any limit to the depths of degradation to which this country can be drawn at the command of America?

Catesby smiled. The dots were joining up. He had met Willie Gallacher at a party in the late forties. Gallacher was one of the two last communist MPs elected to the UK Parliament. It was a pretty drunken party, but Gallacher was more sober than most and had deduced, via an indiscreet host, that Catesby was in SIS. They had talked at length and the communist MP was surprised to find that Catesby was a lefty too. Catesby had, of course, laid it on thick to gain Gallacher's confidence. It was all part of the game – Catesby had even written a brief report about the encounter. You needed to cover yourself.

One of the library's fluorescent lights began to blink and flicker. It made Catesby feel anxious, under surveillance. It was as if the light had discovered his secret self and was sending out a Morse code signal. Catesby now understood why Eisler had picked him out. His 'fellow comrade' pose with Gallacher had finally paid off.

When Catesby got back to his office, he leaned against the plate-glass window. There was something about the Bonn embassy that made him uneasy. It was a modern post-war building with lots of glass and steel. The idea was to convey, falsely perhaps, the openness of Western democracy. But Catesby found it too light and airy,

9

especially at night. Anyone passing by on the street could see him leaning against his office window and looking thoughtful. But what if they could read those thoughts?

Catesby listened to the night. The nocturnal chorus began with the high singing whistle of a Rhine barge – and a second later the low base whistle of a steam locomotive. The great hulking iron mammoths of the Rhine seemed to have their own language. The thought of inanimate objects talking to each other made Catesby queasy. It reminded him of his own job. Espionage was a nightmare world of the unnatural. It was a Hieronymus Bosch hellscape where house plants have ears and fountain pens take pictures. There was no such thing as an innocent object. Every telephone was a predator waiting to trigger a tape machine. The human was becoming irrelevant. It wouldn't be long, Catesby knew, before radar dishes spoke directly to missile silos. The human factor was too slow – and maybe too sentimental. Catesby hated the bomb, but he had to keep that secret too – because part of his job was spying on other people who hated the bomb.

There was a new noise, one that was much nearer. Someone was knocking hard on his door and calling his name. When Catesby opened the door he found the NDO, the Night Duty Officer, holding a cable marked URGENT in his hand.

'I'm glad we could find you, it's always our fault if we can't.'

Catesby unfolded the cable printout. The perforated strips from the telex machine were still clinging to its sides. The message was simple, not a word wasted. It was typical of Henry Bone.

RETURN TO LONDON IMMEDIATELY

Bone didn't need to say more. It was clear he wanted help with the Fournier op.

Henry Bone was as cadaverous as his name: tall, slim, high-browed and hollow-cheeked. Catesby thought that the black cassock with velvet piping suited him perfectly. Bone wasn't the sort of priest you'd find striding across a sheep-shitten hill in Galway. Oh, no. Monsignor Bone was every inch a Vatican inner-sanctum priest: 'His Holiness will see you now, Ambassador.' Just as the real life and secular Bone was an inner-sanctum spy chief. Catesby, on the other hand, wore his Roman collar with less assurance and wasn't always sure when to turn the page of music.

The two men were staked out in the organ loft of Brompton Oratory. It was an excellent surveillance post. You could see everyone who entered the church and hear every syllable of the most faintly whispered Hail Mary. Catesby had set up a pair of cameras with wide-angle lens that covered most of the nave. He operated the shutter releases with a foot control so that he could take snaps while still turning pages of eighteenth-century organ music.

'Let's try the d'Agincourt again.'

Catesby leafed through the sheets of music until he found *Dialogue du 2e Ton* and propped it on the stand above the four rows of keyboards.

'Do you like François d'Agincourt?' said Bone.

'No, he's boring.'

'You're not very musical are you, Catesby?'

'That's not true. I like Jacques Brel and Charlie Parker.'

'But not at the same time.'

'No. They're for different moods.'

Just as Bone pulled out a stop and began to play, there was the sound of a door opening and the echo of footsteps from the nave.

'He's here,' whispered Catesby, 'keep playing.'

Bone glanced down at a viewing lens as he held a long unstopped note. Catesby had got technical services to provide periscope pipes with magnification lens. The periscope eye and a wide-angle camera lens were hidden in the ornate wooden frame of a clock mounted on the organ loft railing. 'Don't turn around,' whispered Bone, 'he's giving us a good look. But you need to turn the page.'

Catesby folded back the music and watched the 6x magnified image of a man genuflecting in front of the altar. The surveillance target held his trilby in front of his heart in a gesture of piety. Meanwhile, Catesby took pictures by working the remote cable shutter release with his foot. When the man was standing again, he turned and walked to the right. Catesby worked his foot up and down to get a couple of profile snaps before the target disappeared from view.

'He's gone into the St Theresa chapel,' said Bone. 'That's where they always meet, bad security.'

'Shhh, this place echoes.'

When Bone reached the end of the *Dialogue*, Catesby replaced the music with a *Sanctus* by François Couperin. Bone fiddled with a number of the organ's 45 stops and began. Catesby remembered the words of the Latin mass that went with the music: *Pleni sunt coeli et terra gloria tua.* He'd had enough of that stuff as a child.

Bone tried to play as normally as possible, but both he and Catesby were listening intently to the sound of rapid footsteps on the parquet flooring.

'He must have made the drop,' whispered Catesby.

They both looked at the viewing lens and caught a glimpse of Vasili Galanin as he hurried through the nave. Galanin was the most important Sov agent in London. He was the *rezident*, the KGB Head of Station, and operated under dip cover from the embassy.

'Our Russian friend,' said Bone, 'looks more like a poet than a spy.'

As soon as Catesby heard the street door close, he put a hand on Bone's shoulder and whispered, 'Stay here and keep playing; I'm going downstairs to make sure he hasn't brought his own watchers.'

The nave wasn't empty. There were three people. Two of them were bent in prayer. They were elderly regular visitors. Catesby and Bone had noted them during the previous days of watching and waiting. They were almost certainly 'civilians'. The third person was a man in his thirties with a black moustache and heavily Brylcreemed hair. He wasn't praying. He was walking around glancing at the dome mosaics and the Mazzuoli apostles as if passing time. His presence worried Catesby. He didn't want the fellow hanging around while he ransacked the Theresa chapel for Galanin's drop. He needed to get rid of him.

Catesby stopped at a display table and picked up a handful of pamphlets advertising parish events and groups. The Brylcreem man was standing near the Lady Altar, described in the Oratory guide as 'an extreme example of flamboyant baroque'. Catesby walked up beside the visitor. 'Magnificent, isn't it?'

'What?'

'The altar piece,' said Catesby. 'It was commissioned in the late seventeenth century for the *Duomo Nouvo* in Brescia, but seems to have ended up here among the *buoni cattolici* of Kensington.'

The other man appeared to be biting his lip or chewing the end of his moustache.

'I don't believe I've seen you here before,' said Catesby, 'but that could be because I'm new to the parish myself.'

The man put his hands in his pockets and shifted nervously.

Catesby waited patiently for an answer. He wanted to hear the voice again; he thought he had detected a North American diphthong in the 'what'. Catesby flourished a pamphlet. 'I wonder if, perhaps, you would be interested in joining the St Philip's Servers Guild. It's a very worthy organisation indeed, and gives a layperson a rare opportunity to take part in the liturgy.'

The man cleared his throat as if he were about to speak, but seemed to be looking over Catesby's shoulder at something or someone else.

'The Servers Guild,' said Catesby, 'is named after our founder, St Philip Neri – an extraordinary priest. After years of prayer, the Holy Spirit finally came to him during the feast of Pentecost in 1546.' Catesby paused; then lowered his voice. 'It happened in the catacomb of St Sebastian. The gift of divine love came as a ball of fire that entered his mouth and plunged into his heart with such force that it broke three of his ribs.'

For the first time, the other man looked at Catesby. His face was cold and vacant, but his eyes were burning. The words came slow and deliberate. 'Would you like to suck my cock?'

Catesby put on a look of priestly disgust. 'I think it's best,' he said, 'that you leave the church.' For the first time, he noticed that the organ music had stopped.

'Father Emile, have you found those hymn books?' It was Henry Bone. 'They ought to be collected after every service. Have you looked in the Theresa chapel?'

'No, Father, I'll do it now.' As Catesby walked to the side chapel he sensed the stranger's eyes boring into his back. – and knew his cover was blown. He began the search in the back row. Unlike the nave, the Theresa chapel was fitted with pews. He moved slowly, genuinely searching for hymn sheets and missals; not wanting to give anything else away, not wishing to shed the last thin veneer of his priestly cover. Finally, there was the echo of footsteps and the sound of a door opening – once again, he sensed a final glance – and then the door slowly closing. Catesby peeped over the back of a pew and saw Bone looking down at him.

'Did your friend introduce himself?'

'Not quite,' said Catesby, 'but he's an American. And I'm sure he's from Grosvenor Square.'

'Diplomat?'

'No, he's one of us – or one of the FBI guys that Hoover uses to spy on the dips.'

Bone looked concerned. 'They're on to Fournier.'

'It looks that way.'

'We can't waste time – we need find the drop before Fournier turns up. Look underneath the pews and I'll keep a look out.'

Catesby got down on his hands and knees to search the underside of the pews. He was surprised to see how many worshippers had used the space to stash their chewing gum. The chewing thing came with the war. He remembered the cry of schoolboys as soon as they spotted an American serviceman, 'Got any gum, chum?'

It didn't take long to find the drop. Vasili Galanin had attached a brown envelope with a strip of brown packing tape. Catesby carefully peeled back the tape so they could re-use it. He then tucked the packet under his surplice and rejoined Bone. They then went back to the organ loft. Bone played Olivier Messiaen's *Transports de joie* while Catesby photographed the fake passports that the KGB had forged for Kit Fournier, the CIA Head of Station, and his lover. Fournier was being very naughty and it was important that the Brits got to him before the Americans – and had the evidence to black-mail him all the way to the Ninth Circle of Hell, where traitors were frozen in ice for all eternity.

As soon as Catesby had finished, he put the passports back into a brown envelope that was identical to the original. They had also brought genuine Soviet envelopes in case the *rezident* had used his embassy's own stationery, but Galanin was too professional to make a mistake like that. This was an op where you didn't want to leave any fingerprints.

When they went back downstairs to replace the drop, Bone stationed himself by the Oratory's only street entrance. He had a set of keys to lock the door, and a sign apologising for the closure, in case Fournier turned up too soon. Meanwhile, Catesby put the envelope back beneath the pew and carefully stretched the wrinkles out of the packing tape. The two elderly parishioners in the nave, an old woman with leg ulcers mumbling her way through a rosary and a threadbare man staring fiercely over his walking stick were oblivious of the drama around them. Catesby wondered if they were 'civilians' after all: the trade made you suspect everyone.

Henry Bone now had to turn his own pages. Catesby had to keep out of sight because Fournier would recognise him. There was little room to hide in the organ loft because you could see through the railings. The only cover was behind the large clock that concealed the periscope and camera lens. It meant that Catesby had to lie scrunched on top of the periscope pipe, which dug into his ribs, and not move at all. As the afternoon wore on, there were more visitors, but still no Kit Fournier. The general rule with DLBs, dead letter boxes, is that you should pick up the 'drop' as soon as possible after the box is 'filled.' The risk that someone unintended will intercept the drop increases with every hour. Catesby looked at this watch; it was more than three hours since the *rezident* had made the drop and still no Fournier. He waited another fifteen minutes and whispered to Bone, 'I don't think he's going to show.'

'Shhh, keep your voice down.'

'It doesn't matter.' Catesby got up and stood next to the keyboard.

Bone frowned. 'You shouldn't have broken cover.'

Catesby picked up Widor's *Marche Nuptiale* and spread it across the music score holder. 'Play that for Kit. People have been known to marry their honey traps.'

'Very droll, especially if he turns up.'

'He's not going to turn up.'

'How can you be so sure?'

'Confessions begin in twenty minutes. There's a confessional in the Theresa chapel, and there'll soon be a queue of penitents not ten feet from the DLB. He's not going to empty a box under the nose of an unshriven sinner. I'm going down to have a look around.'

On the way to the Theresa chapel, Catesby picked up a couple of hymnals to keep up his cover as he briskly walked to the pew. He slid along the DLB pew as inconspicuously as possible; then put his hand under it at the very place where he had taped the envelope. It wasn't there. He double-checked to make sure that he was in the right place; then looked underneath to make sure it hadn't come unstuck and fallen on the floor. Still nothing. It was gone.

Catesby made his way back to the nave and looked around. The man with the walking stick hadn't moved and was still staring fiercely, but the mumbling old woman with the rosary was gone. At that moment the triumphal strains of Widor's *Marche Nuptiale* filled the Oratory.

'What do you think of this umbrella?' said Bone.

They were in the middle of Green Park; no longer priests, but suited and bowler-hatted civil servants. Their walk back to SIS Headquarters wasn't the shortest route, but it was the most pleasant. Catesby looked at Bone's brolly. 'It looks just like any other umbrella, except perhaps for being more expertly rolled.'

'Look,' Bone held his umbrella next to Catesby's, 'what's different?'

'It's got a bigger handle.'

'How perceptive. Now then, why would someone order a bespoke umbrella with a larger handle?'

Catesby thought hard for a few seconds. 'To make it distinguishable from other umbrellas, so you can easily find it among a dozen or so otherwise identical brollies in a stand or on a rack.'

'Excellent, Catesby – that was Eliot's idea exactly.'

'Eliot who?'

'T.S. Eliot.'

'So,' said Catesby, 'you went out and ordered one for yourself.'

'No, that would have been far too expensive. Eliot's quite well off nowadays – he can afford such luxuries.'

'You nicked it.'

Bone raised the umbrella and gestured at Lancaster House, just visible through the trees. 'It happened there, a couple of years ago. The British Council gave a little musical soirée for the diplomatic community – and Eliot was a guest of honour. I overheard him bragging about his clever umbrella idea to Sir Thomas Beecham – and something about Eliot's tone annoyed me. So, I decided to have a look at the famous umbrella as I was leaving. It was, indeed, easy to find – and just as easy to pinch.'

'Is this story top secret?'

'In a way, it is,' Bone held the umbrella in front of Catesby as if he were pointing at something. 'What else is different?'

Catesby looked carefully. 'The spike on the end looks newer than the rest of the umbrella.'

'That's why I need to scruff it up a little.'

Catesby guessed that a spring-loaded hypodermic syringe had been inserted in the spike. He'd heard that such a device was being developed. 'Cyanide or ricin?'

'Don't worry,' Bone smiled, 'it's not loaded. But, if it were, the boffs at Porton Down seem to think that ricin would be easier to administer. Pity, it doesn't kill as cleanly and provides a long painful death.'

'Why not VX, that swish new nerve agent?'

'Fingerprints, Catesby, fingerprints. We're the only chaps that have VX. If you use ricin for a wet job, you can plant false flags anywhere from Moscow Central to an obscure religious cult.'

'And, if you leave that brolly at the scene, you can stitch T.S. Eliot.'

Bone laughed. 'I don't think that's on, but it is a tempting thought.'

'Are you going to use that umbrella to kill Kit Fournier?'

Bone paused and looked across the park. 'How many trees can you name?'

'The most numerous seem to be London plane, and,' Catesby pointed behind him, 'there are also lime, silver maple …'

'But surprisingly few native oak.'

'No, I haven't seen any at all.'

'The question is, Catesby, are you a native oak?'

'Is this a way of getting at me because my mother is Belgian? I've had a stomach full of this. At every selection interview from officer training to Special Operations Executive it's come up. And now this new Positive Vetting gang at Central Registry are having a go too.'

'Maybe it's because we're trying to promote you, to give you more responsibility.'

'Thanks, but maybe Vetting should pay more attention to your purebred native oaks – like Burgess and Maclean.'

'It's not the Belgian connection – there are other issues and you very well know it.'

'I don't vote Tory, so what? I'm a socialist – and don't hide the fact.'

Bone smiled. 'That side of you is very useful, but it's a legend that needs to be cultivated with care and cunning. And both sides need to be convinced, and absolutely sure, that you are a totally genuine product.'

'We've had this conversation before – and it frightens me. It's a big ask.'

'But if we do ask it, we need to pump you up to make you more attractive. It might mean Head of Eastern Europe P Section, or even Controller Eastern Area. And to do this I need to convince Central Registry that you really are one of us.'

'Who are "us"?'

Bone laughed. He clearly wasn't going to answer the question. Instead, he tapped the footpath with the umbrella. 'I hope I don't have to kill Kit Fournier with Mr Eliot's umbrella, but it is an option. The Sovs, of course, would get blamed – and Washington would lean on us to expel a load of faux dips, among them of course, the *rezident*. And we don't want that, do we?'

'I suppose not.'

'And we don't want to kill Fournier. We don't want him dead *or* alive. We want him dead *and* alive. How well did you know him?'

'Obviously not as well as I thought I knew him. Otherwise, I would have stopped him killing Horst.'

'But it was pure textbook.'

'And totally unnecessary.'

The killing of Horst was one of several incidents – including the recruitment of ex-Nazis as intelligence operatives – that turned Catesby against the Americans. The death of Horst had been unnecessary, but it had been a work of art. Fournier and his colleagues had kidnapped the supposed double agent and drove him away in his own car. They then faked a late-night autobahn breakdown, and pretended to let Horst escape before chasing him across the central reservation of the autobahn – except there was no central reservation, they were on a viaduct. They then siphoned the remaining petrol out of Horst's car and left the scene. The police investigation concluded that Horst had run out of fuel, then accidentally fallen 300 feet to his death while trying to cross to the other carriageway so he could hitch a lift to the nearest town. No fingerprints.

'If we get Fournier in the bag, we might want you as part of the interrogation team. How would you feel about that?'

'Mixed. I liked Kit. He wasn't like the other Americans. He was understated and modest – and loved poetry. In fact, he's very fond of Eliot – be awfully ironic if you killed him with that brolly.'

Bone tapped the path hard with the umbrella spike. 'I don't like Eliot – his politics are obnoxious and his poetry pretentious. But, I suppose, he's the sort of thing Americans think of as serious culture.' Bone leaned hard on the umbrella, as if trying to break it. 'When Americans like culture, which fortunately isn't very often, they want it with a capital "K" and lots of priestly portentousness.'

Catesby smiled. Something had touched a raw nerve in Bone. 'Well, Henry, if you take Kit alive, you can educate him and improve his flawed judgement.'

'Not before we've turned him inside out. Harvesting the contents of Kit Fournier's brain could be our best intelligence coup since the cracking of Enigma.'

Catesby smiled wanly. Bone was off on a rant.

'Don't smile like that. You still haven't any idea the extent to which Washington has kept us in the cold, treated us like lepers.'

'I'd have to be stone deaf not to know.' Moaning about the lack of intelligence cooperation was a constant background noise at Broadway Buildings, SIS HQ. The Americans had begun to be sparing about what they shared with the British in the late forties because they didn't feel comfortable with Atlee's 'socialist' government. But after the defection of Burgess and Maclean in 1951, the sharing of intelligence and military secrets dried up almost entirely.

'And,' said Bone, 'the Treasury doesn't like it either. Being left out in the cold is expensive. We've had to develop our own nuclear weapons from scratch.'

'We shouldn't bother – it's a waste of money.'

Bone pointed to a park bench. 'Sit down.'

Catesby sat down.

'Watch what you say at Broadway Buildings. You know I'm trying to build you up, to be a member of the inner circle. I want the others to trust you – and accept you as one of us.'

'You didn't answer my earlier question, who are "us"?'

Bone closed his eyes and leaned forward on his umbrella. 'If you don't know by now, you're too stupid to be in the service.'

A chill ran down Catesby's spine. It was a warm early September day, but he began to shiver. He suddenly knew it was time to ask the question, a question that had been burning a hole in the back of his mind since Oakley Street. Catesby said a name. It was the name of someone who had been one of Bone's closest colleagues. He then asked, 'Is he a traitor?'

Henry Bone gave a dry laugh. It sounded like a saw blade scraping a rusty nail. 'Let's go.'

They walked in silence until they emerged from Green Park opposite Clarence House, the home of the Queen Mother. Catesby gestured towards the royal townhouse. 'Someone once told me that you're a friend of hers.'

'Who told you?'

'One of the women who works in Personnel. It was Ley's leaving bash. She was a bit tiddly and, you know, the sort of person who's impressed by that sort of thing: "Cor, there's Mr Bone, he travels in very high circles, takes tea with the Queen Mum."'

Catesby noted that a nerve in Bone's left cheek had begun to twitch. The twitch occurred on the rare occasions when Bone was worried, embarrassed – or caught out.

'That's an exaggeration. I've been to two dinner parties at Clarence House, hardly intimate affairs – a dozen or so guests.'

'Did she ask you to arrange a wet job on the Duke of Windsor?'

'You're being banal, Catesby. No, she wanted to show me some enamels from her collection.'

'To make sure they were the real thing?'

'Yes, that is what Her Majesty wanted. And I was pleased to reassure her.'

Catesby bit his lip to stop from smiling. Mental flashbulbs had begun to pop and sizzle. It was like that comic opera moment when you break down the bedroom door and start snapping those naked writhing bodies. But he wasn't going to embarrass Bone further. He wasn't going to mention the Cambridge classmate. He wasn't going to say, *I suppose he asked you to Clarence House to verify his own opinion as an eminent art historian …*

They crossed the Mall and entered St James's Park. Catesby felt he had to say something to break the awkward silence. 'This used to be a royal zoo, didn't it?'

'That was during the reign of James I. Camels, elephants, exotic birds – he used to keep crocodiles in the lake. But in the Middle Ages it was a leper colony.'

Catesby gestured to a large web-footed bird swimming through the overhanging branches of a weeping willow. 'I like the pelicans.'

'They were a gift from the Russian Ambassador in the seventeenth century.'

'And they're still here.'

'And so are the Russians.'

They started to cross the bridge over the lake. 'D'you know,' said Catesby, 'I once saw one of them eat a pigeon alive?'

'He must have been a survivor of the Siege of Leningrad.'

'I didn't mean the Russians, Henry, I meant the pelicans. It happened by that flower bed.'

Bone stopped in the middle of the bridge and looked eastwards towards Horse Guards. 'I'm worried.'

'About Fournier getting away?'

'No, about the Americans getting him first. That would be …'

'Be what, Henry?'

'The worst, the very worst outcome.' Bone pointed over the lake. 'This is, you know, one of the best views in London.'

Catesby looked eastwards. The setting sun had bathed Whitehall's Ministries of State with burnished gold. Foreign Office, Treasury and Defence seemed, for a moment, no longer British. As they rose above the shimmering waters of the lake and its exotic birdlife, the turrets, spires and roofs of Whitehall flowed into each other like the jumbled palaces of an exotic Oriental satrapy where silky courtiers stalked each other with long curved knives.

'We need,' said Bone, 'to tame Fournier into a songbird who sings for us alone. Otherwise he could do a lot of damage.'

Catesby had a good idea of what Bone meant by 'damage'. He suspected that Kit Fournier's still ongoing attempt to defect to the Russians hadn't been orchestrated by the Russians alone. The truth could be embarrassing.

'By the way, Henry, who were the gorillas in the black Wolesley?'

'What black Wolesley?'

'The one that kept driving back and forth up and down the Brompton Road. Do you think they might have been from Five?'

'Good Lord, I hope not.'

Catesby wasn't convinced that Bone was telling the truth. He rather suspected that if Fournier had turned up, the American would have got coshed and bundled into the Wolesley in front of all Kensington. It would have been a horrible risk. Fournier was a desperate man who carried a gun. But it looked like Henry Bone was a desperate man too.

They descended from the bridge and followed the path out of the park towards Birdcage Walk. The streets were filling as most of Whitehall reached the end of its working day.

'Is it true,' said Catesby, 'that Kit was widely tipped for the NSC – or even as future Director of the CIA?'

'He may have had the brains, but not the temperament – as is now obvious. In any case, Fournier is going to be *our* crown jewel. The Americans owe us five years of withheld intelligence – and most of it is in Fournier's brain. And we're going to squeeze out every precious drop.'

Catesby lowered his voice. 'Do you suppose Fournier knows about the RYBAT business?' RYBAT was the CIA cryptogram for 'extremely sensitive'. It had only been used twice since the war.

'What RYBAT business?'

Catesby smiled. 'Are you teasing me? You really don't know?'

For a second Bone's face became so blank that it seemed his features had been erased. Then he said, 'What do you know?'

'One of the Yanks at BOB drinks too much. He tried to impress one of our girls by hinting that the American station chief was grooming the biggest defector ever. The Yank didn't say anything else, but smirked and winked as if the awaited prize was the head of the First Directorate – or even Serov himself. The girl thought he was just telling tall tales so he could get his leg over. I told her that was certainly the case.'

'Is that what you think?'

'I did until the heavy drinking Yank disappeared.'

'Sent back to the States as a security risk?'

'Maybe, I don't know. But the swiftness impressed me.'

'On the other hand …'

'It could just be chat up bullshit – or canteen gossip.'

'I understand that Mr Fournier is somewhat of a gossip himself.'

'It sounds, Henry, as if you're trying to change the subject.'

'Is Fournier a gossip?'

'He certainly is. Kit knows *everyone*. He knows what they have for breakfast; who they shag over lunch; how much they drink and the secrets of their bathroom medicine cabinets. Fournier is the consummate Washington insider – he even knows where J. Edgar Hoover buys his man-size dresses and lingerie.'

'Catesby.'

'Yes.'

'Next time you hear that RYBAT rumour, try to look even more bored and cynical than usual.' Bone stared closely at Catesby. 'Has anyone ever mentioned AV/ORIOLE and AV/CATCHER?' AV was the CIA digraph that prefixed the code names of double agents.

'No.'

'Don't mention them either.'

'Are there *two* of them?'

'I hope not.'

As they emerged from St James's Park, Birdcage Walk was filling with rush-hour traffic from the government offices of White-hall. Black taxis for EOs and HEOs; Humber Hawks for SEOs and chauffer-driven Humber Super Snipes for Permanent Secretaries. Meanwhile, the lesser ranks plodded on foot to bus stop and tube station. Catesby wasn't a lesser rank, but he preferred walking when the weather wasn't filthy.

They were at Queen Anne's Gate, less than a couple of hundred yards from the Broadway Buildings HQ, when Bone suddenly stopped. 'I'm not going back just yet. Would you mind updating the op ledger yourself?'

'Fine.' But Catesby knew it wasn't fine; it was going to be a late night. First of all, he needed to go back to Brompton Oratory disguised as a pipe organ maintenance engineer to recover the surveillance gear they had left hidden in the loft – and then he had to develop the snaps he had taken of Vasili Galinin and the fake passports. None of this could be delegated to technical staff however trusted, it was all too sensitive.

Bone smiled wanly, 'Sorry to drop this on you.'

'Not to worry.' Catesby turned away and began to walk down Queen Anne's Gate. After about thirty paces, he stopped and looked back to see if Bone was still there. There was something furtive about his senior colleague; he half expected to see Bone waiting to watch him disappear. But when Catesby looked back towards Birdcage Walk, it was full of identical men in bowler hats carrying identical rolled umbrellas. It was easier to pick out a guardsman on parade than identify a suited Whitehall mandarin in a rush-hour throng. Except if the mandarin had done something to annoy a taxi driver. Catesby didn't see what happened, but it must have been outrageous for the taxi's horn blast was long and full of self-righteous indignation. He then noticed that a black Wolseley had pulled up on the park side of Birdcage Walk – and someone in a regulation bowler was getting in the backseat. But Catesby couldn't see more for one of the new Routemaster buses hove in to block his view. Two seconds later the bus was gone, but so was the Wolseley.

Catesby had been given one of the desks reserved for officers on temporary duty at Broadway Buildings. There were, in fact, four desks – all grey steel – in a cramped cubbyhole of an office lit by two hanging fluorescent lights. There was one telephone, non-secure, and a small combination safe that was bolted to the wall. The combination had long since been forgotten. Catesby had wasted two hours the previous night trying to reset the combination. He began by sketching the 'relocking devices' to remember how they had been attached to the lock. Then he disassembled the 'wheel curb' and carefully aligned each new combination number with the index line. He was feeling pretty good about his efforts, but when he dialled the new combination it didn't work. He then went through the process two more times, and it still didn't work – whereupon, he slammed the door shut. And it was locked, for good. Catesby shouted 'fuck' so loud that the Broadway Buildings NDO came up to see what was wrong.

When the NDO was gone, Catesby had a rummage through the three untenanted desks. It was a professional habit. The drawer of one desk, one of the big lower ones where you put hanging files, contained five empty bottles of Bell's whisky. For a minute or two, Catesby toyed with the idea of finding out who had been using the desk – and then writing a confidential note to Vetting. But maybe, he thought, the tippler had enough problems – or maybe he just liked a drink. The finds from the other desks included a very dog-eared Farsi dictionary, a half empty packet of Polo mints, an *Old Berkhamsteadian* alumni newsletter, a copy of *Racing Post* annotated with tips, and some loose change in West German *pfennigs*. Catesby put the *pfennigs* in his pocket and hoped they belonged to the old Berkhamsteadian.

Catesby was tired and hungry, but the sooner he started the sooner he would be free. He began by phoning the motor pool in Vauxhall; they shared the garage with MI5. He needed an unmarked van for the Brompton Oratory tidy-up. The motor people were very good and would paint fake liveries on your vehicles if you asked. Catesby had decided a plain van would be fine; he wasn't going to drive around London with Organ Servicing on his side panels.

As soon as the van was arranged, Catesby went to the 'props cupboard' to find a flat cap, toolbox and stained grey mac. He had to look the part – and certainly felt more comfortable dressed as a worker than a priest. When Catesby checked himself in the mirror he felt he was looking at his *real* self – not the bowler-brolly impersonator. It had, after all, been Henry Bone who had insisted that Catesby dress as a 'city gent'; otherwise, he wouldn't 'get on'. During his early days in SIS, Catesby had sported a trilby and his Montague Burton 'Demob Suit' with the loose-cut trousers of the period. Bone said he looked like 'a bookie's runner'.

Catesby grabbed the toolbox and went down five floors of the dimly lit backstairs. When he reached the ground floor he pushed open a heavy steel door that led to a dank service area at the back of the building. Before shutting the door he checked his pockets to make sure he had keys and wallet, because once the door locked behind him there was no way he could get back in. Catesby hoped the driver had been instructed to meet him there – and had a set of keys to get through the gated alleyway. Otherwise, he was going to be trapped for hours in an urban wasteland with only a stray cat for company. It was a black tom with white paws and a white muzzle that was purring and rubbing against Catesby's trouser leg. Catesby held out a finger and the cat rose on its hind legs to nuzzle it. He noticed that one of the cat's ears had been bitten off – poor warrior puss.

Catesby looked at the luminous dial of his watch. They were late. He wouldn't have time to do a 'surveillance detection run'. Whenever you go on an op, however routine, you're supposed to make a dummy run to make sure you haven't 'grown a tail'. But it was, in Catesby's view, usually a waste of time. If 'the watchers' were any good you probably wouldn't detect them in any case. But sometimes, they really *weren't* any good. Catesby remembered an MI5 surveillance operation that was blown when the target under observation noticed that a suspicious car parked outside his flat had a different registration number every day, and that the reg on the front bumper was different from the one on the back. Bone always sniffed at MI5 as a retirement home for dimwitted former colonial policemen. Or maybe he didn't like them for other reasons.

Catesby was relieved when he heard engine noises and the clank of the gate. And even more relieved when he saw the headlights of a second van. The extra motor meant he wouldn't have to waste time by taking the delivery driver back to Vauxhall. The driver winked at Catesby as he handed over the van keys. 'It's got a full tank, sir. Can you make certain it's full when you bring her back?'

'Sure.'

'Or just leave her in Russia.'

'Cheers.'

The van was certainly inconspicuous. It was a ten-year-old Z series Morris 8. Catesby could tell it was former GPO because it had rubber wings instead of metal ones; posties and telephone engineers weren't always careful drivers. The British were pragmatists, not perfectionists.

Brompton Oratory had closed to the public when Catesby arrived at quarter past eight. This meant he could get the stuff out of the organ loft without any, or many, prying eyes. The Oratory surveillance had been more than a secret op, it had been an illegal one too. It wasn't just the Americans and Russians who needed keeping in the dark, but MI5 as well. SIS was forbidden to carry out clandestine operations within the UK – that was why the Commander Crabb debacle in Portsmouth Harbour had created such a stink. And chasing spies around London was strictly MI5's job too. SIS turf began at Calais. For the SIS, spying on foreigners in London was almost as bad as spying *for* them. And Brompton Oratory itself was an extremely sensitive location. MI5 was perfectly aware that the *rezindentura*, the KGB section in the Soviet Embassy, used the Oratory as a post office. Nonetheless, Five refrained from putting the Oratory under surveillance for, if they did, the Russians would have scattered their dead letter boxes all over London. It was better to have spy traffic concentrated in one area. MI5 simply didn't have enough watchers to cover all of London. It was almost a tacit gentlemen's agreement where the Sovs said: 'You don't watch Oratory and Kensington Gardens too closely; we don't go south of the river or north of Regent's Park.'

Catesby knew that messing up this agreement would be like pissing in the punch bowl at the Queen's garden party.

Catesby turned the Morris up a narrow private lane that ran along the side of the Oratory and provided access to Holy Trinity, a much smaller Anglican Church squeezed into the shade by its larger Catholic rival. He parked, an atheist interloper, in the dark shadows between Rome and Canterbury. Catesby used a skeleton key to let himself in a rear door of the Oratory. The door opened directly into the sacristy, the room where the priests and their attendants vested themselves for services. The light was on and there was a strong smell of candle wax and mothballs.

'Hello.'

Catesby froze in place; then slowly turned towards the voice. A plain slim woman was standing next to a sink where she was measuring communion wine into a cruet. She wore a high-collared white blouse that was buttoned tight below her chin with a sapphire brooch.

'You must,' she said, 'be here for the organ.'

'That's me all right; Morgan the Organ.'

The woman laughed more than the joke was worth; rocking back and forth on her flat brogues and wiping her small shiny eyes with a cloth she kept tucked in her sleeve.

'Well, Mr Morgan, I'm sure you know where to find it.'

'Yes, it's just a quick routine service. I won't be long.'

The woman had now finished with the cruets and was unhooking something from a wardrobe where vestments and altar linen were kept. As Catesby left the sacristy, the woman was stretched and bent over the vesting table as she neatly arranged a rose coloured silk chasuble and stole for morning mass. The woman was neither young nor pretty, but there was something strangely erotic about her posture and the way the coarse wool of her skirt stretched tight across her buttocks.

Once in the organ loft, it didn't take Catesby long to pack up the surveillance devices and camera fittings. He quickly put them in a long canvas holdall, but it was too soon to leave. The Oratory wasn't as empty as he had hoped: doors opened and closed and footsteps echoed in the nave. Catesby took a screwdriver and spanner out of his toolbox and undid the panelling under the keyboard. If anyone turned up, he would say he was inspecting the mechanical linkages that connected the keys and stops to the pipes. Catesby beamed a battery torch around the mechanisms. Everything was covered in thick dust and rodent droppings; there were two huge mouse nests largely constructed of paper, string and wire. Catesby tapped a section of metal frame with his spanner for a minute or two to make workman-like noises, then screwed the panelling back into place. He heard footsteps on the spiral stairs just as he finished.

As Catesby crawled out from beneath the keyboard, he found himself looking up into the face of a very young and fresh-faced priest. 'How's it going?' The priest had the sort of Irish accent you usually heard in an academic seminar: friendly, but deadly earnest.

Catesby put on the persona of a bluff workman in a hurry to finish. 'Nearly done, just got to lubricate the blower.'

'Well, I'll let you get on with it then.'

But the priest didn't let him get on with it. He stood there silently watching while Catesby folded back the carpet to find the inspection plate that gave access to the air reservoir and blower. The priest was still there when Catesby began struggling with the bolts on the blower itself. Catesby was stalling for time because he hadn't a clue what to do next or what to lubricate. In desperation, he let the spanner slip and scraped a knuckle. 'Fuck.' Catesby said the word under his breath, but it echoed through the Oratory like a pistol shot. He immediately covered his mouth and looked up at the priest. 'Sorry, Father, it just slipped out. I'll put a couple of bob in the collection box.'

The priest's face turned red, then pale. 'Well, I'd better let you get on with it then.' And this time the priest really did leave.

Catesby left the Oratory the way he had come in. He used his torch to find his way through the now darkened sacristy. The London air was fresh and clean after the cloying odours of incense and candles. Catesby had enough of church; he was looking forward to pub and pint. He opened the van door and slung his toolbox and holdall into the passenger side. Catesby settled in the driver's seat and pulled out the choke before turning the ignition. For a second, it seemed that the sweet cloying scents of the Oratory had followed him into the Morris van. But maybe not. Catesby flared his nostrils and sniffed the night air. Something was wrong. A shudder ran down his spine that signalled both fear and pleasure. The scent around him wasn't burned incense. It was musky and sensual: jasmine, citrus, sandalwood. It wasn't church; it was bedroom. Catesby remembered something that made him happy and sad. But the bittersweet reverie lasted only a second. It was broken by the cold steel of a gun barrel jammed hard behind his left ear.

'Where are the passports?' It was a woman's voice. The accent was American, but the sort of softened American spoken by expats of long standing. It was the sort of voice you often heard at embassy functions or on ski slopes.

'I don't know,' said Catesby, 'I thought you took them.' The last bit was a wild guess, but intended to confuse.

'We don't need them, Jennie.' The new voice belonged to a man, an Englishman.

'But I, *I*, would like to have them as a backup.' She then spoke to Catesby. 'Pass those bags into the back – and I will fucking shoot you if you do anything funny.'

Catesby handed the bags back as gently and innocently as possible. He knew that she meant it. He then put his hands on top of the steering wheel to further assure that he wasn't going to do 'anything funny'. For a second or two he felt the pressure of the gun barrel disappear, he looked into the rear-view mirror to see what they were doing. They were busy emptying his bags looking, presumably, for the passports. Just as Catesby tensed up ready to leap, the woman's eyes met his in the mirror. They were dark pools, empty of anything except madness and desperation. 'Don't,' she said, 'don't try anything. Or I will kill you.'

Catesby remained looking into her eyes and felt his stomach churn. All at once he understood what had happened to poor Kit; the wheel of unattainable desire on which every bit of him had been broken. It wasn't just her beauty, every day one saw a dozen women just as pretty on the streets of London. It was the dark secret that no one could ever touch. Yes, she would give you her body in the sweetest imaginable ways, but would never release that dark secret – the only thing you had ever wanted. Catesby looked away: oblivion scared him.

The couple had finished going through his bags. The man said, 'They're not here, Jennie, I don't think he has them.'

'Why,' said Catesby, 'don't you ask Kit where they are?'

Catesby felt the barrel of the pistol prod hard into the back of his head. 'Why don't you,' said the woman, 'close your fucking face?'

'You shouldn't swear – it doesn't become you.'

The shock hurt more than the actual pain. The woman had swatted the side of Catesby's head with the barrel of the gun; the raised half moon of the front sight had caught his temple and opened up a small cut. Catesby dabbed away the blood with his fingers and started laughing. It reminded him of France. The first time that he thought he was going to die, he was completely terrified and almost literally shit-scared. Then one night, when things were totally hopeless, it ceased to be frightening and became a great cosmic joke. He was no longer a tragic figure falling into a dark hole that went on for all eternity; he was just an insignificant insect waiting to be crushed. And that was funny.

Catesby listened to the couple having a whispered argument about what to do next. The woman wanted to shoot him then and there and take the van to make their getaway. The man thought that would be a mistake, but didn't want to explain why with Catesby listening. Suddenly, there was a new gun sticking in the back of Catesby's head. The van's rear door opened and a moment later the woman was sitting in the passenger seat. 'Start the engine – and don't try flooding it by leaving the choke out.'

Catesby turned the key and the old van shook into life. He felt something touching his crotch. He looked down and saw the woman's pistol. 'If you don't do as you're told I'm going to shoot your cock off and leave you to bleed to death.'

'Okay.' It was no longer funny.

'Drive north out of London.'

Catesby came out of the church slip road and turned left towards Mayfair. Before they got to Wellington Arch, the man said, 'We want you to leave London on the A12 towards Chelmsford. Do you know it?'

'Yes.' There were few roads that Catesby knew better. It was the way home, to Suffolk. Were they going to end him where he had begun?

The traffic was light and London and its suburbs slipped by like images from a half-remembered dream. It started to rain after Chelmsford. The barrel of a Smith & Wesson .38 was still prodding the base of his penis, but the hypnotic slap of the windscreen wipers created a mood of calm. No one had said anything since they left London. Catesby had begun to dare to hope that it would be over in the morning – and he would still be alive and un-mutilated. The serene rhythm of the wipers seemed to soothe the woman. It was as if the windscreen wipers were singing a lullaby. Catesby's mother had never owned a car, but she did sing lullabies – and always in Flemish: *Slaap kindje slaap, daar buiten loopt een schaap …* Catesby heard the woman yawn and felt the pressure of the gun lessen. *Slaap kindje slaap.*

The place names had become more rural: Wickham Bishops, Little Braxted, Eight Ash Green. They weren't far from Colchester. Catesby wasn't surprised they were heading into East Anglia. He knew who his passengers were, but wasn't sure what they had done. He knew that the man, Brian Handley, was Chief Scientist at the Orford Ness Atomic Weapons Research Establishment. He knew that both he and his wife, Jennifer, were trying to defect to the Soviet Union – and that Kit Fournier was desperately in love with Jennifer. This love had turned Kit into a traitor – and now he wanted to go to Russia too. Espionage had turned into personal tragedy and personal tragedy had turned into bedroom farce. Catesby didn't know any more because that's all, in his role as an operational officer, he needed to know. It was like reading a book with most of the pages missing.

It got scary again after Woodbridge. They were now in deepest Suffolk. They had crossed the Deben at Wilford Bridge and were heading into a wilderness of dark woods, marshes and deserted beaches. It was a land that belonged to poachers, owls and eel catchers. As a child, Catesby had loved its wildness and mystery – and had never been frightened.

They were driving through Rendlesham Forest when Brian Handley told Catesby to turn off the road onto a rutted Forestry Commission track. A pair of roe deer appeared in the beam of the headlamps before disappearing deeper into the wood. The eyes of other creatures briefly reflected in the beams; then they too scattered. Handley ordered Catesby to turn off the lights, but keep driving. They continued at walking pace for a hundred yards or so; then Handley told him to stop and got out of the van. Catesby knew that he was about to be shot and dumped and braced himself to try to escape. Jennifer seemed to sense his tensing and transferred the pistol barrel from his crotch to his head. 'Don't,' she said, 'be stupid, Brian hasn't finished with you.'

'Okay,' Catesby was ashamed of his helplessness. He felt like a twelve-year-old giving in to the school bully. No dignity. He could see the beams of Handley's hand-torch waving about in the under-growth. Catesby closed his eyes: *Slaap kindje slaap*. It was the first time since he was three years old that he realised he loved his mother.

'It's here.' It was Handley's voice. It sounded near, towards the back of the van.

Then Jennifer spoke, the gun digging into Catesby's temple. 'Do you want some help?'

'No, I'll manage. Keep your eye on whatsit.'

Catesby smiled again; he was even less than an insect. He was a 'whatsit'.

'Listen, Brian,' it was her again, 'I don't want you to throw your back out.'

'Stop nagging, woman.' For the first time Catesby noticed the flat Northern vowels: Warrington, Manchester?

Whatever it was, it sounded heavy. Catesby could hear what sounded like a sack of combined barley being dragged along the rough ground. Brian was grunting and breathing hard; he obvi-ously had never been a farm worker. You need a rhythm to deal with heavy objects, but Brian had at least managed to get it to the van and to open the rear door. The weather was now less overcast; the light of a half moon filtered in and silvered the van's interior. Brian gave a great grunt as he hefted the leading edge of the object on to the rear floor of the van; then he must have put his shoulder under it for he managed to get the rest of it in. Catesby felt the van's suspension sag as the object slid forward and bumped hard into the back of his seat. It was a lot more solid than a sack of barley. 'All right,' said Brian, 'turn the van around and let's get out of here.'

When they got back to the road, Catesby was directed to continue towards the coast. They came out of the forest on to Hollesley Heath. After they passed the Stores Corner water tower, Catesby could see the lights of the Hollesley Bay Borstal in the distance. Just then the van went over a huge bump and something flopped out of the sack and landed between the front seats. Catesby looked down: a bloated hand on the end of a fish-belly grey arm was resting on the emer-gency brake lever. The limb was flecked with dirt and leaf mould.

A minute later they passed the entrance to the borstal. Several of Catesby's mates from his Lowestoft childhood had served time there. They had left school at fourteen and turned out bad. Catesby had won a scholarship to go to Denes Grammar – and then on to Cambridge where he studied languages. Some of the bad kids were probably in prison again, but some of the others probably had a decent enough life – kiddies, wives, coal fire and a few pints down The Anchor or The Drifter. But none of them were in that van with that dead body – heading towards … The sickly sweet smell of a ripening body now began to fill the van. Catesby wondered if they remembered him, ever talked about him at the pub. 'Seemed an all right bloke, even though his mother was a foreigner. Didn't see much of him after he went to the grammar – and that sister of his. She was strange, bit stuck up too. Reckon she needed a good shag.' Poor Freddie, Frederieke. Would he ever see her again?

They were now less than a mile from the sea and Catesby could see the loom of Sunk Sand lightship on the horizon – and the blinking lights of the Harwich Channel buoys in the near distance. He counted the red and white running lights of two ships leaving Harwich, and the green and white lights of two ships going in. No one could understand how much he loved that stretch of sea. Sometimes when he walked along the beach at night Catesby fancied he could hear the bones of sailor ancestors rolling in the tide. But they didn't say much.

Catesby noticed that the woman had become very subdued since they had picked up the body, but maybe that was hearse etiquette. The road dipped lower. He slowed down for the sharp left turn at Dum-boy Cottage. Catesby remembered the cottage from a childhood visit: it was where the cowman lived. He imagined that Friesian cows were still grazing in the dark fields on either side of the road.

They finally came to the creek bridge. It would, Catesby thought, be a good place to jump out of the car. The bridge abutments were only a foot or two in height. If the tide was high, he could dive off the bridge into the creek and they'd never find him. If the tide were low, he would either break his neck or be hopelessly trapped in waist-deep Suffolk mud – the most glutinous and glorious mud of all. It wasn't a good idea, even though the woman was crying and distracted. There was a high-pitched communal piping of oyster-catchers as the van lurched over the bridge. They were almost there. Catesby could smell the salt tang and almost hear the gentle whisper of sea lapping on shingle.

'Slow down.'

Catesby was startled to hear a voice from the back of the van; he had forgotten that one of the rear passengers was still alive. They continued for a few hundred yards at walking pace. There was sand and marram grass on both sides of the road. They were nearly on the beach.

'There's a ramp,' said Handley, 'between those anti-tank blocks. Drive over it, towards the cottage.'

Catesby turned off the road and wondered if there would be lights in the cottage. It was called The Beacon and overlooked the confused waters where the River Ore joined the sea. He had stayed there once, as a boy of sixteen, and had overheard a secret that utterly shocked him. At that age he still expected adults to be what they seemed to be. In later years, he got to know the person better – and began to understand, and even sympathise. How he wanted to see candles and Tilley lamps glowing behind the cottage windows – but there was only blackness.

'Stop here.' It was Handley again. They were halfway between the ramp and the cottage. It was as close as they could get to the sea, for otherwise the van would have sunk up to its axles in the shingle. There was a scrabbling noise in the back of the van as Handley opened the door and jumped out.

The woman had stopped crying and had stuck the gun in Catesby's crotch, but this time she seemed to be caressing his privates with the barrel. Or maybe she was just nervous and her hand was shaking. Her husband meanwhile was standing on a tank block and staring out to sea. A red glare of flashing light reflected on the shingle in front of him. Handley was signalling with a torch. Catesby watched and counted. There was a rapid group of six flashes, then a ten-second interval followed by a single long flash that lasted three seconds. Handley kept repeating the sequence for about fifteen minutes. Then he shook his head and came back to the car.

The woman put her free hand on Catesby's thigh as she leaned across him to talk to her husband through the van window. 'Nothing?'

'Nothing,' repeated Handley.

She sighed deeply. 'I told you that we would need the passports.'

Handley put one hand on the van roof and leaned down to the open window to talk past Catesby to his wife. 'Jennifer?'

'What, asshole?'

'You can fuck off. Just fuck off back to London.' Handley stuck a finger in Catesby's shoulder. 'Muggins here can be your chauffeur.'

'You're ...' She didn't finish, she just sat back and put two fingers on the bridge of her nose. 'I've got a splitting headache.'

Handley turned away and walked back up the shingle bank. Then Catesby turned to Jennifer and said, 'What should we do?'

'Keep out of this.'

Catesby looked down and saw her gently stroke the dead hand between them. She was crying again. Meanwhile Handley had resumed his futile signalling: five quick, one long; five quick, one long. Catesby watched the red flashes reflecting on the shingle, like coals in his mother's cooker, and remembered that he hadn't eaten since breakfast, but he wasn't hungry at all. He closed his eyes, *Slaap kindje* ...

Suddenly Handley shouted. There was triumph in his voice – and vindication too. 'They're coming, lass. I told you they would.'

Catesby looked up and saw Handley running back to the van. He jerked open the driver's door and stuck a gun in Catesby's face. 'Get out.'

Catesby got out and raised his hands above his head. He could hear an outboard motor approaching from the sea. Jennifer was standing next to her husband. 'Do they know,' she said nodding at Catesby, 'that he's coming too?'

'Aleksandr said it would be a bonus.'

'But what about ...' Her voice was full of quaver.

'We'll do him first, there's a pile of old anchor chain by the cottage. We don't want him drifting around.'

There was little sea running that night; the tiny waves were less than whispers. Catesby felt Handley's pistol press hard in the base of his back. 'Okay, I get the message.'

'You're lucky, Catesby.'

'Why am I lucky?'

'Because, even though it's a pain in the arse to bring you along, Aleksandr wants you alive. He thinks you're a good catch.'

'I'll probably be the only thing that trawler's ever caught.' The SIS called the trawlers IGAs, intelligence gathering auxiliaries, but the Russians still pretended they were fishing. There was always one off Suffolk.

35

'You might,' said Handley, 'end up liking Russia.'

It was turning, thought Catesby, into an awful irony. He'd always been considered dangerously left-wing by many of his SIS colleagues. He'd caused a stir when he first joined by trying to obtain trade union membership rights for SIS employees. He was nearly sacked, but escaped with a stern warning not to do it again. The 'lefty' label stuck which was probably the real reason he had been submitted to so many 'positive vetting' interviews. And now this. The corridors of Broadway Buildings would soon be echoing with a chorus of smug Blimp voices grunting, 'I told you so.' The Blimp mentality could never get its brain around the fact that it was possible to be a socialist *and* to love your country. Catesby looked south towards Bawdsey: the silhouettes of two Martello towers that had guarded England's shores since Napoleonic times looked like sandcastles made with buckets. That's how he had taught Freddie to make sandcastles, on North Denes beach just below their home in Lowestoft. Catesby knew he'd miss her more than anything.

The whine of the outboard motor abruptly ceased. Catesby heard a boat crunch on to the shingle. He looked towards the noise and saw the shadow figures of two men jumping out and hauling a boat up the beach. They were probably less than thirty yards away. Handley shouted out in bad Russian, 'We're up here – and we've got a prisoner.'

The two shadow figures didn't answer, but started walking up the beach. Both men held their right arms rigid against their thighs. Handley shouted something else in his garbled Russian. It sounded to Catesby that he was asking for *vyeryevki*, ropes.

Catesby breathed deep. The night sea air and lack of food had tuned his senses so fine that everything had suddenly turned champagne clear. The toll of the bell buoys marking the river entrances sounded like the clinking of crystal glasses. Even the stars were ringing and jigging. The steady crunch of sea boots on shingle came nearer. The men were wearing black oilskins and watch caps. Hunger had turned his senses so sharp that Catesby could even smell the thin layer of lubricating oil on the breach operating handles. The white knuckles of the men glowed like pearls in the dark. And below those pearl knuckles, still tucked so closely to their thighs, were the long silencer tubes of the Welrod 9mm automatics.

Handley either hadn't noticed, or thought the guns were normal kit for Soviet Naval Spetsnaz ex-filtrating agents from English beaches. But his wife was quicker off the mark: she knew, but didn't get far. By the time the bullets hit the back of her thigh her husband was dead.

It lasted less than two seconds, but to Catesby it seemed like a ballet *coda* that had been carried out in slow motion. He had watched, with bleak fascination, as the gunman on the left lifted up his Welrod to shoot Handley in the chest. Catesby stiffened and braced himself for pain, knowing that Handley's pistol was poised to blow a hole in his own spine, but then – and it was a reflex action that must have lasted less than a quarter of a second – he felt the barrel slide across and away from his back. Handley must have been trying to defend himself. When the gunman finally pulled the trigger, the Welrod was almost touching Handley's chest. Handley shouted 'ouch' and the Welrod made a dull bark, like a muzzled Alsatian. It's not as quiet as other silenced pistols, but it fires a bigger, more killing bullet. Catesby remembered the Welrod 9mms from France – and how they jerked upwards when you pulled the trigger.

While Handley was busy getting killed, there had been the quick rustle of someone trying to run on shingle, then two more Alsatian barks – and then the sound of a woman moaning. Catesby turned to see what had happened. The gunman who shot Jennifer Handley had turned her over. There was enough starlight for Catesby to see the two dark stains on her beige skirt: blood from the 9mm exit wounds. Just as the gunman raised his pistol to finish her, a voice next to Catesby called out: 'Don't kill her, not yet.' The voice wasn't Russian; it was pure South London spiv. Catesby turned to look at the Londoner, just in time to see him pump two more rounds into Handley, who had been lying on his back but still twitching. Finished with that, the Londoner looked over to his fellow gunman. 'Can you give me a hand with this geezer?'

'All right, mate.' The second gunman had an unmistakeable accent too. Before going off he looked down at Jennifer Handley and said, 'Don't try walking on that leg, *kleintjie*, I'll be back in two shakes.'

Kleintjie. Catesby knew the word: it was the Afrikaans form of *kindje*, small child. He watched the two gunmen pick up Handley and begin to half carry and half drag him down to their boat. He then went over to Jennifer and kneeled down next to her. 'I wish,' he said, 'that I could do something.'

'You can get my gun – it's in my handbag in the van.'

'You want me to shoot those fellows?' Catesby couldn't bear to admit to her, to tell her, that it was pretty likely that he and the gunmen were playing for the same team.

'No, I want you to shoot me.'

Catesby touched her cheek with the tips of his fingers. Her tears had smeared streaks of mascara down the side of her face. He hated what he was doing, and the way he was going to do it.

'Your husband,' whispered Catesby, 'mentioned Feklisov.'

He knew full well that Handley hadn't said Feklisov, he had merely said Aleksandr. And almost every other Russian boy of a certain generation was an Aleksandr, but was theirs the Aleksandr Semyonovich Feklisov who had been head of the London *rezidentura* in the early fifties? 'Is all this Feklisov's doing?'

'I don't know, I don't think so. Aleksandr was a kind man. Now, will you please shoot me? Aleksandr would do me such kindness.'

'You're right. I don't think it was Alex. I think it was … someone else.'

Jennifer's face contorted with pain. 'Don't make me laugh. It hurts my leg – God it hurts!'

'I'm sorry.'

'I can't believe you're so crass, so stupid. Why are you pumping me for information when I only want to die?'

'Because you might want revenge – you might want to get the person who tipped us off.' Catesby didn't know what he was talking about. He was following instinct and making it up as he went along.

Jennifer smiled. 'What a stupid question. You already know.'

'Me? I don't know anything; I'm just an ignorant spear carrier. But maybe I want to be something else.' He paused for dramatic effect. 'One day I'm going to stick the knife in and I want to make sure it goes through the right set of ribs. Kit must have told you – was it ORIOLE or CATCHER. Which one?'

Jennifer shook her head. 'I don't know what you're talking about.'

'There's a cuckoo in Section 3 of the First Chief Directorate.' Catesby was improvising and guessing like mad. 'Three' was the Moscow Central section responsible for the United Kingdom and Scandinavia.

'You stupid bastard.' Jennifer was laughing and crying at the same time. 'The parasitic bird you're referring to won't be flying out of Moscow.'

For a second Catesby thought she might be off on a disinformation riff, but a deeper instinct said this was deathbed truth. There wasn't much time; he heard heavy footsteps crunching back up the shingle. 'Who is he?'

'It is a he, but I don't know his name. He's one of Mischa's boys.'

'Who's Mischa?'

'You mean,' Jennifer almost choked with laughter, 'you don't know who Mischa is?'

The first gunman to arrive was the South African. He looked down at Jennifer. 'You're lucky, *kleintjie*, we've got some morphine for you.' The South African pulled up her skirt exposing her stocking tops and underwear. He then took the top off the morphine syrette and pulled the wire loop to break the seal. It was a form of analgesia made for battlefield use. 'Useful piece of kit,' said the gunman. He then leaned forward and pushed the needle into the bare flesh of Jennifer's unwounded thigh.

The Londoner was now there too. 'How are we going to carry her? I think you might have smashed the bone.'

'No problem, mate, like a dead springbok.' The South African grabbed Jennifer by the wrists and hoisted her on to his back. She screamed with pain. Her gunman turned to start off down the beach with his prize hanging on his back like a loose cloak.

Jennifer looked at Catesby one last time. She still had enough strength to whisper. 'Find him and get him – I want you to do it for me.'

Catesby looked at her and mouthed a 'yes'. He understood the wheel of desire that had broken Kit Fournier, for he was strapped on it too.

The Londoner was shining a torch on the shingle and picking up the spent cartridges. When he finished counting them, he came over to Catesby. 'I've been told, sir, that you have to go back to London.'

'Who told you?'

'The gaffer.'

Catesby knew it was pointless to ask more.

'Is the van all right, Mr Catesby? If you need petrol I can get you some.' The South London accent had changed to Sandhurst cadet from a council estate who's grateful for the chance, but not ashamed of his background. It was a familiar journey and Catesby knew the signposts because he had followed them himself.

'I can manage, but there's a body I'd like to lose.'

'Another one? Where?'

Catesby nodded towards the Morris 8.

'I'll give you a hand, sir, just leave it to us.'

Without passengers and corpse the van was a lot lighter on the bumps, but it still carried the confused odours of putrefaction and bedroom perfume. The ghosts were still there. Catesby didn't turn on the headlights until he got back to the main road. He'd only driven a couple of hundred yards when he stopped to admire a barn owl that was perched on a gatepost. The bird was caught in the full beam of the van headlights, but remained perfectly still for at least five seconds. Finally, the owl turned its head to look at Catesby, then flew off over the field behind the gate. Catesby's eyes followed the soundless flight of the barn owl as it dipped and swooped in the moonlight. The owl disappeared, but something else reflected in the moonlight. It was parked on a farm track and its metallic glitter caught the eye. The car was partly hidden by an overgrown hedge, but it was easily recognisable as a black Wolseley. Catesby looked away and put the van back in gear and continued driving. After-wards, he regretted not having taken the registration number. But later, when he thought about it more deeply, he was glad he hadn't. There were a lot of black Wolseleys in the world – and some of them belonged to farmers.

It was four o'clock in the morning when Catesby got back to London. He parked the van illegally in front of Broadway Buildings and reported to the NDO. There were no messages. He could see that the NDO was looking at his cut temple, but the man had been in the service too long to ask questions. Catesby dropped his holdall on the duty officer's desk.

'Firearms?'

'No, cameras and surveillance stuff.'

'We'll sort it. Need a lift?'

'I'd love one.'

'I'll wake up young Manton.'

The driver was one of the Signal Corps dispatch riders who couriered for SIS. He was a tall lanky lad who was more used to motorcycles and had to push the van seat all the way back. 'Where to, sir?' he said.

'Tachbrook Street, Pimlico.'

'Near the Tate?'

'That's right,' said Catesby. 'Do you know the gallery?'

'Yeah, I used to go there a lot. I wanted to go to art school, but you know how it is.'

Catesby did know. Dreams were for others, but it didn't have to be that way. 'So what happened?'

'I got a GPO apprenticeship and then the army ...' The dispatch rider suddenly flared his nostrils and started sniffing. 'You know there's a bit of a pong in this van?'

'Yeah, I noticed it too.'

They had just passed the coroner's court on Horseferry Road. 'What do you think of this Suez thing? My boss says I'll probably get sent out.'

'I think we're going in. Eden wants to get rid of Nasser. Who are you with?'

'14 Signal. I hope I don't get deployed. I'm supposed to be going on a telecommunications course at Cranfield. I want to transfer to GCHQ.'

It was, thought Catesby, a good decision. His own sister, Freddie, worked there. She was a bright girl who always made the right choices. Freddie had read Slavonic Studies at UCL and then joined GCHQ as an interpreter translator. GCHQ specialised in Signals Intelligence which everyone knew was the future. SIS specialised in Human Intelligence, which was sloppy, unreliable and old fashioned. Freddie and her friends worked in a shiny new building in the green fields of Gloucestershire. They didn't have to get rat-arsed on vodka at three o'clock in the morning babysitting a contact reeking of body odour and self-pity. And in the end what did you get? Four hours of sentimental slush over-seasoned with long passages of Pushkin recited in the lugubrious accents of a stage drunk:

It's better to have dreamed a thousand dreams that never were
Than never to have dreamed at all ...

The young driver was just coming up to Tachbrook Street. 'Which end, sir?'

'Turn left, it's the one with the bicycle on the black railings.'

As Catesby got out of the van, he remembered something. He reached into his pocket and found two quid and a ten-bob note. He handed them to the driver, 'You'll need to fill her up with petrol before you take her back to Vauxhall, otherwise they'll do their nut – and can you get a receipt too?'

'What about the change?'

'Keep it.'

'Nah, I can't do that.'

Catesby could see he had hurt the young man's pride. 'Okay, put the change in an envelope and leave it with the NDO.'

The young man smiled and put the van in gear, 'Cheerio, sir.'

The flat was located in the basement of a Regency townhouse that belonged to Catesby's in-laws. He had lived there off and on with his estranged wife when they were not so estranged. After they started to split up, the wife said he could keep it on for a silly rent. Catesby said no at first, but then his sister Freddie told him she would like the flat for Tomasz. It wasn't as complicated as it sounded. Tomasz was Freddie's lover. He was an expat Pole who worked for the Polish Service of the BBC. Freddie stayed at the flat when she wasn't on duty at GCHQ in Cheltenham. And, since there were two bedrooms, it gave Catesby a foothold when he was in London. He felt guilty about the arrangement and always tried to press money on his wife in exchange for his using the flat, but she always flung it back at him. It eventually occurred to him that she preferred the guilt to the cash. At least, reasoned Catesby, he was paying *something*.

Catesby opened the railing gate and walked down the stone steps. He heard the electric hum of a milk float turning into Tachbrook Street. London was coming to life. As usual, the door key was attached to a piece of string that you reached by sticking your fingers through the brass letter flap. Convenient for burglars and it saved Catesby the trouble of using the lock-picking skills he had learned at Fort Monckton.

He called out, 'Tomasz? Anyone home?' as he let himself in. There was no answer. Maybe Tomasz was sleeping. He walked over to the bedroom door and slipped it open to have a peep. The bed was empty beneath its candlewick cover and the curtains were drawn. Good, thought Catesby. He wanted to be alone and he needed a long hot soaking bath – even though the hot water gas geezer was as lethal as a flame thrower. Catesby didn't much like his functional flat in Bonn, but at least you could have a bath without the risk of being napalmed.

Catesby couldn't remember how long he had been lying in the bath. He must have fallen asleep for the water had turned tepid. Something must have woken him. He sat up and listened hard: there were footsteps, and then the sound of someone breathing on the other side of the door. He waited. The door handle began to turn; then stopped. Catesby looked around for something that he could use as a weapon. The only thing at hand was the Lowestoft china jug that Freddie used to wash the shampoo out of her hair. Oddly enough, he was more afraid of breaking the jug than of being hurt. Freddie had won it for finishing top of her class in languages at the girls' grammar. It was her favourite prize. Catesby remembered how her eyes had filled with tears as she clutched it to her narrow chest. The jug's blue and white design depicted a chinoiserie landscape in which a woman carrying a parasol was crossing a bridge. To what?

The person on the other side of the door now seemed to be leaning against it and listening. He finally cleared his throat and said, 'Is that you in there, Frederieke?' It was Tomasz.

Catesby lay down in the cooling scummy bathwater and felt the tension drain. 'No, it's me.'

'William, I didn't realise you were in town.' Tomasz was one of the very few people who called Catesby by his first name. Even his mother called him Catesby. There were, however, a few others – the closest – who called him Will. Apparently, his father had called him that, but Catesby couldn't remember because he was only two years old when he died.

'Sorry to trouble you,' Catesby had to shout because he was running the water to clean the bath, 'but I was called back rather unexpectedly.' Catesby didn't feel like explaining why he had spent four nights sleeping on a camp bed in a corridor at Broadway Buildings. Instead he said, 'And where were you last night, Tomasz? If you've been two-timing my sister I'm going to horsewhip you.'

'Ah, whips again. You want to convert me to *le vice Anglais*. But I am not going to give you the excuse for which you are searching. You are a wicked man. There is no other woman; I am on night shift at Bush House.'

'You didn't need to give a speech.'

'What do you mean, give a speech?'

'Never mind, it's just my way of saying that you are a tedious bore.'

'And you are very impolite and rude. But I have excellent manners, so I am going to ignore your insults and make some tea.'

Dressed and combed, Catesby arrived in the kitchen to find a pot of freshly brewed tea and a table spread with bread, cheese, cold meat, honey and jam – a sort of Anglo-Polish compromise. 'Thank you,' said Catesby.

Tomasz was staring at Catesby's cut temple. 'Being a Cultural Attaché must be a very dangerous job.' Tomasz knew perfectly well that Catesby was a spy, but maintained the polite fiction of his cover story. The Pole poured the tea and said, 'Have you seen this new play, *Look Back in Anger*?'

'Not yet.'

Tomasz laughed and gestured at Catesby's injury. 'It looks like one of those "angry young men" got angry with you.'

'I cut myself shaving.'

'What were you shaving with? A gun barrel?'

Catesby felt a bit unnerved by the accuracy of Tomasz's guess. He got up to toast some bread under the cooker grill and said, 'I ran out of razor blades.'

'I can lend you some.'

'What calibre are they?'

'Poor William,' Tomasz seemed genuinely concerned. 'They shouldn't use someone like you to deal with common thugs. But I know you won't talk about it.'

'Maybe I got in a fight over a woman. It's happened before, you know.'

Tomasz whistled gently under his breath. It was an incident that friends and family pretended had never happened. The only person who didn't seem embarrassed about it was Catesby. Tomasz placed a thin round of *kielbasa* on a slice of rye bread. 'You know,' he said to change the subject, 'that Bertolt Brecht is dead?'

Catesby sat down and buttered his toast. 'I was at the funeral.'

'Ah, as Cultural Attaché.'

'That's right,' smiled Catesby, 'and, as you said, it is a dangerous job – all those intense young poets off their heads.'

'Was Czeslaw Milosz there?'

'He's the one who hit me.'

'That's not true,' Tomasz leaned forward and playfully prodded Catesby's shoulder with his forefinger, 'but I wish he had hit you. No, Milosz couldn't have been there – they would have arrested him and sent him back to Warsaw.'

'I'm not sure. It was all pretty civilised and there weren't many Vopos around.'

'You shouldn't apologise for those regimes. You British are too soft on them.'

Catesby bit his tongue. He didn't want to get into yet another political argument. Tomasz was fanatically anti-communist and anti-Russian. And, perhaps, he had reason to be. Many of his family had been executed in the Katyn Forest when Lavrenty Beria ordered the Soviet NKVD to liquidate the Polish Officer Corps in 1940. Catesby looked at Tomasz. The Pole seemed to have gone into a little trance. His eyes were closed, but his lips were faintly moving.

'Are you all right?' said Catesby.

'Shhh, I'm translating. Wait a second. Okay, now listen:

Grow your tree of lies from small seeds of truth,
Show no contempt for what is real.
Make your lie more true than truth itself.

What do you think?'

Catesby shrugged his shoulders; then looked blankly across the breakfast table. 'So what? That's what we all do.'

As soon as Catesby saw Henry Bone he knew the news was good. Bone was sitting behind his desk with his coat off and hands on top of his head as if he were trying to stop his overjoyed brains from jumping out.

'You look happy,' said Catesby.

'We've got him.'

'Kit Fournier.'

Bone nodded.

'Alive and well?'

'Alive.'

'Where is he?'

'At the moment in a secure location in Suffolk, but we've got plans to move him to a safe house in Norwood.'

'Have the Americans noticed that Fournier's gone AWOL?'

Bone smiled weakly. There were nervous lines around the sides of his mouth. 'I'm sure they have, but we haven't heard a peep from Grosvenor Square.'

'Have you got a private line to the DPG?' Catesby meant the Diplomatic Protection Group, the Scotland Yard unit responsible for protecting embassies and diplomats. 'Wouldn't they get the first call?'

Bone steepled his fingers in front of his lips and shook his head. 'Not for someone of Fournier's rank. The first UK contact would be the Foreign Secretary via a discreet call from the US Ambassador.'

'Has that happened?'

Bone suddenly looked cross in the way of a professor who had been asked a silly question by a dim undergrad. 'How should I know? Am I supposed to ring up the Foreign Secretary and say, "We've just kidnapped a senior American diplomat who also happens to be CIA Head of Station. If you hear anything from Grosvenor Square could you give us a bell, ta very much."'

Catesby was surprised by Bone's sarcasm. It wasn't like him. He looked closely at Bone and saw something in his face that he had never seen before: fear and cruelty. In normal life, the two emotions seldom go together. But fear can turn people ugly.

Bone's face softened and he tried a half smile. 'Sorry, I snapped at you.'

'Don't mention it.'

Catesby looked closely at Bone and realised that he didn't know him at all. It reminded him of France. You were never certain if you were among those who would shield you or those who would betray you. And their faces could turn so quickly. Likewise, Bone might be a true member of the Resistance – or he might be a greedy peasant about to turn him over to the Vichy militia.

'In any case,' said Bone, 'I believe you had a rough time last night.'

It took Catesby a second to realise that Bone was talking about his midnight trip to Suffolk and not the jump into the forests of Limousin. 'Was it,' said Catesby, 'planned to turn out like that?'

'No, to be frank. We thought Handley was going to use his own car to get to the rendezvous, but he must have realised that his motor was under surveillance. But we certainly didn't expect them to grab you to drive them there. We were quite shocked when we realised what had happened. For a time we even thought you might be part of the gang. You were lucky not to get shot.'

'Thanks.'

'In fact, you weren't supposed to know anything about that part of it at all. So don't tell anyone.'

'Does the DG know about the Fournier abduction?'

'Very much so. He was personally involved in the planning stages. Would you like a cup of tea?'

Catesby watched Bone go to a sideboard to pour the Earl Grey from an Echinus Demotter tea service. The cups and saucers had gold rims and elaborate spiderweb patterns.

'Henry?'

'Yes.'

'Does the DG know all the details of what happened last night? Does he know a man was killed?'

Bone looked hard at Catesby. His eyes were fire and ice at the same time. 'No.'

Catesby was a little shocked – and also frightened. He knew that Bone's job required him to 'compartmentalise' operations and restrict access to information. But to exclude the Head of SIS seemed a step too far. Could it even be what the disciplinary code called 'gross misconduct?' On the other hand, Bone was awfully high up: he was

Director of Requirements – or DR. Although he was on the same salary scale as four other directors, in terms of hierarchy Bone was the third most powerful figure in SIS after the management reorganisation. It was, in fact, a reorganisation that Bone had led. SIS now resembled a capitalist economy in microcosm. Bone's 'R' sections determined 'intelligence consumer wants and needs'. Catesby was a 'P' section man. The Ps, the Production Sections, employed the worker bees who produced the goods.

'How many,' said Catesby breathing in the bergamot aroma of the tea, 'have access to the Fournier ledger?'

'You mean the full ledger, the complete op plan?'

'Yes.'

'Only myself, of course.' Bone seemed surprised that the question had even been asked.

'How many have least privilege access?' Catesby was referring to operatives drafted in on a strictly 'need to know' basis. These were the close-mouthed foot soldiers who pull the triggers, dig the graves and burn the evidence without ever having a clue why they're doing it.

'Six at the moment, but eventually we're going to have to include up to ten or a dozen.' Bone smiled wanly, 'But the nice thing is, you can always *reduce* the numbers *if* they get too talkative.'

'But what about the Americans? How much do they know?'

'They've handled it very badly. The ambassador's deputy, a newcomer who fancies himself an intelligence whiz, suspended Fournier before he even had a clear idea of what Kit had done. As a result, Grosvenor Square has turned into a rumour hive. Even the Brits working as filing clerks and doormen know something is out of joint.'

'What if the press get hold of it?'

'What's the headline? "US Diplomat Goes Home Owing to Personal Problems." That's the sort of line the press attaché will put out. The Americans are good at cover-ups and disinformation – or unintended misinformation, because half the time they don't know themselves what's going on. They call it "security through obscurity". They put out so many rumours and counter-rumours that the truth becomes hopelessly lost in the mire.'

'But will they, the ones that matter, know the truth?'

'It won't,' said Bone admiring his teacup, 'make any difference.

And it's for the same reason that they would never dream of asking us for help to track down Fournier.'

'Which is?'

'You must know. For years the Yanks have been rubbing our noses in it over Burgess and Maclean, and spitting with rage over ...' Bone stopped before he said the name; then continued. 'The last thing they want now is to have to admit that one of their own shiniest and brightest all-American boys tried to spy for the Russians because ... because he was "in love".' Bone laughed. 'Greed would have been less shameful, more American. In any case, Washington will want to pretend that nothing happened, that Kit Fournier never existed – airbrushed out of history like a Politburo member from a May Day reviewing stand. It won't matter to them whether Kit spills his secrets in Moscow, London – or wherever we stash him. The milk's all over the tablecloth and that's that.'

'And what if it doesn't work out that way?'

Bone stared at Catesby as he picked up a thick fountain pen that was lying on his desk blotter and began to unscrew its body from the nib. As the pen separated into two, a cyanide capsule fell on to the blotter. Bone continued to stare at Catesby. 'That's what makes this job interesting. You take risks – and make decisions that really matter.' Bone reassembled the pen and held it up. 'Would you like one of these?'

'No.'

'One day you might change your mind. In any case, I want you to have a word with Fournier when we move him to London. I think he used to like you.'

Catesby watched Bone pick up a document as if he were about to get on with paperwork. He thought the chat was over and turned to leave.

'Just a second,' said Bone.

'Yes.'

Bone stood up and handed a document ledger to Catesby. 'You've got some homework to do before you meet Fournier.'

Catesby glanced down at the cover classification: SECRET/ DELICATE SOURCE/UK EYES ALPHA.

'I've also attached an "R" guide at the end.' Bone meant a 'Requirements' guide. In other words, a shopping list of 'products' that Catesby was to obtain from his interview with Kit Fournier.

49

Catesby tucked the ledger under his arm and turned to leave.

'Where are you going?'

'I'm going to read the file you just gave me.'

'That ledger, young man, does not leave this office. You will sit here and read it – and no note-taking.'

Catesby pulled a chair to the opposite side of the large mahogany Victorian 'partners desk'. The office furniture clearly was Bone's own and not civil service standard issue. Catesby opened the ledger and began to read. He quickly saw why Bone didn't want the document to leave his office. He felt he was handling primed explosives; he had never seen such sensitive material before. At one point he looked up at Bone as he read a passage aloud and said, 'Did they really do that?'

'Yes, the details are in the attached appendix.'

'Then someone's going to jail.'

'Only if it gets out – and only if they get caught.'

'Or if it goes to court.' Catesby looked back down at the ledger. 'It seems to me that Kit Fournier was dropped from the loop before a lot of this happened.'

'But he still knows.'

'Then why didn't he tell the DG?'

'I don't know. Perhaps a sense of lingering professional pride: a last scrap of self-respect that he is still clinging to one gem that he hasn't given up. Or maybe he couldn't see the relevance.'

Catesby continued reading, but watched Bone out of the corner of his eye. Bone was going through some sort of catalogue richly bound in red leather. At one point, when Bone got up to make tea, Catesby leaned over and read the title: Government Art Collection. The British government owned a vast art collection that included Constables, Gainsboroughs and even a Picasso lithograph. Ambassadors, ministers and senior civil servants could choose items from the GAC to decorate their offices. When Bone was back peering at the catalogue, Catesby tried to see what had caught his fancy. One page in particular was drawing Bone's attention: it featured reproductions of what looked like eighteenth-century enamels. Catesby got up to take his empty teacup back to the sideboard and glanced over Bone's shoulder as he walked past. He just managed a fleeting look before Bone slammed the catalogue shut. 'I don't like it, Catesby, when you spy on me.'

'Sorry, I was just curious to see what you're going to hang on your wall.'

'I think you had best watch your step.'

Catesby was surprised by the menace in Bone's voice, but understood his embarrassment. Catesby tried not to smile as the dots joined up. Suddenly, Bone's cosy visits to Clarence House to help his 'art historian friend' identify the Queen Mother's enamels slotted neatly into place. Catesby had only managed the briefest glance, but the artist's name had clearly registered: Bone, Henry 1755–1834.

Catesby slept badly that night. He had his recurring nightmare of being taken out and shot. They always found him cowering in a hole in the ground badly camouflaged by twigs and leaves. And Catesby always tried to talk his way out of it as they led him away: 'No, I was only pretending to work for them – I was really working for you all along. Please, please, don't do this. Please, I can prove it.' He always woke up just as he felt the cold steel pressing into the back of his neck – and could never get back to sleep.

Catesby was also worried by the upcoming Fournier interrogation. It was important that he didn't botch it and that he pressed the right buttons and turned the right screws. The most difficult task in the trade was interrogating another intelligence professional who had been trained in the same techniques that you were about to use. But it was possible. Catesby was not one given to bursts of national pride, but he did know that the British were the best interrogators in the world. They were good actors – and playing villains like Richard the Third were the roles they did best. So maybe it wasn't something to be *too* proud of.

Catesby had almost fallen asleep when the memory of his first prisoner interrogation came back to haunt him. The German was in his early thirties and the only survivor of a *Maquis* ambush. They brought him into the cowshed which was lit by hurricane lanterns. Catesby started off by asking what seemed to be most banal questions: about food, frequency of letters from home, leisure, leave rotas. The German answered the questions without guile or hesitation while eating the bread and cheese that Catesby had offered him – and even complimented Catesby on his almost fluent German. At one point, the captured soldier took some family photos out of his pocket to show Catesby. There was little Gretchen and the older boy and the Frau holding the baby. Catesby admired the photos, then continued the questioning – which now focused on more sensitive military matters. Afterwards, the German shook hands with Catesby before the *Maquisards* led him off into the night. Catesby was left alone in the cowshed with an old farmer who spoke only *Lemosin*, the local dialect of Occitan, a language that hadn't changed since the fall of Rome. In the near distance there was a single pistol shot. The old man looked at Catesby and said, *'Plòu.'* 'It's raining.' Later on, Catesby reminded the *Maquisard* commander that prisoners should be stripped of *all* documents – and that included family photos.

Kit Fournier was lying on his back on the bed with his hands behind his head. He was fully clothed and still had his shoes on, although the laces had been taken away. 'Why,' he said, 'did they wallpaper the ceiling?'

'I don't know, maybe the plaster was crumbling and loose – like this chair.' Catesby got up and once again pounded together the joints of the wooden chair with the palm of his hand.

'You need some glue,' said Kit.

'Or maybe some matchsticks to wedge in the joints. Have you got any matches?'

'You know I don't smoke – and you don't think, for a second, that they'd let me keep matches.'

'I suppose not.'

'Ah,' said Fournier still staring at the ceiling.

'"Ah" what?'

'I know why.'

'You know what why?'

'I know why they wallpapered the ceiling.' Fournier spoke quickly, like a child just finding the answer to a riddle. 'It's because that's where they've hidden the bugs.'

'But they haven't bugged this room.'

Kit looked at Catesby and smiled bleakly. 'Stop being silly. What's the point of interviewing me in a room that hasn't been wired? Even the cops in Poughkeepsie aren't that stupid.'

'This is a new safe house. It's scheduled for wiring up, but Tech Services are too busy at the moment. I don't want to offend your ego, Kit, but at the moment Suez is more important than you.'

'Who are you bugging?'

Catesby laughed. 'Listen, Kit, you're the one who's supposed to be telling me secrets.'

'Sorry, I forgot.'

'But since you asked, we're doing the Egyptians, the Jordanians, the Czechs and the French.'

'I thought the French were your allies in this business.'

'You mean,' smiled Catesby, 'you don't spy on allies?'

'Touché.'

'How are you feeling?'

'A bit bruised,' said Kit touching a swollen split lip.

'Looks like they played a few rounds of "slappy face". They shouldn't do that.' Catesby knew that some of Fournier's interrogators held the American responsible for Lionel Crabb's death in the Portsmouth op.

Fournier looked at the bruise on the side of Catesby's face. 'Do you guys practise on each other?'

'I suppose it's something we have in common.' Catesby smiled as he remembered Jennifer whacking him with the pistol.

'You're a weird bunch.' Kit paused; then said, 'Why are you here?'

'Just to talk.'

'I've done a lot of talking, mostly to Blanco.' Kit glanced at Catesby and noticed his confused expression. 'Blanco, that's our nickname for your DG, because his name is White and because his hair is white. I know it's a bit childish. What do you call him?'

'I call him Sir Richard.'

'Like hell you do.'

'So what did you tell Lord Blanco?'

'I told him he was a liar.'

'What did he lie about?' said Catesby.

'He lied about Jennifer.'

Catesby had read the transcript of the DG's interview with Fournier in Bone's office. White had certainly lied, but there had been threads of reality too: *Grow your tree of lies from small seeds of truth.* One of White's falsehoods had been the claim that Jennifer had died of asphyxiation as a result of a bondage game with her husband that had gone wrong. The lie was a psychological ploy. It was intended to redirect Kit's anger away from White and SIS. The DG had even showed Fournier a fabricated autopsy report. But the biggest, the most preposterous lie of all, was that Jennifer had been working for SIS all along and only pretended to be a Soviet spy in order to ensnare Kit in a British intelligence honey trap. In the end, it didn't matter whether or not Kit had believed everything. The important thing was to disorientate and confuse, to make reality and falsehood so inseparable that Fournier could no longer tell where one began and the other ended. *Make your lie more true than truth itself*. White had broken him, but hadn't collected all the pieces.

'I don't know,' said Catesby, 'what exactly the DG told you about Jennifer, but I do know that she was betrayed by ... what are you doing?' Fournier was standing on the bed and had begun to peel back the ceiling wallpaper.

'I'm trying to find the bugs.'

'I told you there aren't any.'

As Fournier tore back a strip, lumps of plaster and dust fell from the ceiling. Most of the debris landed on the purple candlewick bed-spread. 'I'd better get a brush and dustpan,' said Catesby.

Ten minutes later the bedspread was clean again, the linoleum floor swept and the plaster and dust shovelled into a cardboard box. 'Shall we,' said Catesby, 'do a proper sweep for bugging mikes? We can take up the lino and pull up the floorboards.'

Fournier was staring intently at a wall switch; he had already checked all the other electric fittings for signs of recent disturbance. Catesby felt sorry for Kit: he was not only broken, but mad. But maybe the paranoid schizophrenia and obsessive compulsion had always been there. There was a grim joke in the trade. Did being a spy make you mentally ill, or did you become a spy because you *were* mentally ill? No one knew the answer.

'What did you say?' said Kit.

'I said we could pull up the floorboards to ...'

'No, I meant before that, about Jennifer.'

'I said she was betrayed ...'

'What are you talking about?' There was real anger in Kit's voice.

'Dick White lied to you.'

'What do you mean?'

'Jennifer and Brian weren't working for us; they were working for the Russians. Even the DG admits it was a porkie too far.'

'Why are you doing this to me?' There were tears in Kit's eyes;

more from exhaustion and confusion than from grief. His mind had been spun too much.

Catesby didn't know what to say next, so he went over to Kit and gave him a hug. It was un-British, but the *Maquisards* in the forests of Limousin had taught him how important an embrace can be. The hug couldn't bring back the son or sister who had been executed, but it said more than words. But Kit didn't respond. His arms hung limp at his sides and his eyes were blank. Catesby stepped back and put his hands on Kit's shoulders. 'We simply don't know.'

Fournier stirred as if a trance had been broken. He looked at Catesby and said, 'What is it you don't know?'

'We don't know who betrayed Jennifer.'

'And you think I can tell you.' All the madness had suddenly gone out of Fournier's voice. He was a fully alert professional again.

'But you probably don't know either.'

'Don't try that one.' Kit gave a bitter smile and began to mimic an instructor's voice. 'At this point the subject being interrogated has his pride hurt and now wants to prove to you how important he really is. So the subject starts shouting, "Oh yes, I do know, I do know, I really do ... "' Kit went back to his normal voice. 'If you want to ask questions, ask questions, but don't insult me with the cheap little tricks you use on Bulgarian Consulate filing clerks.'

'I'm sorry you took it that way. It wasn't intended as a trick.'

Fournier sat down on the side of his narrow bed. 'What time,' he said, 'does the bar open? At least Blanco gave me a drink.'

'His expense account is bigger than mine.'

'Don't worry. It probably won't do me any harm to dry out a bit.'

'Does Angleton drink a lot?' Catesby was referring to the CIA Head of Counterintelligence.

'Like a fish – and so does Bill Harvey. But do you know who the real lush is?'

'Mamie Eisenhower?' Catesby had heard rumours about the First Lady.

'No, that's unfair. A lot of people say that because they don't know about her inner ear problem. It makes her lose her balance, but Mamie's not a drunk.'

'So who's the lush then?'

'Nixon – and he's a vicious shit.'

Catesby could see that Kit was a gossip columnist *manqué*. But it was so otherwise out of character. Maybe gossip was Kit's way of relaxing, of getting out of his private personal hellscape. Catesby didn't want to do it, but he had to reel Kit back in. He did it with one word, 'Jennifer.'

'What about Jennifer?'

'Who betrayed her, Kit?'

'I don't know – and I don't even know what you're talking about.'

Catesby looked hard at the American. He was either pretending to be naïve or needed some guidance. 'We know that there's someone on the other side who gave the tip-off that Jennifer and Brian were working for Moscow Central. He must either have direct access to the agent files at the First Chief Directorate – or knows someone who does.'

'If you got the tip-off, then you guys must know who it is.'

'We didn't get the tip-off, we intercepted it. It was in a communication from your embassy to Washington. Very sloppy security on your part, your new boss doesn't know how to use a secure phone line.'

'The Ambassador was pretty silly about that too; he used to talk to Eisenhower about your Prime Minister on a normal line from the residence.'

'We know.'

Fournier looked thoughtful for a moment or two. 'But you wouldn't have taken action on an unsupported tip-off you overheard on a tapped line from a foreign embassy. Otherwise, anyone from any embassy – knowing their lines were tapped – could wreck your entire intelligence service with false accusations.'

'Of course, but the intercept confirmed intelligence that we had already received from a different source – a source that on its own wouldn't have been credited.'

Fournier smiled. 'Oh yeah, sure. So who was this *different source*?'

'Listen, Kit, I'm just a bit player too. They don't let me see the entire script – just the lines I need to know so I can do my job.'

'So you don't know?'

Catesby didn't answer.

'Why,' said Kit, 'are you playing this game?'

'Because you used to be a friend – and I want to stop you getting hurt.'

'Are you now pretending that our friendship was real – and not just tradecraft cynicism?'

Catesby waited before he answered. 'It was real.'

Kit smiled, but this time the smile betrayed a hint of warmth. 'I'm tired of being lied to. It's worse than getting beaten up.'

'Are you sure you want the whole truth about Jennifer?'

'Yes.' Kit's voice was a little frail.

'One of the reasons that they got caught was that Jennifer had the hots for another man. She wanted to take a spare lover with her to Moscow.' Catesby paused. 'I shouldn't be crude: it wasn't just lust, it was genuine love.' Catesby knew that this was going to hurt Kit even more.

'Henry Knowles?'

Catesby nodded. 'And it was pretty stupid on her part. She must have known that Henry preferred other men, but she really did love him and couldn't bear to leave him behind. The unbearable attraction, I suppose, of the unattainable. In any case, Knowles did the honourable thing and informed us.'

'Did you ever meet him?'

'Only as a corpse.'

'I'm glad he's dead.'

'Knowles was a good man.'

Kit stood up and shouted in Catesby's face, 'Shut up.' He then began to walk around the room like a cat on hot tiles. 'I wouldn't mind a drink.'

'I'll ring room service.'

'You don't understand jealousy, do you?'

'How little you know about me,' said Catesby.

'Then you should know that jealousy poisons the soul.'

'That may be so, but revenge doesn't. It's cathartic, it makes you feel good.' At Denes Grammar Catesby's class had studied Shakespeare's *Othello* for the School Certificate Examination. How sad he thought that, when they took parts, all the boys wanted to read Iago's lines. And Catesby was the best villain of them all.

'She was a bitch,' said Catesby, 'and deserved what she got.'

'No.'

Catesby was surprised by the answer.

'Her being like that,' said Kit, 'somehow increased my desire for her.'

Catesby suddenly realised it was Jennifer, and not just sleep deprivation and confinement, that had driven Fournier to the brink of madness. Catesby wanted to reel him back into the boat.

'You wouldn't,' said Catesby, 'have wanted to hurt her?'

'No, but I would have wanted to make mad love to her.' Fournier paused. He was lost in a world of bitter honey. 'She completely lost herself. She clung so hard and her face was like a runner's stretching for the tape. For that moment at least, she was mine alone.'

'I wonder,' said Catesby, 'what she looked like when they raped and murdered her?'

Fournier's face turned dark and mad. 'You didn't say that happened?'

'I didn't think I needed to.'

Kit sat on the bed with his face in his hands.

'If,' said Catesby, 'you want us to kill them we can do it for you.'

'Bullshit.' Fournier sounded composed and in control again.

Catesby shrugged. 'I thought you could help us find them.'

'Bullshit.'

'Why,' said Catesby, 'didn't you tell Dick White about AV/ORIOLE and AV/CATCHER?'

Catesby looked closely for a reaction, but couldn't tell whether Fournier's look of misapprehension was genuine or feigned. Then all of a sudden the American laughed and said, 'You're having me on. You must be talking about my home town baseball team.'

'I don't understand,' said Catesby, 'what agent codenames have to do with baseball.'

'Our team is called the Baltimore Orioles, after the oriole, a native Maryland bird.'

'And AV/CATCHER?'

'The catcher is the guy who squats behind home-plate wearing a face mask and protective pads – he's sort of like the wicketkeeper in cricket.' Kit shook his head. 'Someone's having you on. Those code-names are a joke.'

Catesby nodded, but there was something in Fournier's manner that was too glib. 'I suppose,' said Catesby, 'you're right. We don't always pick up American humour on this side of the Atlantic.'

'Nor we yours.'

'In Berlin,' continued Catesby, 'there were lots of rumours about an expected high level defection to your side. The term RYBAT was used, but I suppose all that was just another rumour mill joke?'

'Absolutely. RYBAT is a bullshit cryptonym that means extremely restricted access. We use it for scaring children and impressing pretty secretaries.'

Far too glib. Catesby knew that Fournier was lying. 'That would explain,' said Catesby, 'why ORIOLE and/or CATCHER went silent?'

'They went silent because they were always silent – they don't exist.'

'Are there two of them?'

Fournier laughed. 'Only two agents that don't exist? There are millions of agents that don't exist.'

'What I meant was,' said Catesby, 'would you ever use two code-names for one agent?'

Kit looked thoughtful, as if he were searching – or pretending to search – his memory. 'It would be very unusual. Our standard practice is the same as yours, one codename per agent. But sometimes, if the level of secrecy is very high and the security issues very sensitive – as you said, RYBAT – the agent may be assigned two codenames.'

'Why?'

'To create confusion if there's a security breach. It means the other side are going to be wasting resources chasing an agent that doesn't exist.'

'Or,' said Catesby, 'to make the other side think there is only one agent when there really are two?'

'Exactly. You win both ways.'

'Can we go back,' said Catesby, 'to this agent – or pair of agents – that don't exist?'

'Sure.' Kit seemed to be enjoying it.

'We thought that ORIOLE/CATCHER may have been blown when he/they tipped off Washington about the Handleys.'

Fournier suddenly was oddly withdrawn.

'In any case, we assumed from the telephone intercepts that your non-existent man in Moscow had clammed up.' Catesby glanced at Fournier and saw that he was laughing, but continued, 'We thought, perhaps, something had frightened him off and he was lying doggo for a while. No one fancies a no-return ticket to the Donskoi crematorium via the Lubyanka cellars. Why are you laughing?'

'What,' said Kit, 'makes you think that this non-existent double agent is a non-existent Russian?'

Kit's remark touched a nerve. It echoed what Jennifer had said. 'So,' said Catesby, 'you know who he is?'

'No, I'm just teasing you. I like winding you up, Catesby … I wish you could see your face.'

It happened so quickly that Catesby couldn't remember why he had done it. Was it something in Fournier's manner or tone of voice that had made him snap? Catesby didn't know why. He had acted on pure instinct. But Fournier hit the wall so hard that more plaster came down from the ceiling. When he tried to get up, Catesby pushed him down again. 'Listen, Kit, if you fuck with me any more, I'm going to lash you to a plank with piano wire and start by cutting your toes off with a pair of bolt cutters – and then work upwards.'

Fournier remained sitting on the floor with his back to the wall. When he got his breath back he said, 'Another shit interrogation technique. If you torture someone, they only tell you what they think will stop the torture. It may be true, or it may just be what they think you want to hear. You can't torture them into knowing something they don't know.'

'Sorry, Kit, I lost it.' While he was speaking, Catesby had taken a pad and pencil out of his jacket pocket.

'Maybe,' said Fournier, 'you haven't been sleeping well either. They don't let me sleep at all: bright lights and loud patriotic music. It's not a bad technique, much more effective than beating someone up – and I now know every word of "God Save the Queen", "Rule Britannia", "Land of Hope and Glory" ...' Kit was trying to read the note that Catesby had written on the pad.

Catesby showed it to him.

`This room is bugged.`

He winked, took a hipflask out of his jacket pocket and passed the whisky to Kit. While the American took a long hungry drink, Catesby continued writing.

`Keep talking.`

'Oddly enough,' said Kit, 'I've got to rather like "Rule Britannia" ...' He continued talking, but leaned over to read what Catesby was writing. Despite the shot of whisky, Kit turned pale.

`One of the listeners is the SIS officer who ordered the death of Jennifer.`

'... "Land of Hope and Glory", on the other hand, is too sugary.'

`And I'm sure he did this to protect his own identity as a double agent. Will you help us nail him?`

Kit nodded. 'We once,' said Kit, 'tried breaking some Koreans with round-the-clock doses of Miles Davis and Charlie Parker. It didn't work – they bopped into the interrogation room snapping their fingers and begging for more.'

Catesby wrote his first question.

Who is Mischa?

Kit took the pencil. 'Country and western, on the other hand, is lethal.'

Mischa is Head of East German foreign intelligence.

Catesby remembered Jennifer's response – 'You mean you don't know who Mischa is? – and realised he ought to have known. Mischa was the Russian nickname of Markus Wolfe, the chief of East German Foreign Intelligence, the HVA. 'Didn't they play you "Jerusalem"?' Catesby had the pad again and wrote as he spoke.

Have you heard of ORIOLE and CATCHER?

Kit took the pad. 'No, they didn't play "Jerusalem".'

Yes, but I can't identify them. I don't even know their nationalities. And I'm not sure there are two of them.

'Isn't "Jerusalem" the one with "England's green and pleasant land"?' said Kit.

'That's right. It's my favourite – it's closer to my personal politics.' Catesby was writing furiously.

If you want to destroy Jennifer's murderer tell me everything.

'They also,' said Kit scribbling, 'played something called "I Vow to Thee My Country". Do you know it?'

I'm sure that ORIOLE isn't from Moscow Central. He must be one of Mischa's boys because he's being handled by Berlin. I'm not sure he's also CATCHER, but there's a rumor that Mischa's 'Romeo ops' have spread to London.

'The music is by Holst. We often play it at military funerals, but I can't remember who wrote the lyrics:

The love that asks no question, the love that stands the test,
That lays upon the altar the dearest and the best ...'

Kit looked at Catesby. 'Is that a tear in your eye?'

'Could be. I'm a bit of a simpleton.' Catesby took the pad and wrote.

Is Washington worried about plants, false defectors?

'No, you're not,' said Kit. He quickly wrote the answer.

Counterintelligence, especially Angleton, are too para-noid even to talk about being paranoid.

Catesby stared at the pad. Something about Angleton's history was playing around the edge of his mind. He was a literary man as well as a spy. Angleton had connections with Pound and Eliot and had once edited a poetry review. An idea was starting to form. 'I'm sorry I hit you,' said Catesby. 'Maybe you haven't got anything else to tell us.'

'No.' Kit started writing again. 'Sing me some more "I Vow to Thee" – I like it when you get misty-eyed.'

'No thanks, it's embarrassing.'

'Go on,' said Kit while writing furiously.

'The love that never falters, the love that pays the price,
The love that makes undaunted the final sacrifice.'

Catesby continued singing while he read what Kit had written. He felt a wave of relief. Fournier was broken. He had finally given them what they wanted.

Angleton's prize defector hasn't checked in yet. He's called Butterfly, but that's his nickname, not his code-name. Butterfly is too secret to have a codename. He works for Mischa. If anyone is running your doubled SIS colleague, it must be Butterfly. Kill them both.

A loose thread was still nagging Catesby, like an itch you can't quite reach. Why had Jennifer known the former KGB *rezident*?

If Mischa's running Butterfly, how does Aleksandr Feklisov fit in?

Kit took the pencil and smiled.

We thought Feklisov was running you.

Catesby looked at the words and felt his whole body turn cold. Espionage was a ruthless trade where rumour, or even a hint of rumour, convicted. It was bad enough in London, but witch-hunt paranoia had become epidemic in America. It started with McCarthy and the House Un-American Activities Committee and had become part of the culture. In every American school children and teachers had to begin each day by pledging allegiance to the flag. The eradication of communism was a holy crusade that justified injustice.

'Do you think,' said Kit, 'that they will let me sleep tonight?'

Catesby looked at the American. Kit was pale, drawn and obviously extremely tired. 'I'll see what I can do. I think you've had enough.'

Kit nodded and lay down on the bed.

As Catesby turned to leave, he saw that Kit was curled up against the wall like a child. He turned out the light as he closed the door.

'William.'

Catesby looked up. The Director General, Sir Dick White, was another of those who called him by his first name.

'William, your interrogation of Fournier was first class. If it wasn't UK EYES ALPHA, I would recommend its use for training purposes. You were superb.'

They were back at Broadway Buildings and had just finished replaying the tape. The notepad was lying open on a table between the DG and Henry Bone.

'I don't think,' said Catesby nodding at the pad, 'that he would have fallen for that trick if he hadn't been so tired and disorientated. They did a good job breaking him down.'

The DG picked up the pad. 'I liked the touch about a "double agent" within SIS who had Jennifer Handley killed to "protect his own identity".'

Catesby looked at Sir Dick and wondered how much he really knew. Then he looked at Henry Bone. Bone's face was completely relaxed and impassive. He looked thoughtful, but his thoughts seemed focused on interpreting Fournier's written answers.

'I was a little concerned,' said Bone, 'to realise how little we know about the HVA.' Bone was referring to the East German Foreign Intelligence Service by its German title, the *Hautpverwaltung Aufklärung*.

Catesby stiffened. He regarded the comment as a criticism aimed at him because providing information about the HVA was part of his job.

'I don't think,' said Catesby, 'that's a fair comment.'

'And no one,' said Bone, 'seems to have picked up that Markus Wolf and Mischa are, in fact, the same person.'

'And the French,' replied Catesby, 'don't even know that Wolf is head of the HVA – and the Italians don't even know what HVA means.' Catesby was furious that Bone had made the criticism in front of the DG.

'Who is Wolf in any case?' Bone continued the attack. 'Where can I find his picture in the photo files?'

'There are no photographs of Markus Wolf,' said Catesby, 'absolutely none – and that's a well-known fact.'

'I suppose,' said Bone, 'Wolf must be like Dracula with mirrors, his image just doesn't imprint on camera film.'

Catesby turned to the DG for help. The DG winked at Catesby and made a calming gesture to Bone.

'Markus Wolf,' resumed Catesby, 'was born in 1923. His father was a physician who gave up medicine to write plays. His family were communists. In fact, his father wrote a book called *Comradely Marriage* – a guidebook for couples living in a communist system. It recommended a form of open marriage with sexual freedom for both partners. Jealousy was simply bourgeois possessiveness ...'

Bone interrupted with a yawn.

'I have,' said Catesby, 'managed to obtain a copy of *Comradely Marriage* for the registry. A wife isn't a possession – she's a comrade.'

'Why,' said Bone, 'are you wasting our time with this rubbish?'

'Because I'm trying to explain the way Markus Wolf thinks and operates.'

'The use of sexual desire,' said Bone wearily, 'to entrap an agent is hardly an original innovation.'

'No,' said Catesby, 'but Wolf uses honey traps in a far more sophisticated way. His Romeos, and his women agents too, provide more than sex. They provide what seems to be genuine love and companionship. In fact, some of them are not even very good looking.'

'And,' said White, 'Fournier thinks Wolf might be using Romeos in the UK?'

'We have,' said Catesby, 'a lot of lonely people here too.'

Bone laughed. 'All that "love" stuff won't work in Britain. We're not sentimental fools like the Germans. Can we move on to Butterfly?'

Dick White began. 'We've heard rumours that Washington has been grooming a high profile defector. The gossip suggests that he's a deskman working in Moscow Central – and that the Americans are going to get him out via Finland. If what Fournier says is true, it looks as if Washington has been planting misleading rumours.' White looked at Bone. 'Why, Henry?'

Bone suddenly looked very weary. 'The Americans,' he said, 'are afraid we'll get to Butterfly before they do.'

'Or,' said the DG, 'Butterfly has tales for Washington that aren't in the UK's interest?'

'That,' said Bone, 'may be so.'

The DG looked at his watch, then at Bone. 'Henry, can you come back to me later? I've got to prepare for tomorrow's JIC meeting.'

As soon as Dick White was gone, Catesby turned on Bone. 'Thanks for slagging me off in front of the gaffer. What you playing at?'

'Don't play the offended prole, Catesby, the pose and vocabulary no longer suit you.' Bone paused. 'I don't want the DG to think that you're my protégé. He's new to the job and wants to stamp his own authority. By the way, do you know Pond is going?'

'Ill health?'

Bone nodded. 'So there's going to be a vacancy for Head of Eastern Europe P Section – and I can't be seen to be pushing your case too strongly.'

'What's the price?'

'Loyalty …'

'To you, Henry?'

'No, I'm not that vain.'

'Loyalty to what then?'

'I don't know how to say it … let's say, to the cause.'

'The cause? What's that?'

'Oh, lots of things: Britain's true national interest for one, but also …' Bone looked away. 'But other things too.'

'Who makes the decisions?'

'We do … and it's a very lonely job.'

'You frighten me, Henry.'

'You can always say "no"; you can always have a confidential chat with the DG about your suspicions – if they are suspicions.'

Catesby felt that he was balanced on a high rock ledge about to dive into a river below. The water was dark and he didn't know what lay beneath the still surface.

'If you can,' said Bone, 'just remember one thing.'

'What?'

'If the Americans decide to fight World War Three, they're going to fight it here.'

Bone meanwhile had picked up the notepad and was re-reading Kit Fournier's responses. 'We need to get this chap.'

'What do you mean by "get"?'

'I'm not sure, but we need to get to him before the Americans.'

'Kit didn't give us much to go on.'

'But,' said Bone, 'it's enough for you to find him.'

'Me?'

'Yes, Catesby, you're the most credible plant we can offer.'

'I never said I would do it.'

'But you will do it. You're almost perfect as you are, but once you become Head of a P Section, you will be simply irresistible – the juiciest piece of bait in the bucket. And they will come for you.'

Catesby stared at the soundproof wall – thick acoustic peg board mounted with reel-to-reel tape recorders. Nothing in the room was natural: no windows, no decoration, no flowers – and the harsh strip lights cast no shadows. It wasn't a sentimental trade. If the plan didn't work, he'd be dropped and denied.

Catesby knew that his request was going to annoy, if not infuriate, the SIS station chief in Washington, but he needed the information too urgently to wait for it via diplomatic bag. In any case, the request he sent to the SIS man in Washington wasn't a difficult one, merely a tedious one because of the encoding involved. UK EYES ALPHA: LIST OF ALL PLAYERS AND THEIR POSITIONS ON BALTIMORE ORIOLES BASEBALL TEAM.

It must have been a dull day in DC, for the station chief responded within less than an hour. The return wire went under the title LATEST NEWS ON GIRLS ROUNDER TOURNAMENT. The Washington man didn't hold baseball in high regard.

As he decoded the wire, Catesby found himself enthralled by the melting pot of names. They all sounded like characters in a hardboiled detective novel: Tito Francona, Babe Birrer, Erv Palica, Hoot Evers, Fred Besana. You don't, thought Catesby, want to mess with those guys. But the important one to look for was ORIOLE/CATCHER. There were four of them, but the first team catcher had the most interesting name: Gus Triandos. Catesby spent half an hour going through a Greek dictionary looking for clues: Gus Three Men, Courageous Trinity, Manly Three. Did this mean that there was a 'third man'? Or did it mean *anthos*, three flowers?

Catesby began to look at the other names. It was one o'clock in the morning at Broadway Buildings. At any moment he expected the door to burst open and Babe Birrer and Erv Palica would be standing there with their trilbies – their fedoras – pulled down over their eyes and dirty great revolvers in their hands. But the door didn't open, so Catesby tried making anagrams of their names – and quickly realised it was impossible.

Catesby was about to give up searching for baseball clues, when another name caught his eye: Willie Miranda. He played at shortstop; which, Catesby supposed, must be something like forward short leg or silly mid on. *Miranda*. The name took Catesby back to his School Certificate English lessons. In Shakespeare's *Tempest* Miranda was the daughter of Prospero, marooned on an island with only her father and the much beaten slave Caliban for mortal company. Catesby had loved the magic language of the play, but had hated Prospero and his obsessive need to control everything – even the weather. And the stuck-up shallow Miranda was just the sort of deb who had patronised him when he was a 'working-class lad' at Cambridge. But the play brought an even more troubling thought to Catesby's troubled mind. Was he Caliban to Henry Bone's Prospero? Was he just an expendable slave in a power struggle that whirled high above his head?

Catesby reached into his jacket to get his hipflask; he needed a drink. He unscrewed the top and put it to his lips – then he shook it to make sure. It was empty; Kit Fournier had finished every drop. Catesby looked at the scribbles he had made on the back of an envelope. It was all nonsense. There are no hidden meanings in codenames: they are randomly selected nouns. Most intelligence activities were a waste of time. You had to know when to stop chasing useless threads. He put his scribbles and the Washington cable in the burn bag.

When Catesby got back to the flat he let himself in as quietly as possible. He tiptoed to the main bedroom and opened the door. There was the sound of gentle regular breathing – and also the sound of someone twisting, turning and sleep-speaking. It was Frederieke. She was a light sleeper and as a child had had awful nightmares. Until the age of eight, she sometimes came into Catesby's bed – and then sat up the entire night talking. Catesby hadn't expected to see her before the weekend, but her shift pattern at GCHQ often changed without notice. He was glad she was there. Being under the same roof with her somehow made the world right. The dragons were either dead or locked out in the dark.

Catesby continued to move around the flat on tiptoe. When he got to the bookshelf, he took out his pocket torch to find the book. It was a large weighty volume. He didn't turn a light on until he was in the spare room. He sat on the bed with the Complete Works of Shakespeare on his knees. It was another one of Frederieke's school prizes. She was a modest girl, but a very clever one. She had won the book for 'excellence in English Literature', but since then had only used the Collected Works for pressing dried flowers. As Catesby opened the book, translucent sprigs of evening primrose, foxglove, violets, crocuses and honesty tumbled on to the bedspread. He picked up a perfect petal of honesty. The drying process had turned the rich purple of honesty into delicate mauves and pinks – and the petal was so fine and frail. He carefully arranged the dried flowers beside him on the bed – and leafed through the book until he found *The Tempest*.

Catesby scanned through the play until he found the lines that he was looking for.

This island's mine, by Sycorax my mother
Which thou takest from me …

Caliban was right: the island did belong to him. Prospero and Miranda were parasites living off his labour, just like the big money men and the toffs lived off the people of Britain. Catesby loved his country, but he also knew it had been taken from him and people like him. He closed his eyes so he could see them. They were all there in their boiler suits and aprons. The builders, the cleaners, the nurses, the cooks, the drivers, the teachers, the miners who traded healthy lungs for heat and light. So many voices, so many faces. The Scousers, the Geordies, the Brummies, the cockneys – and the West Indians too, for without them there would be no NHS. The Taffs, the Jocks, the Micks, the chef at the Canton takeaway, the posties, the clippies, the trawler deckies, the brickies, the welders, the chippies, the Doctors Patel and Niswas. The people. This island belongs to them.

Catesby opened his eyes again. What he felt and believed was his deepest secret of all. And he sometimes wondered what he would do if his loyalty to the state came into conflict with his loyalty to the people. It was a thought that frightened him – and he prayed he would never be tested.

As Catesby prepared for bed, he noticed that Freddie had laid out a pair of pyjamas for him. They were neatly folded and ironed. She liked looking after him. Fussing, he called it. When they were young Catesby had found her big-brother hero worship annoying. He sometimes had got cross with her and told her to stop being a pest – especially to show off in front of his friends. He now hated himself for that. The worst thing you can do – and *nothing* is worse – is to hurt someone who loves you. And yet he had spent much of his life doing just that.

Poor Freddie. She had been a very slightly built girl and had reached puberty long after her classmates. Growing up among kids far rougher than yourself is a good education, but it can sometimes be cruel. It must have happened in a gym or swimming bath changing room. A coarse and ill-favoured female classmate, noticing that Freddie hadn't sprouted a single pubic hair, started the bullying. The nickname 'Garibaldi' stuck and pursued Frederieke all the way to the sixth form. And even as an adult she sometimes heard a taunting 'Garibaldi' hissed from the shadows of a Lowestoft backstreet.

As Catesby slipped into the pyjamas, he vowed once again to be a better, more protecting brother. He liked knowing that Freddie was safe and less than ten feet away lying in the arms of a man she loved. Tomasz was good for her. He complemented her intelligence with his own intelligence – and he understood her sense of humour, no small task. There were times, however, when Catesby wished that Tomasz was *less* glamorous and *less* dashing. Tomasz was one of the 150 Poles who had fought as Battle of Britain pilots – and he was a member of the *szlachta*, the Polish aristocracy. He didn't want Freddie to have her heart broken.

Catesby also hoped that Tomasz wouldn't infect his sister with his right-wing politics. There had been some horrific political arguments. On one occasion Catesby had shouted, 'Why were you flying Spitfires, didn't you qualify with Messerschmitts.' But, fortunately, Freddie was a still a paid-up member of the Labour Party. Maybe she could convert her boyfriend.

Catesby got under the covers and turned off the light. He strained to hear Freddie's breathing through the wall, but there was only stillness – and the noise of distant trains and ships. He wondered if he should tell her about his promotion. There was a bit of good-natured sibling rivalry. At GCHQ Frederieke worked in J section, the division responsible for translating and analysing Soviet communications – and had recently been promoted to an HEO post. Catesby was well aware that she had the brains and the ability to go a lot higher than himself – and wanted her to. His only worry was that, if his own career ended in disgrace, it might affect her chances too. Maybe he should take fewer risks. For his most sacred vow, far more sacred than the Official Secrets Act, was his vow that he would never do anything to harm Freddie. Her happiness was above everything.

The selection board for promotion to Head of Eastern Europe P Section was far more matter of fact than Catesby had supposed it would be. The only problem was the representative from MI5 who spent most of the interview going through Catesby's most recent vetting files. The man from Five used a number of theatrical gestures – eyebrow arching, slow head shaking, sudden intakes of breath – to indicate he didn't approve of the SIS way of doing things. When the MI5 man finally got around to asking a question it was an odd one that appeared, at first, to have nothing to do with Five's area of responsibility. 'Do you think, Mr Catesby, that Russia can win without fighting an all out war?'

As soon as Catesby began to answer he realised that it was a trick question. The MI5 man was really asking, 'Are you a Marxist?' For a Marxist believes that the collapse of the capitalist system is inevitable – with or without war. Catesby put on his blandest smile and also controlled the giveaway eye movements that interrogators look for to assess truthfulness. He cleared his throat and began, 'Well, from a Marxist point of view ...' And was so tedious that he managed to reach the next question without stating *his* point of view. There were no other problems or trick questions. After a brief private huddle, they confirmed Catesby's appointment.

The promotion meant that Catesby now had an office of his own at Broadway Buildings – albeit, not one as grand as Henry Bone's. He had, however, managed to obtain a copy of the Government Art Collection catalogue. Catesby was considering a request for an Augustus Lamplough watercolour entitled *On the Nile (with Camels)*, when Henry Bone walked in without knocking.

'I hope you're not settling in.'

'I'm not settling in,' said Catesby.

'Because we don't you want you hanging around here.' Bone looked over Catesby's shoulder at the reproduction of Lamplough's watercolour. 'It wouldn't be so ghastly if he had left out the camels.'

'That's what I was thinking.'

'I'm glad,' said Henry, 'that you're developing an interest in paintings. When you go back to Bonn your cover story is going up a grade. You will now be *the* Cultural Attaché instead of ...'

'CultAt for Broadcasting and Film. What's happening to Burrows?'

'She's moving on to Warsaw – and could be a useful contact.'

Catesby closed the catalogue. 'I'm still not sure,' he said, 'what I am supposed to be doing.'

'We've been through all this before. And I emphasise, once more, the most favoured outcome is for him to become one of ours.'

'You know that's not going to happen.'

'I agree,' said Bone, 'the odds are against it.'

'Nor do you want it to happen.'

Bone didn't reply; he just looked at Catesby. And there was no expression in his eyes. It was as if he had become as skeletal as his name.

'You, Henry, don't want to take responsibility.'

'That's not true, but I realise that you may have to act according to your own judgement ... without my holding your hand.'

Catesby knew that he was being used, but he used people too. He remembered what he had done to Fournier – and to others before him. It didn't so much make him ashamed – for that was his job – but it made him sad to be part of a world where you got paid and promoted for lies and exploitation of others. And the pity of it was that so many in the game were – when they weren't playing spies – good people. They were often talented individuals who played musical instruments, wrote poetry and spoke God knows how many languages. Many had survived horrendous wars and knew the meaning of personal sacrifice. Many were loved and had loved – but in their trade, no one could risk loving them.

'What's wrong, Catesby, you seem lost in a different world?'

'You don't want me to bring him back?'

Bone didn't say anything or show any sign of an answer. He might, just as well, not have had a face.

As a rule, Catesby didn't like Soho pubs. The thick pall of smoke made his eyes water. But he wanted to meet Otis before he went back to Bonn – and Soho was the place to find him. Soho was good for rendezvous. The pubs were just over a mile from Broadway Buildings, a pleasant evening stroll, and only a brisk fifteen-minute walk from Grosvenor Square. Except that Otis never walked briskly. Maybe he took taxis.

The first pub that Catesby checked was the Coach and Horses on Greek Street. There was the usual after-work crowd, but no Otis. There was a journalist whom Catesby knew by name drinking with two others that he recognised only by face. Catesby ordered half a pint of London Pale and was aware that the hack he knew was looking at him. Out of the corner of his eye Catesby saw someone emerge from the gents doing up his flies. It was SHUTTLE, MI5's codename for a Labour MP that the security service had been trying to frame for years. SHUTTLE's only crime was a penchant for sexual acts that harmed no one, but were still illegal. Essentially, the MP was being hounded for his sexuality and his left-wing political views. But the odd thing about SHUTTLE, from Catesby's point of view, was that he was a devout High Church Anglican – like T.S. Eliot. Apparently, however, MI5 regarded SHUTTLE's liking for vestments, Latin ritual and incense as completely normal and not worthy of inclusion in his file. Catesby quickly finished his half pint and was about to leave when his journalist acquaintance came over to the bar.

'Good evening, Catesby, can I get you another one?'

'Very kind of you, Woodrow, but I'm in a bit of rush.'

'I think you're out looking for someone.'

'Okay,' said Catesby, 'I'll have a half of bitter.'

The journalist ordered the drinks, then said, 'Who are you looking for? Buster Crabb?'

Catesby found the jokey reference to the missing frogman tasteless and tactless, but he didn't want to get in Woodrow's bad books. He was a dangerous journalist and ex-Labour minister. Catesby played along, 'Yes. Have you seen him?'

'No, and ...'

The drinks arrived. 'Cheers,' said Catesby.

'And I haven't seen much of Kit Fournier either?'

The conversation was getting too dangerous for flippant banter. Catesby put on a serious face. 'Listen, Woodrow, this is a bit confidential, but we think that Fournier had some sort of nervous breakdown and has been sent back to the States. How well did you know him?'

'I chatted to Kit once or twice at cocktail parties.'

Catesby knew that he was being disingenuous. Woodrow had

almost certainly received freebies from the CIA-sponsored Congress for Cultural Freedom. One of Fournier's jobs had been to encourage right-leaning Labour politicians to abandon socialism for the free market – and Woodrow was more than willing. Catesby didn't want to rub the shoulder next to him. He quickly finished his drink and winked at the journalist. 'If I hear anything more about Fournier, I'll let you know.'

Catesby was glad to leave the pub. London was just as much of an espionage swamp as Berlin. Catesby continued north up Greek Street feeling more out of place with every step. He felt ridiculous wearing a bowler hat in Soho, but it was a good cover story. He could pass as a banker or stockbroker looking for 'fun' before catching the last train back to Berkhamstead.

Catesby paused to admire St Barnabas at the top of Greek Street. It was one of the handsomest eighteenth-century townhouses in London, and had been a charity for the homeless for a hundred years. Catesby thought there may have been a Christian angle. There was a chapel attached designed in Victorian 'High Church' – perhaps SHUTTLE swung a censer there at matins. Catesby suddenly heard rapid steps behind him. He stepped aside to let a man of seventy cruise by who didn't seem in the mood to brook hindrance. The man, wearing a flat cap and a filthy mac, was bent over nearly double and swearing at the world. A chill ran down Catesby's spine. Will I end up like that? With no pension after a long stretch in Wormwood Scrubs? It was a risky trade. He knew there were no safety nets, no exonerating file was going to leap out of the Registry proclaiming, 'This man is innocent; he was obeying instructions.' No. There would be nothing but denial and distancing. Would even St Barnabas have him?

The Wheatsheaf, thought Catesby, was a pretty stupid name for a pub in the middle of London, but the whole city was full of rural anachronisms: Haymarket, Shepherd's Bush, Fenchurch, Parson's Green. Maybe in the aftermath of a nuclear war London would revert to field and pasture. Catesby imagined an elderly twenty first-century ploughman dandling a grandchild: 'I remember, Billy, when this were all office buildings and concrete, not a blade of grass in sight.' But it wouldn't be that way. London would be a rat-infested, stagnant wasteland of twisted beams, collapsed sewers, loose bricks and broken concrete. Like Berlin when he first arrived in '45, but far, far worse. When Catesby got to The Wheatsheaf, he furtively stuck his head through the door. There were three young writers who appeared to have been drinking all day – even through afternoon closing. But no Otis. Catesby closed the door and carried on.

The next pub, The Fitzroy, was just around the corner. Catesby once heard a scientist say that cockroaches are the only creatures that would survive a nuclear holocaust. In that case, The Fitzroy was going to be the liveliest pub in post-apocalypse London. Catesby pushed open the door. Otis was standing at the bar drinking a double whisky, what he called 'Scotch'.

Otis's official role at the US Embassy was Assistant Labor Attaché. And, as far as Catesby knew, that was his real job too. But you never knew with the Americans: the dips and the intelligence types worked so closely together you couldn't always tell them apart.

'Can I get you a drink?' said Otis.

'I'll have what you're having.'

'On the rocks?'

'Without rocks please.'

As the barman double prodded the optic for his whisky, Catesby looked at the American and tried to figure out old he was. Otis was one of those people who could have been forty or could have been sixty, but today he looked closer to sixty – even though his Brylcreemed black hair, that stuck to his scalp like a layer of lacquer, still didn't have a streak of grey. 'How are you?' said Catesby.

'Fine.' Otis pushed his glass across the bar for a refill.

But Catesby could see that Otis wasn't fine. And this was a pity. For Otis was a 'good American', just as there had been 'good Germans' who emerged from the post-war rubble.

Catesby had first met Otis in Bremen in 1950. At the time Catesby was working on denazification – a process that often brought UK and US intelligence officials into conflict. After a long day with boxes of files in the cellar of the Bremen town hall, Catesby visited a club called Stubu in another cellar. Germany was still a grim place and USIS, United States Information Service, was funding jazz groups to travel around the Western occupation zones. It was, thought Catesby, the only enlightened thing that USIS had ever done. The group was a quartet: sax, drums, double bass and piano. They had lived in Paris in the twenties and thirties, like so many African-American artists, to escape prejudice.

It was a remarkable evening. It was the first time that Catesby realised he liked jazz. The Germans, even the older ones, were going wild and demanding encore after encore. The Third Reich was truly finished.

Catesby felt sorry for the saxophonist. He was an old man who had a bad case of psoriasis. The skin on his fingers was raw and bleeding. But he refused to stop playing. Suddenly, the drummer was up and shouting. He pointed a stick at a group of American officials at a table in the corner. Then the sax player was shouting and pointing there too. At first, Catesby didn't know what was going on. He thought they were shouting 'oats'. Were they demanding instant cash?

Then all of a sudden, a little white guy – wiry and compact like a jockey – found himself being dragged and pushed up on to the stage. Otis seemed reluctant. He finally took over the sax, but not before explaining to the audience in good German that the sax player was an old friend from his home town, Chicago. Otis warmed up his lips with 'Dewey Square' before moving on to 'Billie's Bounce' and 'Moose the Mooche'. He then tried to hand back the saxophone to its owner, who was now on the piano. The original sax refused to let Otis go until he did an 'impro' piece. The Stubu was in a road called *Buntertorsteinweg*, which literally translates as Many Coloured Gate Stone Way. Otis closed his eyes for a second; then said in English, 'I'm going to end on a piece called, "Stoned Again on My Way Through the Rainbow Gate of Bremen".' It was a wonderful impro piece and got a standing ovation.

The Fitzroy had started to fill up with the after-work crowd, mostly from local publishing houses. 'Drink up,' said Otis, 'so I can get you another one.'

'It's my round.'

'Yeah, but it's my going-away party.'

'Where are you going?' said Catesby,

'They're sending me back to Washington. I've got to be interviewed under the provisions of the Federal Employees Loyalty Act. I might get sacked – I might even lose my pension.'

'Then you better let me buy the next drink.' Catesby paused. 'Sorry, I wasn't trying to be funny.'

'No offence taken.'

'Do you still play alto sax?'

Otis smiled. 'I might have to now – for a living.'

'What happened?'

Otis finished his whisky and ordered another double. 'I told a joke – well, not exactly a joke, but it was still kinda funny.'

'Jokes can be dangerous,' said Catesby. 'Who did you offend?'

'Only one person. It was at the Ambassador's Fourth of July party; the one at Winfield House where you guys don't get invited. You know, just for embassy staff – it means we can let our hair down a bit.'

'Were you drunk?'

'Not that drunk.'

'You should have got out your alto sax?'

'Catesby, are you going to let me finish the story?'

'Sorry.'

'I was standing next to the Military Attaché, who isn't really *that* stupid. I mean, you can talk to the guy and he sort of understands what you're saying and his pupils constrict if you shine a light in his eyes. So there is a bit of brain and we were getting on fine. Anyway, he was telling me about the latest H bomb tests on Bikini Atoll – and it all sounded very impressive. And then … I don't why I said it. Maybe I wanted to impress the Press Attaché, a very bright young lady, who was standing next to us …'

'Go on.'

'I said, "Colonel, why did we need H bombs? We've got Charlie Parker, Miles Davis and Gershwin. If we deploy those guys, no one can touch us."'

Catesby touched Otis's elbow. 'Sounds like a good idea.'

'Well, good idea or not, as soon as I said it there was a shadow on the grass in front of me. The whole time I'd been speaking, the new DCM had been standing directly behind me. I'd never heard a silence so loud, it was deafening. The Press Attaché coughed and said she needed to see someone or other and the soldier had already retreated. The worst thing was that hanging silence: just me and the DCM. Him staring at me and me looking at my empty glass. Finally, he said, "Did you like Charlie Parker?" The DCM isn't stupid: he used the past tense because he must have known that Parker had died last year.

'So I said, "His death was a great loss. Parker was a one in a life-time musical genius." I was trying to read the expression on the DCM's face, but couldn't see it because the sun was behind him. There was nothing but this blank black disc with rays coming off it – like an evil halo.

'Finally, I shook my empty glass to show that I was going for a top up. But just then, DCM says, "Did you know that Parker was a heroin addict?"

'I said, "That's a pretty well-known fact."

'And he says, "And that's what killed him."

'I nodded, "That may well be the case, but who knows." I thought this was the end of the conversation, so I started to slope off again.

'But the DCM hadn't finished. I don't know how he stopped me from going, but I'm glad he didn't touch me. In any case, he says, "So you think a negro heroin addict who dies of a drug overdose is the sort of image of national excellence that America should show to the world?"'

Otis smiled. Catesby thought that Otis suddenly seemed very pleased with himself. 'Well,' said Catesby.

'Well what?'

'What did you say?'

Otis was still smiling. 'I looked at him for about two seconds; then I said, "You're an asshole." And I walked away.'

Catesby walked with Otis after they left the pub. Although Catesby wasn't a tall man, Otis only came up to his shoulder. It was usually the other way around: Americans of his generation usually towered over Brits. But then Otis was older. Once again he wondered whether Otis had ever been a jockey. The American certainly knew about horses and racing – especially the flat. He passed on tips to trade union officials he met in the course of his Labor Attaché job – and the tips usually landed in the money. Catesby noticed that Otis walked with a slight limp. He wondered if it was childhood polio, a war wound – or the result of a bad fall from a jazzed up thoroughbred. Or maybe a slug from a gangster's gat on the streets of Chicago. In the coolness of the autumn night Catesby realised there were mysteries about Otis that he would never know. Was it coincidence, for example, that both he and Fournier had mentioned Parker and Miles Davis? Or was it something else?

They were walking north up Charlotte Street. 'Are you going on the Underground?' said Catesby.

'You don't know where I live.'

'North London?'

'Hampstead.'

'Do you like it?'

Otis shrugged. 'It was Gladys's idea.'

It had never occurred to Catesby that Otis had a Gladys or a wife of any description. Or maybe Gladys was someone in personnel who handed out accommodation. He didn't like to think of Otis as someone with a family. He liked to imagine him sitting under a bare light bulb practising alto sax in the small hours of the morning with a glass of whisky close at hand.

'I never could figure out,' said Otis, 'what your job was? You kept popping up doing different things.'

'When I first started off I was involved in the Denazification Commission, but while we were busy banning ex-Nazis, your colleagues were busy hiring them.'

'Why are you saying, Catesby, that they were my "colleagues"?'

'I wanted to give you the opportunity to deny it.'

'And I'll take it. Don't ever put me in the same basket with those sons of bitches.'

'But you knew about PAPERCLIP?'

'You should call it by its proper name.'

'What was that?'

'Pact with the Devil. We sold our souls for a bunch of grubby rocket scientists and a simpering band of two bit intelligence officers who should have swung at Nuremberg. But no one would listen to me; I was just an embarrassing leftover from Roosevelt's New Deal. I used to say, "Nazis are poison: once you let one of them in, you poison your whole system. Okay, you don't have to hang them all, just don't make them respectable."'

'And you never got promoted?'

'Not promoted – I got *de*moted. Well, it's amazing I lasted as long as I did.'

They were now on Goodge Street, a couple of hundred yards from the tube station. 'What,' said Catesby, 'happened to Kit Fournier?'

Otis stiffened as if a pain had suddenly shot through his bad leg.

'You don't have to tell me.'

'Then why did you ask?'

'I like Kit; I like him a lot. I wonder why we don't see him around any more.'

Otis laughed. 'Who the hell do you work for, Catesby? Have you gone over to Five?'

'No, I'm still at the Foreign Office.'

'Can you say that without smiling?'

'I'd need to practise first.'

'Okay, Catesby, I'll tell you about Kit Fournier. He's one of those thoroughbreds that never panned out. His owners and trainers thought he was going to win the Preakness and the Derby, but he spooked in the final furlong and threw his rider. He then went crazy and ran completely off the course. When they found him he had a broken leg, so they had to shoot him.'

'Who was his jockey at the time?'

'That's a good question.' Otis paused. 'Listen, Catesby, I don't really know what happened to Kit. There's never been a statement from the bosses, but lots of rumours that no one is denying.'

'What do you think happened?'

'I think he might have fallen out with the same people that are out to get me. They might have shipped him back to the States and put him in Shepherd Pratt.'

'What's that?'

'It's the Agency's private insane asylum. Once you're locked up in there, you're out of it for good. Or,' shrugged Otis, 'he might have killed himself and we'll never find the body.'

'Or defected to the Russians?'

'Who knows? They'd certainly keep quiet about that one.'

Catesby was relieved. It seemed to be turning out just as Bone had predicted. They arrived at Goodge Street Underground.

'Well,' said Otis, 'we'd better say goodbye.'

Catesby looked closely at the American as they shook hands. Otis's little brown eyes were as shiny as sloes – and looked full of mischievousness.

'And remember,' said Otis, 'that the Bird still lives.'

Catesby was taken off balance. He didn't mean to say it, but it just came out. 'You mean ORIOLE.'

The American's face suddenly turned cautious, furtive. 'No, I meant Parker. We used to call him Charlie *the Bird* Parker. Didn't you know that?'

'I forgot.'

'Well, don't forget this. When that other bird comes out of his cage, he's going to shit over everything. That's what he's been trained to do.'

'Who trained him?'

Otis slowly shook his head. 'I don't know, but those old poisons are going to flow.'

'Thanks, Otis. It's been good to know you.'

The American began to make his way into the Underground, but after a few steps, turned and looked back. 'And, Catesby, there's one more thing.'

'Yes.'

'Next time you see Kit Fournier, give him my very best wishes.'

Catesby felt relieved to be back in Bonn. His promotion had raised his status in the embassy. Colleagues, who previously had ignored him, struck up casual conversations and sought his advice. The Head of Chancery, second in rank to the Ambassador, even popped in to Catesby's office to ask him about the growing crisis in Hungary. It was the 24th of October: Soviet tanks were parked outside the Parliament in Pest and Imre Nagy had been named Prime Minister by popular acclaim. Everyone was waiting to see what the Russians were going to do next. Meanwhile, Britain was about to invade Egypt.

'What a mess,' said Catesby, 'just when Suez is primed to explode.'

Catesby and the Head of Chancery were both privy to top secret cables containing the latest intelligence summaries and British battle plans. The Egyptians, as expected, were going to nationalise the Suez Canal on the 29th. The Israelis were poised for a surprise attack the same day. The British and French would land at Port Said on the 5th of November with the aim of seizing control of the canal.

'The timing of Suez,' said the Head of Chancery, 'could scarcely be worse. The Prime Minister seems totally unaware of what's going on in the rest of the world.'

'Such as how Suez will affect the Russian response to Hungary?'

'Absolutely. What's your view?'

Catesby was enjoying himself. 'It means Khrushchev will have to put down the Hungarians to appease the hardliners in Moscow. He created a lot of enemies last February when he made that speech denouncing Stalin. But now Khrushchev has to watch his back – and with us going in to Egypt, he can't afford to look weak.'

The Head of Chancery was staring out of the window with a faint smile. 'And what do you think of the way the Hungarians are dealing with the situation?'

'I don't think the Hungarian rebels see the wider picture and realise Khrushchev's own precarious position. They ought to take any deal on the table and forget about leaving the Warsaw Pact. And RFE, by the way, is totally irresponsible in the way they are egging on the Hungarians. The Ambassador really ought to have a word with the Americans about that.' RFE, Radio Free Europe, was a CIA-sponsored station broadcasting out of Bavaria. Catesby felt RFE was making the situation worse by raising hopes that could never be fulfilled and by hinting at possible US military help. 'In any case,' said Catesby, 'I'm glad that I'm watching from a distance. Budapest sounds like a nightmare posting. I suppose they'll be sending a regional boff from London.'

The Head of Chancery was still smiling. 'By the way, Catesby, there's a UK EYES ALPHA cable waiting for you in the Communications Room.'

Catesby had managed to get the last MASZOVLET – Hungarian Soviet Civil Aviation Company – flight into Ferihegy, the main airport ten miles east of Budapest. All the other passengers were young Hungarians who had been working in Vienna. Presumably, thought Catesby, they didn't want to miss out on history. Spirits were high and there was a lot of loud laughter. A bottle of pálinka, a brandy made variously from plums, prunes, apricots, apples, cherries, was being passed around.

As the Russian-built MASZOVLET plane circled to land at Ferihegy, Catesby looked out the window. The airport was surrounded by Russian tanks and troop carriers. The only vehicle that wasn't Russian was a Humber Hawk with a Union Jack spread over its bonnet. Henry Bone was waiting.

Catesby saw that getting through customs was a pretty nasty business for the Hungarians. Their passports were being checked by guards from the ÁVH, the State Security Department, who were armed with submachine guns. There was a lot of shouting and pushing. There were uniformed Russian officers in the background who seemed a little drunk. The Russians were laughing and seemed to want to make light mischief by telling the new arrivals to stand up to the ÁVH.

Catesby tried to present his diplomat's passport to an ÁVH, but the guard waved him through the partition to where Henry Bone was waiting. Bone was wearing a trilby and a long overcoat. Catesby had never known him to look so scruffy, but then again they were in the middle of a revolution – and Henry was as always, *un homme comme il faut.*

As they shook hands, Catesby said, 'You realise I don't know a single word of Magyar.'

'But I'm sure you can speak bad Russian with a German accent.'

'I don't know about the accent.'

'Just imagine one of those soldiers is standing on your testicles.'

The road to Pest was straight and flat. On the left was a railway line. On the right, clumps of farm cottages and boring fields of root vegetables stretching to the horizon. It reminded Catesby of Norfolk. They often had to slow down to overtake horse-drawn wagons carrying produce into Budapest. All the wagons were mounted on much-patched worn-out lorry tyres. Most of the motor vehicles were lumpy light blue Pobeda passenger cars that hared along at speed. Bone nearly collided with one while overtaking a horse-cart.

'Henry,' said Catesby, 'will you remember that it's me in the FDS.' FDS was British Forces slang for 'fucking death seat'. Most UK government cars in Europe had right-hand drive which meant the passenger had to sit helplessly facing mad Magyar, French or German drivers closing in fast.

'It helps if you don't look.' Bone took a hand off the steering wheel to fish a document out of his pocket. He tossed it to Catesby. 'Read that instead.'

There were two pages. Translucent carbon copies typed in Cyrillic Russian. The text was set out like the minutes of a meeting – but not just any meeting. It was a meeting of The Presidium of the Central Committee of the Soviet Communist Party – and it had taken place only two days previously. Catesby felt his mouth go dry as he read the proceedings. Once or twice he looked up at Bone and tried to read his face. Catesby was convinced that Bone was playing a dangerous game.

'How,' said Catesby, 'did you get these?'

'There were passed on by a Hungarian contact.'

'How did the Hungarian get them?'

Bone shrugged and said, 'Can you translate, please? Your Russian is far better than mine.'

'Khrushchev begins: "We are responsible for this and must face the facts." Sorry, the type is a bit faint.'

'Try your best.'

'"The question is whether the Hungarian government will be with us or against us. If they are against us, they will ask for the

85

withdrawal of our troops. Then what will follow? Nagy says that if we intervene in the crisis, he will resign. Then the Hungarian coalition will collapse. The uprising may spread to the provinces; the army may side with the rebels."'

'How,' said Bone, 'would you feel reading that if you were a hothead Hungarian rebel?'

'I would feel that we had Moscow by the balls.'

'Continue.'

'"We have two choices ..." But then there's a break in the text as if something's been left out. The next comrade to speak is Shepilov: "Developments have shown that our relations with the people's democracies are in a crisis. There is now a widespread mood of anti-Sovietism. We must look at the underlying causes. There must be no ordering about of others." Shepilov ends by suggesting the Presidium issue a statement: "1) We profess the principle of non-intervention by armed force 2) We are ready to withdraw our forces with the agreement of the Hungarian government."'

'And, after reading that, how would our Hungarian rebel feel?'

'Game, set and match. By now he'd be collecting the Russian's balls and putting his racket back in the press. And there's more of the same from Marshal Zhukov. He says he "agrees entirely with Comrade Shepilov" and ends with, "This has been a military and political lesson for us all." Catesby waved the pages. 'Is this a forgery?'

'No, it is genuine.' Bone pulled off the road and pointed to a set of initials at the bottom of the sheet. 'The minutes were taken by Vladimir Nikiforovich Malin, the Head of the General Department of the Central Committee and the initials next to his are Anna Lebedeva's, his high security typist – and it's her usual machine, an ancient Yanalif.'

'It still doesn't ring true. Something's missing.'

'There's a great deal missing,' said Bone, 'the comments, for example, of the hardliners: Molotov, Kaganovich, Suslov.'

'Half-truths are always better than lies. It's a black propaganda classic'

'Of course it is.'

Catesby looked across the road to the railway line. A long train was approaching from the east. Each wagon carried a large lumpy object covered in canvas. Catesby counted fifty T-34 tanks and twenty self-propelled artillery pieces before the train disappeared towards Budapest. 'Are there more copies of these minutes?'

'Thousands. They've been printed and distributed all over Hungary – some have even been dropped from airplanes.'

'Whoever got access to this stuff in the first place must be awfully high up.'

'Who do you think it is, Catesby?'

'You have to look at motivation first. Who gains most?'

'And who is that?'

'The Kremlin hardliners. If you stir up the rebels and make them over-confident you wreck the chances for a moderate settlement and you've got an excuse to send in the tanks. I put my money on Molotov. It's obvious.'

Bone put the Humber in gear and drove back on to the main road. 'You seem to have forgotten that Russians are chess players and chess players don't make obvious moves.'

'You think it's Butterfly. Don't you?'

'I don't know.' Bone suddenly sounded very weary. 'Sometimes trails seem to join together and a picture begins to form – like on photo-paper in a tray of developer. Then a second later it fragments and there's nothing but grey turning black.' They were now on the outskirts of Pest. To their left, steam was rising from locomotives in the sprawling rail yards.

There was no British embassy in Budapest, only a legation headed by a Head of Chancery. The legation was located in the former head offices of the Hazai Bank, a grand neo-classical building located at Harmincad utca 6. 'When you get out of the car,' said Bone, 'keep your head down and face towards the legation. Don't look, but on the opposite side of the road there is a dry cleaning shop under a sign that says Patyolat. The ÁVH have installed a surveillance camera in the "o".'

The legation entrance was guarded by a pair of depressed looking ÁVH cops who were leaning against the wall staring at the ground – as if searching for clues to their future. They didn't even look up as Bone and Catesby made their way through the heavy doors.

The upper, and presumably safer, floors of the legation had been turned into emergency accommodation for the families of the staff. Catesby and Bone had to make do with camp beds in the large echoing bank hall on the ground floor. It was cold and dark and hadn't been used for years. The floor was marble with diamond-patterned mosaics.

'It's not so bad,' said Bone. He was still wearing his hat and coat and inspecting the premises with a cup of coffee in his hands. 'There aren't any ground floor windows and the walls here are the thickest in the building. I can't see why they didn't put the dependents down here. It's much safer than upstairs.'

'Maybe they don't want to catch pneumonia.'

'Look at those fireplaces. If they're not blocked up we could get some coal.'

'How long are we going to be here?'

'I haven't a clue.'

The hall was full of dusty relics of the capitalist past: long mahogany tables with scales for counting gold; an inlaid box full of bank seals and stamps; padlocked strong boxes, inkwells, blotters, bells. The bank counters, splendid nineteenth-century affairs with ornate brass grilles, had been disassembled and were scattered around the hall. Henry put his coffee down on the ledge of one and looked through the grille at Catesby.

Catesby peered through the counter grille from the cashier side. 'How can I help you, sir?'

'I want *Babushka*.'

Catesby laughed: it was a common Russian word. 'Do you want your own grandmother or will any old woman do?'

'In Hungarian, not that I know much, they call him *Pillangó*.'

'Is that,' said Catesby, 'their word for grandmother?'

'I'm not sure, but I assume it is.'

Catesby almost felt the memory flit across his brain. It was something Fournier had said. 'What exactly, Henry, are you talking about?'

'The Hungarian contact who passed on the Presidium minutes ...'

'Who is?'

'I don't know his name, but I wish you would occasionally let me finish a sentence.'

'Go on.'

'This contact suggested, or at least I think he suggested, that the source of the Presidium minutes was *Pillangó*. I asked what it meant, but he didn't know the English equivalent. He then flapped his arms around – and, of course, I immediately thought of ORIOLE, but then he said, "In Russian, you would call him *Babushka*."'

'How good, Henry, is your Russian?'

'Not brilliant, but I get by.'

'What's the difference between a *babochka* and a *babushka*?'

'Ah,' said Bone looking thoughtful, 'now that I've heard you say it, I think it was the first one.'

'So your contact said *babochka*?'

'I'm certain.'

'He wasn't referring to your grandmother, Henry, he was talking about a butterfly. You suddenly seem very pleased with yourself.'

'It does confirm my reasons for asking you here.' Bone paused. 'Isn't there a Russian legend about butterflies?'

'Yes, I think it's because the word for old woman is a pun on butterfly. They believe that the *babochka*, the butterfly, can be an evil spirit that may be hiding a witch, may even be a witch.'

Bone smiled. 'The coincidence of beauty and evil residing in the same creature.'

'Something like that. You think you've cracked it. Don't you, Henry?

Bone shook his head. 'I might be wrong. This *Babochka*/Butterfly could be a completely separate entity – and, likewise, ORIOLE and CATCHER might be one person or may not exist at all. On the other hand, we could be chasing three people – and, even worse, we don't even know ...' Bone's words were cut off by the sound of automatic gunfire in the near distance.

'Are they celebrating or fighting?' said Catesby.

'I think they're fighting, it's too soon to celebrate.'

'This place needs a good clean.' Catesby wiped dust from his hands and came out from behind the cashier's grille. 'I think you're wrong about Butterfly. The person stirring up trouble here is a Russian agent working for the Kremlin hardliners. If Butterfly is on the verge of defecting to the Americans it just doesn't make sense that he would want to sabotage a Hungarian freedom movement.'

'On the other hand ...'

Catesby smiled and continued. 'On the other hand, there are cynical bastards in Washington and the CIA who would relish the propaganda value of Russian tanks going in to crush brave freedom fighters. Exploiting the threat of the Russian bear is a big money racket for the US military industrial complex.'

'Do you really believe that?'

'I don't understand what the Americans are up to – there are too many of them. On one hand, Dulles preaches containment rather than liberation. But then you've got Radio Free Europe taking the liberation line. No one seems in control. I think we're heading towards World War Finito. Why have you gone so quiet?'

'You might be right.'

'Thanks.' Catesby paused. 'Who, Henry, do you think Butterfly is working for? Bad Russians or bad Yanks?'

'Have you ever heard of chaos theory?'

'Vaguely.'

'It doesn't matter who he's working for. Butterfly only needs to be himself.'

'You know him. Don't you?'

Bone looked closely at Catesby. 'Have you ever met anyone who was truly evil?'

'I'm an atheist. I don't believe in evil – it's a concept that went out with angels and miracles.'

'I thought you were at Oradour.'

'I don't talk about that – and you know it.'

'Then stop pretending that you don't believe in evil.'

'If you're so clever, why do you need me?'

'You are here because you speak fluent German – or at least fluent enough to convince the Hungarians that you are a native German speaker.' Bone reached deep into his coat pocket and took out two documents with stiff covers that had been suitably distressed and aged by Tech Services. He handed them to Catesby. 'Your name is Walter Telemann.'

Sporadic small arms fire had, after a lull, started up again. Catesby looked at the larger document. It was a German passport, but the one that bore a hammer and a draughtsman's compass superimposed on a red background. The other document carried the same coat of arms, but on a flag waving from a rifle held aloft by a muscular arm. It was the identity card of a colonel in the *Ministerium für Staatsicherheit*, the East German secret police.

'Memorise Telemann's place and date of birth,' said Bone, 'but it's best you make up the rest of your legend yourself.'

Catesby looked at his new cover documents as if they were poison pills. He didn't think he could pull it off; he didn't even know what he was supposed to be pulling off. He looked up for explanation.

'The ÁVH and the Hungarian authorities will talk to you as

Comrade Colonel Telemann. They won't talk to me – or any med-
dling Brit.'

'What am I going to say if I run into another MfS officer?'

'You'll think of something.'

'What am I likely to find out?'

'It could be a lot. The ÁVH are uncertain about how East Berlin,
and Warsaw are playing the situation.' Bone paused for a second and
looked closely at Catesby. 'Would Mischa Wolf, for example, send in
an agent provocateur to ensure that the Hungarians get thumped?
Or is Butterfly a rogue agent acting on his own. The ÁVH could be
streets ahead of us on the case.'

'I don't think Warsaw Pact satellites have even formed policies.
They're still waiting for a lead from Moscow.'

'That's good for you, Catesby, the ÁVH will believe any story you
tell them. But before you become Telemann, I want you to meet
some of the *Pesti Srácok*.'

'Who are?'

'The "Budapest boys" – and most of them are just that, boys.'

When he left the legation the next morning, Catesby looked directly
into the 'o' of the Patyolat dry cleaner's sign. He wanted the ÁVH
to see the swarthy, moustached and bespectacled diplomat. The
make-up made Catesby look distinctly Anglo-Indian, a bit like the
agent who got PNG'd in Washington. It was a necessary precaution.
It wouldn't be a good idea for an ÁVH to see the spitting image of
Colonel Telemann hanging around with the *Pesti Srácok*.

As Catesby walked with Bone through the streets of Pest, he
felt like Faust following Mephistopheles to the *Walpurgisnacht*, the
Witches' Sabbath. When they got to the first intersection, a burned-
out tram was lying on its side and two side roads had been blocked
off by piles of paving stones. They passed Magyar Rádió where the
revolt had begun in earnest after the ÁVH had opened fire on a crowd
of protesters killing many. Catesby noticed that all the windows had
been blown out and the street was covered with glass as if the violence had been the first snow of winter. A banner on the top floor
proclaimed a name change: *Magyar Szabad Rádió*, Free Hungarian
Radio. A number of buildings and lamp posts were festooned with
flags with holes in the centre. The rebels had cut the communist red
star from the red, white and green Hungarian tricolour. And there

was graffiti too: *Ruszkik haza*! It didn't, thought Catesby, take a linguistic genius to realise that the words meant, 'Russians go home'.

'Where are you taking me?' said Catesby.

'I want you to meet József.'

'Is that why we're walking on a boulevard called József?'

'Just a coincidence.'

József körút was one of the main boulevards through the centre of Pest. Catesby was aware of a large sea of people surging along with them. Many were carrying flags with holes in the middle and chanting *Ruszkik haza*. The mood was mean and tense. Something was going to happen. The boulevard was loud with angry voices and stamping feet. But suddenly there was another noise from the near distance. 'Tanks,' said Catesby.

The petrol bomb first became known as the Molotov cocktail during the Russo-Finnish War when the Finns manufactured them in mass to use against Russian tanks. It had, however, been used earlier against tanks in the Spanish Civil War. The best Molotov cocktails contain a mixture of ethanol, tar and petrol and have high-temperature storm matches taped to the outside of the bottle. You light the storm matches before you throw the bomb. But you can also make a Molotov cocktail with just petrol and engine oil and a rag stuck down the mouth of an empty Slivowitz brandy bottle. This, observed Catesby, seemed to be the Hungarian method. There were people running past carrying crates of the homemade bombs.

There was very little shelter on either side of József körút. The footpaths were narrow and four- and five-storey buildings towered on either side of the boulevard with no openings or alleyways for hiding. The crowd had thinned out as if action was imminent and a convoy of lorries hurtled past at speed. Most of the people still in view were either armed or carrying supplies. Practically all of the rebels were wearing long dark overcoats and berets that the Hungarians called *micisapka*. The Head of Chancery had been thoughtful enough to provide *micisapka* for Catesby and Bone to help them fit in and look inconspicuous.

'Can you still hear the tanks?' said Bone.

'No, they seem to have stopped.'

They continued walking forward. They came to the T-junction

where Prater utca came into József körút. There were signs of heavy recent fighting. The buildings were pitted by high calibre shells. A top storey of a tenement had been blown away; glass and paving stones littered the roadway. Catesby looked up Prater utca. The wreck of a Soviet army truck blown sideways blocked the road. The truck, torched into a white skeleton beneath layers of white ash, was resting on its axles. In front of the truck were the twisted bodies of two Soviet soldiers. The dead Russians were also ash white, but not so much from burning as from the quicklime that had been heaped on their corpses to stop the stench and discourage vermin.

Catesby suddenly stopped and stood still.

'What's the matter?' said Bone.

'I can hear the tanks again – they're nearer.'

The street had emptied of pedestrians, but people were shouting from open windows. Someone standing on a rooftop was looking up the boulevard with a pair of binoculars. Suddenly the man on the roof shouted something and disappeared. Catesby pushed Bone into a doorway of what seemed to be a block of flats; there were buzzers and nameplates on the side of the entrance. Catesby pushed against the door to try to get into the foyer, but the door was locked and too heavy to force open.

Catesby stuck his head out of the entrance to see if the coast was clear for a dash back up József körút the way they had came. The boulevard was clear – except for a single Soviet tank that had come to a halt about sixty yards away. Catesby was mesmerised. He watched the turret of the tank turn so that the gun was pointing up Prater utca towards the burned-out wreck. Then the turret hatch opened and two tank crew scrambled out and jumped to the ground. They were carrying ropes. It suddenly made sense: they had come to recover the bodies. And then it happened.

The first thing that Catesby heard was shouting and then the sound of automatic weapons fire coming from all directions. The two tankers crumbled and their bodies bounced up and down on the paving as bullets continued to hit them. Then the gunfire suddenly ceased and Catesby saw why. Two figures, who were hatless and looked like boys of fifteen, had dashed out from nowhere and threw two petrol bombs at the tank turret. The bombs exploded and the boys were quickly out of sight. There was a line of jagged orange flame licking the rear of the tank, but not enough to disable it. The driver put the tank into reverse and was backing up József körút, but not in a very steady line for the treads on the right-hand side had mounted the footpath. It was a mistake to manoeuvre so close to the tall overhanging buildings. Catesby felt the heat strike his face. It was like a Guy Fawkes bonfire that suddenly leapt out of control. The Molotov cocktails rained from window and roof. The tank became a helpless Guy trapped in a storm of fire and hate. Catesby watched the tank being consumed in flames with neither fear nor horror. It was just the way things were.

A moment later there was the iconic clanking of steel treads on paving stones. Two tanks had come up in support. The first shell hit the top storey of the building directly above the hulk of the burned-out T-34. Catesby shielded his face against flying rubble; a piece of masonry the size of a Labrador landed less than a yard from his feet. Meanwhile, Bone was pressing all the bell buttons on the entrance wall.

The Russian tanks were raking the buildings from where the Molotov cocktails had come. There was also machine-gun fire. Catesby saw bullets chipping the road surface just feet in front of where they were standing. He pressed hard against Bone crushing him against the door. Catesby was worried about ricochets. Bone, determined to get inside the relative safety of the building, was pressing the bell buttons with both hands.

At first, Catesby thought that Bone had been hit; his body was no longer a cushion between him and the door. In fact, Bone was no longer there at all. It was as if he had disappeared into a hole. But it wasn't a hole; the door was open. There was a voice speaking rapid Hungarian from the shadows of the foyer. Catesby felt a hand tugging frantically on his coat-sleeve. He found himself in the foyer with the door shut behind him just as a ricocheting shell fragment splintered the thick wood.

Bone was expressing his gratitude in stilted schoolboy German. The useful thing about getting by in Hungary, as Catesby had noticed, was that the residents were language-coded according to age. Almost all the under twenties spoke Russian and almost all the over forties spoke German. And the woman who had let them in was certainly over forty. She was wearing a flowing mauve dress, her hair was done up in a chignon and she was carrying a silver chain heavy with large keys. 'Come,' she said, 'my apartment is in the back – overlooking the gardens. It is a little quieter there.'

As Catesby followed her up the dark staircase, he noticed that she was wearing backless slippers with high heels. But that wasn't why she swayed back and forth and had to grab Bone to keep her balance. She was drunk – and who could blame her. The woman leaned on Bone and whispered in his ear. 'Where are you from, treasure, you're obviously not German?'

Bone smiled.

The flat was more austere then Catesby would have thought from his first impression of the woman who lived there. There was an upright piano, a worn brocade sofa, a modernist-style 1930s table and thousands of books. The books were mostly on shelves, but there were also piles of books on the parquet floor or wherever there was a surface to hold them.

Once she had bolted the door, the woman turned on Bone. 'Now,' she was still speaking German, 'where are you from?'

'We are journalists from London,' said Henry.

'So,' said the woman effortlessly changing languages, 'we should speak English. Journalists, eh?' She paused and smiled as if she didn't believe a word of the cover story.

'You were very kind to rescue us,' said Catesby.

'What makes you think you are rescued?' There was a slight hint of American in the woman's accent. She laughed and turned to a dresser which was preciously old and hand-painted with flowers. The dresser's rustic naivety seemed out of place in the flat. 'But maybe we should celebrate with a bottle of *Tokaji* or …' A nearby shell explosion rattled the crockery on the dresser. 'Or *Hárslevelü*, this wine is made from a grape that tastes faintly of lime.'

'It would,' said Bone, 'be a pity to drink such a fine wine un-chilled. Please save it.'

The woman gave Bone a stern look. 'What makes you think that I wasn't going to chill it? There is plenty of time; you are going to be here a while.' She turned away to put the wine in a lead-lined ice box in the kitchen corner. 'Meanwhile, there is always Slivowitz.'

'No proper journalist,' smiled Bone, 'ever covers a revolution sober.'

'No one from Fleet Street,' added Catesby, 'ever covers *anything* sober.'

The woman filled their glasses from a bottle that was half-empty. The label on the bottle bore a bunch of ripe plums and the type of red star that the rebels were busy cutting from the national flag. Catesby looked closely at the woman and could see that she had been, and still was, stunningly beautiful. It wasn't a beauty that promised a bright future with bouncing babies, but the beauty of refinement ripened by experience. It was impossible not to think of *Der Rosenkavalier*. On impulse, Catesby raised his glass, 'To the Marschallin.'

But before the woman could reply, Bone had raised his glass and sang, '*Wie du warst! Wie du bist!*' The line, 'How you were! How you are!', was from the opening act of the opera.

The woman smiled and touched both their glasses. 'I am,' she said, 'far more blessed than the Marschallin, for I have two Octavians.' She gave Bone a light peck on the cheek.

Catesby looked out of the window. The wind had changed direction and black smoke was drifting over the rooftops. There was still heavy machine-gun fire. He wondered if the Russians were going to send reinforcements to clean out the quarter. He shrugged and drank the Slivowitz.

'You must,' said the woman, 'stay until after dark. Maybe the Russians will go back to their barracks.'

'What do you think of this business?' said Bone.

The woman made a Central European 'pftt' noise. 'I have mixed feelings – life has made me a sad pessimist. Have you seen enough – to report back?' It wasn't clear what the woman meant by 'report back'?

'What,' said Bone, 'is the best way to get to Corvin köz?' He had a map of Pest opened on his knees. Corvin köz was a series of narrow passageways shaped like a wishbone. It contained the headquarters of the largest resistance group.

The woman laughed. 'You want to go to the cinema?'

'Precisely,' said Bone, 'that's exactly where we want to go.' The rebels had barricaded the cinema building with its thick windowless walls into the bunker of last resort.

'What film do you want to see?' she said.

'The one by József starring the *Pesti Srácok*.'

'József who?' said the woman.

Bone gave his full name.

'I am not sure that József is a good director. His film may turn out to have a very sad ending. And he's a …' the woman leaned over and pretended to take a nip out of Bone's neck. 'József is a Transylvanian.'

'But,' said Catesby, 'we need to interview him – otherwise, our editor will be furious.'

The woman closed one eye and smiled. 'Well, I might help you, but you must wait until after dark. That's when he comes out of his coffin. Meanwhile, you must eat. But there isn't much. I haven't been shopping today.'

It was a simple meal: a thick vegetable stew called *fözelék* and some apples and cheese. Catesby felt sorry for her. She had so little and she wanted to share everything. He looked around the flat for evidence of her past, but there was none. No family portraits, no holiday photos, no diplomas, no keepsakes. Catesby sensed that something awful had happened – and it was best not to ask questions. It was one way of coping with a lost past. You pretend it's not there, that maybe it never happened at all. And you have to respect it. Each hurt human heart has the right to an empty space.

After they had finished eating, Catesby began surreptitiously to look at her books. He knew a person's books said more about them than their furniture. More than half her books were in foreign languages – mostly German, French and Russian. Catesby noticed the collected works of two Russian women poets, Anna Akhmatova and Marina Tsvetayeva, whose lives had hovered constantly on the very limit of human endurance. Except that Tsvetayeva eventually stopped hovering and hanged herself. Stacked on the floor, next to the brocade sofa, were the first three volumes of *À la recherche du temps perdu*. The books showed signs of recent study. There were dozens of strips of paper marking pages.

The woman saw Catesby looking at the books. 'You like Proust?'

'I never finished reading him.' Catesby had begun reading Proust at Cambridge, but when the war interrupted his studies he decided that carrying all seven volumes of *À la recherche du temps perdu* off to officer training might be regarded as a bit pretentious. In the end, he wished he had.

'How much of Monsieur Proust have you read?' The woman sounded a little sceptical.

'I got to the end of *Du côté de chez Swann*.'

'And what,' she said, 'was your favourite section in that volume?'

My god, thought Catesby, she's *testing* me. He thought a moment; then said, 'I love the bit when young Marcel turns up at his uncle's place on an unannounced visit. At first the servant refuses to let

Marcel in, for his uncle is entertaining an "actress", a woman of loose morals.' Catesby noticed that the woman's eyes had gone flinty, but continued, 'Nevertheless, the actress begs the uncle to let …'

'Is that what you think of actresses?'

'I…' Catesby looked at Bone who was trying hard not to laugh.

'You think,' she said, 'that every actress is an … *éjszakai pillangó?*'

Just as Catesby registered the word *pillangó*, the room shook. It wasn't tank fire this time, but artillery. Plaster dust fell from cracks in the ceiling.

'What about "Butterfly"?'

'Ah, you know some Hungarian, but I meant a "night butterfly", a moth perhaps – it's slang for whore. But,' the woman continued with increasing rage, 'you eat a whore's soup and drink a whore's brandy.'

'I'm sorry, but it wasn't me who suggested that the actress was a whore. It was Marcel Proust. Blame him.'

'But *you*,' the woman was pointing, 'you chose the passage, because you want to call me a whore!'

'I didn't know that you were an actress.'

'*Everyone* knows that I am actress – don't play stupid.'

The artillery rounds were dropping nearer. The windows and the cutlery were rattling; a row of books fell off a shelf. The woman, sitting on the sofa next to Catesby, suddenly threw herself back and burst into laughter. She finally sat back up dabbing at her eyes with a handkerchief and turned to Bone. 'Wasn't,' she said, 'wasn't the expression on his face absolutely priceless?'

Bone nodded agreement.

'I didn't mean to offend,' said Catesby.

'Oh, don't be silly! I was teasing you.' She suddenly started sniffing the air. 'I hope the building's not on fire. Can you smell smoke?'

'Not yet,' said Catesby.

'Good,' said the woman, 'then there's still time to open the bottle of *Hárslevelü.*'

While their hostess got the wine from the ice chest, Bone sat down at the piano. He began to sift through a large pile of sheet music. 'What sort of acting are you involved in now?' said Bone as the woman brought him a glass of wine.

'None, I'm just a teacher now. But I worked in Hollywood in the thirties – for a little while.'

'And you came back,' said Bone although Catesby was gesturing for him to keep quiet.

'Yes, I came back.' She paused. 'It was for my family: I knew the trouble was coming and I wanted to ...'

Bone sensed that it was difficult for her to go on, so he quickly said, 'And poor you, the end of your acting career.'

'Well, not completely,' the woman sipped her wine and smiled, 'there has been some work. Two years ago I went to East Germany for a part in a film called *Einmal ist Keinmal*, how do you say in English, "Once is Never".' She laughed. 'Well, I suppose "once was never" for Koni never called me back.'

'I think,' said Catesby, 'that Koni made a very bad mistake.'

'Everyone knows what Koni Wolf is like. He prefers the younger girls, the prettier girls – just like his father.'

Catesby looked at Bone as the memory slotted into place. Then back to the woman. 'Didn't Koni's father write a book called *Comradely Marriage*?'

'I don't know. Friedrich wrote lots of things, but drama mostly. I acted in two of his plays. He was much more handsome than his son.'

'Which son?'

'Koni, of course.'

Bone looked at Catesby and mouthed 'back off'.

'Friedrich Wolf,' said Catesby pretending to try to remember something, 'I recently heard something about him, but I can't ...'

The woman looked into her wineglass. 'Poor Friedrich, I went to his funeral. The whole world was there: Russians, Poles – from when he was Ambassador, of course – and so many beautiful women.'

'And,' said Bone, 'is that where you met Mischa?'

'Yes, and he was just as good looking and charming as his father.'

Bone sat down at the piano and said, 'Do you like Bartók?'

The woman smiled. 'Only when I'm drunk, so I might like him now.'

'Will you turn the pages for me?'

The woman picked up the music for Bartók's Piano Sonata (Part One) and spread it open on the rack stand. It was dark now and there were still the sounds of shellfire: sometimes distant. As Bone began to play, Catesby realised that the sonata was apt music for a revolution. It was a modernist piece and the notes sounded like marching feet. Catesby sipped his wine and no longer cared where he was. The wine was the colour of gold and tasted like dry cool honey scented with lime. He watched Bone with admiration as he crossed his hands on the keyboard to do a particularly difficult set of chords. The woman was gently leaning on Bone's shoulder.

After he had finished, Bone chose the next piece of music. It was an old score and the sheets were dog-eared and stained. As soon as Bone began to play the solo piano arrangement of Tchaikovsky's *Pathétique*, Catesby realised that there was a subtle coded message. The longing that can never be fulfilled. When Bone had finished there were tears on the woman's face. The wine was finished too and the shellfire now sounded like summer thunder. She leaned down over Bone to kiss him with open mouth. Catesby couldn't take his eyes away. It was unbearably sad, but revealed so much that couldn't be said. Bone's eyes were wide with something like fear, embarrassment or confusion. Then he too opened his mouth and they kissed. It was not a kiss that could be measured in time; only in meaning and unspoken words. The woman was the first to break off the kiss. She looked at Henry Bone and stroked the side of his face which was wet with her tears. She understood.

It was now time to go. Time to go out on the rubble-strewn streets to find József and the *Pesti Srácok*. The woman was dressed in black boots, black coat and a dark scarf. She suddenly seemed very sober. 'The worst thing,' she said, 'will be getting to the other side of József körút. The Russians are trying to seal off the Corvin quarter.'

When they got on to the street there was the acrid smell of burning. There were glowing embers in the shells of the buildings opposite. A petrol generator clattered in the near distance. The three moved slowly up the boulevard with their backs pressed hard against the sides of buildings. Whenever there was an alcove or entrance, they crushed into it and waited. Catesby didn't feel that he was there as a real person in real time. He felt that he was in a cinema watching an image of his self in a very corny film. 'We need,' whispered the woman, 'to get to a passageway that leads to Corvin köz. There's a wooden gate next to the *kozert*, the government food shop, but one of the girls always leaves it open for her boyfriend.'

'So he can steal things?' said Catesby.

'No, so they can make love.'

A searchlight played down József körút. The shadow of the wrecked tank moved against the building walls like a beached sea monster creeping inland. The searchlight then swept upwards to examine the roofs and upper stories of the buildings. The light moved further away and Catesby could sense the woman tensing for a dash across the boulevard, but at that moment someone started shooting at the searchlight. The light extinguished and a heavy engine rumbled into life as the searchlight crew moved their truck to another position. Meanwhile, another light had taken over and a machine gun started firing into the darkness. Catesby watched green tracer bounce off the rooftops and pour into suspect windows. 'Let's go,' said the woman, 'it's only going to get worse.'

As they dashed across the boulevard, Catesby tripped over a paving stone and went sprawling. His palms were scraped, but otherwise he was all right. The woman shouted from the shadows. 'Come on!' Just as Catesby got to his feet, he was caught in the full glare of the searchlight. He started to run, but halted in his tracks when he saw a large figure running towards him. There was more machine-gun fire and he watched a line of tracer stitch the figure who was dashing across the facing wall, but miraculously the apparition kept running. Catesby started to run again and reached the other side before he realised he'd been chased by his own shadow.

The three of them had escaped the sweeping light and were crushed in a heap against the gate. 'Oh God,' said the woman, 'Maria has locked it.' The searchlight crept towards them again and seemed to be examining each metre of footpath like a dog sniffing for a place to pee. 'Hey look,' said the woman, 'the *kozert* is wide open.' Tank fire had blasted out the windows as well as the steel shutters of the shop front. They felt their way through the broken glass and twisted metal into complete darkness. They continued to feel their way along empty shelves and into the storerooms at the back. After a few more metres of blind groping they found the rear door. The keys were in the lock. They drew the bolts, pushed back the door and emerged into an alley. It was a dank place that smelled of cabbage and cats' piss, but the stars were out and the night was sweeter than ever.

One of the things that Catesby liked most about the *Pesti Srácok* was their nicknames. There was Cápa, the shark; Róka, the fox; Mackska, the cat; Pók, the spider – and Janko of the Wooden Leg. In fact, it was Janko who had led them through the barricades. The wooden leg looked like something that Janko had turned on a lathe, but he spun on it with surprising agility. Janko was well armed. He had a bandolier of machine-gun bullets around his neck, a submachine gun draped on one shoulder and a bolt-action rifle in his hands.

Janko took them to the barricaded cinema building that was rebel group headquarters and left them with Cápa who spoke good German and English. Cápa-the-shark seemed to recognise Bone, but didn't seem particularly happy to see him. 'You English,' he said, 'it's Yalta all over again.'

'What do you mean?' said Bone.

'You've done a deal with the Russians. You say to them, "If you let us take Suez, you can do what you want to Hungary."'

'Who told you that?' said Bone.

'Radio Free Europe – they tell us the truth, not like your BBC.'

'Be careful where you walk,' said Cápa pointing to the floor in front of him.

The floor was covered in large dinner plates that two boys of about fourteen were busy painting matt black.

'Clever, eh,' said Cápa. 'What do you think?'

Bone shrugged his shoulders.

'We lay them down in the road. The Russians think they are anti-tank mines and so they turn their tanks around to go another way. And the other way means the Russians have to drive their tanks down a slope, but we pour oil down the slope so they can't reverse or turn around. And then,' Cápa said, 'we finish them off with petrol bombs.'

'I believe,' said Bone, 'that József is expecting us.'

József's headquarters, festooned with maps, was located in the projectionist's cabin. An oilskin cloth covered the projector and piles of film canisters were stacked on the floor around it. There were two radios. One was tuned into RFE who were broadcasting Benny Goodman dance music. The other radio was being monitored by Pók-the-spider who kept fine-tuning the dials to pick up Soviet army frequencies. Meanwhile József, a strongly built man in his forties with thick black hair, was having a heated argument with Róka-the-fox. The shouting reached a crescendo and József rested his hand on his pistol holster. Róka ignored the threat and shouted back even louder. The only words that Catesby understood were

Imre Nagy and *kommunista*. Finally, Róka turned on his heel and left the room.

József looked at Bone and made a gesture at where Róka had been standing. 'He thinks we should go along with a load of piss bucket reforms. He thinks we can trust the Russians.' József seemed to be speaking as much to himself as to his visitors. 'I say we keep Nagy, but only if he meets our conditions.'

'And what,' said Bone, 'are your conditions?'

'The Russian troops must leave immediately and Hungary must withdraw from the Warsaw Pact. If that is too much for Imre Nagy, we will have to educate him.'

'No compromise,' said Bone.

'Why should we compromise? We're winning,' he said, 'the army has come over to our side and the Russians have stopped sending reinforcements.'

There was a table against one wall piled high with leaflets. Catesby picked up a copy. It was a Russian statement followed by a Hungarian translation. Catesby read the Russian version and was abashed. He turned to József. 'How did you get this?'

'Someone gave it to me. He is an excellent source of information, but I can't reveal his identity.'

'What is it?' said Bone in English.

József frowned. 'Please speak a language I can understand.'

Catesby shifted to German. 'This is an edited copy of Khrushchev's secret speech denouncing Stalin.'

'Very important speech,' said József, 'it shows that the old Soviet system is finished.'

'We've heard rumours about it – and we thought that if the speech was true our newspaper would publish it.'

Bone spoke next. 'We'd love to meet your "excellent source".'

'He doesn't speak to newspaper people. Even if that,' laughed József, 'is what you really are.'

Catesby picked up another leaflet with Russian text. It was another version of the Soviet Presidium meeting that suggested a Russian military withdrawal. It reminded him of Czeslaw Milosz's poem:

Grow your tree of lies from small seeds of truth

The leaflets gave the impression not only of Russian withdrawal from Hungary, but of the Soviet Union's imminent collapse. The brave street fighters of Budapest were being deliberately misled about their chances of victory. If there was an honourable side to the spy trade, it was preventing false intelligence from leading your country to disaster. Hungary needed an honourable spy.

'What do you call him,' said Catesby listing the Hungarian, Russian and German for butterfly, '*Pillangó*, *Babochka* or *Schmetterling*?'

'We call him all three, but when I speak to him I call him "my dear *Herr Schmetterling*".'

'Because,' said Catesby, 'he's German.'

'I don't know what nationality he is. He will never say.'

'But,' said Bone, 'he speaks to you in German.'

'Not always – he knows some Hungarian, but his Polish is excellent.'

Catesby remembered that József, himself, had been born in Transylvania – and that Austria-Hungary had been an empire of thirteen languages. The most important task of the empire's rulers had been to stop the various nationalities from attacking each other – and even to show some respect and tolerance.

'I think,' said József picking up a bottle, 'you try to make me talk too much. Have some Slivowitz and maybe you will talk too much.'

After finishing their drinks, Bone and Catesby left the room. They found their woman friend slumped asleep in a chair in the back row of the cinema hall. She was smiling, as if dreaming of herself on the screen in front of her. Bone gently touched her shoulder and she opened her eyes. 'My *Rosenkavalier*,' she said looking at Bone, 'has come back to me.'

'Is there,' said Catesby, 'a less exciting way to get back to your flat than the way we came?'

'They won't let us leave,' said the woman, 'there is a curfew – and anyone who breaks it will be shot on sight. We must stay here for the night, but some of them are happy. Too happy. They say that a big change is coming in the morning. I don't believe them.'

Catesby looked at his watch. It was after midnight. He watched Bone recline on one of the cinema seats and pull his beret down over his eyes. Catesby admired his ability to sleep anywhere. One of the nice things about the seats was that you could pull up the armrests. It facilitated comradely cuddling. She slid into the seat next to Bone and rested her head on his shoulder. It was a mistake, but she needed a happy illusion as much as anyone else.

Catesby stretched out and waited for dawn. He knew that he wouldn't sleep, but closed his eyes to pretend. After an hour of pretending, sleep finally came in the form of a sailing dream. They were on the River Ore and had almost reached the end of Havergate Island. At first he thought a gust of wind was making the boat heel, but then he realised that someone was shaking his shoulder. He opened his eyes. It was Róka-the-fox. 'We must talk,' he said, 'follow me.'

Róka led Catesby to a trapdoor and then down a narrow set of stairs to the cellars. The space was illuminated by weak voltage electrical bulbs. There was a great deal of rubble. The rebels had knocked down the walls between the neighbouring cellars. They were creating a vast subterranean network to move underground and unseen across the city.

'Look,' Róka pointed to a wall that was stacked high with boxes of hand grenades, ammunition and mortar rounds. There were even two flamethrowers. 'We are ready for big war.' Róka wasn't as fluent in German as József, but spoke as passionately. 'But if big war come,' Róka lowered his voice, 'we lose. Most of us die.'

'Is that what you want?'

'I don't want to die for nothing. No one wants to die for nothing unless they crazy.'

'Do you like József?'

'We argue all the time, but József is a good man – even if he wrong. Me, I want revolution to make better socialism. It don't matter if we stay ally with Russians. At first, József almost agree with me. But then he change.'

'Why?'

'He talk to someone who say you can't trust Russians to make a deal. This person also say that Russians are weak and that their soldiers won't fight – and ready to come over to our side.'

'Do you believe that?'

'No, I'm not so stupid – and a lot of people agree with me. This revolution start as good thing, but someone ruin it.'

'Have you ever heard of someone called,' Catesby said the name in German then repeated it in Hungarian, 'Butterfly, *Pillangó*?'

Róka's face turned dark. '*Pillangó* is a devil sent to destroy.'

'Where can I find him?'

'Why do you want to find him?'

'To help you.'

'I don't know where to find him. Maybe you should ask the *Ávö*. They know everything.' Róka had used the old hated name for the secret police 'And you must ask quick, for soon *Ávö* will be *kaput*.'

'What does *Pillangó* look like?'

'He look like angel, but act like Satan.' Róka smiled and shook hands; he had nothing more to say.

The next morning was a far from sleepy Sunday. The mood in the Corvin köz was jubilant. There were rumours that the Russians were preparing to pull out of Budapest – and perhaps all of Hungary. At 13:20 Prime Minister Imre Nagy came on *Magyar Rádió* and announced a ceasefire.

The first thing that Catesby did when he got back to the British legation was to remove his disguise and have a hot shower. He wanted to cleanse himself of politics and intrigue. He felt sorry for good honest men and women, like Róka, who only wanted to make things better for everyone. It starts fine. You set off with the other brave pilgrims on a sunny morning, but then the fog comes down. And when you get to a crossroads, you find that someone has swapped the signposts around. You can't ask strangers for directions, because you won't know whether they're lying or telling the truth – or even if they know the difference.

When Catesby finished dressing he joined Bone in the bank hall. Bone was at their work table encoding a report to wire back to London. 'Any thing to add, Catesby?'

'No, Henry, you're the brains.'

'Don't put yourself down.'

'That's usually your job.'

'Don't get in a mood.' Bone picked up his report. 'I wouldn't want to be one of them.'

'One of whom?'

'The ÁVH, the secret police. Their days, if not hours, are numbered. The average Hungarian hates the ÁVH more than the Russians – and I can't say I blame them. No one knows how many people the ÁVH have tortured and executed – I imagine they are burning the files as we speak. So you'd better get cracking.'

'What do you mean?'

'You need to pay the ÁVH a visit as soon as possible, while they are still above ground.' Bone paused. 'That fellow you talked to …'

'Róka.'

'Róka was right. If we want to track down Butterfly the ÁVH are our best bet.'

Catesby held up his forged East German ID. 'Are you coming with me?'

Bone smiled. 'No. Let's look at the map. Their headquarters are here on Népköztársasság út, which according to my dictionary means People's Republic Avenue. And the people have, in fact, surrounded it. You best get there before the place is overrun and sacked.'

'Thanks.'

'I reckon there are two possibilities. Either the ÁVH are acting in collusion with Butterfly in the hope that his activities might wreck the revolt – or they are desperately afraid of Butterfly and want to hunt him down. What's your view?'

'I think,' said Catesby, 'they want to get Butterfly just as much as you do – and for the same reason.'

'Which is?'

'Fear.'

'How little you know about me.' Bone fixed Catesby with an unblinking stare. 'I'm not afraid of him – but I know he can inflict a lot of pain.'

'Have you told me everything?'

'I've told you everything you need to know.'

'When are you going to see your girlfriend again?'

Bone smiled wanly. 'You're jealous.'

'A little.'

'I'm sorry that I can't come with you, my presence would bust your cover. But they'll trust you. The ÁVH are desperate for fellow tradesmen who understand their appalling situation.'

'What if they realise I'm an imposter and lock me up?'

'Don't worry,' said Bone, 'in a few days the rebels will free you.'

'What should I tell them?'

'Oh … you'll have plenty of time to make up something while you're in the cell.'

'Thanks.'

Népköztársasság út was one of the grandest boulevards in Pest. The ceasefire had brought out the crowds. Many were carrying stubby Russian PPSh-41 sub-machine guns which, with their round drum magazines, looked like the Thompsons that Chicago gangsters carry in violin cases. The gangster gats, carried by men wearing trilbies and long coats, gave the scene a filmic quality. There were also wagons stacked with bodies.

The ÁVH headquarters was located a good way up Népköztársaság út, past the opera house and towards the quarter where many foreign embassies were located. It looked like there had been relatively little violence in the quarter – although the Soviet war memorial had been vandalised and defaced with *Ruszkik haza* slogans. When Catesby got to the secret police headquarters he found it surrounded by a milling crowd, many of the crowd were armed and had angry faces. There wasn't yet a suggestion of imminent violence, but the mood was simmering.

The ÁVH HQ was located in a stately nineteenth-century grey neo-classical building. The windows on the ground floor were shuttered and the heavy oak doors of the main entrance were firmly closed. There were no guards on the outside. The windows of the three upper stories were un-shuttered and seemed like watchful eyes peering on the scene below. From time to time a curtain would twitch and a face would appear. It was clearly a building under siege.

As Catesby walked up to the entrance doors he felt dozens of eyes boring into his back. Someone was shouting in Hungarian, but he didn't understand the words or even if they were directed at him. But the voice wasn't a friendly one. Catesby pressed a buzzer on the side of the doorway and waited, but nothing happened. He pressed again, still nothing. There was no more shouting from the group milling in the street. The fact that the ÁVH obviously weren't expecting him seemed to count in his favour. Finally, Catesby started hammering on the door with his fist. After a minute or two, the door opened a crack. The face of a middle-aged woman wearing glasses peered out at him and said something in Hungarian. Catesby held up his MfS identity card. The woman's eyes grew large as she read the details; she nodded and closed the door leaving Catesby outside.

Catesby folded his arms and tried to stop his foot from nervously tapping. Someone in the crowd shouted, '*Ruszkik.*' Shit, thought Catesby, they think I'm Russian. He sensed an ugly mood and people moving nearer. Catesby turned and said in a slightly bored voice, '*Je suis journaliste Français.*'

Someone in the crowd who was an excellent French speaker

began testing him. Catesby made a feeble joke comparing Budapest to Paris in 1789 and how they needed a guillotine. No one laughed, but Catesby felt less threatened. A moment later the door opened and a uniformed ÁVH let him in.

The scene inside the secret police quarters was utter chaos. There was paper everywhere as files were emptied and put in bags for incineration. Eleven years of brutal history had to disappear. The mood of fear was tangible. The barrel of a heavy machine gun jutted from a sandbagged emplacement inside the foyer and pointed at the main entrance doors.

The policeman who greeted Catesby led him to a paternoster lift, a system common to Germany and central Europe. The lift, like the continuous circle of prayer beads on a rosary chain, never stopped. There were no doors. You stepped into a paternoster while it was still moving and, when it reached the floor you wanted, you stepped out while it was still moving. Catesby used to hate paternosters because he feared he wouldn't get out in time and would be ground to mincemeat by the mechanisms in the roof. Then someone told him that you could ride them all the way around. He tried it once and was thrilled to see the secrets of the huge wheels and chains in the loft space.

The office of Major Gábor was on the top floor. There was a copying machine in the corridor outside his office that a crowd of officers were using to fabricate new personal identity cards – and bags and bags of files for burning. Gábor stood up and greeted Catesby as Comrade Colonel Telemann. They shook hands and Catesby sat down on the other side of Gábor's desk.

'We tried to get through by telephone,' said Catesby, 'but it was impossible.'

'They have cut the lines, but we still have radio communication. Surely, you have our frequencies.'

'Yes,' said Catesby, 'but we can't risk having our communications compromised by monitoring. I have been sent here to deal with an extremely sensitive issue.'

'Ah, well if it's that sensitive you should have used the Fialka/ Violet. Our machines are still working and our code pads are up to date.'

Catesby felt a prison cell beckoning. The Fialka/Violet was the standard eight-rotor cipher machine used for secure Warsaw Pact communications. 'That may be true,' he said, 'but Hungarian Army Fialka/Violets have fallen into the hands of the insurgents.'

'Well,' shrugged Gábor, 'Moscow still use them for encryption.'

'Yes,' said Catesby, 'and that's why Soviet communication security is shit – as you well know.'

Gábor leaned forward and touched his brows with his fingertips. His eyes were closed and he looked exhausted. Without opening his eyes, he reached out a hand. 'May I see your identity documents, please?'

Catesby handed over his East German passport and State Security ID.

Gábor looked at them professionally, studying the watermarks, ink and security threads for any sign of forgery.

'If you like,' said Catesby, 'I'll wait while you put them under an infra-red magnifier.'

Gábor handed the documents back. 'That won't be necessary, Comrade Colonel.'

Catesby smiled. 'I can understand your being suspicious. These are very difficult times for you. It was like that for us during our uprising in '53, but what is happening here is much worse.'

'At least,' said Gábor, 'you didn't lose your job. There are rumours that Nagy is planning to abolish us.'

'Don't worry. You'll later be re-formed under a different name. They need people like us.'

Gábor looked at Catesby with weary hooded eyes, 'I hope, Comrade Colonel, that your optimism does not prove unfounded.'

'These uprisings,' droned Catesby, 'seem to follow a pattern. We noticed it last summer in Poznań and now it's happening here too.'

'At least,' said Gábor, 'the Poles managed to put down the insurrection without Russian help.'

'Maybe our friend was just getting practice in Poznań.'

'What are you talking about?' Gábor snapped at Catesby. He was annoyed. 'What friend, who?'

'You don't know?'

Gábor wearily shook his head. He now seemed too tired to talk.

'In your language he is *Pillangó*; we call him Butterfly.'

Gábor glanced furtively at the door. 'We can't discuss any of that here.' He lowered his voice. 'Meet me tomorrow at Anonymous.'

Catesby looked blank.

Gábor smiled. 'Don't you know Anonymous? He's famous.'

'No.'

'In any case, you will find him in Városliget Park. I will meet you there at noon.'

As Catesby got up to go there was a loud splintering noise followed by a harrowing shriek of metal grating and grinding that momentarily shook the floor beneath his feet. Then everything stopped. For a second Catesby wondered if the building had been hit by a tank shell. There were angry voices shouting from the direction of the paternoster lift.

'I think,' said Gábor, 'there has been an accident.'

The policeman got up and Catesby followed him down the corridor to the lift. The barrel of a large calibre gun was firmly wedged between the ceiling and the floor of the paternoster compartment. It looked like the gun barrel had shifted while the weapon was being moved and then jammed the paternoster and stripped all its gears.

'I'm sorry,' said Gábor, 'but you'll have to take the stairs.'

Városliget was Pest's main park. It was located at the upper end of Népköztársasság út behind Heroes Square. Catesby walked through the long solemn square and thought how nice it would be to live in a country that had no need of heroes or war memorials. They were both signs that something had gone wrong. But he liked the heavily wooded park that stretched out behind the paved square. There was a castle rising above the trees, a large lake and thermal baths.

It was easy to find Anonymous. He was cast in bronze and seated on a pedestal in the middle of the park. He was pretty frightening to look at. Anonymous was wearing robes and a hood. The heavy hood cast his face in shadow. He looked like the Grim Reaper, except he had a pen in his hand instead of a scythe. Maybe, thought Catesby, his job was recording the names of the dead instead of actually killing them. The pen was the only part of the statue that was polished. It shone like burnished gold, while the rest of Anonymous was weathered verdigris.

Catesby heard footsteps crunching on the gravel behind him. He touched the handgun weighing down his coat pocket and turned around. It was Major Gábor, five minutes early. He was dressed in civilian clothes. 'You had no trouble,' said Gábor, 'finding Anonymous?'

'No.' Catesby gestured at the statue, 'Why do you call him that?'

'Our oldest Magyar chronicles have no named author, but we think it was one person – so we wanted to honour him.'

'And the pen?'

'If you want to be a writer or a poet you have to touch the pen of Anonymous for inspiration – and there are so many hands touching his pen that it never loses its lustre.'

Catesby smiled, but kept his hands in his pockets.

'Are you a writer, Comrade Colonel?'

'No.'

'Not even,' smiled Gábor, 'poems when you were a student?'

'Maybe one or two – but I was good at writing unsuccessful love letters.'

'Ah,' said Gábor, 'we all write those hopeless letters. For when you are successful, there is no need to write love letters.'

'Do you really believe that?'

'No, I write love letters to my wife.'

Some people, thought Catesby, might think it odd that a villain like Gábor could appreciate poetry and write love letters. But culture didn't make you good. He wondered if Gábor really was a villain – or just a good cop doing a dirty job. Judging others wasn't an easy job – particularly when they burn the files. It meant everyone was guilty and everyone was innocent too.

It suddenly occurred to Catesby that Gábor looked awfully scruffy for an off-duty major. He was wearing a greasy beret and a frayed leather jacket. The ÁVH were supposed to be overpaid fat cats. Then Catesby realised that Gábor had been to the costume cupboard. He wanted to look like the humblest worker. When there's a revolution the top layers have to go undercover.

'What,' said Gábor, 'do you know about *Pillangó*?'

'We think he played a role in the uprisings in Berlin and Poznań?'

'Does he work for the West?'

'We're not completely sure who he works for. That's one of the reasons I'm here.'

Gábor sagely nodded.

'But during all three insurrections,' said Catesby, 'radio broadcasts from the West seem to have been in coordination with Butterfly's activities.'

'So he must be a Western agent?'

Catesby looked closely at Gábor and placed a hand on his shoulder to draw him close. One of the most difficult things to teach Western agents going undercover is to remember that Eastern Europeans speak to each other with their faces much closer together than Westerners, especially British Westerners.

'There is,' said Catesby, 'bad blood between Mischa and Mielke. Mischa is a reformer; Mielke is a hardline Stalinist.'

'But Mielke is Comrade Wolf's boss; why doesn't he just sack him?'

'Because it is not possible. Mischa Wolf has built up too much of a power base, so Erich Mielke may be trying to undermine him in other ways.'

Gábor squinted. His secret policeman's reasoning had shifted into gear. 'If you think *Pillangó* is working for Mielke, you must be one of Mischa's boys.'

Catesby fixed Gábor with a hard stare. 'I didn't say that – and don't assume I'm one of Mischa's arse-kissers. We're not even sure if Butterfly is one of ours. He may be a German-speaking Pole. He may even be Russian. I've come here to find out who he is and who he's working for.'

'And why should we help you find him?'

'Because if things get bad for you, I can get you and your family out of Hungary and into the GDR.'

Gábor looked at the statue of Anonymous as if expecting the statue to give advice. He then looked at Catesby and said, 'I know someone who can tell you about Butterfly. In fact, he knows who he is.'

'Why hasn't he told you?'

'I don't know why. Maybe he thinks the information is a gem that he can trade to save himself and his own family.' Gábor looked sharply at Catesby. 'Make him the offer and see if he bites.'

'Where can I find him?'

'I don't know where he is now, but tomorrow he will be on duty at party headquarters on Köztársaság tér. So far, the rebels have left the building alone. And there is no reason for them to attack the building: there are no weapons, no secret files. You will find it much easier than Népköztársasság út. I'm surprised they let you in.'

'How will I know your friend?'

'He isn't my friend, but his name is Captain Lajos. He is a tall handsome man with wavy brown hair.' Gábor began to walk away, but stopped and pointed at Anonymous. 'You must, Comrade Colonel, touch his golden pen. It will help you tell better stories.'

Köztársaság tér, Republic Square, reminded Catesby more of London's Green Park than a paved urban space. There was grass, trees and gravel paths. The headquarters of the Hungarian Working People's Party, where Captain Lajos was supposed to be on duty, was on the northwest side of the square. The building, as Catesby could see through the bare trees, was modern and functional. And to his right he could see a tank with its gun facing the party headquarters.

At first, Catesby couldn't understand why people were lying on the grass in the middle of the square. It was hardly a warm summer's day. Then he heard two popping noises go past his head. All of the people in the square who weren't lying down were crawling behind trees. Catesby thought the nearest trees looked too small for cover; but to his left there were wheelbarrows and a shed. He ran towards the shed and threw himself down behind it. He wasn't alone. There was a young man lying there with a camera around his neck and blood running down his left arm.

'Are you all right?' said Catesby before he realised it was a stupid thing to say.

'I got shot.' The man answered in American English.

'Is it bad?'

'I don't know. It felt like someone hit me with a baseball bat.'

Suddenly there was a loud bang from the direction of the tank followed by the sound of tumbling masonry from the party headquarters.

A girl dressed in a white coat was running towards them with a medical satchel. She didn't look over sixteen. There were two boys, who didn't look any older, following her with a stretcher. The bullets were still flying.

The American tried to wave the boys away with his good hand. 'Don't worry,' he said, 'I can walk.'

Catesby helped the American up and then watched him and the girl run bent double towards a waiting car. One of the boys remained squatting behind the shed with Catesby while the other went off to look for more wounded.

'What's happening?' said Catesby.

The boy didn't understand. Catesby switched to Russian, but quickly explained that he was German before he repeated the question.

'The ÁVH have taken hostages and the fighters are trying to free them. And the ÁVH are firing at all of us.'

There was the sound of more tanks clanking into the square. Catesby turned and counted four of them. An older woman wearing a white coat joined them behind the shed. She put her arm around the boy and said something to him. Catesby asked what was happening in German.

'Don't move,' she said, 'just lie still and hope for the best. They've come to help the ÁVH.'

'Who?'

'*Die Panzer.*'

Catesby looked at the newly arrived tanks. They were flying Hungarian tricolours with round holes in the middle. 'But,' he said, 'they are your tanks.'

The woman made the sign of the cross. 'Someone told me they were Russian.' She and the boy then went off in a crouching run looking for casualties.

There was still a lot of shooting, but Catesby got up and ran towards one of the newly arrived tanks. He thought being behind a tank would be safer than the shed. Then something strange happened. The tank's turret turned away from the party headquarters. For a second the gun was directly in Catesby's face. Then the gun traversed the square. There was a minute or two of sheer panic and uncertainty. People were shouting and running in all directions. Were the tanks wearing false flags and had they, in fact, come to rescue the besieged ÁVH?

Catesby curled up on the ground and waited. When he finally looked up, the gun was aiming at the party headquarters. The tank crew, he supposed, had just been getting their bearings. In any case, the tank was now firing at the building. Catesby was so close he could feel the heat of the gun barrel and smell the stench of burnt gunpowder.

The rebels were now moving closer to the building and several of them were being hit by machine-gun fire from the ÁVH. Catesby couldn't understand the logic of their tactics. Why were the rebels rushing the building on foot and getting killed? Why didn't they simply wait for the tanks to reduce the building to rubble? Then he remembered the rumour about hostages who needed freeing. War was about dealing with confusion – and this was war.

Catesby ran behind the tank where he crouched and waited. He suddenly remembered why he was there. Amid all the excitement and danger he had forgotten Captain Lajos. Was Lajos still alive? And if he was alive, how was Catesby going to find him in the middle of a battle?

The firing continued and more people arrived in the square. Almost everyone was carrying a gun or rifle. Catesby turned to look at a truck full of boys and women that had pulled up behind the tank. They were shouting and flourishing a variety of vintage weapons, some of which must have gone back to the nineteenth century. A boy of about fifteen crumpled on the paving after jumping down from the truck, he had shot himself in the foot. Could, Catesby thought, *Walpurgisnacht* happen at ten o'clock in the morning?

Ten minutes later there was a lull in the shooting and the crowd surged forward. Catesby saw something white being waved from an upper floor. He left the shelter of the tank and pushed forward with the others. He recognised some faces from the Corvin köz. One of them was Farkas-the-wolf. Catesby elbowed his way through the throng to get closer to Farkas. Something serious was happening at the party headquarters building. There was a lot of screaming.

Catesby stood on tiptoes to see over the heads of the crowd. Armed rebels had surrounded the building. The front entrance had either been opened or blasted open. Catesby pushed his way through; he needed to catch up with Farkas. He shouted his name several times, but Farkas was either ignoring him or hadn't heard him. Catesby put his head down like a crazed rugby back heading for a try. Someone gave him an ugly jab in the ribs as he went through, but Catesby managed to reach Farkas. He grabbed him by the elbow and shouted, 'I need to find Captain Lajos.'

Farkas pried off Catesby's grip with the butt of his submachine gun. 'Are you crazy? Why do you want Captain Lajos?'

Catesby realised that Farkas didn't recognise him. 'I need to find Lajos,' said Catesby, 'it's important.'

Farkas shouted something in Hungarian that made the people around him laugh. Catesby pushed away and tried to get to the front of the crowd. There was a space ahead of him that seemed like an empty hole in the pushing throng. Catesby pushed to the edge of it. A woman was weeping over a body with a Hungarian flag draped over it. He edged around the casualty and managed to get on to the footpath in front of the building. Catesby could see that the tanks had done a good job. All the windows were knocked out and the area in front of the building was covered in concrete rubble. He sensed something ugly was going to happen – and there was nothing he could do to stop it.

Catesby was about ten feet from the building's main entrance. He saw one of the rebels stick his head inside the doorway and shout something. A few seconds later, an ÁVH officer came out. He was smiling and talking. It looked like he was trying to explain that there had been a misunderstanding. It happened so quickly that Catesby wasn't sure what had happened. He first thought that the officer had tripped on the rubble and fallen down, but then he realised there had been gunshots at the same time.

A few seconds later two more policemen in uniform came out. Their hands were raised and their faces drained of colour. They didn't say anything or try to make eye contact. The square seemed strangely quiet. Catesby braced himself to hear gunshots, but none came. The silence was eerie. One of the policemen had a nervous tic: his left eye kept blinking like a light bulb that was about to go out. When it happened it wasn't just one person or ten, it seemed that half the crowd had surged forward at the same time. In less than a second the two policemen had disappeared under a sea of pounding rifle butts, fists and kicking boots. Catesby felt he was going to be sick; then he was sick. He looked at the vomit lying at his feet. He used his foot to scrape a layer of rubble over it; then he wiped his mouth with his handkerchief. Catesby looked over the shoulder in front of him and watched as the two policemen were stripped to the waist and strung upside down on the nearest trees. Catesby hadn't heard shots, but hoped that they weren't still alive – for now was the kicking time. He felt his empty stomach churn at the crunching sound of boot on face: cheek, nose, brow, chin – and lips that had once kissed someone. Kick, kick, kick, kick.

Catesby felt the crowd's attention shift back to the building. There were angry shouts when a group of six more officers emerged from the entrance. They marched out at gunpoint with their hands raised. It looked like one of the officers had been whacked in the head with a rifle butt for a trickle of blood was running down from his ear. It was impossible to tell their ranks for their shoulder boards had been ripped off. The six seemed to represent the ethnic diversity of Hungary: two were blond, one looked Scandinavian, two were Mediterranean dark and one looked almost Chinese. But they all looked frightened, except for a small Slav-looking blond who seemed simply resigned. Oddly, one of his eyes looked blankly outward while the other looked inward.

Catesby wondered if the blood lust had abated and the officers were going to be treated as prisoners. Once again, there was a tense silent interval. But the respite was a brief one. Catesby didn't see who fired the first shots; it might have been Farkas. It seemed to happen in slow motion. The first person shot was the Chinese-looking man. Catesby remembered how he raised his hands in an almost prayer-like gesture to ward off the bullets. The six collapsed in a heap; one on top of the other against the base of the building. The executioners kept firing into the body heap. One of the dying officers briefly raised his foot as if the heel of his boot could stop bullets. Catesby could see the fabric of their uniforms dimpling as the bullets struck.

When the firing finally stopped, the mood of the crowd changed. There was pushing, shoving and loud arguing. Catesby sensed that there was a faction who thought things had gone too far. He looked at the pile of bodies; one at the bottom of the heap was still moving. It was the Slav-looking blond of the inward eye. Catesby wanted to help him, but was afraid that his help would be a signal for another bullet.

Catesby heard shouting from inside the building. Another group of officers were brought out. The first was a good-looking man in his late thirties with wavy dark brown hair. He had the relaxed confident air of an experienced teacher called in to deal with an unruly class. He was still wearing shoulder boards – and the boards carried the three stars of a captain. There wasn't time to waste. Catesby sidestepped the pile of bodies and put a hand on the captain's shoulder. 'Are you Lajos?'

The captain at first seemed confused that someone was speaking to him in German. He finally smiled and said, '*Ja*, I am Lajos.'

'Stick close to me. I'm going to get you out of here.'

There was now a lot of shouting behind him.

'What,' said Catesby, 'are they saying?'

'They're saying, "Who the hell is that?" and "What does he think he's doing?"'

'Listen, there's a car on the other side of the square that's been taking wounded to hospital.' Wounded rebels, thought Catesby, that Lajos may have personally shot. He put his arm around Lajos's waist. 'If I can get you there, I think you'll be safe.'

Hands were tugging at Catesby trying to pull him away from Lajos. Catesby felt a fist hit the side of his face. He wondered if he should reach for the automatic in his coat pocket and try to grab one of the rebels as a human shield. Instead, Catesby tried to ingratiate himself with the crowd by chanting *Ruszkik haza*. The chant convinced at least one pair of hands to let him go. He managed to get Lajos into the parkland in the centre of the square. Their flight was aided by the distraction of more ÁVH officers being dragged from the blasted wreck of the party headquarters. There was another round of retribution gunfire as more policemen were executed. Catesby was desperate to get Lajos as far away as he could. On the other side of the trees he could see white coats and an ambulance.

Just as Catesby thought their luck was improving, a group of rebels blocked their way through the park. He recognised a face or two from the Corvin köz. Suddenly they were surrounded by a large pushing crowd that materialised from nowhere. Someone slammed a rifle butt into Lajos's face; Catesby felt a spray of blood spatter his own cheek. He instinctively pulled Lajos down to protect his head from the pounding rifle butts.

Catesby had his arms around the Hungarian's face and was cradling his head against his chest when it happened. The gun barrel came up from a low angle like a blue-black snake. The front sight brushed Catesby's elbow before it pressed into Lajos's chest. Lajos saw it coming and started screaming. The press of the crowd was too tight for Catesby to move his arms. They swayed back and forth for a second like a rugby scrum. When the shots came he felt Lajos shudder in his arms and then become a dead weight. Catesby turned to look at the gunman. Most of his face was covered by a scarf and hat brim, but the part that Catesby could see – the blue eyes, the high cheekbones – had an unearthly beauty. Lajos was looking at him too. As he slipped through Catesby's arms and on to the ground, the dying secret policeman uttered one word, '*Pillangó*.'

Catesby turned to look at the gunman, but he was already gone. He then tried to kneel down next to Lajos to see if he was still alive, but he was pushed away by the crowd. They still had things to do. It wasn't enough to kill the ÁVH, they had to humiliate the corpses as well.

Catesby felt dizzy. His knees started to give way and he felt the ground coming up to meet him. It was fear vertigo, but he managed to stay upright. He sensed that the crowd was turning on him. People were shouting at him and pointing – and someone gave him a sharp elbow in the back. Finally, a boy of about fifteen jumped up behind him and grabbed his hat. The boy ran off spitting on the trilby and then, incongruously, put it on his own head. Catesby watched the boy prance about – and then noticed the crowd seemed to have lost interest in him. The boy's antics had humiliated Catesby enough to forestall more violence.

Catesby began walking, almost running, across the square. He wanted to get away. He hadn't gone far when he saw two women in white coats with red crosses sitting on a bench, but the younger one was only a girl. He realised that he had seen the woman before. She had been with him sheltering behind the shed with the wounded American photojournalist. The woman was now holding the girl in her arms. Catesby sat next to them. 'What's wrong?' he said.

The woman's eyes were closed and her face was wet with tears. 'I don't want my daughter to see this. She is too young to remember the war. I don't want her to see what men can do.'

Catesby put his hand on top of the woman's hand which was on her daughter's head. There weren't any words – particularly from someone like him, in his trade.

The woman looked at Catesby. 'Are you hurt?'

'No.'

'But you've blood on your face.'

'It's someone else's,' he said.

The daughter, who may have been fifteen, had lost all pretensions of adulthood and was clinging to her mother like a child.

Catesby looked back towards the party headquarters. The crowd was dispersing and there hadn't been any gunshots for some time. He remembered something. 'There's someone,' he said, 'who needs help.'

The woman looked up.

'They shot a group of ÁVH policemen, but one of them, under the pile of bodies, is still alive. Can you help him?'

The woman nodded and stroked her daughter at the same time. 'But,' said Catesby, 'your girl … I can stay with her here.'

The woman spoke briefly to her daughter in Hungarian and then turned to Catesby. 'She wants to stay with me, so she has to come too.'

Catesby looked at the girl, but the girl didn't look at him. She looked through him. Her childhood innocence was a half remembered dream.

The woman set off towards the wrecked party headquarters with one arm around her daughter's shoulder. There were no more tears. She was a doctor on her rounds. She was a well-known figure and the crowd parted as she approached. Some of the gunmen turned away with looks of shame, but not all.

The pile of bodies at the base of the building had diminished by two. One body had been laid out in the road with a coin stuck in his mouth and his officer's pay book open on his chest. The other, who had half his head shot away, had been strung up from a tree to provide more kicking practice. The woman showed no emotion as she made her way to the remaining four bodies. She confirmed that three were dead and ordered members of the crowd to move them. But, as Catesby had noticed, the one at the bottom of the pile was still breathing. The woman kneeled down next to the Slavic-looking blond and checked his injuries. The worst bullet wounds were to his left thigh which was badly mangled. She gave him an injection of morphine before tying off the wounded leg with a tourniquet. The woman then got four men to lift the ÁVH officer on to a stretcher and carry him to the ambulance.

The officer had lost a lot of blood and had very little breath. As he was carried past, the officer's inward-looking eye turned outwards and stared directly at Catesby. The secret policeman's voice was less than a whisper, 'Who are you?'

Catesby didn't know the answer.

As soon as the woman and her ambulance were gone, the mood in the square turned ugly again. A body hanging from a tree had petrol thrown over it and was set alight. Catesby was surprised that many of those lynched were wearing civilian clothes. They might, he supposed, have been ÁVH who had changed out of their uniforms to try to escape – or they may have been civilian party officials. The lack of discrimination, the deafness to pleas of innocence, frightened Catesby and confused him too. Most of the rebels he had met were brave men fighting for an ideal. Sure, some of them had quick tempers – but he didn't imagine that it could turn to this.

Catesby turned away. He had seen enough. It began to drizzle as he walked back across the square. The bare trees, black with damp, were no longer living things, but the scorched remains of broken ideals. Catesby paused as he passed the body of Captain Lajos. Someone had stuck a tablespoon in his mouth; the spoon distorted his lips into a grotesque smile. His arms were flung out over his head as if he was still surrendering. A gold wedding band gleamed from a bruised finger smeared with blood and dirt.

'You seem rather quiet this evening.' Henry Bone had done a great deal to make their quarters in the cold echoing bank hall comfortable. He had found coal for the fireplace as well as armchairs and a large mahogany table for working and eating. Bone was sipping whisky he had purchased from the legation's stores. He held up the bottle, 'Top up?'

'Thanks,' said Catesby as he held out his glass.

'If you don't mind my saying so, you seemed very upset when you came back – and you need some ice for that eye.'

'I'm sorry,' said Catesby. 'I shouldn't have been so … so earnest when I told you about it.'

'You have to put things in context.' Bone paused. 'I don't suppose you would like to …'

'Talk? No.' Catesby stared into his whisky glass. 'Okay. The last time we had a conversation like this you mentioned Oradour-sur-Glane – and I told you to shut up.'

'You didn't tell me to shut up – you said you didn't want to talk about it.'

'But I want to talk about it now.' Catesby stared at the fire. 'We didn't get there until two days afterwards. We'd heard rumours, but couldn't believe they were true. The bodies had already been removed, but the church was still smouldering – and the smell. Identifying the bodies of the 190 men was easy – they had been machine-gunned. But the 247 women and 205 children had been burned alive in the church, so …' Catesby continued to stare into the fire. None of the flame patterns connected to anything. He wondered if the black lumps on the grate were really coal. 'It didn't make sense.'

'What didn't make sense?'

'That the sun was shining and that cows were still grazing in the pastures. Why? How could they?'

'Did it make you hate?'

'Yes. Before Oradour, I wanted to fight the Nazis. After Oradour, I hated them – destroying them became a mission.' Catesby paused. 'And the general who ordered that massacre is still alive … and his ideas.'

'Perhaps' said Bone, 'you can understand what happened today. You can understand their hate.'

'No, Henry, you're wrong. You don't get rid of Nazis – or anyone like them – by mob violence. If you do that, you're drunk on the same poison that they're drinking. But you don't give them any quarter either. If you don't kill them in battle, you put them in front of a court – and then you hang the bastards.'

'Sometimes courts and hangmen are a luxury of civilised life.'

'Maybe you're right, Henry.'

'We'll see. In any case, Imre Mezö was one of those who were shot today. I think he was a friend of yours.'

Catesby looked confused. 'Mezö's here in Budapest?'

'Yes.'

'Is he dead?'

'No, but unlikely to survive.'

Catesby had known Mezö in France when the Hungarian-born communist had fought with the Resistance. Mezö used to enjoy speaking Flemish with Catesby. He had learned the language after immigrating to Belgium in the twenties where he became a member of the Belgian Communist Party. In 1936 Mezö had gone to Spain to fight with the International Brigade and had been severely wounded.

'Why,' said Catesby, 'didn't you tell me he was here?'

'I thought you knew.' Bone paused. 'But maybe it was best that you didn't know.'

'Can you explain that?'

'We didn't know what game Mezö was going to play, but when we found out it was too late.' Bone sipped his whisky. 'I was afraid that if you went to see him it would have blown his credibility and your cover.'

'You could have ordered me to stay away.'

'You don't always obey orders.'

'What exactly was Mezö doing here?'

'He returned to Hungary in '45. He served his time as a party apparatchik and became a member of the Central Committee.'

'Did you know that he was going to be at party headquarters this morning?'

'If I had known, I definitely wouldn't have let you go.' Bone looked into his glass. 'Mezö was supposed to be meeting with Nagy at the Parliament. He was going to offer to join his government.'

'So,' said Catesby, 'the crowd shot someone who was on their own side.'

'It would seem that way.'

'You don't think Mezö is going to pull through.'

'No, his kidneys are gone.'

'How long's he got?'

'Two days, maybe three.'

'I've got to see him.'

The Szent János Hospital was a complex of buildings on the Buda side of the Danube. It was more modern than most of Budapest. Imre Mezö was on a ward with other victims of the fighting. At first the nurses didn't want to let Catesby see him because he wasn't family, but Mezö intervened and they let him through.

As soon as Catesby saw Mezö he knew that the old fighter was a goner. His skin looked like yellow parchment. The Hungarian raised a hand that was festooned with drips and Catesby grasped it.

'Whose side are you on?' said Mezö in French.

'I'm at the British legation. We're not allowed to take sides in case we pick the one that loses.'

'Very wise.'

A nurse came over and whispered in Catesby's ear that there were other visitors waiting and he should be quick.

'What did she say?'

'She said that you're the bravest man she's ever seen.'

'I think,' said Mezö, 'she might have said I'm the stupidest man she's ever seen.' The Hungarian grimaced as if he felt a wave of pain. 'I walked straight into it.'

The nurse was tapping Catesby's elbow to indicate that his time was up.

'Straight into what?' said Catesby.

'Straight into …' suddenly Mezö shifted to Flemish, 'into the *Vlinder*.'

Catesby reached down to take Mezö's hand. 'I promise you, I swear to you.' He didn't need to say what he was promising. For they both knew and they both could see the *Vlinder* spreading its bright wings and fluttering in front of the swooping net.

The next seven days were more eventful for the Hungarians than they were for Catesby and Bone. On the 1st of November new Soviet military units entered the east of Hungary for the purpose of 'protecting the withdrawal of the Soviet units' that were already in Hungary. Meanwhile, Nagy had assumed the role of acting Foreign Minister and announced Hungary's 'immediate withdrawal from the Warsaw Pact.' On the same day, Imre Mezö, who would have counselled otherwise, fell into a deep coma from which he never awoke.

Catesby spent most of his remaining time in Budapest writing assessment ledgers and liaising with the dips to monitor the situation. There were confirmed reports that Soviet war graves and war memorials had been desecrated; and unconfirmed reports of more lynchings. Although the ÁVH no longer existed, the secret police had been abolished by decree, Catesby spent most of a day pounding the streets of Pest trying to find Major Gábor or any former member of the security service. But they had buttoned up and gone to ground. What struck Catesby most as he walked the streets of Budapest was the total unawareness of the people. Couldn't *anyone* see it coming?

On the 3rd of November a Hungarian commission began talks with the Soviet military authorities in the Parliament buildings in Pest. The aim was to arrange an orderly withdrawal of Soviet units. The meeting was friendly and helpful. The talks were reconvened later that evening at the Soviet headquarters at Tokol. At midnight, KGB General Serov ordered the arrest of the Hungarian delegation. At four o'clock the next morning eight Soviet divisions with air support seized control of Budapest.

There were pockets of fierce, but hopeless resistance. Most of the tank crews stayed buttoned up in their tanks and navigated only by the use of periscopes. There were reports of Hungarian girls jumping on tanks and smearing the periscope lenses with plum jam. Another tactic was to hold up a piece of burning paper in front of the lens to panic the tank crew into thinking they were on fire. But in the end, it was all futile. Imre Nagy was tried for treason, found guilty and hanged.

On the 5th of November, Guy Fawkes Day, Catesby and Bone drove as part of a diplomatic convoy to the Austrian border.

'What,' said Bone, 'have we learned?'

'We've learned that Butterfly has blue eyes and a pretty face.'

'I bet you've been busy.'

Catesby and his sister Freddie were walking through the North Denes dunes towards the North Sea. Freddie's frizzy blond hair framed her head like a halo against the early morning sun.

'At GCHQ, we're always busy,' she said with regimental pride. 'We don't spend all our time slushing champagne at cocktail parties waiting for a wink from an undercover KGB colonel.'

'Well actually, Freddie, parties are excellent places to recruit agents.'

'Have you ever done it?'

'Dozens of times.'

'I don't believe you.'

'I exaggerated the numbers.' Catesby had done it exactly four times. Three of his cocktail party conquests had subsequently been found out and executed. The surviving one was lying completely doggo. The executions haunted him. He couldn't understand how his newly recruited agents had been uncovered so quickly.

'Did you,' said Freddie, 'ever bring any of your girlfriends here?'

The North Denes dunes were the lovers' lanes of North Lowestoft. They were fixed dunes thick with bramble rose and hawthorn. There were hundreds of private hollows where privacy was complete.

'I might have.'

'Who did you do it with?'

'I'm not going to tell you – they might be friends of yours.'

'I'm not surprised that you said that.'

'Why?'

'Because sex and espionage are almost the same thing.'

'In what way?' said Catesby.

'If you get caught doing it with the wrong person, it can ruin your whole life. You lose your wife or husband, your kids. You can even get kicked out of your house.'

'I know,' said Catesby.

'Is being unfaithful to someone who loves you worse than being a traitor?'

Catesby leaned close to his sister and whispered. 'I think so, but that's a secret.'

'It's a good thing you didn't tell *them* that?'

'Who?' said Catesby.

'The selection panel. Otherwise, they would never have promoted you. Congratulations.'

'Thanks. How did you know?'

'That's a secret.'

They walked out of the dunes on to the broad beach. A trawler, so close to shore that you could see the helmsman's face, was heading for the harbour entrance. The trawler was one of the older ones that still mounted a mizzen sail to lessen the rolling in a following sea.

'That's Jumbo's boat,' said Catesby waving. Someone on the bridge waved back.

'He wants,' said Freddie, 'to get back in time for Christmas.'

Catesby remembered the harbour from his childhood. Around Christmas time the fishing basin was so packed with returned trawlers and drifters that you could walk across the water from Hamilton Docks to the seawall. And when they steamed up to go back to sea after the first of the year the whole town was covered in a smog of sweet-smelling coal smoke.

Freddie put her arm through her brother's as they walked down to the sea. The wind was from the northeast which meant bitter cold, but clear weather. They squinted as the wind whipped sand and salt spray against their faces. A feeling of cleansing came with the sting. It was as if the winter sea was a vast antiseptic that stripped away dirt.

Freddie looked out to sea, leaned her head against her brother's shoulder and recited their version of the poem:

'Full fathom five our father lies
Of his bones are coral made,
Those are pearls that were his eyes,
Nothing of him doth fade ...'

'You never knew him,' said Catesby.

'And neither did you – even though you pretend to.'

Catesby was a year and a half when his father died; Freddie was five months. Their father hadn't been lost at sea, but buried at sea after he had died of severe concussion during a passage to India. He had slipped on a wet deck in rolling seas and bashed his head on a bollard. It was so unfair. He had survived the war and a bad bout of Spanish flu – which had killed off the two oldest children. Catesby remembered a teacher, who meant well, once telling him that his father's death wasn't a tragedy. 'His death was what we call bathos, a banal anti-climax. It was as if Odysseus had fallen off a stepladder and broken his neck the day after he got back to Penelope.'

Catesby turned into the wind and looked up the beach towards Yarmouth. No one from Lowestoft ever called it *Great* Yarmouth, the name you see on the map. That was tantamount to treason.

'When is Tomasz arriving?' said Catesby.

'On New Year's Eve. You know that he's doing the Christmas shift at Bush House.'

'Is he going to broadcast a Polish translation of the Queen's speech?'

'I think he is.'

'I hope he doesn't add anything extra of his own.'

'Such as?'

'"And finally I would like to say to the people of Poland. If you rise up against your communist oppressors I will send the full force of my army, navy and air force to assist you." Sorry, I'm not very good at royal accents.'

Freddie smiled. 'Tomasz might very well like to add those words to the Queen's message, but he knows that he would get into terrible trouble with the BBC if he did.'

'Maybe he should get a job with Radio Free Europe.'

Freddie frowned. 'Don't joke. Tomasz has considered RFE – and often threatens it when he's having a bad time at Bush House.' She paused. 'In fact, I even think that RFE may have offered him a place.'

'How would you feel if he went?'

'I'd be devastated. It means he'd have to go to Munich, but I don't think he will do it.'

'Because he wants to be near you?'

'I hope so. At least, that's what he tells me.'

Catesby looked out to sea. There was a fair breeze, Force 4 or 5, and he could see the spray flying high above the offshore sand-banks. It was a deceptive and dangerous coast. A frequent drama of childhood was hearing a maroon go off. The maroons were flares that summoned the lifeboat crew. Even if you didn't see the maroon, you heard its almighty pop – and seconds later the sound of boots running towards the harbour. And there was something about his sister's relationship with Tomasz that set off maroons in his mind.

Catesby had mixed feelings about the house on Dene Road. It was larger than the house on Roman Hill where he had been born – and closer to fields and woods and beaches – but it was his mother's house, a Belgian house, and not a home for him and Freddie. It was, of course, at Dene Road that Catesby first realised that he was a spy. The big problem, and one that was never completely resolved, was that Catesby wasn't sure whom he was spying for and whom he was spying against. Or was he secretly working for both? At times Catesby thought he was a Belgian agent working undercover to spy on the English. And at other times, he was an English agent sent to spy on the Belgians. His cleverest ruse of all was that he could speak all the languages – as if he were a real Fleming, a real Walloon or a genuine Englishman. But no one knew which was real and which was false.

Catesby had few memories of Roman Hill, but he did remember the house and the neighbourhood as being English. And you could tell it was a *seagoing* English town. Every terraced house had a salvaged ship's mast at the bottom of the backyard for the washing line – as well as block and tackle for raising and lowering the washing. In those days even his mother seemed almost English. In fact, as a child of three or four, it never occurred to Catesby that she wasn't English. True, she spoke Flemish and French in the privacy of the home, but at that time the languages were just word games, like riddles or hangman. It was fun. Freddie liked to mix all three languages together to create a linguistic Frankenstein that even their mother couldn't understand. The extra languages also gave Catesby and his sister secret codes that they could use between themselves. But as a young child Catesby never thought of himself as English or Belgian, he thought of himself as a loyal supporter of Lowestoft Town Football Club.

Catesby's earliest memory was being bitten by a hen on the way to a football match at Crown Meadow. A lot of families kept chickens in those days. It happened, Catesby was sure, in the alleyway between Seago Street and Wollaston Road. Catesby was with Uncle Jack and

Jumbo at the time. He was excited about going to the match – it was the local derby against Yarmouth – but also fascinated by the sleek hens clucking behind the gates. He managed to get his child's hand through a gap to stroke a hen, but the hen must have thought his finger was a pale worm and nipped it hard.

Catesby couldn't remember whether or not he cried. But he probably didn't cry, because even by the age of three the children of Roman Hill knew that tears were useless things and more likely to earn a slap than a cuddle. But the hen had drawn blood and Jumbo, the trawler skipper, lifted him on to his shoulders from where he watched Lowestoft beat Yarmouth.

During the Roman Hill days Catesby was too young to understand how poor they were. The house was a two-up two-down terrace, but so were all the other houses on Roman Hill. Nonetheless, the family had been comfortable and well fed until Catesby's father died. After that the abyss opened and there wasn't a safety net. It turned Catesby's mother into a hard desperate woman. She left the children with a neighbour and cycled ten miles each day to Beccles where she kept the books for a cattle merchant. She accepted help from her in-laws, but she knew that they were almost as poor. She kept up her charade of independence for almost three years, but then one winter's evening she fell off her bicycle on her way back from Beccles. She was exhausted and malnourished and lost control of her bike when it hit a patch of ice. A fish merchant found her sprawled in the road and brought her and the bike back to Roman Hill in the back of his ill-smelling van. In the morning her knee was too swollen to cycle so she had to 'waste' a precious shilling on rail fare. That evening Catesby knew that something must have been wrong when his mother came back to his bed after she had already tucked him in. She had never done that before. He remembered her hot tears falling on his cheek.

'Slaap kindje, slaap.
Daar buiten loopt een schaap...
Slaap kindje, slaap.'

It must have been about that time that she made the deal with the Belgians.

The house on Dene Road was much bigger than Roman Hill, but

there were a lot more people living in it. Catesby's mother shared a bed with her mother, *Grootmoeder* Bastin, in the front bedroom. His mother's sister, Marieke, who was much older and not completely in her right mind, slept in a tiny box room that was hardly big enough for a single bed. Uncle Théo and his wife Irina had the best bedroom: it had a good fireplace and overlooked the backyard. Catesby and Freddie shared the back bedroom, which was roomy, but freezing even though it faced south. It was a cold house – and damp and draughty too. It would have cost a fortune to heat it all, so they economised by heating just the kitchen and one other room. Catesby remembered doing his homework wearing hat, coat and gloves. On the other hand, there were indoor toilets – a luxury completely unknown on Roman Hill.

Catesby never knew what sort of deal his mother had struck with the Belgians, but it seemed to entail taking on family commitments in exchange for help with expenses. The Belgians were from Antwerp, but his mother's father had been a French-speaking Walloon. Catesby knew they had owned a bar near the docks – and he always assumed that that was where his parents met. He wasn't sure that his mother had always been 'a good girl,' but couldn't imagine her otherwise. From the later perspective of adulthood, Catesby imagined they must have sold the bar to finance the move from Belgium to Dene Road. But he never found out, for the Bastins were more secretive than any intelligence service he had ever encountered. They always seemed to be hiding something dark, something not completely legal.

The only non-Belgian was Irina. She was a Russian *émigrée* who had fled the revolution with her husband, who was allegedly of noble birth. And like many other noble Russian *émigrés*, he made a living by driving a taxi in Paris. Catesby never found out what happened to the princely taxi driver – or how Uncle Théo ended up married to his wife. Once again, the wall of secrecy descended. But Irina, with her dyed red hair and her furs and her perfumes, was wonderful – and she loved Freddie as the daughter she never had. By the time she was ten, Freddie spoke fluent Russian. By the time Catesby was ten he realised he was leading a double life – and wasn't sure who he was.

Catesby knew that he had had an English father and lived in an English county, but when he came home from school and shut the door behind him he was no longer in England. The curtains on the windows behind him were Flanders lace, the words that greeted him were French or Flemish and the smells from the kitchen were European too. And there was the religious tat as well: Irina's Orthodox icons and his mother's rosaries and Blessed Virgins. At least his mother provided him a cover story. Whenever a school friend asked why they were Catholics, Catesby said it was because of the Belgium connection.

That was a lie. The Catesbys were Catholics too. True, they weren't very religious and only attended St Mary's Star of the Sea for christenings, marriages and funerals. But the tradition had never been broken and no Catesby had ever been an Anglican or any other form of Protestant. It was very unusual for a working-class English family without Irish connections to be Catholic. And there was another odd thing too: Guy Fawkes Night. No Catesby ever made a Guy or went to the bonfires. Catesby remembered his Uncle Jack telling off one of his sons. 'We don't go to them things. We never have and we never will. And don't you ask why. Someday you'll find out.'

Burn him in a tub of tar.
Burn him like a blazing star.

Dene Road now had a lot more room, too much. *Grootmoeder* had died when they were still at school. And Uncle Théo and Irina had mysteriously packed up and went back to Belgium in 1945. Catesby thought that Théo might have got involved in the post-war black market – or maybe he had fallen out with his sister, for they seemed to be out of contact. Some families are like that. And poor Marieke had died the previous year. Catesby's mother had found her on the floor wedged in between the base of her narrow bed and the wall. Marieke was already stiff and cold. Catesby couldn't understand why his mother stayed in that cold lonely house. She was nearly seventy. He knew that Christmas was going to be a chore.

Catesby knew there was going to be a lot of spare dull time, especially before Tomasz arrived to cheer things up. Catesby had brought a packed briefcase with him. Not just to pass the time, but because it was work that needed to be done. None of the stuff that he had brought with him was UK EYES ALPHA, but a lot of it was fairly confidential – not the sort of papers you would want to leave behind in a train carriage.

He was working at the same bedroom desk that he had used for homework when he'd been at the boys' grammar. Except that, instead of translating Caesar's *Gallic Wars*, he was preparing budget estimates for various agent networks. It was dull work, but not something that could be delegated because of the level of security. Catesby worked for nearly two hours. It was now dark and getting cold. He could hear his mother and sister talking in the kitchen. It didn't seem fair to leave Freddie alone with their mother, but Catesby was fancying a pint and a game of darts at The Anchor.

As he started putting the files back in his briefcase, Catesby had a funny intuitive feeling. It was like when someone is staring at your back; you can't see them, but you know that they're there. He looked at the compartments of his briefcase. Everything looked normal, but something didn't feel normal. He still had the uncanny sense of being watched. Catesby left the briefcase on his desk and picked up his hairbrush from where he had left it on the chest of drawers. He picked two hairs from the brush. It was the most primitive form of counter-surveillance imaginable, but always worked. He placed one hair between the first and second sheets of the file he had just been working on, and the other between pages 29 and 30 of a briefing document on the UB, the Polish security service, that he had yet to read. He shut and locked the briefcase. The lock was a feeble combination thing that a child of twelve could crack in ten minutes, but it meant that anyone who wanted to sneak a look would have to make an effort. It wouldn't simply be an impulse peep.

As Catesby walked to the pub he felt vaguely ashamed of himself. He felt that his trade was turning him into a paranoid schizo who could trust no one. Maybe that's why his marriage hadn't lasted – or maybe that was wishful thinking. The night was misty and still. Catesby regretted the passing of the gas street lights of his youth. He liked the way they had hissed and pulsed. He wondered what he would have been if he had come back to Lowestoft after the war: town hall official, solicitor, teacher. Probably a teacher. The thought terrified him more than being under fire.

In fact, many of the teachers at Denes Grammar School in the 1930s had served as officers in the Great War. And many were not completely in their right minds. The teacher that Catesby remembered most was Captain Pearse, who taught Greek and Latin. The captain was always impeccably dressed. He wore three-piece tweed suits that looked like they had been woven out of barbed wire under his academic gown. He also carried a great fob watch under his gown that ticked away like a time bomb. Catesby's mother reckoned that Captain Pearse lived beyond his means. He was a member of the local hunt and owned a gleaming yacht that he raced out of the Royal Suffolk and Norfolk Yacht Club. Catesby remembered that Pearse had the most perfect moustache, but the maddest blue eyes. Many of the other boys were terrified of Captain Pearse, but Catesby – even at the age of thirteen – felt sorry for him. One winter morning he found the captain staring out to sea from Gunton Cliff. The wind was coming from the southeast and blowing wintry showers on to the coast. It was as if the dust of Flanders had turned to ice crystal and was being thrown in Captain Pearse's face again. At first, Catesby thought the drops on Pearse's face, as he stared steadily across the North Sea to Flanders, were melted sleet.

It happened about a week later. It was the last class on Friday afternoon and the boys were being little shits, but Captain Pearse was oddly oblivious. He had written the conjugation of the present tense indicative mood on the board. *Amo, amas, amat, amamus, amatis, amant.* He then repeated each word in a voice that was, at first, scarcely above a whisper. The boys were supposed to repeat after him, but they were too busy flicking things and talking. Captain Pearse then said the words in a normal voice, *Amo, amas, amat* … but as he pronounced each word his fist hit the wall. He then repeated the process again, but in a much louder voice and hitting the wall harder. By now the boys had stopped flicking things and were looking at their teacher with bemused interest. This time Captain Pearse was screaming the words in a shrill voice, *Amo, amas* … and hitting the wall so hard that the blackboard was rattling and board rubbers and chalk were falling to the floor. Captain Pearse hadn't got all the way through the conjugation when he slumped to the floor with his back against the wall. His face was covered in sweat and tears and he looked like a heap of rags. The words now came in English: 'I love, you love, he loves, we love, you love, they love … No, not for years, no more, no more …' The exact place – Ypres, Loos, Somme, Passchendaele – no longer mattered. It was all over for Captain Pearse.

When he got back to Dene Road Catesby let himself in with the flower pot key. His mother had already gone to bed, but Freddie was curled up in front of the sitting-room fire with a book. Catesby had paid for a big load of coal so that they would be warm over Christmas. He put his head in the door; the warmth was delicious. 'You should have come to the pub, Fred, you might have got pulled.'

'That's why I stayed here.'

'See you in the morning, sleep well.'

When Catesby got to his room he picked up his sponge bag and headed for the bathroom. He looked at his briefcase and remembered the telltale hairs he had planted. Why bother, he thought.

After he brushed his teeth, Catesby looked at his face in the mirror. The eyes looked like they belonged to someone else: tired, drained, furtive. And why shouldn't they be? They *were* after him: the Sovs, the Americans, the vetting people in personnel, the spy chasers in Five, Butterfly, Bone. They wanted to get him down with both thumbs on his jugulars. Maybe they watched him change trains at Ipswich and followed him to Lowestoft. And Freddie? Not Freddie, surely not her.

Catesby went back into the bedroom and stared at his briefcase. He was calm now. The madness was under control again. He went over to the desk and lined up the combination numbers on the briefcase locks. He opened the case and took out the two files. He held them tight to make sure the telltale hairs wouldn't fall out by accident. He opened the file with the budget estimates and closed his eyes, afraid to look. He opened his eyes again. The hair, brown and greasy, was still there, curled like a question mark that was its own answer. Catesby breathed easy. He then found the Polish security service briefing folder and put it on top of the innocent budget file. He held it down tight and closed, only bending up the page corners to look at the numbers. When he found pages 29 and 30, he slowly opened the folder taking care not to dislodge the hair. The pages shone bright and white under the glare of the desk lamp. The hair wasn't there.

Catesby put everything back in his briefcase and locked it again, which was a bit pointless. He knotted his dressing gown tight around his waist and carefully opened the bedroom door to silence its eerie coffin-lid creak. He didn't want to wake his mother who was a light sleeper. Likewise, he knew through long experience which floorboards and steps to avoid in order to get downstairs without causing disturbance. A crowded childhood home teaches covert action more thoroughly than the best spy school.

When Catesby got downstairs he looked in the sitting room. Freddie had nodded off in front of the fire. Her book lay open on her knees, her chin on her chest. Catesby went into the kitchen and poured a whisky for himself and one for his sister too. He carried the drinks back to the sitting room and put his sister's on top of the fireplace. He sat in the armchair opposite her and looked at her sleeping face. She looked so vulnerable. He could never hurt her; would never hurt her. No matter what.

He didn't know how long he waited, but Freddie eventually yawned and stretched her arms. She opened her eyes and looked at her brother. 'Are you still up?'

'Yes.' He nodded at the fireplace. 'I've poured a drink for you.'

'Thank you.' She sipped the whisky. 'Is something wrong, Will? You look very pale.'

'A maroon went up.'

'I must have been dead to the world, I didn't hear it.'

'It wasn't that sort of maroon.'

Freddie turned her head to one side and looked closely at her brother. 'You seem in a strange mood. Why are you talking riddles?'

'Why are you putting on an act?'

'I'm not sure,' she said, 'what you're talking about.'

'You've been spying on me.'

Freddie flushed and squeezed her glass with both hands. 'I still don't know what you mean.'

'Stop acting, Freddie. You opened my briefcase and went through my files while I was at the pub.'

She looked at the floor; then looked at her brother. The only sound was the tick pulse of the mantel clock. Finally she said, 'Yes, I did. Does that make you feel better?'

'No, I want to know why.'

Freddie shrugged her shoulders. 'Because I was bored. And because you've done the same thing to me.'

Catesby sighed and sipped his whisky. She was right. On a visit to her flat in Cheltenham he had gone through some BJs, the distinctively blue jacketed files used for secret signals intelligence, that she had left on her desk. 'But,' he said, 'they weren't locked in a briefcase.'

Freddie smiled. 'I suppose fiddling the lock was a bit naughty. Are you going to write a report? You could probably get me disciplined.'

'Don't be silly.'

Freddie dropped her voice to a whisper. 'You know, I should probably pass more things on to you.'

'Did you say to me *too*?'

'No, Will, I just said, *to you*. You really are getting paranoid.'

'Sorry.'

'I suppose,' said Freddie, 'that you've seen the latest Pitovranov transcripts. It's my own translation, by the way.'

Catesby smiled. 'Pull the other one, Freddie. The Pitovranov tapes don't exist. The general only uses secure landlines from the Karlshorst compound. No one can touch them. Why are you looking so smug?'

'Because these calls weren't made from Karlshorst. They're from the family flat in Unten den Linden. Madame Pitovranov insisted they move out of the barracks because she wants a more glittering social life.'

Catesby suddenly felt off guard. There was something in Freddie's words that sounded uncomfortably true. 'Go on.'

'I have to admit they don't contain any military secrets – just personal stuff. Pitovranov makes frequent phone calls to his wife when she's in Moscow, and to a woman, that we think is his wife's sister because she shares the same patronym. And sometimes, Pitovranov asks his wife to "kiss Natashka and Mama for me". Unfortunately, Mama seems to have died. And that's about it.' Freddie paused. 'It's sometimes difficult to remember it's the enemy when you hear them sending kisses to Natashka and Mama – and poor Mama.'

Catesby stared into the fire. It was odd that he didn't know about the tapes, however banal. Lieutenant General Yevgeny Petrovich Pitovranov was the KGB *rezident* in East Berlin, a shadowy security-conscious figure who was notoriously difficult to track down. The demons of paranoia began to leap and hiss. Surely, as head of the East Europe P Section, he ought to have known. 'What's the source,' said Catesby, 'where did you get it?'

'It's listed as a "clandestine source of established authenticity".'

'We don't use that sort of terminology – and neither does GCHQ.' Catesby felt something tighten in his chest. 'You got the tape from the Americans.'

'Well,' said Freddie, 'I suppose we did.' She paused. 'You see, Will, they share things with us that they won't share with you. GCHQ has never had a Burgess or a Maclean.'

Catesby smiled. 'Yet.'

'I shouldn't have told you about it. The Americans share their sources with us because we've got better language skills, but none of it is supposed to go outside GCHQ.'

'They're trying to turn our intelligence agencies against each other.'

'But we gave them a head start – just look at yourselves and Five.'

'Listen, Freddie.'

'What?'

'Be careful. I don't want you to get in trouble.'

'So you don't want me to pass anything on to you, no matter how useful?'

'It's not a good idea. I'm going to bed.'

'But I want to, Will. I want to make up for peeping at your poxy budget figures.'

Catesby leaned forward to give his sister a goodnight kiss. '*Slaap kindje slaap.*'

Later, Catesby found it difficult to sleep. He got up twice to adjust the curtains to stop the moonlight from coming in, but it didn't make any difference. The telltale hair in the budget folder had still been in place. Freddie had been in his briefcase and reading his files long before he went to the pub. That evening had been her second go, at least.

It wasn't, thought Catesby, such a bad Christmas dinner. There was *marcassin des Flandres*, *aardappel kroketjes*, *endives au gratin* – and, of course, Brussels sprouts. The only guests were Monsieur Lemaire and Father Sinclair. They rhymed. Lemaire was Lowestoft's only spare Belgian. He had been an RAF pilot during the war and had crash-landed his damaged Hurricane in the Pas de Calais. Lemaire spent the next four years as a PoW, but what really bothered him was the guilt of having lost the expensive fighter plane with which his host country had entrusted him. Since the war he had earned a living as a French teacher, but devoted all his spare time to charity work – as if he had to pay Britain back for the lost Hurricane. Lemaire was the most *correct* person that Catesby had ever met. His manners were impeccable without being grand. His shoes were always perfectly shined; his shirts a tribute to the art of *blanchissage*, and his overall appearance effortlessly walked the tightrope between understatement and elegance.

Father Sinclair was more fun. He looked the sort of bloated priest or cardinal that you see in anti-clerical cartoons. His father had been a British diplomat who had married a French countess. His mother's family owned a chateau in Bordeaux. Sinclair always arrived for a dinner party with two bottles of claret from the family estate – and then spent most of the evening apologising for the wine's deficiencies.

Sinclair turned to Catesby after serving himself a second helping of *aardappel kroketjes*. 'Are you still in Bonn?'

'Yes,' said Catesby keeping to his cover story, 'but recently I've had to spend a lot of time at the Foreign Office.'

'I suppose the upcoming Treaty of Rome must be causing some headaches in Whitehall.' Sinclair was referring to the treaty that was due for signing in three months' time. The treaty was going to lay the foundation for the European Economic Community, 'an ever closer union among the peoples of Europe'.

'It's a pity,' said Catesby, 'that we can't join.'

Sinclair had the instinct of a Jesuit for the nuances of words. 'Why,' he said, 'do you say "can't" rather than "won't" join?'

'Because they, particularly the French, wouldn't have us even if we wanted membership. They think that Britain would be a Trojan horse for the Americans to get into Europe.'

'Is that true?'

'Sadly, yes. The Suez debacle means that we're going to become more and more dependent on Washington. It's a pity we don't spend more time looking across the Channel and the North Sea instead of across the Atlantic.'

Father Sinclair smiled and looked across the table at Monsieur Lemaire.

Catesby felt a little naughty. Talking to a Roman Catholic priest about Britain going in to Europe was like discussing the possibility of a UK workers' revolt with the Soviet *rezident*. European integration wasn't treason now, not quite, but it had been in 1605.

Rememember, remember the 5th of November,
The Gunpowder Treason and Plot ...

Catesby felt sorry for Lemaire. His mother always invited him in the forlorn hope that somehow a relationship between Freddie and

Lemaire would spring up – and that Freddie would ditch Tomasz. It wasn't going to happen. Lemaire was far more likely to join an order of ascetic monks than become a lover or husband. Catesby imagined that if you did get Lemaire's clothes off, you would only find layer after layer of impeccably starched white linen. But, on the other hand, those types could sometimes surprise.

Tomasz arrived at midday on New Year's Eve, just as Catesby was leaving. North Lowestoft Station was conveniently located at the end of Dene Road. Catesby shook hands with the Pole as he got off the train.

'I'm sorry you're not staying,' said Tomasz.

'We've got the same deal as you – either Christmas or New Year, but not both. Listen, I've got to go, my train's coming in now.'

'Sure, Will. Have a happy New Year.'

Before he crossed to the other platform to catch the London train, Catesby grabbed Tomasz by his coat collar and pulled him close. Catesby was smiling so it was impossible to tell whether or not it was a joke – and Tomasz was smiling too. Two lads playing about.

'If,' said Catesby, 'you ever do anything to hurt my sister, I will fucking kill you.'

The party at the *Volksbühne* in East Berlin was a pretty drunken one. But it proved to be an important one. It changed Catesby's life. The guests included a large cross section of dips and other officials from both East and West, but most of the arts crowd came from the East. Catesby recognised a lot of them from Brecht's funeral, but he didn't know the dark bearded man who was swaying back and forth in front of him – except that he was a professor. He was stinking drunk.

The professor, who spoke good English, looked Catesby directly in the eye and said, 'I know you – you're a spy.'

Catesby smiled wanly, half wondering whether his cover was really so transparent. 'I'm sorry you think that, but I'm not.'

The professor swayed dangerously, but continued to stare directly at Catesby as if that was the only way he could keep his balance. 'Would you like to know how I know you're a spy?'

Catesby gave a conspiratorial wink and nodded his head.

'It's because you pretended to enjoy that film – it's boring shit.'

'Well, I did enjoy it, but if I am only pretending, it's not because I'm a spy, it's because I'm a bloody *diplomat*.'

The drunken professor seemed a little taken aback by Catesby's apparent annoyance. 'Ah,' he said, 'maybe ...'

While Catesby waited for the professor to finish his sentence, he was eavesdropping on another conversation a few feet away. A member of the Soviet delegation was introducing himself to the Australian Cultural Attaché. The Russian introduced himself. 'My name is Vladimir Volkov.'

The Aussie smiled and said, 'My name is Richard, and so can you.'

Catesby didn't recognise the Australian; he must be new. But Volkov – who didn't get the joke – worked for the Soviet Export Film Office. Meanwhile the professor had disappeared. Catesby turned to the Russian to say hello and then winked and raised his empty glass to show that he was going for a refill. But what Catesby really wanted to do was to circulate and sniff around. For that's what spies do at receptions and cocktail parties. They are uncouth dogs who sniff in uncouth places. And Berlin was a spy dog's fondest nose dream. Every kerb stone led to a lamp post sprayed with conundrums and come-ons – and which were real and which were false? The city could drive a dog mad.

1950s Berlin was a gap in the iron curtain. People could move freely between the Soviet and Western sections of the city. And there were even a number of East Berliners who worked in the West and vice versa. The anomaly turned the city into a Western listening post, a NATO intelligence island, located 110 miles inside East Germany. And likewise, Berlin was a port of entry for agents from the East.

Khrushchev called Berlin an 'espionage swamp'. And he was right. Catesby reckoned that espionage was the single biggest source of employment in Berlin. Spying provided the main income for one out of thirty of the city's working population – including foreigners of course. And if you added in the part-timers, the IMs – the *Inoffizieller Mitarbeiter* – it was one in ten who made money out of espionage. Not all of these people, of course, were fully trained intelligence professionals. But there was an army of watchers, couriers, drivers, informers, locksmiths and engineers who supported those who were. If you went to a party in Berlin, you could assume with good reason – as had the professor – that the person you were talking to was a spy. And if that party was put on by DEFA, the East German state film company, you were likely to meet spies – especially ones pretending to be Cultural Attachés.

The party was to celebrate the debut of *Lissy*, a film about a working-class girl who decides to leave her Nazi husband. The film's ideology wasn't subtle, but Catesby had been impressed by the acting and cinematography. He was still hanging around because he wanted to meet the film's director – who was regarded as a pretty hot contact for reasons that had nothing to do with cinema. But it wasn't easy to get near the director. He was protected by a wall of DEFA colleagues and a pair of state security minders as well. It was easy to pick out the MfS. They were fitter and better looking than the film types. The only people who seemed to get access to the director were young attractive women – who, Catesby was sure, had been vetted for Western honey trap infection by the MfS. Making contact with the director seemed a hopeless task.

Catesby decided he needed another drink. As he made his way to the bar, Catesby felt someone at his elbow. It was Elmo Buckner from the US Embassy. Elmo wasn't pretending to be a Cultural Attaché; he was pretending to be a representative of the USIS, the United States Information Service – which was pretty useful cover, for the USIS worked hand in hand with the CIA in any case. Maybe Elmo did both jobs.

'How you doing, Catesby,' said Elmo, 'did you manage to stay awake?'

'Actually, I thought it was quite a good film.'

'Ah, come on pal, all that party line crap was more boring than a Walter Ulbricht speech. Typical DEFA stuff, just a load of commie bullshit.'

'How d'you know? I thought you fell asleep?'

'You only need to see the first five minutes. Propaganda brainwash.'

'It's a lot better than most of the rubbish coming out of Hollywood since McCarthy got your best directors and actors blacklisted.'

Elmo gave Catesby a playful punch on the upper arm. 'What you drinking?'

Catesby told him.

Elmo turned to an unsmiling woman who seemed to find serving drinks to Westerners a distasteful duty. *'Ein Schnaps für Ihren sozialistischen englischen Kameraden.'*

'Thanks,' said Catesby, 'your German is better than your English.'

Elmo ignored the comment. 'All you Limeys are socialists – that's why you liked that lousy film. But I have to admit that dame playing the lead was pretty hot stuff. What's her name?'

'Sonja Sutter,' Catesby gestured to the group surrounding the director, 'that's her over there. Would you like her autograph?'

'I wouldn't mind her something else.'

Catesby looked at Elmo. He was one of those Americans whose head seemed to grow straight out of his shoulders. 'Go on,' said Catesby, 'have a go. Tell Sonja you're a talent scout for Cecil B. DeMille.'

'Look at that director guy,' said Elmo, 'big bear of a man with thick glasses. Not much to look at, but I bet he gets more pussy every week than both of us ever will get in a lifetime.'

'Are you married?' said Catesby.

'Yeah, most of the time.' Elmo pointed to the director. 'Do you remember that guy's name?'

'I don't know. Let me see.' Catesby reached into his pocket to get the leaflet with the credit details. 'Konrad Wolf. Have you ever heard of him?'

'No,' said Elmo, 'can't say I have.'

Catesby bit his lip to stop smiling. They were both pathetic actors.

'But I know that I don't like his films.' Elmo sipped his drink and made a face. 'And East German whisky is crap too – and they charge three bucks a bottle for this poison.'

Catesby suddenly felt uneasy. Maybe he was wrong. Maybe Elmo hadn't been lying about not knowing Wolf. And if the CIA didn't realise the significance of Konrad Wolf, then maybe he had no significance at all. Perhaps Elmo's acting had seemed so poor because it hadn't been an act. Catesby began to feel dizzy – and it was only partly owing to the drink and the empty stomach. The game was an endless tossing of coins – and half the time the coin rolled under a dresser where it was lost in the dark mess of spiderweb and mouse dropping.

'Listen,' said Elmo, 'I want to ask you a question. Were you at Cambridge with those queers?'

'Which particular queers?'

'You know, the traitors, Burgess and Maclean.'

'Not quite, they were about ten years ahead of me.'

'But you, uh, most have known some of the same guys, same professors, breathed the same air?'

'I don't want to sound patronising, but …'

'I've never heard you or any other Englishman sound any other way?'

'You make it difficult not to.'

The American raised his glass. 'Touché.'

'Sure, Elmo, I went to Cambridge, but it wasn't the Cambridge of Burgess and Maclean. They came from the upper-class elite, the aristocracy. I was far removed from that – and still am. You see, Elmo, I am common – I am working class.'

'Then why do you sound so upper-crust?'

'I may to you, Elmo, but you haven't English ears.'

The American finished his drink. 'You guys are strange. Listen, I'd better circulate – otherwise people might get the wrong idea about *us*. Nice talking to you.'

Catesby felt relieved to see Elmo waddle off. He suspected,

however, there was another side to Elmo behind the role playing. Whenever an American spoke a foreign language fluently it meant there was something odd, something hidden. Catesby needed to circulate and sniff around. He tried to avoid eye contact with other Westerners. His job wasn't to hang around with diplomats and intelligence officers from the West. Too often it happened that way at East Bloc social events. All the Western intelligence agents end up talking and drinking with each other – like journalists interviewing other journalists.

The reception room was severe and functional. The only decorations on the bare concrete walls were cinema stills and posters. One of the posters proclaimed International Women's Day. The woman in the poster was wearing blue overalls and a red headscarf. She was standing next to a factory machine and had a huge spanner in her right hand. Catesby did a double take. A tall blonde woman standing in the crowd around Konrad Wolf was the spitting image of the woman on the poster. Catesby saw his chance and, ignoring the stern glances of the MfS minders, walked over to the woman.

'Excuse me,' he said gesturing clumsily towards the poster, 'but is that …'

'No, it's not her poster, it's mine.' The answer came from a small dark woman. She wasn't the sort of woman one noticed in a crowd. Her sudden appearance reminded Catesby of a wren darting out of a hedge.

'I meant,' said Catesby nodding at the tall blonde, 'that …'

'No, I painted it, so it is mine. Katrina was only the model.'

'All right, I agree, it's yours.'

The tall blonde excused herself. 'I must go see Ute, I come back later.'

The dark woman looked at Catesby with something like disdain. She seemed, he thought, to have placed him as a womaniser who chases blondes. 'And who,' she said, 'are you?'

'Pablo Picasso.'

'That's not very funny.'

Catesby could see that the woman was not overly charmed. But when he looked at her more closely, he found himself attracted. Her face was alive and full of changefulness. There was something odd about her, but an intriguing oddness that held the eye like a magnet. She was beautiful in a way that a beautiful woman can never be. She reminded Catesby of a woman who used to keep snails for pets – and for whom all Cambridge longed.

'Ahhh …' It was a very long 'ahhh' and came from someone who had just joined them. The voice was familiar. 'I know this man, Petra, he is a British diplomat.'

Catesby turned to face the man. It was Gerhard Eisler.

'We last met,' said Eisler, 'at Brecht's funeral and before that we met in …'

'I am sure,' said Catesby, 'that the funeral was the first time we met.'

'Memory is a strange country. When you go back there after a long time it is always different.'

Catesby was aware of Eisler's intent stare and wondered if the German was a shark sent to inspect the bait. Catesby felt nervous under Eisler's eyes and turned to Petra, the dark artist.

In response, she looked away from him and spoke instead to Eisler. 'I think,' she said, 'I should go see Katrina. I think she's upset about something.'

'It was nice to meet you,' said Catesby.

The woman walked away without answering.

'Petra can be difficult,' said Eisler, 'but she's a talented artist.'

'At painting propaganda posters?'

'Raising the people's awareness is a very important function. Nonetheless, I take your point, posters are not always the most creative outlet for an artist, but Petra does other things too – you ought to come to her studio.'

Catesby finished his schnapps.

Eisler took the empty glass. 'Let me get you another one.'

'Thanks.' Catesby knew the script. He had to play a role that included drunkenness, loneliness and ideological disillusion. Many a diplomat and spy had paced the same boards before him. It was an easy role to play.

Eisler didn't need to go to the bar to get served. He was Head of East German Radio, the bar came to him. A waiter suddenly appeared bearing a tray. As soon as Catesby sipped the schnapps he knew it was colder and better quality. The Party looks after its own.

'How,' said Eisler in English, 'is your old pal, Kit Fournier?'

Catesby was surprised at the boldness of the question. 'I don't know – I haven't seen him for ages.'

'A little birdie told me that Kit has been a very bad boy,' said Eisler.

'That's interesting. Who was this birdie?'

'He was one that travels a lot. How do you call them?'

'We call them seasonal migrants: swallows, cuckoos – and winter visitors from Siberia.'

'It might have been one of those. So how is Kit?'

'I wouldn't know,' said Catesby.

'That's very strange.'

'What's strange?'

'That you don't know. Didn't you become good friends when he was assigned to Bonn?'

'I knew Mr Fournier – I know a lot of people from the US Embassy. We try to show them the ropes, how not to make mistakes.'

Eisler smiled. 'And they didn't always appreciate a helping hand from their older, oh so wiser British allies.'

'Not always.'

'What a pity. Maybe if Kit Fournier had listened to you, he wouldn't have got in trouble.'

'I've got a big enough job keeping myself out of trouble.'

'Ah,' said Eisler, 'I find that hard to believe.'

Catesby looked at the short, plump, balding man in front of him. Eisler's cover was perfect. The exterior was a disguise that hid ruthlessness, bravery and romance. Eisler won five decorations for bravery during the First World War. And he was a seducer too. The American press had described his first wife as a 'vampish Viennese actress'.

'Listen,' said Eisler, 'you must meet Koni.'

Catesby let Eisler guide him by the elbow through the group surrounding the film director. The MfS minders were more relaxed. Eisler put his arm around Koni Wolf as if he were a Hollywood impresario sealing a deal.

'Koni,' said Eisler, 'I want you to meet my English friend, William Catesby. He speaks Russian.'

Catesby smiled blandly. Eisler had clearly, perhaps with the help of a secret MfS file, done his homework and wanted to show off the fact.

Wolf blinked in Catesby's direction through thick spectacles. The lenses made it difficult to catch the director's eyes. Catesby wasn't sure if Wolf was looking at him – and, if so, whether the look was one of interest or disdain. He remembered what the Hungarian actress had said about Koni: not as good looking as the father or brother. And Catesby could see what she meant. Wolf's features were thick and ungainly. But there was also something gentle and intelligent.

Finally, Wolf leaned towards Catesby. Despite Eisler's advice, Koni spoke in English instead of Russian. In a voice just above a whisper he said, 'The brave don't cry.'

Catesby was taken aback. He was sure that the words were a code, but didn't know what to reply. 'I don't know,' whispered Catesby, 'what you mean?'

Wolf looked disappointed. He blinked a few more times and said, '*The Brave Don't Cry*: it's about a mining disaster in Scotland. It's an excellent film.'

'Oh, that one.'

'You mean there's another film by the same name?'

'No ...'

Another large man had just arrived who was giving Koni a bear hug and speaking to him in Russian. It reminded Catesby that Berlin was an espionage swamp so full of fauna that even the juiciest prey had to queue up and wait to be eaten. But at least he had met Konrad Wolf, the only brother. He wondered how many onion layers he would have to peel off before he found his way to Mischa – the spy without a face. Who knows? Maybe Mischa was there. It would have been churlish for him not to come – Mischa's office at MfS HQ was only a ten-minute drive. Catesby looked around at the milling guests and wondered which face belonged to the man without a face.

Catesby couldn't remember exactly how he left the *Volksbühne* party. But he had a fuzzy recollection of a heated political argument with Elmo Buckner. It must have been a good argument because he vaguely remembered Elmo grabbing him around the neck and someone dragging Elmo away. Catesby touched his shirt collar. It really was torn, so the fight really must have happened. Catesby smiled. Fancy that. He hoped the incident compared favourably to the embarrassing wobblies that Guy Burgess used to throw in Washington. The best one required an apology from the British Ambassador. Burgess, bored and drunk at a dinner party, had drawn an obscene cartoon of a senior CIA officer's wife. He then presented it to the husband. But Catesby hadn't misbehaved because he was bored or drunk; he had misbehaved because he was playing to an audience.

The fresh winter air must have made Catesby calm and sober for he clearly remembered walking home with Petra. They had left the party separately, but at the same time. Catesby remembered watching her unlock her bicycle from a railing. He walked over and said, 'Why do you need to lock your bike? I thought we were in the German Democratic Republic.'

'I need to lock it so it doesn't get stolen by a thief from the West. One day,' she said, 'we'll have to build an anti-fascist protection wall. Shit.'

'What's the matter?'

'I've got a puncture.'

'Shall I help mend it?'

'No, you're too drunk and I haven't got a repair kit.'

'Shall we find you a taxi?'

'I can walk – it's less than two kilometres.'

Catesby put his hands in his pockets and started walking beside her. He was surprised that she didn't ask where he was going. They were walking along a long straight empty boulevard called Torstrasse. For a while the only sound between them was the click-click of her bicycle sprocket.

As they turned off into another wide empty boulevard called Chausseestrasse, Petra said, 'Do you know Gerhard's brother Hanns?'

'I've heard of him.'

Petra laughed. 'Hanns wrote the national anthem.' She began to sing, '*Auferstanden aus Ruinen … Rising from the ruins and turning to the future*. But Hanns does other things too – he wrote a lot of music for Brecht.'

'He writes national anthems like you paint posters for International Women's Day.'

'There's no comparison. Our national anthem is a beautiful piece of music that is also accessible to the masses. My poster is not beautiful – and I'm not even sure it's accessible. I should have made her prettier, more feminine. It's a difficult balance – the worker, the woman.'

'They're both beautiful.'

'You'd make a good Party member.'

'Are you a member?' asked Catesby.

'Of course.'

Catesby recognised the Dorotheenstadt Cemetery coming up on their left. Something about Brecht's funeral, an odd sense of déjà vu, floated into his mind. Something about Petra had triggered it. He had heard her voice before.

Catesby looked at her. 'Can you sing again, please?'

'What, more GDR national anthem?'

'No, I want you to sing something by Brecht-Weill.'

'I like the bit at the end of the MacHeath song.'

'Go on.'

'*Und die einen … And some are in the dark*
And some are in the light.
But you only see the ones in the light
You don't see the ones in the dark.'

'I remember you singing it at Brecht's funeral. I couldn't see you, but I could hear you.'

'We were very drunk.'

'Are you drunk now?'

'I must be, otherwise I wouldn't be walking with you.'

'Thanks.'

'You're welcome. By the way,' Petra pointed to the top floor of a building opposite the cemetery, 'that's where Brecht used to live. He was a great man. He could have stayed in Hollywood and become a millionaire with a Cadillac, but he chose to come back here and live in a socialist state.'

'But he could criticise the system because of his status.'

Petra shrugged. 'That's true – and it's the same with Koni Wolf.'

'And because he's Mischa's brother?'

'Is that a question or a statement?'

'That depends on your answer.'

'I think,' said Petra, 'that Koni and Mischa use each other. But they can only do that because they love each other dearly.'

'Should you be telling me these things?'

'I told you I was drunk. This is where I live. Are you going to come up?'

'Do you want me to?'

'Yes.'

'Is it because you work for Mischa?'

'I don't work for Mischa.' Petra turned away to lock her bicycle. Then said over her shoulder, 'Maybe it's best you just go.'

'I shouldn't have said that.'

'No, you shouldn't have.'

Catesby gently touched the back of Petra's neck under her thick dark hair. 'I'm sorry.'

'Katrina works for Mischa. You should have gone with her.'

'I'm sorry that I offended you. It was wrong of me.' Catesby took his hand away. 'I must go. Goodbye.'

Petra turned to face him. 'You shouldn't say bad things.'

Catesby put his lips against her forehead. 'I don't want to go.'

Petra took his hand in both hers. 'Listen, if I invite you up for sex, don't think you're going to get a cup of coffee too. I'm not that sort of girl.'

Petra's room faced east. There weren't any curtains and the morning sun just walked in. Petra was curled up against Catesby with only the top of her head above the *Federbett* duvet. He felt her breath against his chest, but was afraid to move lest he wake her. Without getting up the only thing that Catesby could see through the windows were factory roofs and chimneys. He could have been in a northern English mill town – except that one of the chimneys was adorned with a red hammer and sickle.

Catesby put his face close to the top her head. Her hair had a faint smell of musk, like a cat's. He wanted to hold her close to him again, but was afraid of waking her. The parts of her touching him seemed almost accidental, like a train traveller who falls asleep against you – but much more intimate. Her face was against his chest, her hand lay on his ribs; one knee was firmly tucked into his thigh and a toe tickled his ankle.

Catesby lay still and assessed the damage. He didn't have a hangover. It had been good schnapps and he hadn't mixed his drinks. He was in bed with a complete stranger. Not a new experience, but not a bad one either. And there had been bad ones – and not just with strangers. He suddenly realised how lonely he had been – and how loneliness can be dangerous. And it was odd – and a bit silly – to be happy.

Catesby squinted. The sun had just risen over the factory roofs.

A ray of sharp light started to tap its way through his forehead. The message was getting through. The sun was annoyed that Catesby was lazing about in bed and not doing his job. Whatever it was that had made him happy jumped up and ran for the door. Catesby felt himself turn so cold that he was afraid the sudden chill would wake Petra. But what did it matter if she did wake up? He was a player – and despite her denials – so was she. Petra was a Party member and Party duty would make her report the liaison and all its details to the MfS. And that, of course, was exactly what Catesby wanted her to do. The sun seemed to be smiling.

Petra suddenly stretched and yawned, but her eyes were still closed. Then she opened her eyes and looked directly into Catesby's. He tried to stay cold and rational. If they did make love again, it was only going to be sex – that other stuff was too dangerous. Once you went down that route you were a goner. Catesby didn't want to turn into another Kit Fournier.

Petra put her arm around him and whispered, 'Listen, I shouldn't have done this.'

'Then why did you do it?'

'Partly because I was drunk, but mostly because I was lonely. I hope you're not disappointed.'

'Thank you for being honest.'

'But listen, I wouldn't have invited you back here if I hadn't liked you.' Petra smiled. 'Why are you doing that?'

'Let's find out.'

Afterwards, Catesby ground coffee beans while Petra laid out breakfast: black bread, quark curd cheese, honey, jam and tinned milk. The kitchen area was so tiny it was difficult not to get in each other's way. Catesby was glad there were tasks. It was still too soon to talk. When the coffee was ready, they drank it out of bowls without handles. Catesby could see that Petra enjoyed feeling the warmth in her hands. She closed her eyes and looked as full of bliss as a Pre-Raphaelite angel on morphine.

While Petra washed up the breakfast things, Catesby went downstairs to repair the bicycle tyre. The bike was outside in the Chausseestrasse and this suited him perfectly. He was going to take his time with the repair because he wanted to be seen by as many people as possible. The GDR was a surveillance society and the least he could expect was being reported by an unpaid informer. But as this was *Berlin Mitte*, he should also be able to attract the eye of an IM part-timer or an MfS professional. He had, after all, just spent the night with a member of the SED, the ruling Socialist Unity Party, and it would be very unlikely if no one noticed. Catesby was sure a report would get back to MfS headquarters in Normannenstrasse before the end of the day.

It was also likely that the news would travel in the opposite direction too – for East Berlin was riddled with Western agents too. Catesby imagined a report winging its way to Washington: Subject has established contact and is on friendly terms with ... The CIA was going to love it. But, if a similar cable went to London, Catesby could only hope and pray that Henry Bone would cover for him. It was a dangerous game – and deciding who to trust was the most difficult call.

When he was finished, Catesby spun the tyre to make sure that it was true. Just as he was about to turn the bike upright, an elderly woman spoke to him.

'Are you Walter?' she said.

Catesby felt a cold shiver go down his spine. Walter Telemann was the cover name he had used while posing as an MfS in Budapest. He didn't know what to say.

'Walter, is that you?' The woman blinked and stared at his face. She seemed to have difficulty seeing.

Finally Catesby said, 'Walter who?'

'Walter Hartmann, my son.'

'No, I'm not him.'

The woman suddenly seemed to shrink. 'Oh, I'm sorry. I thought maybe Walter had come back. It's been fourteen years, but I still haven't seen his name on any of the lists.'

The woman sighed and continued on her way up the Chausseestrasse. Catesby turned the bike upright, chained it to a lamp post and went back to Petra's flat.

'I've repaired your tyre.'

'That was very kind of you.'

'I'd better wash my hands and be going.'

'Do you have to go so soon?'

Catesby was taken aback. She seemed disappointed. 'What did you have in mind?'

'Maybe a walk along the Spree or through Volkspark.'

Catesby took her hand. 'It's a difficult situation. I've got to go back to work.'

'Will you get in trouble if you're late?'

'Possibly, but it won't be for being late.' Catesby looked at her closely. 'What do you think I do for a living?'

'Oh … I'm not sure. I heard someone say you work for the British government.'

'Yes, but they don't own me – they just pay my wages.'

'Okay.'

'I would like to see you again.'

'That would be nice.'

Catesby kissed her. 'I have to go to London for a while, but I will come back.'

Petra touched his neck. 'Poor you, your shirt collar is torn. Can I sew it for you?'

'It'll do for now, but I'll bring it with me when I come back.' Catesby paused. 'It was nice meeting you.'

'It was nice meeting you.'

'And can you pass on my best wishes to Frau Hartmann?'

'That poor woman. She doesn't understand that her son is never coming back – she is a little mad.'

'History is a cruel master.'

Petra's eyes flashed. 'Only if you let it be.'

'I'm very impressed by how well this is going.' Henry Bone was leaning back with his hands behind his head. Catesby wondered if he was doing some sort of exercise. Earlier, he had been surprised to see a rowing machine tucked away in a dark corner of Bone's office.

'I'm not sure,' said Catesby, 'Eisler seems to have taken the bait too readily.'

'He remembers you from his Oakley Street interrogation in '49. He's probably had his eye on you ever since.'

'But, Henry, Eisler isn't even part of the MfS. He's the propaganda *Meister* for radio.'

'That makes it easier for both of you – especially you. He's not an intelligence officer, so you're not a traitor.'

'I can't see the point of these fictions.'

'It also makes it easier for Mischa Wolf.'

Catesby yawned. Bone had a habit of thinking aloud.

'As you know,' continued Bone, 'there seems to be bad blood between Wolf and his boss, Mielke. Erich Mielke is a puritanical communist from a poor working-class background. He resents Wolf's airs and graces and is always looking for an excuse to bring Mischa down a peg or two. Therefore, Wolf isn't going to risk making a pass with one of his professionals in case you turn out to be a planted "dangled double". It's all office politics. Wolf doesn't want to give Mielke another stick to beat him with.'

Catesby yawned again.

'I'm sorry you find this so boring.'

'Not at all, Henry, please go on.'

'I intend to. It already seems that Mischa Wolf is using Eisler and the arts crowd as unofficial "access agents" to see what you're like.'

Catesby was now more alert. 'It still doesn't make sense. If Mischa accepts the advice of Eisler that I might be a genuine double, then at some point Wolf must risk making an official MfS recruitment pitch. He could still get a face full of custard.'

'Ah,' said Bone, 'and that, Catesby, is why Mischa is an artist and you are a mere craftsman.'

'When Mischa repaints the Sistine Chapel I hope he puts in some girls.'

'Sometimes, Catesby, you are a perfect example of the English philistine. But it appears that Mischa has already put girls into the picture.'

'But not Petra.'

'Surely,' said Bone, 'you don't think Petra is an innocent civilian.'

'She may not be, but she isn't a honey trap professional either.'

'We'll see.'

'Fine,' said Catesby. 'By the way, I thought you were about to tell me Mischa's master plan.'

'I'm not sure there is one, but I do know that Mischa has more cunning and guile than his boss.' Bone paused. 'You must realise that Mischa is a lot more intelligent than Mielke.'

'I'm not sure I agree,' said Catesby, 'I detect a strong whiff of class prejudice.'

'May I continue?'

'Please.'

'Mischa,' said Bone, 'is master of the double and triple bluff. If Eisler and the others report back to Mischa that you are ripe to double, Mischa is going to say no. He's going to refuse to recruit you.'

'End of story.'

'Of course not, it's a Mischa ruse – and the others, at least Eisler, will be in on it too.' Bone walked over to the rowing machine and seated himself.

'Next step?'

'Eisler – and maybe even Koni Wolf – will arrange a private meeting with Mielke. They're going to say something like, "We have come as loyal Party members and we all are very concerned about Mischa's decision. We are worried about him. Mischa has been drinking a lot lately and there are marital difficulties ..." etc. Mielke is going to love it.' Bone had begun to pull on the oars and was sliding back and forth as the oarsman's seat slid on its greased tracks.

'And override Mischa's decision.'

'Abslolutely. And give him a direct order to recruit you whether he likes it or not.'

'I'll bet you a fiver you're wrong.'

'Good ... but in some ways I hope I lose the bet.'

'Why?'

'Because if I win, and it really works out that way,' Bone stopped rowing and looked at Catesby without smiling, 'you'll probably think I've been working for Mischa all along.'

Catesby looked away and said, 'There's another issue we need to discuss.'

'I'm sure there are many.' Bone got up from the rowing machine and went back to his desk.

'If they do recruit me,' said Catesby, 'who I am allowed to betray?'

Bone looked down at his desk blotter as if the names were materialising from the ink stains. It was the most painful part of planting a fake double. In order to prove 'genuine', the plant has to provide real intelligence and sacrifice real agents. Making the list is an awful decision.

Finally Bone looked up. 'We'll get you a list and it's going to mean giving up a few jewels. But it's worth it if we find Butterfly.'

Catesby wondered if 'find' was a euphemism, but something else was bothering him too. 'What about ORIOLE/CATCHER – he, she or they seem to have gone off the agenda?'

Bone looked slightly annoyed. 'I'm wondering whether ORIOLE and/or CATCHER ever existed.'

Catesby could tell there was something odd about Bone's demeanour. It was as if he was keeping something back. He wondered if Bone had made a mistake; if he had got codenames confused. Or if he had resolved ORIOLE/CATCHER by other means. It was, he thought, best to change the subject.

'Have I got,' said Catesby, 'an insurance policy?'

'You want us to cover your back?'

'That's right.'

'And by an insurance policy, you mean something like a top secret ledger signed by all the members of the JIC with copies to the Cabinet Office, the FO and the National Archives saying something like, "William Catesby had the full authority of HMG to pass on classified information to a foreign intelligence agency, etc."?'

'That would be lovely.'

'Well, Catesby, that isn't going to happen and you know it.'

'Listen, Henry, if anything goes wrong, it's just your word between my freedom and twenty-five years at Wormwood Scrubs.'

Bone smiled and nodded towards the rowing machine. 'That's why I'm keeping fit. I want to be there in case you need me.'

'On the other hand, Henry, you might end up in the dock beside me.'

Bone stared blankly back.

It was late evening when Catesby got back to Tachbrook Street. It was a weekend, but Freddie was there alone because Tomasz was on duty at Bush House. As Catesby hung up his coat, Freddie nudged his briefcase with her foot.

'Have you got any new secrets for me?' she said.

'That's not funny.'

'You're in a ratty mood tonight.'

'That's because I'm a rat.'

'Are you hungry?'

'I'll make my own supper.'

Freddie sat next to Catesby as he ate tinned corned beef, boiled potatoes and cabbage. It was the sort of meal they used to eat during the war. Rationing hadn't finally ended until 1954, but Catesby missed it. He thought rationing had been a good thing – a leveller – and provided a healthy diet. It was another of his views that wasn't very popular at Broadway Buildings. But such lefty quirks did add to his cover story persona. Catesby wondered if the MfS had started profiling him at meetings in East Berlin: 'His colleagues in the intelligence service think Herr Catesby is strange. He approves of rationing and state schools.'

'Would you like another beer?' said Freddie.

'Only if you share it with me.'

'All right.'

As his sister poured the beer, Catesby picked up the corned beef tin. 'I wonder,' he said, 'if this beef comes from an Argentine ranch being run by one of the ODESSA Nazis that the CIA helped escape?'

'You're not very happy, Will.'

'I'm just tired.'

'Are you still angry about my looking through your files at Christmas?'

Catesby didn't answer.

'I'm worried,' said Freddie, 'about GCHQ not passing things on.'

'If you do the Americans will cut off your supplies of chewing gum and nylons.'

'And Hershey bar chocolate.'

'No wonder their secrets are safe with GCHQ.'

'Will?'

Catesby looked at his sister. There was something strange about her face. She was flushed and upset in a way that he had never seen before.

'What is it, Freddie?'

'I've got something for you.'

'Don't show it to me.'

'No, Will, I've got to.'

Catesby stared at his sister's empty glass. She had downed the beer in one. In the background he could hear her undoing the snaps on the ancient brown leather Gladstone bag she used to carry her papers. He then heard her behind him, breathing hard and swallowing. She put her hand warmly on her brother's shoulder as she laid the document in front of him.

It was the briefest of messages, but Catesby couldn't take his eyes away. He felt the shock waves start in the pit of his stomach and spread outwards. He took his sister by the arm and made her sit next to him.

'Can this copy be traced back to you?'

'No, I retrieved it from the burn bag when no one was looking. That's why it's so wrinkled.'

'You could get in a lot of trouble.'

Catesby looked at it again. The distribution list was as interesting as the content. It had originated in Warsaw at the UB, Polish Security Service – and still contained the original Polish. It then winged its way to Normanennstrasse in East Berlin where an MfS linguist had translated it into German. At this point one of Berlin's army of spies, perhaps a cleaner or a bored typist, had nicked a copy from Normanennstrasse and passed it via courier to a CIA agent handler. Catesby was, however, a little surprised that the document had ended up so quickly in Cheltenham. The Americans usually did their own German-English translations; it was Russian they needed help with.

'How,' said Catesby looking at his sister, 'did this end up on your desk?'

'They wanted someone to verify the accuracy of the translation from Polish into German.'

'But your Polish isn't that good.'

'It's not that bad. I did some at UCL – and I've learned a lot from Tomasz. In fact, I've been translating his poetry into English.'

Catesby laughed. 'Tomasz writes poetry?'

'You shouldn't mock. His poems are good. I might show you one or two.'

Catesby looked again at the document. It was itself poetry of a sort. It dealt with the main themes: truth, betrayal, death. And maybe even love. The most disturbing line needed no translation. It had been added as a file note by a CIA field officer in Berlin. It was, of course, written in American English.

Catesby looked at his sister. 'Have you ever done anything like this before?'

'No.'

Catesby knew she was lying. It was all over her face. Freddie was shit at lying and always had been.

'Do you know, Freddie, that I would die for you?'

'Why are you telling me that?' She suddenly seemed cross and pointed to the stolen document. 'Do you want more?'

'You didn't answer my question.'

Freddie looked down at her folded hands. 'I know that you care about me – and I think that you would be stupid enough to …' She couldn't say the word.

'Don't get involved.'

'Okay.'

Catesby knew that she was lying again. He picked up the document.

'Can I keep this?'

She nodded. Her face was drained of colour.

The Director didn't have a particularly grand office. In fact, it was considerably less grand than Henry Bone's. But that was Dick White's style. He regarded himself as a colleague rather than a distant mandarin on high. When Catesby requested a meeting about a 'personal and sensitive issue', White immediately granted him one without fuss or diary fumbling.

As soon as Catesby entered the office White was on his feet and making him feel welcome and at ease. And instead of sitting behind his desk, Dick White sat on an armchair next to Catesby as if Catesby were his fondest nephew just down from Oxford.

'I'm glad you've come to see me,' said White.

For a second Catesby wondered if the DG already knew what he had to say, but then he realised that White was merely trying to make him feel relaxed. It occurred to Catesby that the boss was a natural born interrogator.

'I don't know whether you know this,' said Catesby, 'but my sister works at GCHQ.'

'Yes, I do know. I've never met her, but I understand she is highly regarded.'

Catesby didn't know whether or not this was manager bullshit, but it didn't matter. 'Freddie, or Frederieke, that's her name, has passed on some information that gives me concern.'

White was leaning forward and attentively nodding.

'I'm also concerned, for her, that she's passed on this information. That's why I want this meeting to be completely confidential.' Catesby looked at the worn civil service issue Indian carpet and knew that it was a stupid thing to say. No meetings in Broadway Building were confidential. They were all on the record.

'And, you,' said White, 'want to protect her.'

'Yes, I do …' Catesby backtracked, 'but I'm not certain that she's done anything in breach of the Official Secrets Act.'

The DG smiled. 'In that case, she is a very rare bird indeed.'

Cunning, thought Catesby, but obvious. The DG was trying the we-all-break-the-rules trick – 'therefore, you can tell me all about it and no one will get in trouble'. Sure.

'But,' said Catesby, 'Freddie is very conscientious and loyal. And I think she was motivated by loyalty when she told me about it.'

'Which is?'

'Freddie says that the CIA is passing on intelligence to GCHQ with a condition attached. The Americans say that GCHQ can have the stuff, provided the intelligence doesn't leave Cheltenham. In other words, the Americans trust them, but don't trust *us*.'

'Well, that's nothing new – and we all know the reasons why.'

Catesby looked at the DG. 'I suppose …' He stopped because he knew it would be presumptuous to ask the boss questions.

'Yes,' said White as if reading Catesby's thoughts, 'I know about this arrangement and have known for some time. One has to admit that our American cousins are a bit naïve.'

'In what way … if I may ask?'

White smiled. 'Naïve in that they believe that GCHQ is simply going to sit on that intelligence and not pass it on to us. Of course, we have to be very discreet and pretend we don't have it – and not pass it around ourselves.' White got up and walked to the safe behind his desk. 'That's why the file never leaves my office. There aren't even any copies in Registry. It's all done person to person between DG GCHQ and myself.'

White worked the dials on his safe with his back blocking the view. After a few seconds, the door wheezed open with a lubricated hiss. The DG turned around with a brown file in his hand. 'If the Americans did discover that Cheltenham was double dealing, I suppose they might very well terminate the arrangement. But I can't say that any of this would be a very great loss. It's mostly "cabbages and kings".' The expression was secret intelligence slang for irrelevant chit chat. Most intercepts were largely just that – and combing through them was the most tedious job in the business.

White handed the file to Catesby. 'Have a look and tell me what you think.'

'Thanks.'

The first thing that Catesby did was check the dates. The file was current and the document that Freddie had passed on was well within the time frame. Catesby was aware that the DG was watching him as he went through the file and was careful not to do anything suspicious. The telephone intercepts between the Berlin KGB *rezident*, Yevgeny Pitovranov, and his family were all there. They were the same calls that Freddie had bragged about at Christmas. There was a new telephone intercept as well. It was a conversation between Pitovranov and the general commanding the Soviet garrison. Pitovranov wanted to go wild boar hunting at night with high-powered rifles fitted with infrared night vision scopes. The garrison commander thought the idea was 'vulgar and unsportsmanlike' – and might pose a 'danger to the local population'. The Russians stationed in Germany had come a long way from 1945.

When Catesby had finished reading he checked the file again. He tried to be as casual as possible, as if he were a normally conscientious officer. The separate documents were fastened together with green treasury tags. He couldn't have missed anything. It just wasn't there. He hoped that the DG didn't notice his face turning pale or hear his heart beating. It wasn't there.

When Catesby got back to his office he locked the door behind him. He took off his jacket because he had started to sweat and sat down at his desk. He reached into his pocket, took out the crumpled piece of paper and spread it on the desk blotter. It was the document that Freddie had passed on. The one she said she had stolen from the GCHQ burn bag.

Catesby read it again, although he had long since memorised everything – even the distribution list and the typists' initials. The document had started as an urgent request from the *Urzad Bezpiec-zenstwa*, the Polish Security Service, in Warsaw. The Americans had supposedly intercepted it on its way to MfS HQ in East Berlin.

```
Urgently request further information concerning SB/
KONUS. No reported contact since 28/01/57. Courier (SB/
ORZAK) reports DLB procedure breach. Has ex-filtration
signal been received?
```

Catesby had seen messages like that before. It meant an agent had dried up – or been dried up. KONUS was presumably the agent's UB codename and he was obviously working in the West, otherwise he wouldn't need a courier for a cut-out. The procedure breach meant he hadn't left a signal, something as simple as a chalk mark on a bin, to indicate that, although he had nothing to report, he was still in place. You had to keep contact – and lack of contact was an agent handler's nightmare. An 'ex-filtration signal' simply meant 'get me the hell out of here!'

So far, there was nothing extraordinary about the message. Catesby had sent dozens of similar ones himself. Usually, the agents got scared or tired or emigrated to Canada. But this agent hadn't been so lucky. There was a handwritten note scribbled at the bottom by a CIA field officer in Berlin: *terminated with extreme prejudice*. It was CIA euphemism speak for killing someone. But Americans don't pee or defecate either, they go to 'restrooms'. Catesby felt a trickle of sweat roll down his spine as he looked again at the code name of the terminated agent: AV/ORIOLE-CATCHER.

He stared at the document and realised what his sister was doing. ORIOLE-CATCHER wasn't dead. The document was a forgery. Otherwise, there would have been a copy in Dick White's Chel-tenham file. Catesby knew that Freddie hadn't created the forgery;

the document itself had clearly been produced by a team of professionals. But she had intentionally passed it on. She knew ORIOLE-CATCHER and wanted to put the intelligence service off his trail. It was desperate stuff.

Catesby began to tear the document into tiny pieces. He put each piece in his mouth and chewed it until it was small and wet enough to swallow. It was too dangerous even for a burn bag. Not dangerous for him, but dangerous for Freddie and whoever passed it on. When Catesby had swallowed the last piece he unlocked his door and made himself a cup of tea. He wanted to get rid of the taste.

As Catesby sipped his tea he thought about Freddie. She made a big deal of tea-making: warming the pot, mixing two or three different blends, not using water that had over-boiled. She called it 'mashing' the tea. It wasn't a Suffolk word. It must be a West Country word that she had picked up around Cheltenham. Yes, and he hadn't lied, he would die for her. But Catesby wasn't sure that his sister would return the compliment. Freddie loved someone more than him. And there wasn't anything wrong with that. It was supposed to be that way.

But she had lied to him. She had not just passed on false intelligence – 'disinformation' – but she had done it in a very professional way with a very professional forgery. Why had she had done it and who was she working for? That was obvious. But who was *he* working for?

The door opened and Bone walked in. Catesby could see he wasn't happy. He must have been talking to the DG.

'You need some fresh air,' said Bone, 'let's go for a walk.'

As they walked up Horse Guards towards the Mall it began to rain and they put their umbrellas up. Bone was still carrying the large-handled brolly he had stolen from T.S. Eliot. A rear admiral was walking towards them. He was wearing a rope of gold braid on his right shoulder and getting wet. Service personnel in uniform are not allowed to carry umbrellas. The rear admiral was trying to dab the raindrops away with a white handkerchief. Catesby smiled: the admiral's vain gestures were so quintessentially British.

When he got closer, the naval officer looked at Bone and said, 'Hello Henry.'

'Who was that?' said Catesby after they had passed.

'John Gower, we were on the Olympic team together.'

'Same boat?'

'No, I was in the eight-metre boat; John helmed our six.'

'If Admiral Gower had listened to the shipping forecast, he'd be wearing oilskins. Nelson wouldn't have got caught out – and he was from Norfolk.'

'You shouldn't be so mocking. John Gower is the best sailor I've ever met. By the way, do you know the significance of that gold rope he's wearing on his shoulder?'

'It's called an aiguillette,' said Catesby, 'and it means he's on the Defence Staff.'

'Very good, but do you know the history of the aiguillette?'

'Can't say I do.'

'The aiguillette, the name referring of course to the spike on the end of the rope, goes back to Napoleon. An officer, who behaved very badly during a battle, pleaded with Bonaparte to be given another chance. Napoleon agreed to reinstate him, but he made him wear a piece of braided rope on his right shoulder. The rope was a reminder. If the officer failed again the rope would no longer be on his shoulder, but around his neck.' Bone paused; then said, 'Catesby?'

'Yes.'

'Did you ever wear an aiguillette?'

'No, I never achieved sufficient rank.'

'Well maybe you should wear one now.'

It happened late on Sunday morning – and, in retrospect, none of it surprised Catesby. It would have happened even if Catesby hadn't quietly passed on a message of 'concern' to an acquaintance in Five. He wanted to protect Freddie and it was better that way than to let things drag on.

It was nearly noon and Tomasz was still in his grey silk dressing gown. He was doing weekend 'lates' at the BBC Polish service and didn't get back from his shift at Bush House until six in the morning. As usual, Tomasz slept no more than a few hours before he got up again. And he was in fine form – unusually fine form thought Catesby. There was something about the Pole that was almost manic. He was sitting in an armchair balancing a cup of strong black coffee and a manuscript. Sunday was often poetry day. The form was for Tomasz to read a verse in Polish and then for Freddie to read an English translation, sometimes her own.

'Why,' said Tomasz flourishing the manuscript at Catesby, 'do you never have anything to read?'

'Perhaps I have, but I'm keeping it as a surprise.'

'I look forward to such a surprise – for I am sure, William, that you are a man full of surprises. In any case, may I now begin?'

'Please.'

As Tomasz began to read in Polish, Catesby looked at his sister who was sitting on the settee next to him. She was looking at the English translation and all the blood seemed to have drained from her face. Catesby had picked up enough of Tomasz's Polish recitation to understand why.

Tomasz finished the poem and looked across at them. 'I think,' said Tomasz, 'it would be better if I read the English too.' He came over and picked up Freddie's sheet of paper, then stood over Catesby as he began to read. The words came loud and fierce.

'Our fear
does not wear a night shirt
does not have owl's eyes
does not lift a coffin lid
does not extinguish a candle

does not have a dead man's face either

our fear
   is a scrap of paper...'

Tomasz stopped and stared at Catesby. 'What do you think, William?'

'I think the poem is by Zbigniew Herbert ...'

'Don't be silly, you know what I'm asking.' Tomasz smiled. 'Tell me about *fear*, William, tell me how you use it.'

'I don't understand what you're talking about.'

'Don't lie. You understand everything, William – except how to be an honest human being.'

Freddie had stood up and was next to her boyfriend. 'Please Tomasz ...'

'Don't worry, my dear, your brother and I are not going to have a fight – that would be too honest, too human. You know that he has no warmth, no feeling. He is a lizard.'

Catesby looked at Tomasz. His first impulse was to deny everything, but that would only prove the point.

Tomasz stared back. 'You're not a friend, William, or a brother. You're just a secret policeman and that's all you'll ever be.'

Freddie put her arms around her boyfriend. Her eyes were closed and she was shaking. 'Tomasz, things are getting too emotional. Can we just …'

'No, Freddie, it isn't me who's causing this. It's your brother. William thinks he knows everything; he wants to accuse me. Maybe he wants to have me arrested and kicked out of the country.'

Catesby now wanted to calm things down too. 'It sounds like Special Branch or MI5 called you in for a talk. It's normal procedure to check up on foreign nationals – particularly if they have a relationship with someone with a job like Freddie's. Nothing to worry about.'

'And you know nothing?'

'No.' Catesby was surprised at how glibly he lied.

'Sure, sure.' Tomasz suddenly spoke in a quiet voice, less than a whisper, 'Remember, William, you know nothing.'

Catesby walked over to the bookcase and picked out a worn hardback. 'It's my turn for poetry. Do you know John Donne?'

'Of course, I know all your poets.'

'What do you think of this?

I HAVE done one braver thing
Than all the Worthies did,
And yet a braver thence did spring,
Which is, to keepe that hid.'

'What does it mean, this *braver thing*?'

Catesby shut the book. 'I can't tell you.'

Tomasz smiled. 'I like your sense of humour.'

Catesby returned the book to the shelf and put on his coat.

'Where,' said Freddie, 'are you going?'

'How should I know? Your boyfriend says I,' Catesby imitated Tomasz's accent, '*know nothing*, so I don't know where I'm going.'

Tomasz got up and walked over to Catesby with his hand outstretched. 'Come on, William, sometimes I get too emotional. Let's be friends again, eh?'

Catesby took his hand. 'Sure, no problem, we're still friends. We were never anything else.'

'Then you stay here,' said Tomasz, 'we go to pub when it opens.'

'Maybe some other time.' Catesby shook hands. 'But I need to go for a walk, by myself. I'm not feeling very well.'

'Sure, William, sure. Don't worry, we're still friends.'

'I'm glad you think so.'

The weather was sunshine and showers. A strong south-westerly was blowing straight down the Thames against the incoming tide and making the brown water ripple like a washboard. Catesby loved the Thames. It was, once it left London behind, just another muddy East Anglian river kissing the Essex marshes. It was a little like being home again. In fact, his grandfather used to skipper Thames barges between the capital and the ports of Suffolk. It was an interesting trade. The barges – known as 'stackies' – had to travel under short-ened sail because the London-bound cargoes of hay were stacked halfway up the main mast. And the Thames was always the 'London River' and nothing else. When they finished offloading the hay, the stackies then filled their holds with London horse manure for the trip back to Suffolk – a by-product of the hay they brought down in the first place. In a way, thought Catesby, they were just sailing the same cargo back and forth. A perfect harmony of wind, land and horse; the human was just there to hold the tiller.

Catesby liked walking the Embankment on a Sunday. There was little traffic, other than lovers strolling hand in hand under the plane trees. He wondered what Petra would think of London. He could take her to visit Marx's grave in Highgate Cemetery. He would tell her that the grave was a 'communist plot', but would her English be good enough to get the joke?

When Catesby got to Lambeth Bridge he had to leave the Thames behind. The Houses of Parliament got in the way. Just like the people in them made a foreign policy that got in the way of Petra coming to London. Or was it Moscow or Washington that got in the way? It didn't matter. The important thing was not to care and to get your pay cheque at the end of the month. Because, when you came down to it, being a spy was just another job. And Petra was just an office romance with a rep from a rival firm.

Catesby was now walking past the Cenotaph. It always gave

him a queasy feeling. He remembered how the classics master who replaced Captain Pearse had told them that cenotaph came from the Greek, *kenos taphos,* and meant 'empty tomb'. Catesby hated all the Remembrance Sunday stuff. What were they trying to do? Make us feel guilty about not having got killed too? As if we didn't already. Or getting us prepared for the big one? The mega-death that would obliterate Britain and Europe. Sure, the United States and Russia might survive in some fashion, their land mass was huge. They might even learn a lesson or two. But not us, we're all going to be dead – and the Thames will vanish in a hiss of steam like spilt water on a hot stove. Catesby turned and looked back at the Houses of Parliament. Don't they understand? Are they really that stupid? He was now passing Downing Street. Catesby began to walk faster. He was afraid that the policeman outside Number 10 might come and grab him by his collar. It was like the motto on the passport – *Honi soit qui mal y pense* – you weren't even allowed to think such things.

By the time he got to Trafalgar Square Catesby was feeling better and knew he wasn't cracking up. But if he did crack up, he wouldn't be the first one. American spies, however, had far more mental breakdowns than British ones. British spies didn't go mad, they went to Moscow instead. Or drank themselves to death. Or both, which was exactly what Guy Burgess was doing.

The National Portrait Gallery was just off Trafalgar Square opposite St Martin-in-the-Fields. Compared to the columned grandeur of the National Gallery, it was a modest building. Catesby had never been inside before, but there was someone he wanted to see. And he didn't need to make an appointment because the person had been dead for 123 years.

He found him in an exhibition room hung with eighteenth-century worthies. Some of worthies had earned their way into the gallery as inventors, soldiers, politicians and scientists. Others were there simply because they had inherited great wealth. The aristocrats looked far more at home than the self-made types – as if a portrait gallery was their natural habitat. The person Catesby had come to see also looked perfectly at ease in a gilt frame. But his ease as a sitter didn't come from inheritance, it came from being an artist himself.

There were four portraits of the artist. The earliest was an oil painting dated 1799 when he would have been forty-four. The nose was longer than his descendant's, but his lips were just as thin and dry. In many ways, the resemblance was stunning. The eyes were the most complex and disturbing aspect of the portrait. They are looking away from viewer and into space. Not focused on anything outwards or inwards, but into a world that only the subject can see and fully apprehend. It was a look that Catesby had seen before.

Catesby was about to move on when he heard someone breathing close behind him. There had been no warning of approaching foot-steps. Whoever it was had entered the room as silently as a stalking cat. Catesby turned around – and found himself looking into the same brown eyes that he had seen in the portrait. The resemblance was uncanny.

'I thought it was you,' said Bone.

'It looks like your lot have surrounded me.' Catesby tried to make it sound like a joke, but it fell flat.

Outside the context of SIS and Broadway Buildings, Bone seemed to have shrunk and aged. He was wearing a black jumper that was frayed around the neck. Catesby wondered if he had been drinking for he looked hung-over.

'I didn't expect to see you here,' said Bone. 'Why are you here?'

'I went for a walk – and decided to have a look at your famous ancestor. It wasn't planned.' Catesby was annoyed at having to explain himself.

Bone nodded at the portrait. 'My great-great-grandfather wasn't really an artist. But he was an excellent craftsman. He had a great talent for copying other artists' paintings on to enamel surfaces – things like lockets, watches, snuff boxes, ornamental plaques of course. Eventually, he became enamel painter by appointment to George III.' Bone laughed. 'I suppose, in Civil Service terms, his post was about on the same level as mine.'

'At least you haven't gone down in the world.'

'Thank you, Catesby. In fact, many of Henry Bone's works are still in the Royal Art Collection, but not all of them. Occasionally they come up for auction at Sotheby's.'

'Have you bought any?'

Bone frowned. 'Yes. It cost a fortune. It was quite a rare piece.' Bone paused before going on. 'It was, in fact, a chamber pot that Henry Bone had painted for George III, the design was based on Sir Joshua Reynold's *The Death of Dido*. The pot cost me a lot of money, but I had to buy it.' Bone looked closely at Catesby. 'No ruler of this country, no matter how grand, is ever going to shit on a Henry Bone again.'

Catesby noticed the odour of whisky, partly disguised by mint, on Bone's breath. It was apparent that Bone hadn't bothered to shave that morning. A picture of lost lonely weekends began to emerge.

'Let us have a look at your famous ancestor,' said Bone.

'I haven't got any ancestors. People like me are lucky to have grandparents.'

'That's not true – follow me.'

Catesby knew what Bone was on about. His family name was an embarrassment; an English master had been fond of teasing him about his namesake who was the first murderer in *Richard III*. But the worst embarrassment was the later Catesby.

'Have you seen this before?' said Bone.

They were in a dark side gallery. The group portrait was a print from a line engraving. They were all there: Bateses, the Wrights, the Winters and Thomas Percy; Catesby was standing between Thomas Winter and Guido Fawkes. Catesby was drawn in profile and the only conspirator shown carrying a weapon, the hilt of his sword rising over his left hip.

'No relation,' said Catesby, 'we're peasants from Suffolk. Those Catesbys were toffs from Oxfordshire.'

'I think your forbears ran away to Suffolk because it was as far away as they could get.' Bone smiled. 'Imagine your ancestors being met by Jesuit spies at midnight on a lonely Suffolk beach. You wait night after night, but the rescue ship from the Spanish Netherlands never arrives.'

'Henry?'

'Yes.'

'Are you drunk?'

'No,' said Bone, 'just a bit tired. It's been a busy week.'

They came out of the gallery to a loud flapping of pigeon wings. London, thought Catesby, needed more sparrowhawks. The fresh air seemed to have revived Bone.

'Which way are you going?' said Bone.

'I'm heading back to Pimlico.'

Bone didn't seem to be going anywhere. He was just standing there with his hands in his pockets.

'See you tomorrow,' said Bone.

Catesby headed off across the square through more pigeon flap. When he was a hundred yards away, he surreptitiously looked behind him. Bone had mounted the stairs of St Martin-in-the-Fields and was looking across the square. It was obvious that he was waiting for someone. Catesby sensed it was personal rather than professional. At least with Bone the two were separate. Or were they?

Catesby had a lot on his mind. The morning had left him shaken and he wasn't looking forward to returning to Tachbrook Street. He needed to talk to Bone and he wasn't sure it could wait until morning. Catesby wanted to do something, anything, to protect his sister. He was minded to turn around and go back, but didn't want to interfere in Bone's personal life. It was an odd British reticence, that drawing of boundaries between home and office.

There was a large equestrian statue of George IV – another one of Henry Bone's patrons – in the middle of Trafalgar Square. When Catesby realised that the statue was blocking the line of sight between himself and Bone, he retraced his steps to the base of the statue plinth. He peeped around the corner and saw that Bone was still waiting. Catesby began to realise that Trafalgar Square was the worst place in London to do covert surveillance. It was too open. Catesby knew that Bone couldn't see him from where he was hidden behind the plinth, but anyone crossing the square to meet Bone at St Martin's would see him. Catesby decided to move on. Lying in wait to spot Bone's contact was a bad idea. But it was too late.

Catesby recognised him at once. It was Henry's art historian friend. He was a tall man who walked with long graceful strides. His air of perfect patrician poise was effortless and understated. A nouveau-riche millionaire would have paid a fortune to acquire even part of that manner. Except you couldn't acquire it, no matter what you paid.

Catesby was caught in the open. He knew it would be senseless to turn away or hide his own face. It would only attract attention. Instead Catesby looked at his watch, then folded his arms and tapped his foot as Bone's friend approached. Catesby was pretending to be just another ordinary Londoner waiting for someone who was late. The friend, who was hatless and looked about fifty, passed within three feet of Catesby, but there was no sign of recognition. And why should there be? The art historian had left the service the year that Catesby joined.

It was only a twelve-minute walk from Tachbrook Street to his office at Broadway Buildings. It was a brisk Monday morning and the daffodils were in full bloom in the garden of the Coroner's Court on Horseferry Road. The weekend fug had gone and Catesby felt like a vibrant senior civil servant as the spike of his umbrella tapped a brisk cadence on the way to Whitehall. At last, he was going to *do* something.

It had just gone eight when Catesby hung his bowler and brolly on the hat stand behind his desk. He thought he would do his quarterly requests for agent and courier funding that he needed to submit to DD/Finance before Friday. He was sure he was well ahead of the other section heads in P3 – and didn't mind making his colleagues look bad.

After two hours of crisp head-clearing admin, Catesby went upstairs. Bone no longer had to do his own budget requests. He had an HEO as a full-time admin officer who did all the routine stuff from an adjacent office. The HEO was a former Signal Corps captain who had lost an eye in Palestine. The glass replacement was an excellent one and Catesby was never certain which eye was looking at him. But on this occasion both eyes looked surprised to see him.

'How can I help you, Mr Catesby?'

'I just wanted to pop in and have a chat with Henry.'

'I'm sorry, but Mr Bone isn't here.'

'Is he going to be back any time soon?'

'I wouldn't know.'

There was something in the HEO's manner that made Catesby uneasy.

'Actually, I need to contact Henry rather urgently. We could probably deal with it on the phone.'

The HEO didn't respond. Catesby was annoyed that his hint had been ignored.

'Have you a contact number where I can reach him?'

'Mr Bone has not left one.'

'In that case, may I have his home number?'

174

'Mr Bone's number is ex-directory and I am not allowed to give it out without his permission.'

Catesby was tempted to give the HEO a smack. In any case, the refusal was pointless because Catesby already had Bone's address and phone number in his own diary.

When Catesby got back to his office he stared at the phone for a while before deciding not to use it. An inner caution told him that it wasn't a good idea to try to contact Bone through the SIS switchboard. Instead, he removed his brolly and bowler from the hat stand. He needed some fresh air.

Catesby's first stop was a phone kiosk on Birdcage Walk. He put a tuppence in the slot and dialled the number. He let it ring a dozen times before he pressed the B button to get his tuppence back. Catesby then went back to his office, not to work, but to get his tools.

It was a genteel part of Kensington, even more so because of its faint patina of seediness. The house was in one of those early Victorian white terraces with pillared porticos and black iron railings. Bone lived in the ground floor flat. Catesby was certain the door locks wouldn't be any problem, but he pressed the doorbell to make sure that no one was home. He examined the lock. It was a simple mortise with a cylinder. It wasn't worth bothering with the skeleton keys. He pressed the bell again. No one was home. He slipped a tension wrench into the lock which would hold the mechanism in place while he did the picking. Catesby then inserted his pick starting with the barrel at the back. You did it with a gentle up and down movement. He managed all five barrels in less than ten seconds and then popped the entire mechanism open with the tension wrench. He did it so quickly and smoothly that anyone passing by would have thought Catesby was an honest resident with a worn key. He was, however, a little surprised that Henry paid so little attention to security at home.

As Catesby let himself in and closed the door behind him, he noticed that there were stronger locks but that none of them had been set. That was a bit odd. Bone's flat had a slightly musty odour. The room to the left of the entrance hall seemed to be a formal sitting room that was seldom used. There were glass-fronted bookcases and armchairs with antimacassars of stiff white crochet-work. Catesby knew what he was looking for and knew that he wasn't going to find it in there.

The next room looked more promising. The door had a more difficult lock, but it wasn't locked at all. Catesby pushed the door open. There was a desk, a filing cabinet and shelves crammed with files and books. This was Bone's home study. There was a half empty bottle of gin on the table and an empty glass with a slice of lemon. Catesby felt a shiver run down his spine. There were two ice-cubes in the glass. At the same moment, Catesby noticed the reel-to-reel tape machine on a table next to the desk. The tape machine was plugged in; a red 'on' light was glowing – and the reels were still turning, the loose end of a tape making a 'slap-slap' noise. Catesby decided it was time to leave.

It happened just as he was backing out of the study. The barrel of the gun pressed firmly into the V where the back of his skull connected with the top of his neck.

'Is Henry expecting you?' The voice was languid and refined without being overdone or pretentious.

'He didn't come to work today,' said Catesby, 'and I feared that he might be unwell.'

'And you were so concerned you decided to pay a visit.'

'Something like that.'

'Lean against the wall, please, with your hands above your head.'

Catesby did as he was told while the man frisked him for concealed weapons.

'You're clean,' said the languid voice, 'or as they say in the films, "not packing heat". You can turn around.'

Catesby turned already knowing who he was going to face. It was the art historian, the same man he had seen the day before.

'You're Catesby, aren't you, Henry's protégé?'

'I don't know about the protégé bit.'

'You're wrong about that. Henry rates you highly – he even trusts you, but you obviously don't trust him.' The art historian looked at the gun in his hand. It was an old-fashioned Webley revolver, the same version that officers had carried at Ypres and the Somme. 'I'm not sure what I was going to do with this. I was afraid that it might have been someone from MI5.'

'What would you have done if it had been?'

'I might have made a citizen's arrest for illegal entry and rung the police. Or I might have blown his brains out and then killed myself.'

The art historian went over to the desk and put the gun in a drawer. He then turned off the tape recorder.

'Henry was very kind to get me that tape; he must have gone to a great deal of trouble. There's a danger that they might be interviewing me again sometime soon and I need to remember what I said last time. It wouldn't look good if I changed my story.'

Catesby assumed that he was referring to his interrogation by MI5 in 1952 when the art historian first came under suspicion of having been part of a Soviet spy ring. The interrogation revealed nothing incriminating. Catesby was amazed that Bone had managed to get his hands on the tape.

The man picked up the half-empty gin bottle. 'A late breakfast,' he said waving it. 'Let's go into the kitchen.'

The kitchen was a large bright room with French doors leading on to an enclosed terrace with iron garden furniture and modern sculpture. While slicing up a lemon for his gin and tonic, the art historian said, 'Do you ever do interrogations?'

'From time to time.'

'Can you give me any advice?'

Catesby smiled. He was amused by the request, but also felt that he was being wrapped in charm and drawn deeper into a web.

The older man looked at him. 'How much tonic?'

'A lot, it's pretty early for me.' It wasn't even noon.

'I hope this isn't too strong. But any advice on dealing with interrogations would be most welcome.'

Catesby sipped his gin. It was too strong. 'MI5 have a nasty trick they play with tape-recorders. From time to time, particularly in a one to one, the interrogator turns off the recorder to get the subject to talk more freely. You think, it's off the record – there's no proof. But you're wrong. The room itself is bugged and every syllable is recorded.'

The art historian smiled. 'They've already tried that one.'

'And you didn't fall for it?'

'My dear young man, I had nothing to hide so nothing incriminating could have popped out.' He paused and looked closely at Catesby. 'But there are a few things that I would like to tell you. In fact, I'm glad that you turned up. It will be good to have a one to one chat without Henry shushing and shaking his head.'

'By the way, where is Henry?'

'He's in Cheltenham. There's some sort of mess at GCHQ.'

Catesby felt he'd been hit in the stomach. He swallowed the rest of his gin and tonic.

'Would you like another one?'

Catesby held out his glass. 'Yes, please.'

'But before I begin my own *apologia pro vita sua*, I would like to ask you something.'

'Go on.'

'Why did you break into this flat? What did you hope to find?'

Catesby looked at the gin splashing into his glass. 'I wanted to find something to use against Henry.'

'Good Lord, you mean blackmail?'

'That's putting it crudely, but I suppose so.'

'Why?'

'To protect someone close to me.'

The art historian looked out the French doors. There were daffodils and crocuses in pots. 'We've all done that.' He paused to sip his drink. 'And it's bloody dreadful when we do.' He turned to look at Catesby. 'You look pale. You're not used to drinking on an empty stomach, are you?'

'No.'

'Have some fruit.'

There was a bowl on the kitchen table piled with apples, pears and bananas. Catesby paused as he reached for an apple and looked at the bowl. It was a chamber pot decorated with a scene from antiquity. A bare breasted woman in a white gown appeared to be dying while an angel and another woman flapped over her.

'Don't worry.' The art historian had noticed Catesby's hesitation. 'It hasn't been used for its original purpose for over a 150 years.'

'Thanks for telling me.'

'But it is an unusual piece. The design is, as you can see, based on Sir Joshua Reynold's *The Death of Dido*. The pot was originally commissioned by George III, but Edward VII gave it away as a joke present when he was Prince of Wales – and, of course, it eventually made its way to Sotheby's. Do you like Reynolds?'

'Not greatly.'

'Neither do I. But Sir Joshua had impeccable taste – he was an avid collector of Nicolas Poussin.'

Catesby looked at the art historian. As soon as the subject turned to art, his face became both serene and animated. He had left spying for a world that he loved. He was a lucky man. His eyes turned to Catesby.

'But you don't want to hear me going on and on about Poussin.'

Catesby picked up an apple and said, 'And you don't want to hear me going on about double agents?'

The art historian seemed momentarily taken aback and turned a little paler than normal. Catesby was sorry he had said it. There was a long silence.

'The problem,' said Catesby, 'is that we all have to walk a tightrope.'

'You don't need to tell me that.' The art historian poured himself another gin. 'And that tightrope stretches and sways between loyalty and treason. But in the end it doesn't matter on which side you fall, you still break your neck.'

'But you're out of it.'

'Don't be absurd, you're never out of it. Why d'you think Henry found me that tape?'

'Why,' said Catesby, 'does he want to protect you?'

The art historian touched his fingers together. It was a gesture of great delicacy. 'These things start out as innocent friendships, or not so innocent friendships, but then in later life, what seemed slightly frivolous and fun as an undergraduate, becomes dark and deadly serious. Henry is still a dear friend, but at some point friendship became self-interest. He wants to protect me because that's the best way to protect himself.' The art historian paused. 'There's a lovely couplet from Orwell's *1984*:

Under the spreading chestnut tree
I sold you and you sold me.'

'You met Henry at university?'

'Yes, but he wasn't part of the inner circle.'

'That came later,' said Catesby.

The art historian smiled. 'I'm not sure he ever became part of it. And, if he did, I'm not sure that I would tell you.'

'Were you lovers?'

The art historian didn't seem at all shocked by the question. He paused and closed one eye as if searching his memory for an accurate answer.

'Briefly – and sporadically.'

'I hope,' said Catesby, 'you didn't think I was rude to ask.'

'Not at all. The MI5 man twisted himself in knots trying *not* to ask it. His embarrassment was worthy of the finest *opera buffa*.'

'I suppose,' said Catesby looking around the kitchen, 'that you don't …'

'Live here? Good Lord, no! I have a much larger flat of my own at the Institute. Henry often comes for dinner and *soirées*, but lately he's been in a grump and out of sorts. But you probably know more than I.'

'That might not be true.' Catesby finished his apple and put the core in a bin packed with kitchen waste, coffee grinds and a newspaper folded over to a half finished *Times* crossword. 'What,' he said, 'was Henry like as an undergraduate?'

'Reserved and self-contained. He never committed himself to membership in a particular group, but always seemed on the brink of deciding. He could be awfully good company – he was outstandingly musical and still is – and everyone wanted to know him better. But if you got too close, he withdrew.'

'But you succeeded.'

'Henry and I were very much alike. That's why we've remained friends, but also why we've never been closer. In any case, his great passion as a young man was sailing. Henry's family originates from Cornwall.'

'Do they?'

'So there's a bit of pirate in Henry. He was always off crewing or helming someone's yacht – and was terribly successful at it.' The art historian poured another gin, as if bracing himself for a revelation. 'I suppose you know that he was on the 1936 Olympic team?'

'Yes, I know that.'

'But how much do you really know?'

'I know that he was on the team and that his yacht did not win a medal.'

'But they were beautiful boats, thirty feet long and more graceful than swans. They were, I believe, called "eights" and had crews of six. Henry must have been twenty-nine or thirty at the time and was helmsman.' The art historian paused. 'I suppose,' he said, 'that they might have done better, might have even won a gold, if it hadn't been for what happened in the middle of the series.'

'I didn't know there was an accident.'

'There was no accident. It was something else.' The art historian paused as if searching for a memory. 'Henry used to say that helming requires above all complete concentration. It's like game of chess. If you lose concentration, even for one move or one second, you lose. And, not surprisingly, Henry lost that utter and complete focus that you need in sport – or art. But who can blame him?' There was another pause. 'Has Henry ever told you about this?'

'No.'

'Then it might be wrong for me to tell you.' The art historian took another drink. It was odd that he still looked and sounded so completely and utterly sober. 'But it is something you ought to know.'

'Why?' said Catesby.

'So you don't make any more silly mistakes.'

Catesby stared at the other man. 'Were you there at the time?'

'Yes, not at the actual incident, but I was with Henry in Kiel. The events for the larger yachts were held in the Kiel Fjord rather than the Berlin lakes. As I might have mentioned, Henry and I were not lovers at the time, but we liked, how shall I say, to "hunt in pairs". Are you shocked?'

'No.'

'Disgusted?'

'No.'

'But there are those who are – and we always have to remember that. In any case, Germany used to be a very good hunting ground – even in the early Hitler years. There was a brief interlude of unawareness before the realisation that Nazism wasn't a passing fad like modernist art, but a disease that needed harsh measures to remove. In any case, there was a very handsome *Junker* who was a member of the German crew. He couldn't have been more than eighteen and had a face like one of Titian's angels.

'The weather was filthy for early August, but the setting was intoxicatingly beautiful and intensely romantic. In fact, I knew that Henry was going to fall in love even before he met his Prussian Titian. It must have begun when an afternoon race had been postponed and we all ended up on the terrace of the Imperial Yacht Club drinking champagne. I'm certain that it was the German who started the flirting – Henry was too focused on winning to fraternise with a rival team. In any case, the atrocious weather continued and there were more breaks in the regatta and more champagne at the yacht club.

'For my part, I was more taken by the faded beauty of Kiel's villas and parks than I was by young Germans. I could imagine Thomas Mann striding through the mottled shade of the Hindenburg Promenade. Mature trees – linden, spruce and beech – come to the very edge of the tide-less Baltic and spread their branches over the water. Our coasts are too rough and salty for that. But I digress.

'It started, I believe, with pleasant little walks like the one I've described. The seaside path continued to Bellevue. The light, shade and sky reminded me, rather aptly as it turned out, of Poussin's *Nymph with Satyrs*. The Olympic yacht harbour and village were in Kiel's most elegant quarter. The town, as it stretched north along the fjord, dwindled to a fringe of seaside villas. Behind the villas was a vast parkland called Dürstenbrook Wood. The wood was a scene from German folklore – you half expected to be confronted by platoons of *Rotkäpchens* pursued by wolves.' The art historian paused and looked at Catesby. 'I hope you don't think I'm being too flippant.'

'I'm not sure what you mean by flippant.'

'Inappropriately glib and humorous.' The art historian poured more gin for both of them; the bottle was getting near empty. 'The trouble with life, as well as art, is that events that are truly tragic and awful are often surrounded by little absurdities and little comedies. What happened to Henry took place in a ridiculous little gingerbread house. Kitsch. One imagines joke Bavarian beer mugs that play a drinking song when you lift them up and girls in flowery dirndls – except, of course, there weren't any girls. You want more tonic water?'

'Yes, please.'

'At the time, some of the wealthy residents of Kiel had summerhouses in Dürstenbrook Wood. To cut to the quick, Henry's angelfaced *Junker* said he had a key to one of these summerhouses. It was a stormy night with plenty of *Donner und Blitzen* and the following day's races were certain to be cancelled. And, I suppose, Henry had had a lot to drink – but I'm sure that wouldn't have made any difference. Henry was at least infatuated, if not in love, with the young Prussian – who, to be fair, was not only good looking, but also extremely cultivated and very funny. A real charmer.'

'And a Catholic aristocrat with a blood line going back to Charlemagne?'

'Probably, but Henry has never been a snob – although by your smiling you seem to think so. But he was, and still is, often very lonely. In any case, Henry and his new friend set off through the woods wearing their oilskins against the summer deluge. Henry was carrying a duffle bag with a sleeping bag, a bottle of Mosel and the complete poems of Rupert Brooke. I never understood the point of the poems. I think they were intended as a present – perhaps Henry couldn't find anything else, perhaps he liked them at the time. Who knows?

'The summerhouse was deep in the wood and very isolated. There was a wide porch with wicker chairs. Henry took his oilskins off on the porch so they wouldn't drip over the inside of the house. Meanwhile, the *Junker* opened the door. Henry was surprised that the house hadn't been locked. He noticed, however, that the heavy window shutters were still firmly in place as if the house had been shut up for the winter. Henry was also surprised that his friend was still wearing his dripping oilskins. Nonetheless, he followed his pretty Prussian into the house. It was completely utterly black. He remembered getting wet as the German put his arms around him and began to kiss him. Henry then broke off the kiss to try to find the buttons on his friend's oilskins so he could help get them off. The blind groping in the dark must have, thought Henry at the time, tickled or amused the German. He could feel him shaking with laughter. And that's when it happened.'

'What happened?'

'Something very unpleasant. Henry never managed to count them all, but he reckoned there must have been at least twenty. The first lights and the most blinding were handheld battery torches. A half dozen or so were beamed directly into Henry's face so he couldn't see who was holding them. The room became lighter and lighter as candles and hurricane lanterns were lit – like a stage. There was even someone bearing a fake Olympic torch. They were there to have fun and many of them were stinking drunk. The first person to hit Henry was Ralswiek himself.'

'Ralswiek?'

The art historian paused before answering. 'Henry will never tell you that name. He'll pretend until he goes to the grave that he never heard it before.'

'Who was he?'

'Rudolf Ralswiek was the angel-faced *Junker* – the pretend lover whose soft kiss was immediately replaced by a smashing fist. I tried to warn Henry. I strongly suspected that Ralswiek was as bogus as a vice squad *provocateur* in mufti.' The art historian paused for a moment and stared out the window. 'But perhaps, I was the naïve one.'

'In what way?'

'In not realising that Ralswiek may have been playing a double bluff.'

Catesby stared at the kitchen table. He wanted to find a grain of wood that didn't change its shape the more you looked at it.

The art historian resumed. 'The proceedings turned pretty awful. They started by stripping him and beating him. I wonder if any of them questioned their own "disciplined masculinity" – one of Goebbels' most ineffable terms – as they did so. Once Henry was naked, the physical violence and humiliation began in earnest. Someone stapled a pink triangle to his buttock. They then kicked him outside and used him as a human urinal. They peed all over his body, but particularly enjoyed aiming at his face and hair. And after that …'

Catesby helped himself to more gin.

'And after that …'

'What?' said Catesby.

'I don't know what happened. Henry never told me.'

Catesby knew it was a silly question, because he already knew the answer. But he had to ask it anyway. 'Did Ralswiek survive the war?'

The art historian looked at the gin bottle. 'I think we're going to have to move on to the whisky.'

'No more for me,' said Catesby.

'Of course not, you've got a job to do. In any case …' The art historian no longer sounded *completely* sober. 'In any case, your job now has a name on it.'

Catesby stood up. 'I'd better get back to Broadway Buildings.'

'Just one more thing.'

'Yes.'

'I would appreciate it if you didn't tell Henry that I told you any of this.'

'I won't.'

'Good – and I won't tell him that you broke into his flat.'

As Catesby turned to leave, the art historian spoke again. 'And there's one thing you should never forget – and that you should never doubt.'

'What?'

'Henry Bone loves this country.'

As soon as Catesby got back to Broadway Buildings he went to the staff canteen for a cup of strong black coffee. He had just started drinking the coffee when Ayres, one of the clerks in Registry, came over to tell him that he was on the circulation list for a new batch of UK EYES ALPHA that had just arrived. This meant that Catesby had to go to the heavily guarded archive vault, browse through the documents, write any comments necessary and sign his initials on the circulation chit to indicate that he had dealt with it. Most of the material is incredibly tedious, but if you don't sign the chit you keep getting reminders and it makes you look bad.

The ledger in question was marked with two red stripes to indicate its security level. He began by reading the transcript of the latest Kit Fournier debrief. Nothing new. Poor Kit, he thought, must be well on his way to the South Atlantic by now. Catesby had heard that SIS were going to stash Fournier on some remote island possession. He wondered if Kit was going to St Helena, the windswept island where Napoleon had spent his last five years. The ultimate safe house.

The next document was headed CIA TECHNICAL SERVICES R&D. The Americans' latest espionage developments included horrible-smelling liquids that you could use to disrupt meetings; a fine clear powder that was harmless until disturbed by passing feet or movement, at which point it turned into tear gas, and itching powder that you could spread on toilet seats. And there were exploding cigars too, but not the ones the Marx brothers used. These cigars would kill you – or at least leave you blind and scarred for life. And, thought Catesby, it was good to know that MK/ULTRA was progressing well. ULTRA was aimed at 'mind control' through the use of drugs and other methods. A drug, called LSD, was already in its advanced testing stages.

As Catesby handed back the document, the clerk said, 'Anything else, Mr Catesby?'

'Yes, I'd like to look at the PAPERCLIP ledgers. It would be nice if I could sign them out.'

The clerk consulted the card catalogue system. 'You can take them out, Mr Catesby, but you can't take them home or leave them in the back of a taxicab.'

As soon as Catesby got back to his office and opened the first ledger, the old sense of bitterness and betrayal came back. PAPER-CLIP was still a raw nerve. The original aim of the Allies, as embodied in the 'Denazification Directives', had been to rid Germany of all remnants of the Nazi regime. But, as Catesby and Otis had discovered, exceptions were made in the case of Nazi scientists and intelligence officers.

Catesby was pleased to see Otis's comments in the earliest PAPER-CLIP files. Otis had been the State Department official in charge of reviewing the personnel files of the dodgiest Germans applying for visas to the United States. Most of Otis's recommendations simply stated: 'Ardent Nazi, visa request disallowed.' In more serious cases, Otis wrote, 'Applicant is regarded as a significant security threat.' And in one case: '100% Nazi, extremely dangerous! Refer to War Crimes Commission!!' But, on review, Otis's recommendations were almost always overruled. Catesby flipped forward a few pages to see the final verdict on Otis's '100% Nazi'. *Nothing in the applicant's record indicates that he is a war criminal, an ardent Nazi or in any way objectionable. Approve visa request.* The applicant was a rocket scientist.

But the worst PAPERCLIP Nazi wasn't a scientist. He was a former high-ranking Nazi intelligence officer. Catesby wanted to cross out the word 'former', for as far as he was concerned the ex-Wehrmacht general was still on duty. And it wasn't just the Nazi general alone who had been 'rehabilitated'. The general insisted on bringing his mates with him.

Catesby restrained himself from throwing the file across the room. He looked at the name and said, 'It's a pity you didn't meet Albert.' Albert Pierrepoint was the Nuremberg hangman. He had once swung twenty-seven Nazis in a single day.

He was called 'the Edelweiss general' for he had purchased freedom – and lucrative employment – with the Edelweiss Files. The files were called that because they had been stored in sealed drums and buried in remote Alpine meadows. They contained microfilm copies of all the German army's intelligence records on the Soviet Union. The general and his friends had seen that defeat was inevitable and had begun copying the files months before the war ended. It was a massive archive, even though it proved largely useless. But it did impress the Americans.

Catesby closed his eyes. He sensed a pattern. The Edelweiss general hadn't been the only Nazi cunning enough to plan his post-war survival plan months in advance. But the Edelweiss general had been especially lucky. When the war ended his staff headquarters were only two miles from the American spearhead in Bavaria. But suppose, thought Catesby, a similar survival-minded officer had been on the Eastern Front? Would he have waited until the end? Defeat was almost inevitable after Stalingrad in the winter of '42–43. And the sooner you jumped the greater was the chance that the Russians would believe you.

Catesby picked up the PAPERCLIP ledgers to take them back to Registry, but then he put them down again. He opened the cover to look at the distribution sheet where the Registry clerk stamps the withdrawal date – and where the person taking it out has to put his initials. In SIS your reading choices are not private. Catesby saw that the files, after six years of gathering dust, had been taken out the previous week. The initials were plain and legible – HB.

The phone was ringing as Catesby opened the door of the flat. He dropped his briefcase and answered the phone with his coat and hat still on. He knew it was bad news as soon as he heard his mother's voice. She never telephoned except when there was an emergency or death. It was like a War Office telegram. There was no phone at Dene Road, so she must have walked to the kiosk on Yarmouth Road. And Catesby knew the news was going to be more dire when he heard her speaking Flemish. It's the only language she speaks when she's upset.

'I'm so glad you're finally there,' she said, 'I've been phoning the flat all evening.'

'What's wrong, *mam*?'

'Haven't you heard?'

'No,' said Catesby.

'Frederieke is in jail.'

'That's impossible. How do you know?'

'Two policemen came to Dene Road. And there were two other men with them, but not in uniform. They wanted to search the house.'

'Did you let them?'

'Of course. It was so embarrassing.'

It was then that Catesby noticed something. All the books in the bookcase were in a different order. The flat had been turned over too.

'*Moeder,* don't worry about the embarrassment. Where's Frederieke?'

'I don't know.'

'I thought you said she was in jail.'

'They said she was arrested, so she must be in jail.'

The line went dead. She must have run out of coins. Catesby put the phone back in its cradle and stared at it. He was afraid to ring anyone else in case his mother rang back. It was difficult to think clearly. There was a rattling noise: it was his own knee nervously shaking against the side table. Catesby breathed in and tried to join the dots. The men in plain clothes had obviously been from MI5. Freddie had got caught stealing secrets.

Catesby was glad that Tomasz wasn't back yet. Things had been bad the previous evening, but at least Freddie had been there to calm it down. He now dreaded the idea of being stuck alone in the flat with Tomasz. He knew there would be shouting and accusations – maybe even a fight.

When the phone rang again Catesby's first thought was that it was Tomasz. He hoped that the Pole was ringing to say that he would be late or not coming back at all. He loathed the idea of talking to him. Catesby finally picked up the receiver. 'Hello.'

A woman's voice answered, 'Hello, may I speak to Miss Frederieke Catesby?'

'She isn't available at the moment. I'm Miss Catesby's brother. May I take a message?'

'This is Guy's Hospital. We have recently admitted a Mr Tomasz Król. He gave Miss Catesby's name as an emergency contact. Will she be back any time soon?'

'She's gone out this evening. Is there anything I can pass on?'

'Let me look at the notes.' There was a brief pause. 'Mr Król self-admitted early this evening complaining of stomach cramp and a high fever. We are awaiting the results of blood tests and keeping him in overnight for observation.'

'Thank you. Can I tell my sister that he's not in any immediate danger?'

The voice paused as if looking at the notes again. 'Mr Król is resting comfortably.'

'I'll pass that on. Goodbye.'

Catesby put the phone back, but didn't take his hand away. He was still waiting for his mother to ring back and was angry at Tomasz for having caused an interruption that occupied the line. He imagined his mother catching a chill in the kiosk while the payphone registered a busy signal because bloody little-diddums Tomasz has a tummy ache.

Catesby closed his eyes and started joining dots again. Many were far apart and one or two completely isolated. But one particular dot started to swell and vibrate. He remembered what the art historian had said that morning about Henry not being in London: *He's in Cheltenham. There's some sort of mess at GCHQ.* Of course, thought Catesby, he's busy stitching my sister and getting her put in the clink. Henry's recent aloofness and unease now made sense.

The phone rang and Catesby picked it up. It took him a second to recognise the refined and jolly voice. It was Father Sinclair.

'Hello William. Your mother's here at the rectory. There seems to have been some dreadful mix-up concerning Freddie.'

'So, I've heard.'

'I managed, however,' said Sinclair, 'to get through to someone at Cheltenham police station.'

Catesby was ashamed that the priest appeared to be handling the crisis more effectively than himself. But that's what clergy are for – and the contacts too. The tentacles of the Vatican reach into every dark cranny.

'Is she still there?' said Catesby.

'No, after being arrested – how utterly absurd – she was transferred to London.'

'Have you spoken to her?'

'Unfortunately not,' said Sinclair, 'my inspector friend in Cheltenham was not able to stretch the rules quite that far. But he did inform me that Freddie will be held overnight in a cell at Bow Street Magistrates Court – communing, no doubt, with the ghosts of Oscar Wilde and Dr Crippen. I shouldn't be flippant, but this episode is so outrageous and mistaken that ...'

'You said my mother was there.'

'Yes, she was here earlier and now she's come back. She's in the kitchen with my housekeeper. By the way, I haven't told your mother about the prison cell and the actual arrest.'

'Thanks, she would find it embarrassing.'

Catesby had never been to Bow Street before. It was, he supposed, a sign of his family's upward social mobility that no Catesby had been in prison since an uncle did time for poaching in the twenties. But the arc was now turning downwards. The custody sergeant was an amiable chap carrying a chain and set of keys that looked like they came straight from the props cupboard at Shepperton Studios. The most unexpected thing about the Bow Street cell block was its uncanny familiarity. It looked just like the film set you'd seen a dozen times before. They reached Freddie's cell halfway down an echoing corridor. Catesby knew it was hers because her name was scribbled on a chalk board next to the cell door: *Catesby, Frederieke*. He was impressed they got the spelling right.

The sergeant knocked on the door first. 'Because,' he whispered, 'it's a woman.'

'Yes.' Her voice sounded faint and far away.

'You've got a visitor, love. Is it all right if we come in?'

'Yes.'

'Can you stand back from the door, please?' The sergeant turned to Catesby and whispered, 'It's the rules.' He slid the metal disk from the peephole and looked in the cell. As he unlocked the door the sergeant said, 'I have to lock you in. I'll be back in fifteen minutes, but if you need anything just bang on the door.'

The door clanged behind him and Catesby embraced his sister.

'Thank god you're here. Oh Will …'

'They shouldn't have let me see you, but the cop on the desk was impressed by my ID.' It was obvious to Catesby that Five had been remiss in briefing the police about access.

'It's been a long day,' said Freddie.

'I bet it has. Sit down.'

The cell walls were the same shiny white tiles you see in public toilets. And there was a toilet too, at the end of the narrow wooden bench that served for a bed. There was a barred window just below the ceiling. But the bars were superfluous for only a twelve-foot-tall giant could reach the window.

'How are you?' said Catesby folding her hands in his own.

'Frightened – and a bit woozy too. There was a doctor, a woman doctor, who examined me when I arrived. She was very nice and said I could have a sleeping pill.'

'Do you want to tell me what happened?'

'They were waiting for me when I got to my desk at GCHQ. They were surprisingly nice and polite about it all. They insisted on taking my bag, of course. But I hope I get it back. I loved that old Gladstone.'

Catesby hugged her. 'I'll get you a new one.'

'You're kind.'

'Then what happened?'

'They said I was going to be charged under the Official Secrets Act – and had to go to the police station.' Freddie smiled. 'That was a bit dramatic. I had to sit in the back of an unmarked car between two beefy men. The policeman in the driver's seat said that I had to be handcuffed, but one of the men next to me said, "We're her handcuffs." Everyone laughed and they left it at that. Oh, and there was also a woman in the front who said her name was Janet and that she was from Special Branch.' Freddie paused to brush back a stray hair. 'Have you talked to Mother?'

'She's upset and very concerned.'

'And embarrassed?'

Catesby smiled. 'Not at all. She's bragging about you to all the neighbours in Dene Road.'

She squeezed her brother's hand. 'Thanks, Will, for making me laugh. I wish we could share a cell.'

'Who knows? Some day we might.'

'And Tomasz?'

Catesby paused. 'He's not very well. I think he ate a bad sausage.'

Freddie was staring at the bleak tiles on the opposite wall. The tiles weren't just for toilets and prisons, but for madhouses and morgues too – any place that needed swilling out with a hose. These were the clammy drab tiles that never saw daylight and always stank of disinfectant.

'He's …'

'Don't,' said Catesby with a finger on his lips. He came from a trade that always assumed a prison cell had ears. Maybe Five didn't mind him being there after all. The paranoia again.

'You say,' she said, 'that Tomasz is ill?'

'Yes, bit of a fever and a tummy ache.' Catesby wasn't going to mention the hospital. Freddie had enough worries.

'And he told you about it?'

'Indirectly.'

'That's so unlike Tomasz. He never complains. He's not a hypochondriac.'

There was the sound of keys clinking in the corridor. Catesby put his arms around his sister.

'You're the only one who matters,' he whispered.

'Will you still die for me?'

Catesby smiled. 'Only after I've tried everything else.'

'Thanks.'

'*Slaap kindje slaap ...*'

There was a plaque in the entrance of Guy's Hospital that stated its origins: *Founded in 1726 to treat the incurably ill and the hopelessly insane.* Catesby was tempted to ask if you had to be both, but he assumed their remit had widened. And that's why they were dealing with Tomasz's tummy ache. Except that now, there was a lot more wrong with him. The latest symptoms included vomiting, bloody diarrhoea and hypotension.

The thing that shocked Catesby most about the Pole was his paleness. The very shape of his face had changed. His nose and cheekbones were so prominent it looked as if someone had tightened his skin from behind his ears. And yet, he had been admitted less than twenty-four hours before.

Tomasz was in a general ward with five other patients, who all looked a lot healthier. He looked up as Catesby approached the bed. There was a drip feeding into his left arm.

'Thanks for coming,' said the Pole, 'I thought you had forgotten me.'

'I should have come last night, but I was busy.'

'And I wasn't important enough?'

'Not at the time.'

'Where's Frederieke? Why isn't she here?'

Catesby winced as if he had been hit in the face. 'Why do you think she isn't here?'

Tomasz looked away and didn't answer.

'But,' said Catesby, 'I'm sure that she will come to see you when she's ... free to do so.'

'Is she in trouble?'

Catesby leaned close to the Pole's ear. 'Fuck you,' he whispered.

'You're cross, aren't you, William?'

It was Catesby's turn not to answer.

'But William, being cross is better than being dead.'

'Are you feeling sorry for yourself?'

'No,' said Tomasz, 'I don't deserve sorry, I mean sorrow ... or pity. Or whatever you call it.'

'It's not for me to judge. In any case, what happened to you?'

Tomasz managed a faint smile. 'You mean you don't know?'

'No.'

'They don't tell you anything.'

'And neither, it seems, do you.'

'No, William, you're my friend, so I will tell you.'

Tomasz managed to sit up a little and leaned forward as if confiding a great secret.

'The Central Line is always packed in the morning – and I bet that every lawyer in England gets off at Chancery Lane. They're not gentle people. It's always elbows and umbrellas. I always try to get out of their way, but yesterday ...'

'Go on.'

'I felt this sharp pain. At first I thought I had been bitten by a wasp, but then I remembered it wasn't the season for wasps – and I realised that someone had speared me with an umbrella. Look.' Tomasz pointed to the foot of his bed.

Catesby lifted the sheet. The mark was on the inside of the calf, just above the Pole's right ankle. It looked like an insect bite that had become badly infected. There was a swollen purple circle the size of a shilling.

'I began,' said Tomasz, 'to feel ill in the late afternoon – heavy sweating and nausea. My boss got the radio car to bring me here.'

'What do the doctors say?'

'They say I've got septicaemia.'

'Did you see the person who stuck you?'

'I didn't see his face, but he was wearing a bowler hat and carrying a copy of *The Times*.'

Catesby noticed that a nurse and two porters were approaching the bed.

'They've come to get me,' said Tomasz.

'What's happening?'

'They're moving me to a different ward. They can't deal with me here.' Tomasz looked at Catesby. There was pleading in his eyes. 'I want to see Frederieke.'

'One of us will come,' said Catesby.

'When?' There was desperation in the Pole's voice.
'This evening.'

The Gestapo called the resistance group die Rote Kapelle, *the Red Orchestra. The resistance spies were the 'pianists'; their secret transmitters, 'pianos', and their agent handlers 'conductors'. They were very successful. They reported Luftwaffe strength during the invasion of Russia, plans for the attack on Stalingrad, locations of Wehrmacht headquarters and updates on Germany's fuel reserves. Half the members of the Red Orchestra were women and most had been executed by early 1943.*

Catesby wasn't sure why he had gone to the Registry to withdraw the files. There certainly wasn't any problem getting them out. Their security status had been downgraded to 'confidential', the lowest classification. The Red Orchestra ledgers were now historical documents rather than current intelligence. The story had been told, but thought Catesby, it should never be forgotten. And the post-working day hush of Broadway Buildings was a good place to remember it.

Catesby had got back to Broadway Buildings at the time that most staff were leaving – and this suited him fine. He wanted to avoid the mutual embarrassment of running into colleagues who knew about Freddie. He had decided to stay closeted in his office until it was time to go back to Guy's Hospital. But he hadn't got out the Red Orchestra files just to kill time. There was something about the story – and the faces too – that was nagging at the back of his mind.

The first ledger he opened contained the file on the Schulze-Boysen/Harnack Group. There were mug-shot type photos taken by the Gestapo of four of the women that they had executed in Plötzensee Prison: Cato Bontjes van Beek, Libertas Schulze-Boysen, Eva-Maria Buch, Mildred Harnack. The women were Catesby's secret loves. They had it all: courage, decency, dignity, commitment – and even beauty. In fact, they became more beautiful the longer you looked at them. He loved their very names: Cato, Libertas – and even poor Mildred, an American academic who had married a German. Catesby looked at Mildred's file. Her 'senior thesis' at a college in Wisconsin had been titled: 'A Comparison of Chapman's and Pope's Translations of the *Iliad* with the Original'. She was beheaded on 16 February 1943. Mildred's documents also included her FBI file. The Americans seemed to have regarded her as a threat as well. The FBI file had an X through her face and a handwritten 'deceased' next to the photo.

Catesby was particularly partial to Cato Bontjes van Beek – and wondered why she had a Flemish name. Cato was the least pretty of the women, but the most beautiful the more you looked at her face. She had grown up in the artists' colony at Worpswede near Bremen. Her mother was a painter, who also danced and choreographed, and her father a potter. The family had little money. The only things the children inherited were creativity, intellectual stimulation, humanity, the courage to speak out and the strength to swim against the current. Cato's inheritance made her far wealthier than the people who executed her. She was twenty-two, as was Eva-Maria Buch. Buch lied at her trial by claiming a subversive article was all her own work – she lied to protect the real authors. She gave her own life to save the lives of others.

Catesby couldn't bear reading any more. He picked up a file that went back to the thirties and was only marginally related to the Red Orchestra ledgers. It contained an article from an American news magazine entitled, 'Baroness Beheaded'. In fact, there were two baronesses. The previous one had lost her head the year before. Both women had fallen in love with Jerzy Sosnowski, a handsome Polish spy who claimed to be a baron. The women, who had access to secret files, passed on information to their Jerzy. It was a great story. There were rumours of parties where champagne was served by the bucket and sex orgies soon followed. In the end, Sosnowski was arrested too, but managed to escape execution when he was exchanged in a spy swap. The baronesses were the two last people in Germany to be legally beheaded by axe. No one knows what eventually became of Sosnowski.

Catesby spent a minute or two staring at Sosnowski's photograph. If he had survived, he'd be far too old, but Catesby wanted to see if there was the possibility of a family connection. He decided there was no resemblance between Sosnowski and Tomasz – other than method. He put aside the Sosnowski file and went back to the Red Orchestra.

There was something about Bontjes van Beek's face and file that drew Catesby back. He opened the folder again and emptied everything on to his desk. There were more photographs, but these were not from the Gestapo. These were family photos. There were two other Bontjes van Beek sisters: one was called Mietje – and the other was Petra Bontjes van Beek. She was much younger – and the eyes much more innocent and fresh, but they still belonged to Petra.

Catesby was surprised to see that they had transferred Tomasz to what seemed to be a private intensive care ward. He had a room of his own and he was festooned with monitors and three new drips. But before Catesby was allowed access, a consultant with a bow tie asked to have a word. Normally Catesby didn't trust people with bow ties, but he could see the practical advantages for a doctor wearing one. You didn't get blood and stuff over it. The consultant took Catesby to a glassed-in cubicle.

'It appears,' said the consultant, 'that Mr Król's next of kin are not in the UK.'

'I believe that is so,' said Catesby, 'I've never met them.'

'Is there any way of contacting them?'

'You would have to ask your patient.'

'He isn't forthcoming.'

'You seem,' said Catesby, 'to suggest there is a change in his condition.'

The consultant read from a clipboard. 'Severe dehydration owing to diarrhoea; decrease in urine output and blood pressure, and an extremely high white blood cell count.' The consultant looked up from his notes. 'And he isn't responding to treatment.'

'The outlook isn't good.'

'No. We assumed, at first, that it was septicaemia, but I don't think it is.'

'Have you contacted Porton Down?' Catesby was referring to the Ministry of Defence Chemical and Biological Research Establishment in Wiltshire.

'Are you in the Security Service?'

Catesby showed his ID.

'Yes, we have. Porton Down suggested ricin poisoning.'

'Did that help?'

'No, there is no known cure or antidote for ricin.'

'So what happens next?'

'Two days, maybe three.'

'When he will lose consciousness?'

'Within the next ten hours, I would think. It doesn't happen all at once – there is some drifting in and out for a while.'

'May I see him alone?'

'Certainly.'

Oddly enough, Tomasz didn't look quite as dreadful as he had in the afternoon. They had rehydrated him a bit and he didn't look so gaunt.

'Hello, William.' The Pole tried to raise a hand in greeting, but it was pinned down by the drips. Although Tomasz looked better, his voice was much weaker.

'Freddie sends her love – she's going to be here later.' Catesby didn't mind lying. The lies were as harmless as placebo medicines.

'I wish I had never caused her any problems.'

'In that case,' said Catesby, 'there would have been no point in the relationship.'

'That's not true, William. I loved your sister, I still love her.'

'Then you can help her by telling me what you were doing.' Catesby paused and prayed that no one had bugged the ward. 'It means that I will be able to cover up the tracks a bit, make her seem less guilty.'

Tomasz blinked at the strong overhead light. There were tears in the corner of his eyes. 'And why should I be loyal to those bastards? They've killed me.'

'Are you sure it was them?'

'Who else could it be?'

Catesby wasn't sure either. 'Stay calm, Tomasz, just tell me what happened.'

'About six months ago they changed my control and gave me a new agent handler too.'

'Who are "they"?'

'The UB, of course, Warsaw. They handed over UK operations to Berlin. The idea was that the UB could spend more time cracking down on troublemakers back home in Poland. But Mischa … you know him?'

Catesby nodded.

'Mischa is an empire builder, his budget is enormous – so he has plenty of money left over for England too.'

'And your in-country handler?'

'He's new.'

'You already said that.'

'But not,' added Tomasz, 'a Pole like my previous handler. Sure, he speaks Polish but with an accent – I think he's German, Prussian maybe.'

'Where do you meet him?'

'On the number 23 bus.'

'But listen, William, last time we met, he told me something that you should know.'

'Go on.'

'There's a cuckoo in your nest …' Tomasz's eyes shifted away from Catesby towards the door.

'Who?'

But it was too late for the Pole to answer. Skardon was still wearing his trilby and there were two policemen behind him. Not ordinary bobbies, but Special Branch heavies carrying guns.

Skardon spoke first. 'You shouldn't be here, Catesby. Who gave you permission to carry out this interview?'

'I'm not here professionally – I'm here personally. Tomasz Król is my sister's fiancé – and if you don't know that, you ought to go back to Leconfield House and do your homework.'

'I don't need a lecture from you, Catesby.'

Tomasz was trying to say something. Catesby turned to the Pole and made a 'keep quiet' gesture with his hand that Skardon couldn't see. It was better not to know the 'cuckoo's' name at all than to have it blurted out in front of MI5 and the cops.

Catesby turned to Skardon. 'Don't worry, I'm going.' Then he turned back to Tomasz and put his hand on the Pole's hand. 'Thank you for loving my sister. That's the best thing you've ever done. Goodbye, Tomasz.'

'We're still friends?'

'Yes.'

Catesby got a black taxi for the trip back to Tachbrook Street. As the driver crossed Westminster Bridge, Catesby looked down the Thames. A runny layer of drizzle and road grease made the cab window look like a cine camera lens that had been coated with Vaseline. It was a trick that directors used to soften images and make them look more like Impressionist paintings than film. Catesby wondered if Koni Wolf had learned the trick. But if he came to a wet London he wouldn't need to. Catesby looked into the black void of the Thames and imagined Romans and Vikings riding the flood tide past Gravesend, Greenhithe, Greenwich and Limehouse. Did they rest on their oars to listen to the oystercatchers piping as the tide covered the mud flats? Did they think this damp island would ever be part of Europe? Did they hear the execution axe echoing from the Tower on the necks of those who got it wrong?

The lights were on when Catesby got to Tachbrook Street. As he let himself in he was met by a tall woman who, despite being in plain clothes, was obviously police.

'Hello,' she said shaking hands with a firm dry grip, 'my name is Janet. You must be William?'

'That's me,' said Catesby a little tentatively. He wasn't used to hearing his first name used by strangers.

'I'm here for a while,' said the woman, 'to keep Fred company.'

'I think I understand.'

'But,' the woman lowered her voice, 'she's sleeping at the moment.'

'That's good,' whispered Catesby as he walked into the kitchen. 'Would you like a drink?'

'I really shouldn't, I'm on duty.'

'Poor you,' said Catesby wiping a glass, 'our rules are a little less strict.'

'Well, perhaps just a tiny one.'

'Sherry, whisky or ...' There was also a bottle of Polish vodka that belonged to Tomasz. It wouldn't be right, not then. 'That's all,' said Catesby.

'A sherry would be nice.'

Catesby poured the drinks and carried them into the sitting room. Janet was good looking in a gawky English sort of way; more hockey stick than horse. He handed her the sherry and plopped into the armchair opposite the sofa where the policewoman was sitting.

'I suppose,' she said, 'you want to know what's happening.'

'Cheers,' he said raising his glass.

'Fred has been released on what is known as "police to court bail". It means she has been charged, but has still to make her first court appearance. And until it is certain that she is not going to abscond or ...'

'Or pose a threat to national security.'

Janet smiled bleakly. 'I'm just a lowly constable doing her duty, but there are issues. As far as I'm concerned, I just want to look after Fred. She's been through a lot – and I can see she's a lovely person.'

'You'd have to be blind not to.'

Janet smiled less bleakly. 'I wish my brothers were like you, William.'

'What are they like?'

'Hard hearted, but they're all right really. They just don't like to show it.'

'I used to be that way.'

'Well,' said the woman swirling her sherry, 'it's all part of growing up, isn't it?'

'Has she been asking about Tomasz?'

'You mean the Polish lad?'

'Yes.'

The policewoman lowered her voice. 'That's a difficult one. We've told her that he's in hospital, but that she can't see him at the moment.'

Catesby sipped his whisky. 'I think,' he said, 'that restriction will soon be pointless.'

'You obviously know more than I do.'

'You can have the spare room. I'll sleep on the sofa,' said Catesby.

'That won't be necessary. I've got a camp bed in Fred's room.'

Catesby looked up with surprise.

'We have to keep an eye on her ...'

'And make sure she doesn't do anything foolish.'

'But I'm sure she won't,' said the policewoman. 'Fred's a sensible girl.'

It was six o'clock in the morning when the phone rang. By the time Catesby had got up, Janet had already taken the call. She was wearing a grey dressing gown with a Royal Air Force crest over the breast pocket. Career tramlines. Different uniforms, same employer. Catesby had done the same thing.

The telephone conversation took the form of the policewoman nodding and saying 'yes' and 'right-ho'. It ended when she said 'as soon as possible'. She put the phone down and looked at Catesby.

'It's all right,' she said, 'for Fred to see Tomasz.'

They drove to Guy's Hospital in an unmarked black Wolseley. Catesby could see that Janet was an excellent driver. When they got to the hospital she parked in a bay near the entrance reserved for the police. I suppose, thought Catesby, they spend a lot of time popping in and out of hospitals. Forget your ravens. Cops, docs and priests: they're the omens of the end.

But when they got to Tomasz's ward, there were no cops and no MI5 either. The Pole was still alive, but his mouth was shut forever. He wasn't going to give away any more code words or names. The three of them sat with Tomasz for an hour and made awkward small talk. Janet then told Freddie she had to leave and gave her a hug. She promised, however, that she would be back at Tachbrook Street in the evening. Catesby and his sister then agreed to share the vigil between themselves.

Late that afternoon, a priest arrived when Catesby was alone with the Pole. The priest had an Irish accent and asked if Tomasz was a Catholic. Catesby said yes.

'Would it be all right,' said the priest, 'if I performed the sacrament of Extreme Unction?' It was, Catesby remembered from his childhood, the Roman Catholic ritual of last rites.

'Yes,' said Catesby. He wasn't sure that Tomasz would have wanted it, but it was a Pascal's Wager situation and Catesby didn't want to get it wrong. The French mathematician calculated that, even though the odds may be long, the bet doesn't cost a thing and your winnings would be infinite. Hence, logically, you'd be a fool not to make the wager.

It was a long ritual. The priest anointed with oil each of the five external senses: eyes, ears, nostrils, lips, hands. And as he did each anointing he recited the *quidquid deliquisti*:

Through this holy unction and His own most tender mercy may the Lord pardon thee whatever sins or faults thou hast committed.

The end came the next afternoon when Freddie was alone with Tomasz. She later said he coughed and intuitively she put her arms around him. She felt him shudder as his heart stopped beating. He was gone, but for a minute or two afterwards trapped air continued to exhale from his lungs – as if his soul was leaving in bits and pieces.

In the end, it was the Polish Embassy who took responsibility for the body. But only after the head Home Office pathologist had finished chopping, dissecting, weighing and testing it. A team of scientists from Porton Down was present during the post-mortem. After the coroner signed a release order, most of Tomasz was cremated in a North London crematorium. His heart, however, was flown to Warsaw where it received a military funeral and was interred near the Lane of Honour in Powąskowski Cemetery. There had, apparently, been a brief ceremony at the crematorium as well, but it was attended only by Polish Embassy staff.

Catesby wasn't surprised it had turned out that way, but was concerned about Freddie being denied the chance to pay her respects. Another awful thing was the lack of keepsakes and memories. Before all the bad stuff had happened, Freddie had a box where she kept photographs and Tomasz's letters. It meant a lot to her, but the box had been confiscated during the search of the flat and was now in a safe at MI5 headquarters in Leconfield House. Losing the box was so painful to Freddie that Catesby made a special visit to Leconfield House to ask for its return. Skardon stared at him from behind his desk and shook his head.

'No way, sunshine,' said Skardon.

'But what about the stuff that's of no intelligence value: holiday snaps, birthday cards?'

'It's all intelligence, Catesby, all part of the whole. I'm surprised you don't know that.'

'How about making copies of the stuff – I'll pay for it – and giving back the originals?'

'Catesby, you're wasting my time. The answer's no. And by the way, your sister's lucky she isn't sharing a cell with a Holloway dyke.'

Catesby clenched his fist. He wanted to lay one on Skardon. But he knew that was just what the MI5 man wanted. Instead, he turned around and walked out without saying a word. That's what Skardon didn't want.

The meeting with Henry Bone had been a long time coming. Catesby's position at Broadway Buildings had, of course, been undermined by the Tomasz Król affair and his sister's arrest. He no longer had access to top secret ledgers. It was also obvious that his career was on hold pending an MI5 interview and an in-house positive vetting. In fact, there seemed little point in his turning up for work at all. Catesby spent most of his days holed up in his office avoiding contact with colleagues. In many ways, it wasn't unpleasant. He spent a lot of time dreaming about a walking holiday in the South of France: the Auvergne, the Lot, the Tarn, Provence. Catesby even got out maps and spread them across his office floor – which was exactly what he was doing when Henry Bone walked in.

Catesby looked up. 'Do you think I should buy a donkey?'

Bone looked over Catesby's shoulder at the Lozère and the Gorges du Tarn. 'That's what Stevenson did.'

'I'd be able,' said Catesby, 'to carry a lot more stuff – a proper tent, a camp bed, storm lanterns, a cooker.'

'And you'd have someone to talk to.'

'But I'd insist on a donkey that spoke Occitan as well as standard French.'

'Very wise considering the area,' said Bone. 'You wouldn't want a town donkey who was constantly quoting Molière and Racine.'

Catesby began to gather up the map. 'It's nice of you to come and see me. I was beginning to feel like a leper.'

'In a way, your leper status is a good thing.'

'What do you mean?'

'I'll explain later. We need to have a talk.'

'Have a seat,' said Catesby. He had managed to get a pair of green leather armchairs from 'stores' when his stock was still high.

'First of all,' said Bone, 'I am very sorry that this business has affected you personally.'

'So am I.'

'And the fact that your own sister was involved at the very centre meant that we had to keep you in the dark.' Bone paused. 'It wouldn't have been fair to test your loyalty in that way. I know how much she means to you. I believe there aren't any other siblings.'

'There were twins,' said Catesby, 'but they died of Spanish influenza in 1919 – so I never met them.'

'In any case, when it became apparent that your sister and her lover were ORIOLE and CATCHER it was obvious that I was going to have to remove you from the investigation – and I don't regret doing so.'

'Which means,' Catesby paused and looked closely at Bone, 'that you were able to kill Tomasz without the embarrassment of informing me.'

'I didn't kill him. How could I? I was in Cheltenham.'

Catesby thought Bone's answer was too quick and too glib, but the alibi was a good one.

'Where's your umbrella?' said Catesby.

'It's in my office. If you like, I'll get it for you so you can submit it to a forensic examination. I wish I had never shown it you.' Bone paused. 'The irony is that we designed the umbrella, and the possibility of a crude ricin poison pellet, so that we would have the capability of carrying out assassinations for which others would be blamed. In fact, the umbrella device is an exact copy of one that has been developed and issued by the KGB. One of our Bulgarian friends passed on a blueprint. And now I seem to have been hoist by my own petard – you're blaming me.'

'Your alibis, Henry, are impressively researched, but your acting is piss poor.'

'Come off it, Catesby. It wasn't me. In fact, Porton Down haven't even developed the pellets yet. In any case, I would never have sanctioned the killing of Tomasz for operational reasons as well ethical ones – and you know it.'

'When was I taken off ORIOLE/CATCHER?'

'At the end of last year. Two of our agents, Polish army officers, who had access to Soviet military plans, were arrested. It became obvious that Polish and Russian counter-intelligence had been able to track them down because someone on our side was passing the raw intelligence accessed by our agents back to Warsaw. The finger, of course, pointed to the Russian section at GCHQ. It was narrowed down to four people – and one of them had an Eastern European boyfriend.'

Catesby looked at his shoelaces. In hindsight, it was all pretty obvious. Tomasz had merely pretended to hold right-wing anti-Soviet views as part of his cover. Guy Burgess had done the same thing in the thirties by joining the Anglo-German Fellowship, a pro-Nazi pressure group. At some point, thought Catesby, do you forget who you *really* are? And it wasn't just humans. Orchids pretended to be female bees and cuckoos laid counterfeit eggs. And who was the cuckoo that Tomasz had tried to name just before the cops walked in?

'When,' continued Bone, 'we discovered that your sister was the source, we worked with GCHQ to feed her false information knowing it would soon wing its way back to the Warsaw Pact community. It's, as you know, a risky operation. It wasn't long before Tomasz's controller realised he was sending fake gems. It looks like they came to the conclusion that Tomasz had been rumbled and turned so they ordered a wet job.'

'That's one thesis,' said Catesby.

'Can you think of any others?'

Catesby looked away and decided it was a good idea to shut up. 'Probably not,' he said.

'But,' said Bone, 'I could be mistaken – I'm not an oracle. When I try to read the minds and motivations of others I often get it wrong.'

Catesby looked at Bone. He remembered what the art historian had said about Henry's humiliation in Kiel. In that case, Henry did *get it wrong*. But there were other issues. 'You kept me in the dark about my sister being investigated.'

'I admitted that.'

'What other things are you keeping from me, Henry?'

'A few.'

'To protect me or to protect yourself?'

'To protect the secrets – and the people involved.'

'Because you know I would talk under torture.'

'We assume everyone would.'

'I've heard that line before.'

'Because it's true.'

Catesby kept looking at Henry and wondered how much he did know. Did Bone know about the forged GCHQ document announcing the demise of ORIOLE/CATCHER? Or had Henry, in fact, forged it himself? Did Henry know that Tomasz's control had been swapped from Warsaw to Berlin? And did Henry know about the cuckoo? It was a funny game. It was sometimes a good idea to show some of your cards, but never a good idea to show them all. If you didn't keep something back, you were as worthless as an empty bottle without a deposit. No one would want to keep you. Why should they?

'How are you feeling?' said Bone.

'I feel that I'm a leper in Limbo.'

'That could be useful. One man's leper is another man's spy.'

Catesby remembered Bone once telling him that the land under Broadway Buildings and the adjacent St James's Park had been the site of a thirteenth-century leper colony. How apt a location for an espionage service.

'I realise,' said Bone, 'that it must run against the grain to use your sister's arrest as an operational deception ploy. But it's too good an opportunity to pass up.'

Catesby wasn't surprised. He had seen it coming.

'When you go back to Berlin you're going to be more credible as an agent ripe for turning than ever. None of Mischa's gang is going to think you're a "dangled double" plant. You're going to look more authentic than Lenin's corpse. They'll still have their doubts, of course, but you're going to weave such a wonderful tale of how you were bullied, demoted and mistrusted that even hard men like Erich Mielke will be reaching for their hankies.'

'How long have I got?'

'We want you back in Berlin as soon as possible.'

'What about my sister?'

'I think the legal wording goes something like, "It's not in the public interest that the prosecution should go ahead." Five, of course, will be furious, but the judge will see that providing evidence without compromising signals intelligence security is impossible.' Bone paused. 'Societies without *habeas corpus* find spy trials much easier. In any case, your sister won't go to jail, but she will lose her job. I suppose she can become a teacher. A lot of busted agents end up teaching languages.'

'I'll keep that in mind,' said Catesby.

BOB was more than a mere person. BOB, Berlin Operational Base, was the CIA headquarters in the western part of the city. The Americans at BOB certainly, although unwittingly, helped Catesby develop his cover as a leper. They hated him and they constantly complained to their British and German counterparts about Catesby still having a sensitive intelligence role. In fact, Catesby's socialist leanings were part of the Berlin gossip mill long before the scandal affecting his sister. As Elmo Buckner liked to remind his colleagues, 'That Catesby guy was at Cambridge with all those commie queers – and he likes East German films.'

There were several varieties of rumour about the GCHQ business. The most common was that Catesby had been covering up for his sister – and maybe even using her as courier to pass on secrets of his own. The Americans, more than the British, were inclined to believe that badness ran in families. They didn't just arrest Julius Rosenberg, they arrested the entire family and fried two of them in the electric chair. So the American spook community didn't only whisper about Frederieke Catesby – the foreign sounding first name didn't help either – they whispered about the *Catesbys*.

The wonderful thing about Americans is their indiscretion. They will gossip in front of anyone, even the person they're gossiping about. It was, of course, inevitable that they would gossip and complain about Catesby in front of their German staff. And it was just as inevitable that the Catesby rumours would feed into the myriad of intelligence grapevines that crisscrossed the espionage swamp of Berlin.

After returning to Germany, Catesby's first visit to Soviet sector Berlin was a low-key one. He was still operating under dip cover as Cultural Attaché and had been invited to the *Volksbühne* to give a talk to drama students about Shakespeare's history plays. One of the students, a surly-looking young man in a black roll-neck jumper, kept staring at Catesby. At the end of his talk, the surly student asked Catesby if he was related to the William Catesby portrayed in *Richard III*:

The Cat, the Rat and Lovell the Dog
Rule all England under a Hog.

Catesby smiled blandly and was about to say that his background was 'far too humble', but instead said, '*proletarisch*'. As soon as Catesby said the word, he noted a slight stir from his audience. The students and their profs certainly hadn't expected a member of Her Majesty's Diplomatic Corps to describe himself as a 'proletarian'.

Catesby acknowledged their surprise by adding, 'Sorry, I probably chose the wrong word.'

Catesby's host, the Minister for Culture, eased the tension by saying, 'No problem. This is the German Democratic Republic. We welcome proletarians from all countries.'

The students and their profs didn't know whether to laugh or clap. Most decided it was safer to clap. Catesby had the impression that the presence of the Minister made them all a little nervous. The Minister, a slight bald man with glasses, sensed the unease and made excuses to leave early. He was, thought Catesby, an incredibly shy and inoffensive man to have achieved such high rank.

The Minister shook Catesby's hand as he turned to leave and said, in a voice hardly more than a whisper, 'Thank you for coming, my proletarian friend.'

Afterwards, Catesby attended a lunch that turned into a drama seminar. He recognised some of the people from Brecht's funeral. He was sitting between a director, Benno Besson, and a young playwright called Heiner Müller. Besson leaned towards Catesby and whispered, 'You know that student in the black jumper who asked you about your namesake?'

'Yes.'

'He's just returned to university after two years in an open face coalmine. The authorities thought he needed to become better acquainted with the working class.'

'To be honest,' Catesby whispered back, 'I can't say I disagree. I think it would do some of our own students a lot of good.'

Besson, who spoke German with a Swiss accent, looked mildly abashed. Catesby smiled and winked. He knew that most of what he said would be reported back to the MfS, but he had to be careful not to lay it on too thick.

The next time Catesby visited the *Volksbühne* was a week later.

Heiner Müller had invited him to attend some theatre workshops. The first was on *Macbeth*. The coalmine student was still wearing his black roll-neck and had constructed a throne for King Duncan, the 'good' king that Macbeth murders to gain the crown. But this Duncan wasn't mild and good; he was seated on a throne constructed from human corpses.

'You see,' said Müller, 'Macbeth is just another bloody tyrant carrying on the work of the bloody tyrant who preceded him.'

'What about the end of the play,' said Catesby, 'when Macduff kills the tyrant Macbeth?'

'The cycle of blood, violence and repression will continue. You realise,' said Müller, 'that Shakespeare could only have written his plays under a dictatorship.' Müller lowered his voice, 'And that only those who live in a dictatorship can fully appreciate them.'

'Is *Hamlet*,' said Catesby, 'just as bleak?'

'No, Hamlet is a pre-revolutionary hero. When he says, "What a piece of work is man," Hamlet is anticipating socialism.'

Catesby smiled. It wasn't the way they taught Shakespeare at Denes Grammar.

'Would you like,' said Müller, 'to see the set design for the new *King Lear*?'

'Yes, I would.'

The new *King Lear* was being put on by Wolfgang Langhoff. Catesby knew that Langhoff was a director who was not always favoured by the authorities. Creative artists in East Germany were like the spies who walked the tightrope between loyalty and treason. If you chose the safe option, and kept off the tightrope, you weren't going to be much good as an artist or a spy. And Wolfgang Langhoff was an artist who knew what happened when you fell off the tightrope. He tried to continue his drama work during the Hitler years and ended up in a Nazi concentration camp. Langhoff's face had literally been beaten to pulp. They used a rubber truncheon so they wouldn't fracture his skull and kill him. Instead they knocked out his teeth and smashed all the bones in his face.

Catesby followed Müller into the main theatre hall. One team of carpenters were building a hexagonal stage and another team were constructing large H-shaped wooden structures for use as portals and balconies. Langhoff, who bore a slight resemblance to T.S. Eliot, was talking to a younger man wearing a grey suit with a black jumper and a black beret. And behind them, off in the shadows, a woman was leaning over a sketch pad. It was Petra.

Müller led Catesby on to the stage to meet Langhoff. After they shook hands, he was introduced to the man in the black beret. His name was Heinrich Kilger and he was the chief stage designer. Langhoff explained his view of the play to Catesby as if the Englishman was another director.

'I want a bare stage,' said Langhoff, 'so we can see the decaying social order without the disguise of pomp.'

'Isn't "pomp",' said Catesby, 'a symptom of that decay?'

Langhoff smiled. 'That is a very good question, but others have already done that. I want to make a new *Lear*. And by the way, the king isn't mad – he is simply unwilling to change.'

As Catesby talked to the others, he kept sending furtive looks in Petra's direction. He wanted to catch her eye, but she was bent over her sketch pad. She finally looked up just as they were about to leave. Catesby saw that she was nodding, nodding a certain 'yes'.

It was a simple meal, *Jägerschnitzel* in tomato sauce with noodles. It wasn't the sort of *Jägerschnitzel* they have in the West, made from expensive cuts of veal. East German *Jägerschnitzel* was made from thin slices of lean sausage. It was one of the 300 standard meals recommended by the HO, the *Handelsorganisation*. The HO was the network of state-run shops that provided all the needs of the average East German. You went to the HO for everything from children's shoes to vodka. You could buy your wedding dress in an HO and your coffin too.

They made love as soon as they got back to the flat. It had nothing to do with his job. Catesby needed the oblivion of losing himself in that rosy void of desire and release. He wanted to leave behind his own petty world of secret ledgers, doubled agents, looking-glass lies and poisoned truths.

Afterwards they drank rough Bulgarian wine and cooked the meal together. Petra stirred the tomato sauce while it simmered. The table was set and everything was done. Catesby put his arms around Petra as she stirred the sauce. He wanted to keep kissing the back of her neck, but feared getting in the way.

'What were you drawing at the *Volksbühne*?'

'It's a poster for Wolfgang's *King Lear*.'

'May I have a look?'

'Sure.'

Turning the sketchbook pages was like leafing through Petra's consciousness. There was her bedroom window and the factory chimneys, the staircase leading to the street, the old woman in the Chausseestrasse looking for Walter, the stage designer in his black beret riding a bicycle. Her ideas for the *King Lear* poster started as line drawings and developed into half-finished watercolours. There was something of Picasso's *Guernica* in the stunned cracked faces.

Catesby looked up, 'I like the poster. I hope the play lives up to it.'

'Is it better than the International Women's Day poster?'

'Much.'

'I'm not sure,' said Petra, 'it's easier to do things that appeal to the intelligentsia. They always fall for the same tricks. The manual workers are much more discerning.'

Catesby smiled. He remembered a lecturer saying the same thing at Cambridge in the early forties. Catesby continued turning the pages. There was a design for another poster set out in the Socialist Realist style. The setting was an open face coalmine. There was a grime-stained worker's hand holding a pen. The caption read: *Pick up your pen and write, mate! Our socialist culture needs you!* And what a pity, thought Catesby, that we didn't get Papa Lawrence instead of the son.

'It's nearly ready to serve,' said Petra.

Catesby turned to the final pages of the sketchbook. There was a slim naked man stretched out on a bed with his back turned towards the artist. His head is resting on his left arm as if he is asleep. The man's skin is pale and almost delicate. There are no blemishes except for a large scar on the base of the back and the top of the right buttock. The scar is a purple recess where layers of flesh have been scooped out by a shell fragment. Catesby had seen wounds like that before. They were often found on that part of the body because human beings tend to curl up into the foetal position when shells start landing. The shell fragment must have hit the man at an angle. The resulting scar had a pink plum colour and was an unusual shape. It looked exactly like a Purple Emperor butterfly.

Above the man's reclining body there is the image of a real butterfly that seems to have hatched in the wound and taken flight. And next to the butterfly is a dark drawing of an old woman, but not a kindly one. Her nose has nearly rotted off and her face is pitted with syphilitic ulcers. She is wearing one tiny black earring that is almost invisible: it is a swastika. There are two words in Cyrillic script that fade into each other and then emerge again and repeat: *baboschka, babushka*; *babushka baboschka*. Catesby wondered how Petra had discovered the Russian folk legend: the beautiful butterfly concealing the evil witch.

'Come on,' said Petra dishing up the meal, 'grub before art.'

Catesby sat down and picked up his knife and fork. They were light because they were made from aluminium, as was most East German cutlery. But that was fine – and so was the fake *Jägerschnitzel* made from cheap HO sausage. Catesby had lived in a world of lies for so long that such minor deceptions mattered not at all. He kept looking at Petra. She ate her food with the simplicity of a hungry child. He knew that she wasn't a fake or a plant or a honey trap.

Catesby woke at first light. The factory chimneys were still smokeless, but the hammer and sickle that was bolted to the tallest turned gold in the rays of the rising sun. He looked at Petra's sleeping face beside him. He needed her to be some vestige of truth and reality. Catesby knew he was soon going to have to leap through the looking glass and start running for his life through a Salvador Dalí landscape of melted clocks and lobster telephones. 'Please,' he whispered to her sleeping form, 'please ...'

There were still no boundaries or walls between East and West Berlin. In theory, you could be stopped by customs officials, but this rarely happened. In any case, as an allied official, Catesby couldn't be stopped by any East German official at all. But this didn't mean that they couldn't follow him, photograph him and spy on his every movement. And, of course, the Americans and the Russians did the same. There was no privacy, but this didn't mean there were no secrets. No one had ever photographed Mischa even though he had an office in the middle of the city. And no one could be exactly sure who was working for whom. The swamp was full of chameleons.

It was still early morning when Catesby began to make his way from Petra's flat to the Schwartzkopffstrasse U-Bahn station, but he knew there were dozens of eyes watching him. In order to feast those eyes further, and because it was a pleasant morning, Catesby skipped the U-Bahn station and continued walking to Friedrichstrasse where he could get the S-Bahn train directly to his office at Olympiastadion. Friedrichstrasse was a crossing point with the iconic sign that issued the warning in all four languages: VOUS SORTEZ DU SECTEUR AMÉRICAIN. The Americans played up the drama and there was always a detachment of GIs chewing gum and glaring into the Soviet sector. As he strode out of the East and past a GI lounging behind the wheel of his Willys jeep, Catesby wanted to shout, 'Look. They didn't eat me.' Yet.

Catesby worked in N Block, the North Block of the Olympic Stadium. The stadium had sustained little damage during the war. The British established their headquarters there in 1945 and never left. It was a convivial place. There were fourteen bars and a Naafi restaurant called the Somerset Arms. Most of Catesby colleagues were military, but there was a small contingent of SIS as well as SIGINT personnel from GCHQ. Catesby had a small office of his own with a safe and a dubiously secure landline. The arrangement was very generous since he wasn't officially there at all, he was still in the directory as Cultural Attaché assigned to the embassy in Bonn.

Catesby had also been assigned a barracks-style billet which he had to share with a ginger-haired tank corps major called Ginger. Ginger had been very disappointed when Catesby turned up. Before that, the major had had the room to himself.

'Don't worry,' said Catesby when he first arrived, 'I don't exist.'

'Oh, you're one of those,' said the major who was lying on his bed reading *Horse and Hound*.

As Catesby hung up his spare clothes in the green steel utility locker at the end of his bed, he added, 'I won't be spending a lot of time here. It's just a bolt hole.'

During the weeks that followed the major was pleased to see how little his new roommate did exist. The affair with Petra developed from a liaison into a relationship. No words were spoken; it just happened. They didn't need to say the words. Catesby settled into a routine of commuting between the East Berlin flat on Chaussestrasse and his office at British HQ Olympia. He didn't feel much different from an insurance broker commuting between Putney, say, and the City of London. Except that his daily journey took him from a communist country to the headquarters of a Western spy station. But this was Berlin, the last undrained primeval espionage swamp where dinosaurs rose from the slime to chase … butterflies.

Like any good spy, Catesby varied his route to work. Sometimes he took the S-Bahn, sometimes he took the U-2 from Rosa-Luxemburg-Platz or the Alexanderplatz. Sometimes he didn't go to work at all, but spent the day in Petra's studio reading and watching her paint. Her studio was in a loft that overlooked the huge girder bridge where the S-Bahn trains crossed over the junction of Gartenstrasse and Ackerstrasse. When you looked out the window you felt you could almost touch the rivets which were the size of dinner plates. Every five minutes the studio shook as a train rattled past, but Petra's paintbrush always remained steady. She had been through much worse.

From time to time Catesby had to leave Berlin to spend a few days in his office at British Embassy Bonn. He had, after all, to keep up the pretence of his cover story. Most professional spies operate under diplomatic cover. This means that if they break laws of the host country – often in ways that would earn an ordinary person the death sentence – they can claim dip immunity and be merely PNG'd and sent home instead of to the gallows. It wasn't, however, a complete guarantee. Spies with diplomatic immunity, like Kit Fournier, sometimes did meet sticky ends. They were kidnapped or murdered by groups that couldn't be traced back to the host government. But, in general, a spy with dip cover plied a safer trade than an NOC, a spy operating under 'non-official cover'. When NOCs got caught, they got the chop – as in chopped up – and no one could do anything about it. And yet, NOCs were the poor foot soldiers who did the most valuable work. No fake diplomat could ever go under cover as a cleaner or a plumber to penetrate a Soviet military base with a hidden camera. Catesby's big fear was that one day he would be a NOC instead of a dip.

The Bonn embassy interludes were good for secure communication and intelligence updates. Telephone and radio communication out of West Berlin was notoriously prone to SIGINT intercept by the MfS, but Bonn's lines were pretty safe and there was also the utter security of diplomatic bag and Royal Signal Corps courier. Catesby used the embassy facilities to send long UK EYES ALPHA reports to Henry Bone and to update himself on the latest ledgers in the registry archive vault.

Catesby was pleased to see that Sidney was still the registry clerk, but noticed a coolness in his manner that hadn't been there before. He wondered if the coolness was owing to his promotion or because he spent so much time away from Bonn – or rumours.

'Did you,' said Catesby, 'put that five bob on Ipswich that I told you to last summer?'

'No, sir, but I see that they have gone up.' End of conversation.

Catesby signed for the ledgers and went back to his office.

The most interesting of the updates was a reappraisal of MfS penetration and effectiveness. Mischa's boys were doing extremely well. It was estimated that the East Germans were now accounting for eighty per cent of *all* intelligence on NATO. Catesby could see a pattern emerging that included Tomasz's swap from Warsaw control to Berlin – and even his own mission. Mischa was a rising star, but he had to walk a tightrope too – between his own success and the jealousy of others.

Catesby pushed the ledgers aside and leaned back in his chair. He closed his eyes and listened once again to the counterpoint whistles of steam locomotive and Rhine barge. They seemed, curiously, to have changed roles since last time. The train was now the alto and the barge was the bass. Would, Catesby thought, they ever change back again? Catesby felt like a worm that had been cut in half and was twisting all over the dissection table. He was living in two worlds that could never be reconciled.

It was Catesby's second evening back in Berlin. He had had to work late at N Block on a lot of routine stuff concerning the renting and maintenance of safe houses in the British sector of Berlin. It was a pain: the landlords, cleaners and plumbers all had to be vetted. And how could you securely vet anyone in Berlin? It was estimated that Mischa was running twenty to thirty thousand agents in West Germany. Keeping the safe houses tidy and supplied with clean linen with security vetted staff was a real pain. Berlin was probably the only city in the world where being a cleaning lady was a lucrative profession.

It happened when Catesby was walking up Chausseestrasse from the U-Bahn station. Summer was finally coming and the evenings were getting long and pastel. He was looking forward to Petra. He had brought some wine and cheese from a West Berlin shop and hoped she wouldn't be cross. Anything from the Naafi was a definite no-no, but sometimes a treat from a West German shop – provided it wasn't an expensive luxury – could be acceptable.

Catesby first noticed the car because it sounded different. It didn't wheeze or rattle like most East Bloc vehicles, it richly purred. And, as it hove up beside him, Catesby could see that it was huge. He guessed who it was. There aren't many powder-blue Cadillacs with armour plating and tinted bulletproof windows on the streets of Berlin. And when you see one, and there probably was only one, it's going to be Bill Harvey, CIA Chief of Station. The man from BOB.

The driver slowed to a walking pace and Bill Harvey rolled down the rear window. 'Hey Catesby,' he said, 'long time no see. Get in and we'll give you a lift.'

'Thanks, Bill, but I don't need a lift.'

The Cadillac continued to keep pace with Catesby. It was a bit embarrassing. There weren't many people in the street, but they all seemed to be staring. It wasn't the sort of incident he wanted reported back to the MfS. Catesby knew it wouldn't be easy to get rid of Bill Harvey. He was a dangerous man who didn't recognise boundaries. The car continued to purr along beside him.

'Catesby,' Harvey rolled down the window another couple of inches, 'I want you to get in the car so we can have a little talk.'

'Some other time, Bill, I'm busy this evening.'

Catesby saw Harvey lean forward to whisper something to a hard-looking man in the front passenger seat. CIA operatives called it 'riding shotgun'. And in this case, there was a real shotgun. Catesby could see the barrel of a sawed-off pump action 12 bore sticking up between the bodyguard's legs. Bill Harvey was paranoid about being kidnapped by the MfS or the KGB. His alcoholism made the paranoia worse.

'Catesby?' Harvey's voice was a lot louder.

'Yes.'

'Are you gonna get in the car?'

'No.'

Catesby looked behind him. He was poised to turn around and start running.

Suddenly, Bill Harvey was shouting at the top of his lungs. 'Catesby, get in the goddamn car!'

Harvey's voice echoed off the surrounding buildings like shell-fire. Windows started to open and curious Berliners stuck their heads outside to see what was happening. Catesby was still thinking of running when the front passenger door opened and a tall man stepped on to the footpath. The bodyguard was wearing dark glasses and looked ready for a race.

'Okay,' said Catesby, 'I'll go for a ride.'

He got into the backseat and sat beside Harvey. The CIA man was huge. He must have weighed fifteen stone, but there was still plenty of room on the back seat. American cars were about size and power – and sex too, for those huge car seats were portable beds. And the armoured Cadillac had a cocktail bar too that unfolded from the partition that separated the rear passengers from driver and shotgun.

'Would you like a Martini?' said Harvey.

'Yes, please.'

'Vodka or gin?' Harvey suddenly laughed. 'What a silly question.' The American pressed a button and a soundproof window slid into place between themselves and the front seats. 'You want vodka, don't you, Catesby?'

'Well, actually, I prefer gin.'

'Is that what you tell Blanco when he invites you to the club for drinks with Kim Philby?'

Catesby was intrigued that Kit Fournier's nickname for Dick White had caught on, but played the innocent. 'Who,' he said, 'is Blanco?'

'Don't play games.'

'Blanco means white,' said Catesby in pretend thoughtfulness, 'so I assume you mean the DG, Sir Richard White.'

'God, you Limeys can't stop being deceitful slime balls for five seconds. It's in the genes.'

Catesby looked at Harvey as he made the Martinis. The American looked more intelligent and kind in profile then he did front on. Or maybe it was a trick of the light. Harvey put a slice of lemon in Catesby's glass. Catesby noticed the way Harvey's jacket was distorted by the shoulder holster as he passed him the Martini.

'Cheers.'

'Does Blanco,' said Harvey, 'know that you've moved in with a piece of East German pussy – or are communist girlfriends now mandatory for all British agents who aren't queer? Why are you laughing?'

'Because, Bill, you're so funny.'

But Catesby was also laughing because it was a safe response.

He knew that the Cadillac was wired up to record every word he uttered. And that Bill Harvey had a track record for busting British agents. It was Harvey who spooked Burgess and Maclean. It was Harvey who got Philby PNG'd from Washington. And, Catesby now realised, it was Bill Harvey's first wife who was the subject of the obscene cartoon that Guy Burgess had drawn at a drunken dinner party. Harvey wasn't likely to spend his annual leave at the Chelsea Flower Show. He regarded the Brits as mincing whores.

Catesby could see from the neon lights and the Mercedes that they were now in the American sector. He soon recognised that they were on the Kurfürstendamm – the famous Ku'damm with its noisy glitter – heading towards Grunewald. Harvey had turned silent. He seemed to have guessed that Catesby knew that the car was bugged and that he wasn't going to give anything away.

'Where are you taking me?'

'Where do you want to go, Catesby?'

'I want you to show me something really secret that the Brits aren't supposed to know about?'

It was Harvey's turn to laugh. 'And that, Catesby, is exactly what I'm going to do?'

Harvey pressed a button and the interior soundproof window came down. 'Hank,' he said, 'there's a change of plans. Take us to Teufelsberg instead.'

Teufelsberg, Devil's Mountain, was a 400-foot mound on the western outskirts of the city. It was completely man-made and had been constructed from millions of tons of rubble that had been cleared from Berlin at the end of the war. It was a sinister place and its ruins of war were well seasoned with the broken bones of Germans and Russians lost in the debris. The area around Teufelsberg had never been urban. Although they were still within the city limits of Berlin, the road now twisted through wooded countryside. On two occasions deer appeared in the car headlights as they nimbly skipped out of the car's path and into the dark wood. Catesby wanted to join them.

The Cadillac finally turned off the road on to a rough track. A couple of minutes later they stopped in front of a padlocked gate that was topped with barbed wire. On the right-hand side of the gate there was light from what appeared to be a guard post. A helmeted MP with a .45 automatic on his hip came over to the car, but seeing who it was didn't even bother to ask for IDs.

Harvey rolled down the window and said, 'Can you let us in?'

The MP saluted and opened the gate.

As the Cadillac rolled through the gate, Harvey leaned forward to speak to his body guard. 'Get your gun ready, Rick. Those boar come out at night.'

Then he turned to Catesby. 'When we fenced it in, we trapped a herd of wild boar. You ought to see them. There's one big bastard that must weigh over 600 pounds. I'm not even sure that Rick's twelve-gauge could bring down that son-of-a-bitch. We might have to get the Thompson out of the trunk to finish him off.'

The Cadillac followed a Z-shaped track that looked like it had been recently bulldozed into the hillside. In the dozen years since the war, the rubble mountain had become part of nature. It was covered with thorny scrub and saplings. Catesby could imagine an irate boar charging out of the undergrowth to take on the Cadillac in one on one tusk-to-fin combat.

As the car approached the top of Teufelsberg Catesby could see the lights of Berlin sparkling in the distance. The view was spectacular as well as unique. Because Berlin is located on such a flat plain, Teufelsberg was the only place from where you could see the city in its entirety. Catesby immediately grasped the strategic importance of the mound.

When they finally got to the top, Catesby could see that the summit had been levelled by bulldozers. There was also a lot of construction equipment and building material.

'Let's have a look around,' said Harvey opening the car door.

Catesby followed him into the starlight, his Martini still in his hand.

'This,' said the American, 'is our next big plan. You guys spoiled the last one. You completely fucked it, in fact.'

Catesby stayed silent.

'Didn't you?' said Harvey.

'I really don't know.'

But Catesby did know. Bill Harvey was talking about STOP-WATCH, the Berlin tunnel operation which had tapped into a crucial telephone junction used by the Soviet military and KGB. The tunnel was a work of engineering and technical genius and it had all been Bill Harvey's idea. It burrowed nearly a mile into the Soviet sector under the most heavily guarded border in the world.

It was Harvey's pride and joy, and rightly so. For eleven, what seemed glorious, months, the CIA and the British had tapped and taped hundreds of thousands of top-level Soviet and Warsaw Pact conversations. The intelligence treasure trove required an army of translators and typists to transcribe. Catesby remembered that the information passed on to GCHQ had given Freddie hours of over-time for months on end. But it was all useless.

In fact, the intelligence was worse than useless. The tunnel had been compromised while it was still in the planning stages. The Rus-sians had rubbed their hands with glee and used the tapped cables as a conduit for false information. The tons of bogus intelligence had simply clogged up Western intelligence. Million of hours of valuable time had been wasted translating and analysing rubbish.

'Who was it, Catesby?' Harvey's voice had become slurred with drink. 'We know that the tip-off came from London. Who was it? It couldn't have been Philby – we made damned sure he wasn't any-where near the stuff. Was it one of your pals, or just an acquaintance …'

Catesby turned away from Harvey and looked out over the pano-rama of night-time Berlin. He wondered which flicker of light was nearest Petra. If only he could send her a message saying he would be late.

'Or was it? Look at me, Catesby.'

Catesby turned and found Harvey's revolver pointing straight between his eyes.

'Or was it you? I always thought you were the one.'

Harvey was pointing the gun in the two-handed stance he had learned as an FBI trainee, long before his CIA days.

'No,' said Catesby as calmly as possible.

'I don't believe you.'

Catesby froze as he watched Harvey pull the trigger. And then there was a hollow click and the sound of Harvey's boozy laughter. The American continued laughing as he reloaded the bullets and slipped the revolver back into his shoulder holster.

'But this time, Catesby, there aren't going to be any Brits involved.' Harvey made a sweeping gesture that encompassed the flattened top of Teufelsberg. 'We're going to turn this place into the best god-damned SIGINT listening station in the world. Our instruments are going to be so sensitive that we'll hear Erich Mielke's sphincter dilate when he dumps last night's sauerkraut in the pan.' Harvey finished his Martini and tipped out the ice and lemon. 'And no more Brits are going to be allowed in even if they're wearing kilts and playing the "Star Spangled Banner" on the bagpipes. So have a good look, Catesby, you're the last one.'

Bill Harvey didn't take Catesby all the way back to Chausseestrasse. 'It's nearly midnight,' he said, 'and I don't want to get kidnapped by the KGB. But you're okay, Catesby, you've got an arrangement.'

They dropped Catesby at a U-Bahn station on the Ku'damm that was notorious as a hangout for prostitutes of both sexes.

As the Cadillac pulled away, Harvey shouted, 'You'd better not get the clap, Catesby, they'll send you back to the West.'

As Catesby began to walk down the station stairs he looked at his hands and realised they were empty. He had left the presents he'd bought for Petra in Harvey's Cadillac.

It was nearly one o'clock when he got back to the flat. Petra was sitting at the table in a nightdress and crocheting a flower design on a cushion cover. She was working by the dim light of an oil lamp. There were tear tracks on her face. Catesby tried to kiss her, but she pulled away.

'What's wrong?' he said.

'Nothing.'

'Is the electricity off again?'

'No, but don't turn the light on.'

Catesby knelt down next to her.

'Why?' he said.

'I don't want you to see me. I'm not very pretty.'

Catesby buried his face in her lap and put an arm around her back. He could feel the bony ridges of her spine against his wrist. The thin layer of skin seemed so delicate and tightly drawn. He thought of the bones churned into the rubble of Teufelsberg. If it happened again a few Londoners might survive … but Berlin? Nothing, nothing … not even a bone this time. Berlin wasn't just a spy station; it was an expendable explosive trip wire.

'You're everything,' he said, 'everything.'

He felt her hand stroking the top of his head.

'It can't go on, William.'

'Yes it can, and it will.'

'You're talking nonsense. They won't let us stay together.'

Catesby sensed something had happened that Petra hadn't told him about. He took her hand and kissed it.

'It happened again today.'

'What happened?' said Catesby.

'They came in a car and took me to Normanennstrasse. It was my third interview.'

'Why didn't you tell me about the others?'

'I was afraid that it would scare you away.' Petra paused. 'They say you are a British intelligence officer.' She playfully pinched his nose. 'Well?'

Catesby couldn't see any point in keeping up the pretence. 'Yes, of course I am.' He paused and stroked her cheek with the back of his hand. 'And what about you, Petra?'

'I really am an artist, but … I'm also what they call an *Inoffizieller Mitarbeiter*. Many of us are.'

Catesby wasn't surprised that Petra was an IM. More than 300,000 East Germans did paid or unpaid work for the secret police. It was just the way things were.

Catesby smiled. 'I suppose you have to spy on me.'

'Of course.'

'Can you tell me about the interviews?'

'Now,' said Petra smiling, 'you're spying on me.'

'Then don't tell me. I wouldn't want you to get in trouble.'

Petra put her arms around Catesby. 'I will tell you. I don't want there to be any secrets between us.'

Catesby closed his eyes. He could feel a demon sitting behind his brow chipping away at his brain with a masonry hammer.

'The first interview was just note-taking. No threats, just questions. They asked how I met you, if we made love, where you were from, what you did. That sort of thing.' Petra paused. 'The second interview was awful. It happened when you were away in Bonn. One of them didn't say a thing, he just sat there and watched, but the other one accused me of consorting with a Western intelligence agency that wanted to overthrow the government of the GDR. He made me so angry that I shouted back at him – and called him a cretin. It was funny, the other policeman smiled when I said that. But then the other guy got really angry and started saying all sorts of crazy things like I could lose my job, my flat and even my GDR citizenship.'

'You must have been frightened.'

'Yes, but I didn't show it. I knew it was all bluff and ...' Petra gave a twisted smile that Catesby had never seen before. 'And I could get *him* in a lot of trouble if I wanted to.'

'And today?'

'It was different. The man who threatened me last time wasn't there, but the other one was. It was all very calm and reasonable. They asked me some more questions, but then they started talking about you. They know who you are, but they don't know what you're trying to do.' Petra stopped and put her hands over her face.

Catesby hugged her tight. 'What's wrong?' he said.

'I wanted to say that you're here not to spy, but because ...'

'But because I want to be with you, I care for you.'

'But I know that's impossible.'

Catesby tried to kiss her but she kept turning her head away. 'Let's go to bed,' he said.

'Not yet,' she said. Petra took both of Catesby's hands in hers and stared directly into his face. 'I've got something important to say. Are you listening?'

'Yes.'

'And, William, I really mean what I'm going to say. Listen.' Petra paused. It wasn't easy for her to say the words. It meant renouncing a dream. 'I love you more than the socialist future we are trying to build out of these ruins. I will come with you to the West. I will be your English housewife and prune your roses and make your tea. And if you don't want that, I'll be your mistress or your whore. Why are you looking at me like that?'

Catesby held her close so she couldn't look into his eyes and see his soul. It wasn't a pretty sight. 'I love you,' he said, 'too much to ask that of you. I want to stay here with you. We can build socialism together.' Catesby held her tighter. 'I don't deserve your love ...'

Petra pulled away so she could look at him again.

'Are you serious?' she said.

'Yes.'

'Do you mean you're going to become a *defector*?'

Catesby had known all along that he was going to have to do this, but the word still rankled in his ears. He knew that he was stepping over the edge into an abyss. If there was a safety rope, it might not have anyone on the other end. He was becoming a NOC. There was

223

no immunity for deep penetration agents. And yet, that wasn't the worst thing. The worst thing wasn't betraying your country, even if the betrayal was genuine. The worst thing was betraying someone who loved you.

'Yes,' said Catesby, 'I decided to defect some time ago. It's because I love you and want to share your life and your ideals. We can't do that in the West.'

Petra was staring at him. He wondered if she could still see the Judas look in his eyes. If only, thought Catesby, she had not offered to come with him to the West. Then he wouldn't have had to make the choice. Petra had offered him a way out of the game – to an English rose garden – and he had refused it.

'I hope you mean that, William.' Petra stood up to blow the candle out. 'Let's go to bed.'

The next morning Catesby made his final trip back to the North Block at Olympiastadion. He told Petra that it was to get his clothes and tell lies about his whereabouts, but the real reason was to send an encoded cable to Henry Bone. When Catesby cleared his locker he realised that he couldn't take any spy stuff with him. A search by his new hosts of his person or belongings that revealed a one-time pad, a dead-drop spike or a hollowed-out coin would land him in a basement cell in the Normanennstrasse. He couldn't even be caught with a piece of chalk. Catesby reached into his trouser pocket to find the chalk and threw it in the wastepaper bin. Chalk was an essential spy tool for leaving cryptic marks on lamp posts or dustbins. It was a means of communicating with a courier, cut-out or agent handler. Why would anyone other than a schoolteacher carry chalk in their pocket? Catesby knew he was going into the cold. He had memorised a list of contacts and escape routes, but they were all impossible.

The MfS paid Catesby the compliment of picking him up in one of the new GAZ M21 Volgas. The car had a five-pointed red star emblazoned with gold hammer and sickle on the front of the bonnet. Marshall Zhukov had personally demanded the red star be added after a visit to the car plant at Gorky. The secret police had waited almost a week to call Catesby in for interview. The local band of Chausseestrasse informers, largely pensioners with spare time, had reported that the Englishman was no longer making his daily journey to the West. But the MfS waited just to make sure Catesby had really settled in place.

The policeman arrived early in the morning as they were having breakfast. He was dressed casually in civilian clothes, open-necked shirt and a sports top bearing the emblem of the Dynamo football team, and was very polite. He told them to finish their breakfast and that the interview was completely voluntarily, but that Catesby had to bring his passport and that Petra wasn't to come with him.

The interview panel was led by a colonel. Catesby knew that he was a colonel because he was in uniform and was wearing his medal ribbons. There were two others present who were in civilian clothes: one took notes, the other merely watched. The colonel was a handsome man with a great quiff of grey hair who resembled a famous conductor. The interview lasted just over an hour and concentrated on Catesby's reasons for wanting to stay in the GDR. Catesby was, at first, surprised that the interview had hardly touched on the fact that he was a defecting intelligence officer. He then realised that those present hadn't the security clearances necessary to ask such questions.

The next interview took place the following day and lasted more than an hour. This time there were two policemen and a driver to take Catesby to MfS Headquarters. The atmosphere was more strained and the accompanying police said little. When they got to Normanennstrasse, Catesby was driven through a gate into an inner courtyard. The MfS Headquarters was a huge complex of modern grey buildings, seven or eight storeys high, which towered over the Lichtenberg district. Catesby felt a sudden chill as the gate closed behind the lumpy Volga. There was nothing soft or pretty about the inner courtyard: no trees, no grass, no flowers. Just tarmac, concrete and parked vehicles. There was no hint of an outside world. The buildings were shoulder to shoulder with no gaps.

Catesby was led into a building designed in minimalist Scandinavian style: glass, stainless steel and light pine. There were lifts, but the policemen led Catesby up seven flights of stairs. He had the impression that physical fitness was an MfS trademark. Catesby was seated in a foyer with plate-glass windows that looked out over the city. For the first time he felt a total lack of control. Someone had pressed a button and he was now on a conveyer belt that he couldn't stop. It was a little like joining the army, but the army had been full of cheery, cheeky Brits and a pub was never far away.

Finally, the door opened and Catesby was summoned into an office that was uncluttered and full of light. The office was shaped like a long gallery. On one side were the ceiling to floor plate-glass windows; on the other, filing cabinets and shelves stacked with books and documents. The atmosphere was puritanical without being harsh. In fact, the desk at the far end of the office had vases of flowers. The man sitting behind the desk was about fifty and was signing documents. He had the sort of face you sometimes see on boxers; the more successful boxers who give more punches than they take. Catesby instantly recognised the man from file photos, but hadn't expected the intensely sad eyes. The eyes belonged to Erich Mielke, head of the East German State Security Service.

Mielke stood up as Catesby approached his desk. He was less than average height, but had broad shoulders and a deep chest. Mielke drank little and exercised a lot. On the wall behind him was a plaque bearing the coat of arms of the MfS: a sinewy arm brandishing a rifle. Catesby knew the emblem well. It was the same coat of arms displayed on the fake MfS ID that he had carried in Hungary. Would, Catesby thought, Colonel Telemann ever come back to haunt him?

The first thing that Mielke did was lean across his desk to shake hands with Catesby. His handgrip was firm and dry. The first thing that Mielke said was, 'You can't stay here in Berlin.'

'I realise that,' said Catesby.

'Why do you realise that?'

'Because I would, at best, be kept under constant surveillance by the Americans, the British and the West German security services. At worst, I could be kidnapped or arrested.'

'Why haven't the British arrested you already?'

'They don't know what I've done. In my job, I have a great deal of freedom of movement.'

'Enough freedom of movement to have a sexual relationship with a citizen of the German Democratic Republic?'

'Yes,' Catesby smiled, 'they trust me.'

'Why should we trust you?'

Catesby looked straight at Mielke. 'Because I am going to tell you everything I know – and in so doing I will betray my country.'

'Why have you decided to become a,' Mielke paused as if he were savouring the next word and wanted to throw it in Catesby's face, 'traitor?'

'There are a number of reasons. I come from a working-class background and I've been sympathetic to socialism since an early age. Over the last few years I've become increasingly opposed to British policy …'

For the next twenty minutes Catesby ticked off a list of wrongs that included Korea, Kenya, Iran, Malaya, Suez, subservience to Washington and the Labour Party's betrayal of the working class under Gaitskell. While he spoke Catesby noticed that Mielke was reading a file that lay open on his desk. It was probably his latest MfS biography and Mielke wanted to make sure that all the points tallied.

'And, of course,' said Catesby, 'there's the business concerning my sister, Frederieke.' For a second he thought he might be laying the pitch on too thick like an over-keen second-hand car dealer.

Mielke looked up from the file and stared at Catesby for what seemed a long time. 'Did you know that your sister was passing on secrets?'

'Not at first, only towards the end.'

'And what did you do, Herr Catesby?'

'I tried to protect her.'

'How?'

'By not reporting what I knew about her activities.'

'Did you give her any additional information to pass on?'

'No.'

'Someone did. Who was it?'

'I don't know.'

Catesby stared into space. He did know. Catesby knew that he was going to be put in these corners again and again and he needed to practise his responses. Mielke knew that someone in England had passed false information to Freddie's desk in the knowledge that she would pass it on to Tomasz. It was the same sort of trick that the Russians played with the Berlin tunnel. Catesby had detailed knowledge of British 'disinformation' operations and knew the names of those involved. But it was one of many things that Catesby couldn't reveal. The most precious secrets were branded with the names of real people who could be arrested, tortured and killed. Whether or not they deserved it was another question. No one in the trade was an innocent civilian. On the other hand, if Mielke realised that he was holding back information, the game was up.

'Who do you think it was?' Mielke wasn't giving up.

'I suppose the immediate source would have been my sister's supervisor at GCHQ.' Catesby then suggested real names, but names far removed from the process.

'Have you brought anything with you?' said Mielke.

Catesby bent down, took off his shoe and unscrewed the heel. Inside the hollowed-out heel were five microfilm containers that Catesby emptied on to Mielke's desk. It was the least that could be expected of any defector – even a fake one. The microfilms contained genuine, but heavily edited intelligence. Catesby had also memorised a list of secrets he could pass on and the names of pawns that could be sacrificed. These were agents who had outlived their usefulness – and probably their lives. Bad luck for them.

Catesby watched Mielke take a drawstring pouch out of a desk drawer. He counted the microfilm containers before putting them in the pouch. Mielke wrote the details on a tag and tied it to the pouch. There was something endearing about a man in such a powerful position doing a simple clerical task. Catesby had read Mielke's SIS biography and knew that the German liked to brag about his working-class background. Mielke's father had been a labourer in a sawmill. His mother died when he was three. When he was twenty-three Mielke shot to death two Berlin policemen who were notorious for harassing communists and had to flee to the Soviet Union.

Erich Mielke was certainly hard and ruthless, but where did those sad eyes come from?

Finished with the microfilm pouch, Mielke looked up at Catesby. 'What were you doing in a car with the CIA boss for Berlin?' Mielke looked down at the file on his desk. 'It happened nine days ago?'

'His name is William King Harvey ...'

'We know that.'

'Harvey and his bodyguard intimidated me into getting into the car.' Catesby sensed that his excuse didn't carry much weight with someone who went around shooting policemen.

'Why did Mr Harvey want to talk to you?'

'He wanted to frighten me.'

'Did he succeed?'

'A little.' Catesby than gave a frank and full account of the evening, but left out Harvey's crudeness. He wondered what the two men would make of each other. Mielke would slaughter Harvey in the boxing ring, but they might be more evenly matched in a gunfight if Harvey was sober.

Mielke gave Catesby a searching stare. 'Do you consider yourself a brave man, Herr Catesby?'

'Not particularly.'

'It's better to be brave. Being a coward doesn't help you survive – and it also means no one will trust you.'

They didn't let him go back to the flat in Chausseestrasse. The interrogation lasted four days and when it was over they put Catesby in a car with tinted windows and drove him out of Berlin. Neither his driver nor his two MfS minders would tell Catesby where he was going. They drove late into the night. Catesby completely lost his bearings and had no idea in which direction they were heading. He wasn't even sure they were still in Germany. When they turned off the main road and bounced down a rough track with thick forest on either side Catesby began to think he had reached the end. But then, why had they brought him so far to do it?

The car finally came to a halt. Catesby looked over the driver's shoulder. The car headlamps beamed on a white timber-frame house that looked almost English. The driver turned around and said, 'We're here.'

The next six months were the happiest in Catesby's life. There was no electricity and they had to pump their own water, but there was plenty of firewood. The nearest village with an HO was a ten-minute bicycle ride, including the places where you had to wheel the bike because the track was too rough. But as the collective farms were allowed to sell surplus produce directly to the public, it was possible to get eggs, vegetables and poultry without even going to the village HO. It took Petra a while to get used to the idea. She thought queuing at an HO with a string bag was a daily ritual for any good socialist. But Catesby pointed out that they had already made enough sacrifices for the state.

The safe house was in a remote and thickly wooded part of Saxony. There were lakes nearby where they went swimming when the weather was still warm. The locals were friendly, but showed little curiosity about why they were there. At first Catesby thought they had been warned by the MfS, but later realised it was ordinary rural reticence. He grew to like them, but could hardly understand a word they said unless they made an effort to speak standard German.

'You're supposed to be an Anglo-Saxon,' laughed Petra, 'but you can't understand a single word of Saxon.'

As Catesby learned the dialect, he found some words did sound Anglo-Saxon, like *Muckefuck*, which meant ersatz coffee made from beans. There were other words that had survived the North Sea voyage: *Palaver* was just that and *muddeln* was to go slowly. Catesby also liked *schwoofen*, to go dancing, but he much preferred to stay *Daheeme*, at home, curled up in front of the fire with Petra.

There was a spare room with rough exposed beams that looked west over an overgrown apple orchard. Catesby's big autumn project was to turn it into a studio for Petra. He found an old pot-bellied cast-iron stove in an outbuilding and enlisted the help of Siegfried, the local tractor repairer, to move the stove into the room and knock through a chimney. Catesby was impressed by Siegfried's skill and handiness. There was no *muddeln*, but there were breaks for home-made plum brandy made by Siegfried's wife.

'She makes this,' he said, 'so I keep quiet and fall asleep.'

When Siegfried learned that the room was going to be an artist's studio, he suggested an extra window for more light. The next day he arrived with an oak window-frame on the back of a flat-bed trailer pulled by a new MTZ-2 from the Minsk Tractor Works in Belarus. Catesby could see Siegfried wanted to show off.

Petra loved her new studio and started painting oil portraits of Catesby. He was surprised to see how he looked in her eyes: older and darker than he looked in a mirror. In none of the portraits was he ever looking at her. His eyes were always furtive, always looking away – and sometimes dead and cold. It frightened him. He didn't want to be like that – or, at least, he didn't want her to see it.

But most of the time, it was good, very good. After the first few months Catesby began to think that they had forgotten all about them, that their file had gone missing. He fantasised they were going to be left there in peace for the rest of their lives. He even began to think, recklessly perhaps, about babies, but never mentioned it to Petra. There was a lot they didn't talk about. At some point, the silence would need to be broken and Catesby knew he would be the first to break it.

It happened on a late November afternoon. The light in the studio had started to go and Petra began to pack up. Catesby went over to the bookshelf he had constructed where Petra kept her art books and her sketch pads. He was proud of the bookshelf. It was the most practical thing he had ever done. And more satisfying than anything he had ever done in Broadway Buildings or Bonn or Berlin. It was useful and it didn't hurt anyone. The bookshelf was exactly what it appeared to be. There weren't any hidden microphones or cameras; it wasn't going to explode. Catesby found the sketchbook and carried it over to Petra.

'There's something,' he said, 'I've always wanted to ask you … but never had the courage.' Catesby opened the sketchbook to the drawing of the nude male with a scar the shape of a butterfly.

Petra looked at the sketch. Her face was expressionless.

'Who …' The word came out as less than a whisper. Catesby couldn't finish the sentence. He didn't want to ask the question. He didn't want to know the answer. He just wanted things to continue on as they had been before.

'Would you like some coffee?' she said. Her face was still a total blank.

Catesby made a fire in the sitting room while Petra made coffee. He began to light candles for it was getting dark quickly. His hands shook when he heard a stag roar and he had to light another match. It was the rutting season. Petra came into the room with the coffee in an aluminium pot.

'I hope it's not too strong,' she said.

She poured him a cup and added HO condensed milk from a tin.

'It's Rudolf,' she said. They had spoken of him before, but never in detail.

Catesby sipped his coffee and looked at the fire.

'Rudolf became a friend of my family when we joined my father in Berlin at the beginning of the war. He was closest to Cato, they were the same age. I was only eleven. Rudolf was awfully handsome and I admired him from afar – as girls of eleven, who understand so little, do.' Petra paused. 'I don't know how Rudolf got to know that Cato was a member of the Red Orchestra, but it was an uncomfortable situation for all of us.'

'Was he already in the army?'

'Oh yes, he was a captain, even though he was so young. And what made it worse,' Petra paused and stared at the flames, 'was that Rudolf wasn't an ordinary soldier. He was an intelligence officer – and a very valuable one because of his languages.'

'Which languages?'

'Polish, Lithuanian and Russian. His family owned a vast estate in East Prussia.' Petra suddenly looked thoughtful. 'I think maybe Rudolf got to know Cato through Libertas. You would have loved Libertas, William. She was *stunningly* beautiful – and the granddaughter of the Prince of Eulenburg.'

'Libertas and Rudolf were Prussian aristocrats.'

'Of course, and you know what these people are like. They have their own little clubs – but Libertas was magnificent, she used her club membership to steal the club's secrets.'

Catesby smiled. It happened in England too.

'Harro, the husband of Libertas, was on the Luftwaffe staff, but she didn't have to steal his secrets. He was also a member of the Red Orchestra. They were both executed the same day.'

Catesby put his arms around Petra. She had begun to cry.

'Poor Cato. She wasn't made for that sort of thing. My sister was a very naïve and idealistic girl. She didn't know how to deceive.'

'What happened?'

'When Libertas knew that she was going to be arrested, she passed on the name of her Soviet intelligence contact to Cato.'

Catesby could guess the rest.

'A short time later,' said Petra, '… well, who can be sure?'

'Did Cato and Rudolf become lovers?'

'I don't know – I hope not. But Cato passed on the name of the Soviet contact to Rudolf.' Petra paused, 'It wasn't such a stupid thing as it seems. Rudolf convinced her that he was opposed to Hitler, that he wanted to join the Red Orchestra. And who knows? Maybe Cato did the right thing.'

'What do you think?'

Petra lowered her voice to a whisper. 'I don't know – I will never know.' She paused and stared at the fire.

'What is it?' said Catesby.

'Please hold me – and please never leave me or betray me.'

He held her.

'A few weeks later they came to my father's pottery shop and arrested Cato. For three months we didn't know what was going to happen, but on a cold day in January she was tried by the Reich Military Tribunal and found guilty of "abetting a conspiracy to commit high treason". They sentenced her to death. And then ... it took such a long time we thought there was hope. But ... on the 5th of August 1943, a year after she was arrested, they murdered Cato with a guillotine.'

They sat together for a long time; holding each other and feeling each other's heart beat. Catesby wanted the story to end there, but he knew that it didn't end there.

'Rudolf,' said Petra, 'was sent to the front just before Cato was charged. He was incredibly lucky. He was wounded just badly enough to get put on the last evacuation flight that flew out of Stalingrad.'

'The wound at the base of his back?'

'That's the one. He calls it his Russian *baboschka* tattoo. He was sent to a hospital in Berlin. My father took me there one day to see him. He was thin, pale and suffering from jaundice. I felt sorry for him. My father pleaded with him to do something for Cato; it was just before her trial. It was an awful visit. Rudolf kept telling Father to keep his voice down. I don't think he really wanted us there, but Rudolf promised – in a little whisper when no one was looking – that he would do all he could.'

'What did he do?'

'Nothing that I know about.' Petra gave a weary smile. 'Looking back, I often think that his promise was a ploy to get us to leave. But who can blame him?'

'Why shouldn't you blame him?'

'What could he have done? Cato would still have died and Rudolf might have joined her? In any case, Rudolf recovered and was sent back to the front in the spring. He was reported missing in June, 1943.'

'But that wasn't the end.'

'No, Rudolf came back, but not as we had known him. It was May, '45.'

Petra sipped her coffee, frowned and put it down again. 'I'm sorry, this stuff is awful.'

'*Muckefuck*?'

'It must be.'

Catesby got up and walked over to a sideboard where there was a pewter flask and two silver cups. He had rescued them from beneath a pile of rubble in a collapsed outbuilding. The last lips to touch the cups before his and Petra's had belonged to peasants who had never heard a wireless or an engine.

'Would you like some of Siegfried's brandy?'

'I think so.'

He carried the cups over to the sofa. The reflection of the fire danced across Petra's face. They had both played roles in the European tragedy, but Catesby had just been a walk-on bit player stumbling over his spear. Petra had been centre stage.

'When,' she said, 'the Soviet Army entered Berlin ...'

'Don't go on.'

'No,' she said, 'I want you to know.'

Catesby realised that what happened hadn't been the Red Army's finest hour. He remembered the way Berliners referred to the Soviet War Memorial as 'The Tomb of the Unknown Rapist.'

'My father,' said Petra, 'is a good man, but also a manipulative man. As soon as he found a Russian officer who could speak some German, he explained that we – a bit of an exaggeration – had all been members of the Red Orchestra resistance. He wanted to protect us. But I suppose a lot of other German fathers and brothers were saying the same thing and the Russian officer had heard it all before. Father realised he needed a name, a contact, who could vouch for who we were. He had never doubted Rudolf. My father thought he was a resistance hero. I didn't know what to think, but I was almost certain that Rudolf was dead. Nonetheless, Father kept writing his name on little notes – with "German who spies for Russia" written in Cyrillic script next to it. I thought it was pointless, but a day later before the fighting had even stopped …'

'Rudolf turns up.'

'Like a magic apparition,' she said, 'wearing the uniform of a Soviet captain.'

'What happened to him – or, at least, what is Rudolf's version of what happened?'

Petra shook her head. 'No, William, you are wrong to be suspicious. Rudolf's story about what happened, then at least, is true. It must be. Otherwise, the Russians would have killed him.'

Petra sipped the brandy and continued. 'Rudolf deserted on a moonless night before the battle. And when he left, he took the battle plans for the Kursk offensive with him. He changed uniforms with a dead Russian soldier so he could get through the Soviet lines without being shot. At first, the Russians were suspicious. They thought that Rudolf was part of a German deception – that the battle plans were decoys. But Rudolf was able to give them the details of the Soviet agent who Cato had passed on to him. It gave him enough credibility to stay, as Rudolf says, "with one foot out of the grave". In the end, the Soviet general staff believed him entirely.'

'Why?'

'Moscow had just received a secret communication from one of their agents in London. The British had broken the German codes and decrypted the latest battle orders. The Kursk attack plan sent to Moscow by their agent in London was identical to the one that Rudolf had carried across the lines.'

'How do you know all this, Petra?'

She smiled. 'Rudolf loves to brag – endless bragging about his heroic adventures.'

Catesby could almost see the face in its entirety – an angel face from hell. The same face that had seduced Henry had also tricked the Soviet general staff. 'Do you suppose,' said Catesby, 'that there were other reasons for his bragging than just showing off?'

'He wanted to impress me, of course. But Rudolf also knew that I didn't trust him. And he wanted to seduce me – even if I didn't have a choice.' Petra paused. 'You see, there is something weak in Rudolf – and it's a sickly pathetic weakness. He needs to be loved even by those he hates and despises – especially by them.'

Catesby began to feel sick. Discovering Rudolf was like opening a coffin. You know there's going to be a stench, but it turns out much worse.

'We still lived in Charlottenburg. Our house had been damaged, but not so badly that we had to live in the cellar. Rudolf made sure that we were looked after and protected. One night when everyone was asleep he came into my room and sat down on my bed. I thought he was just going to talk, but he put his hand under the cover and started touching me. I was only fifteen, but I was old enough to know what he was going to do. I asked him not to, but he did it anyway. He took my virginity and he hurt me and made me do other things. When he was finished, I just wanted him to go and leave me alone so I could lie there and cry myself to sleep. But he wouldn't leave. He kept stroking me – gently now – and talking to me sweetly. He even apologised and said he had been "a little naughty". He finally left me, but I knew he was going to come back. And I knew that I couldn't complain. Many girls had suffered far worse.'

Catesby put his hand around hers. It was cold.

'And,' said Petra, 'when he did come back, it wasn't like it had been before. He was friendly and brought us food and cooking oil. It was as if nothing had happened – maybe Rudolf had been just "a little naughty" and he was feeling ashamed.'

Petra sipped her brandy and closed her eyes. Catesby felt her body stiffen next to his. She was suddenly like a corpse with rigor mortis.

'We went for a walk that night through the Tiergarten – which was still a mess. Most of the park's trees had been blasted and the few trees remaining had been cut down for firewood. There were trenches, rusty twisted steel and smashed concrete everywhere. Oddly enough, I was inspired and wanted to paint it all.' Petra smiled. 'I imagined I was a modern Goya. And I said so to Rudolf. He smiled and whispered in my ear.' Petra paused. 'What he said was weird, not frightening, just odd …'

'What did he say?'

'He said that I was "a civilised German" and that "the civilised mind will always defeat the barbarian". I laughed; I thought Rudolf, in his Soviet officer's uniform, was making a joke. But he grabbed me tight by my arm and said, "You will see what I mean."'

Petra went to the sideboard and poured herself more brandy.

'On the north side of the Tiergarten, on either side of the

Spreeweg, there was a huge Soviet supply depot with lines of temporary huts with canvas walls. Rudolf took me into one of the huts. The only light was a dull hurricane lantern that gave off an oily reek. A soldier was sitting at a table drinking vodka. Rudolf said something in Russian and pushed me towards the soldier. He tore my clothes and raped me. The soldier smelled of horse sweat and tobacco. Rudolf watched while it was happening; his own trousers were open and he was touching himself. I was so young I didn't understand what Rudolf was doing. I had never seen a man do that before.'

Petra sipped her brandy and sat down on the sofa. She was still rigid, but Catesby thought the worst of the story was over.

'When the soldier got off me, Rudolf helped me up. I could hear his teeth gnashing like an animal. He suddenly seemed so full of hate. "Now," he said, "you will never forget that these people are *Untermenschen*, subhuman vermin."'

At first Catesby thought that Petra was crying, but then he realised that she was laughing.

'Don't worry,' she said, 'I haven't gone mad. It wasn't funny at the time. I felt so frightened and humiliated – I almost didn't want to live. But afterwards, when I think of Rudolf saying those words, I have to laugh. He had ceased to be a human being and become a cartoon.' She paused. 'In any case, Rudolf's charade wasn't over. He drew his pistol and marched the soldier into the alley between the huts. He shouted something in Russian and several others came running. When he had witnesses and an audience, he pointed at me with my torn clothes. He then gave a little speech and shot the soldier in the back of the head. Rudolf was now a hero. He had punished a rapist and restored military discipline.'

'Why have you never done anything about him?'

'Never?' Petra was wearing that twisted smile that Catesby had seen only once before. '*Never* hasn't come yet.'

'When,' said Catesby, 'did you do the drawing?'

'Just after I met you.'

Catesby felt a tinge of jealousy. 'Did Rudolf model for you?'

'No, I drew the butterfly wound from memory, but … I'm surprised you asked.'

'Why?'

'Didn't you recognise the body of the nude man? It's yours.'

More weeks went by without any word from the East German security service. Catesby began to nourish a faint hope that they really had been forgotten. Or perhaps a decision had been made to let them live out their lives in rural obscurity. In the second half of December there was heavy snow. The lane was blocked, but they had sufficient food to last for weeks – and firewood was all around them. It was a pure dry cold and the sky was crystal clear. Their isolation seemed complete and the outside world a million miles away.

It was the shortest day of the year. Catesby was chopping wood in the shed when he saw the two skiers. They were slipping along on cross country skis and wearing white winter warfare uniforms. They both had large rucksacks as if they were going on expedition. They looked like apparitions as they poled and slid through the trees, their movements almost too graceful to be human. The taller one saw Catesby first. He pushed across the open space between the woods and the house with even piston movements. When he was a ski's length away from Catesby he pushed up his goggles.

'Are you Herr Catesby?' he said.

Catesby put his axe down. 'Yes.'

The tall skier took off a mitten and unbuttoned a pocket on his tunic. For a second Catesby froze, he wondered if he was reaching for a gun. But when the hand emerged it was snapping open a document wallet. The ID was almost identical to the one Catesby had carried in Hungary when he met Gábor, except that the arm and rifle coat of arms looked larger and more menacing. Flashing a secret police ID is always a good starter. It cuts through all the useless formalities and gets straight to the point.

The shorter skier was now next to him. He also put up his goggles. He looked older and more in charge. 'Is Fräulein Petra Bontjes van Beek in the house?'

'Yes, she's making bread.'

'What a pity to waste it.' The policeman looked at the axe lying on a block of wood next to Catesby's hand. He quickly grabbed it and threw it deep into the shed. The policeman looked closely at Catesby. 'I'm sure you wouldn't have done anything foolish.'

Catesby stared back. 'No.'

The front door opened. Petra looked at the policemen without saying a word and came to stand next to Catesby. The smell of baking bread wafted from the kitchen.

The policeman touched his cap and said, 'Good afternoon, Fräulein.' His voice was polite and respectful, as if he knew her family history. 'I am sorry about the bread, but we are going to have to leave now. You are allowed one suitcase each.'

The army uniforms and the skis had puzzled Catesby at first, but it now made perfect sense. It was their cover story. There was nothing secret or sinister about a pair of soldiers going for a cross country ski trip. It was so near Christmas they might even have been on leave. The arrival of the 'soldiers', if anyone had seen them arrive, would not be linked to their own disappearance. Catesby could already imagine the village gossip. *That nice couple who came to stay in the grange house seemed to have gone back to Berlin. Or was it Dresden? But it's no surprise that they didn't last the winter. They were here only for the summer and autumn. She was an artist working on a government project. And that shy man. Someone said he was a university teacher on sabbatical. No, he's a translator. In any case, people like them use the house: it belongs to the Ministry for Culture. Or some ministry.*

'It's a shame to waste the bread,' said Petra, 'and I don't want to leave my paintings either.'

'Don't worry, Fräulein. Your paintings will be looked after – as well as your other belongings.'

It was after dark when they began their walk through the woods. Catesby found it difficult not to think of recent history. How many Europeans had walked through such woods on a winter night without knowing what was on the other side? Petra reached out and took his hand.

They came out of the woods onto a rough lane that led to a wooden shed. The lane on the other side of the shed had been cleared with a snow plough. Inside the shed, there was a GAZ-61 four-wheel drive painted Warsaw Pact green. The car, with its huge engine, raised suspension and cross country tyres, was made for Russian winters. It was pure no-nonsense Soviet engineering. Just what you need for a chauffeur-driven tour of a Gulag. The Gulags weren't, of course, just for political prisoners. They were also for those with unexcused absences from work, petty thieves and for those who told anti-government jokes. It wasn't, thought Catesby, about not having a sense of humour; it was about having the last laugh.

The GAZ-61 was roomy and comfortable. Catesby and Petra sat

huddled together in the back. The car heater, designed for a Siberian winter, generated a warm fug that made them both sleepy. Catesby tried to keep awake so that he could spot the road signs as they flicked into view: Dresden, Cottbus, Luckau. They were heading north, back towards Berlin. After Luckau, Catesby fell asleep. He didn't wake again until the GAZ-61 came to a stop and the throaty soporific noise of its huge four-litre engine ceased.

Catesby couldn't see where they were. Everything was totally black. Suddenly, there was the sound of a car door opening and the faint glow of an interior light before the door closed again. Then the sound of two sets of boots crunching across a hard surface strewn with gravel.

'Where are we?' said Catesby holding Petra tight.

'We're handing you over,' said the shorter man.

'Both of us?'

'No, just you, Herr Catesby.'

'I'm coming with him,' said Petra.

The shorter man turned around and spoke softly. 'Please, Fräulein.'

Catesby held her tight and whispered, 'Stay calm. They're not going to hurt me. They have to talk to me alone.'

'I don't like it.'

'Don't worry, we'll see each other soon.' Catesby kissed her forehead, her lips. 'It's just procedure.'

Catesby had tried to sound convincing, but he hadn't convinced himself. There was every chance that his cover had been blown; that they had discovered that he was a planted defector. The footsteps were coming around to his side of the car. There was a blast of cold air as someone opened the door. It was time to leave. He reached out to touch her hand, but missed in the darkness. There was a heavy hand on his shoulder. He had to go. It was only when he was outside the car and the door closed that Catesby realised he had made a terrible mistake. All those months ago she had offered to come with him to the West. But he had turned her down. He chose duty before life. It was the worst mistake he had ever made.

The handover car was a black GAZ M21 Volga like the one that had brought them south. The two MfS minders were wearing black leather jackets that matched the sheen of the car. If the secret policemen on skis had been furry mammals, these were cold reptiles. Their eyes didn't look, they swivelled.

As the Volga pointed into the night, Catesby sensed they were heading north. The road surface was now damp and clear of snow. There were sleet showers at first and then drizzle. The Volga's windscreen wipers, designed for heavy blizzards, seemed to swat the light rain with contempt.

'Where are we going?' said Catesby.

The two men in the front ignored the question. Catesby leaned back in the corner of the back seat. The leather was new and slippery. He huddled himself inside his coat and tried to sleep, but couldn't get comfortable. After a while the men started talking to each other in low voices. Catesby strained to hear the words, but understood very little. They were speaking Polish. Catesby suddenly remembered what Tomasz had said in his dying hours, how his control had switched to Berlin. It all added up. Mischa was empire building. The foreign intelligence section of the UB, the Polish security service, was coming under his control. Even the KGB had begun to acknowledge Wolf as an espionage genius. If you wanted to penetrate the core of East Bloc intelligence; you didn't go to Moscow Central, you went to the lair of Mischa Wolf.

The kneaded dough sat on an enormous marble worktop. 'We must let that rest for half an hour. While we are waiting we can mix the beef and the pork filling.' Wolf looked at his guest. 'Have you ever had pelmeni before?'

'I don't think I have.' Catesby lifted a heavy tinted glass to his lips. The Georgian wine was dark, almost black, and smelled of earth and berries. He watched closely as his host seasoned and mixed the meat in a white enamel bowl.

'This is good pork, from Poland.' Wolf smiled. 'My father's parents, orthodox Jews of Spanish descent, would not have approved. But we were brought up non-religious and, in any case, my mother was a Rhineland Christian, a flaxen-haired Lorelei. And now my name is Mischa and I'm cooking you Russian meat dumplings. Would you pour me some wine, please?'

Catesby looked closely at his host as he poured the wine. Wolf looked more like a film star than a spymaster. And there was nothing secretive or sinister in his face. Mischa Wolf had warm brown eyes and the reassuring manner of a trusted family doctor. Catesby suddenly felt he ought to be helping. 'Is there anything I can do?'

'You could find a bowl for the sour cream – and some big soup plates.'

Catesby looked around. The kitchen was enormous. The worktops were long and wide. There were great chopping blocks worn concave with use, deep stone sinks and an oak-beamed ceiling hung with burnished copper pots. A traditional German stove, a green tiled Kachelöfen, radiated dry heat. A basket of seasoned birch logs lay close to the stove. Catesby opened several cabinets hand-painted with spring blossoms until he found a bowl and the plates.

As Catesby laid the dishes on the table, he became aware of the total silence and isolation that surrounded them. After a rest day in a safe house, he had been driven there in darkness. He hadn't a clue where he was. The kitchen windows looked out into utter blackness. His Polish MfS minders had left him at a back entrance to the house and then driven off into the night. A second later Wolf appeared and invited him in. The only sounds were the sounds they made themselves.

'Are we alone?' said Catesby.

'Yes, we are completely alone.'

Catesby looked at a knife lying on a worktop. He remembered his training. There were two places to aim your thrust. One was downwards through the suprasternal notch where the neck joins the chest. It was effective because it went straight into the aorta, but it was a small target, only an inch wide. The other target was the substernal notch, just below the base of the sternum. You had to aim straight up, twisting and thrusting at the aortic arch. Catesby felt his hands turn cold and clammy. The idea sickened him. He couldn't do it – and Wolf knew it. A stronger harder agent would have picked up the knife and struck a blow that would have effectively won the Cold War intelligence battle. But Wolf would never have let such an agent anywhere near him. Mischa wasn't an expert on bugs and gadgets, but he was an expert on people.

Wolf smiled at Catesby as if he had just read his thoughts. 'Did you carry a gun when you were back home?'

Catesby shook his head.

'I don't carry a gun,' said Mischa, 'but I'm supposed to. It's a point of contention between Erich and I. Erich's quite handy with a pistol. He shot and killed two policemen just before he fled to Moscow. He keeps the details locked up in a safe, but I think he's quite proud of it.' Wolf paused. 'Did you know about the incident?'

'Yes, it's in his file.'

'It's silly of him to think it's a secret.' Wolf turned away and kneaded the dough. 'Actually, I think this is ready.' He looked up at Catesby. 'Would you like to know a state secret?'

'If you think you can trust me.'

Mischa winked. 'The secret of pelmeni is to roll out the dough as thinly as possible, otherwise you've got pierogi.'

Catesby watched as Wolf rolled out the dough. When it was suitably thin, he used a pastry cutter to cut rounds about five inches in diameter.

'Erich and I,' said Wolf as he began to spoon the meat filling on to the rounds of dough, 'argued about you.'

'I hope it wasn't a serious argument.'

'Oh, it was very serious.'

Catesby sipped his wine to hide his nervousness. Wolf continued to make pelmeni.

'I told Erich,' said Wolf, 'that you were almost certainly a fake defector, a British plant.'

Catesby felt beads of cold sweat form on the back of his neck. He looked again at the carving knife on the worktop.

'Well,' said Wolf, 'what have you got to say for yourself?'

'I can see why you might think that. As soon as I defected, London and Washington would have started a disinformation campaign using doubled agents. Moscow tried the same thing with Deryabin and Petrov.'

'What if the intelligence against you dates from before your defection?'

Catesby faked a casual shrug. 'Then that intelligence is wrong.'

'You sound,' said Wolf as he began to seal the pelmeni for cooking, 'just like Erich.'

'In what way?'

'We need,' said Wolf, 'the biggest pot you can find.'

Catesby found a double-handled one hanging from a beam and took it down. 'I assume you want this full of water.'

'Just over half full, please, and a pinch of salt.'

'You said,' said Catesby as he put the pot on to boil, 'that I sounded like Erich Mielke.'

'You defended yourself using the same arguments, almost the same words, that Erich used in defending you. It was almost as if you rehearsed your answers together.'

'Do you really think that?' said Catesby.

'Of course not, but it's interesting that your minds operate on the same tram tracks.'

'Is that meant as a compliment or an insult?'

'That's a very shrewd retort and a bold one too, but not particularly original.' Wolf sealed the last of the pelmeni. 'It's the sort of thing that Erich says to put people on their back foot.'

'I assume it's not a compliment.'

'You're being Erich again, but ...' Wolf paused to wipe his hands, 'but there's a lot more ...'

Catesby smiled.

'You pretend to be blunt and straightforward with a touch of the shrewd peasant, but you're not that at all.'

'And neither,' said Catesby, 'is Erich Mielke.'

'How perceptive. Erich is a complex man who pretends to be simple. I'm a simple man who pretends to be complex. Has the water boiled yet?'

'No.'

'At first, I wanted to work with you,' said Wolf, 'but I knew that I had to play games with Erich to get him to agree. I knew that if I denounced you as a British intelligence plant that Erich would have to take your side. He needs to keep me in my place, to remind me – and the rest of the MfS – that I am subordinate. But sometimes, Erich sees through my bluff so he double bluffs by agreeing with my decisions because he thought I was trying to trick him into disagreeing. But … I think that the water has started to boil.'

'It has,' said Catesby.

Wolf carefully ladled each pelmeni into the pot. 'But this time it was different. They need about ten minutes.'

'How was it different?'

Wolf looked at his watch. 'We stopped playing games.'

'In what way?'

Wolf looked closely at Catesby. 'I'm going to pay you the compliment of frank honesty. Erich genuinely believes that you are the real thing. He isn't bluffing or double bluffing. That's what he believes.' Wolf stopped to stir the pelmeni. 'You have to be careful they don't break apart.'

'And you?'

'I believe that you've been planted by British intelligence. I didn't believe it at first, but I believe it now. Help yourself to more wine.'

Catesby refilled both their glasses.

'But,' said Wolf, 'if you are a plant, you can still be useful.' Wolf stared again at Catesby, but he was no longer trying to peel off layers to find his soul. Wolf's eyes were neither friendly nor cold. The eyes were those of a schoolmaster explaining a poor exam result to a student. 'You realise, of course,' said Wolf, 'that you no longer have diplomatic immunity. You were struck off the accredited list a day before they picked you up.'

Catesby knew this was going to happen, but was surprised his name had remained on the diplomatic list for so long. It certainly showed that Henry Bone was keeping the Foreign Office in the dark. Had Bone, in fact, informed anyone? Catesby felt like an Antarctic explorer who had been kicked out of the tent because his frost-bite had turned to reeking gangrene. And Mischa Wolf had just reminded him, as if Catesby didn't already know, that he no longer had the privilege of the black diplomatic passport. A spy without diplomatic immunity has no more rights than a common criminal – and may be treated a great deal worse.

They ate the meal in silent civility, like a married couple on the verge of divorce. Catesby felt like the shamed adulterer. He'd been discovered, but his other half was too well bred for tears or tirade. And why should Mischa behave otherwise? He was the one who was going to end up with the house and kids. The situation had an eerie familiarity.

Catesby's bedroom overlooked parkland and a lake. It was obvious that the house was old and grand, but much of the furniture and decoration had an institutional air. The ambience reminded him of the numerous stately homes, like Fawley Court and Audley End, that the SOE had taken over during the war to train their agents. The homes were beautiful, but it was ridiculous that such places had been used to house a single family. When Catesby said as much during a dinner at the end of his training, a colonel looked at him over his claret and said, 'It's a good thing we're sending you to the *Maquis Rouge*.'

Catesby slept soundly for the first few hours. At first, he didn't know what it was that woke him up. He was sleeping under a great plumped-up *Federbett*. He didn't want to leave the warm, but there was something there and he needed to see what it was. The casement window was partly open and the curtain only half drawn. It was there again: a hollow coughing sound from outside. He got up and went over to the window. Starlight and a slim crescent moon cast a pale light over the parkland of centuries-old chestnut trees that sloped gently to a lake. On the other side of the lake was a strip of rough grassland with dark woods behind. The coughs now sounded more like rough barks – and came from a distance. Catesby suddenly noticed movement on the other side of the lake. A dark silhouette was making its way through rough tussocks of winter grass. There were other silhouettes too, but still as statues. Then a statue moved. The statue had broad antlers and was larger than the hinds. Then all at once, as if a signal had been given, the herd of fallow deer ran towards the wood in long loping strides and disappeared.

At first, Catesby wondered if his appearance at the window had spooked the deer. But he noticed something else. On the near side of the lake was a tall dark figure, certainly Mischa, but there was someone else too. The other person was shorter and clad in a dark cloak that reached the ground. The two were having an intense conversation, but their voices were too hushed for Catesby to distinguish the words or even the language they were speaking. The latecomer turned to walk back towards the house and disappeared from view. Mischa remained and stared at the lake; his upper body shook slightly as if he was shivering – or laughing at a private joke. Mischa turned, put his hands in his pockets and walked back to the house. Just before he disappeared, Catesby heard another sound. It was Mischa whistling a tune from a Brecht-Weill song. It was the same song that Petra had sung at Brecht's funeral:

Und der Haifisch ... and the shark has teeth
And wears them in his face.
And MacHeath has a knife
But it's a knife that no one sees.

Catesby was concerned that someone else was in the house. He drew the curtain to darken the room and got back into bed. For a few minutes, he lay awake and worried about himself. He didn't want to die; he didn't want to be tortured. But he was tired and the *Federbett* warmth was like a drug; he soon fell into a dreamless sleep.

He didn't know how long he had been sleeping when he woke again. He didn't know whether it was the door opening or closing that had startled him. But he knew he wasn't alone: there was the faint sound of someone or something breathing. At first he hoped it was a cat, but he knew his visitor was human. The sticky pad of bare feet on varnished oak reminded Catesby of pre-marital midnight trysts with his wife in her parents' country home. But the slim pale figure gliding towards him was not his wife. He felt the mattress sag as his visitor sat on the side of his bed. A minute ticked away and then another. The silence was finally broken by the voice of a man speaking English.

'Are you awake?'

'Yes,' said Catesby. The word felt unaccustomed in his mouth. It was the first English he had spoken in over six months.

'I've wanted to meet you for a long time, but I was afraid I was going to be too late.'

'Who are you?'

The other man sniffed as if stifling a laugh. 'That's a good question, William. Do you mind if I call you by your first name?'

'That's fine.' But Catesby knew it wasn't fine. Something inside him recoiled from the intimacy.

'Listen, William, we need to get you back to England. You're in danger here. It hasn't worked.'

Catesby smiled into the dark. He was surprised that Mischa would try such a crude trick to test him. He stopped smiling. It wasn't a Mischa ploy. Wolf was too sophisticated for that. The visitor had his own agenda. But it was too soon for Catesby to play along or give anything away. 'You've got it wrong,' he said. 'I don't want to go back to England.'

The other man hissed a soft derisory laugh. 'Stop lying. You're a British intelligence plant and you've been busted – and I've been sent to save you.'

'Oh yeah, sure.' It was Catesby's turn to laugh. 'Who sent you?'

'Henry Bone.'

Catesby remained silent. He wasn't going to rise to the bait, if it was bait. If the other man was lying about Henry Bone, it was a brilliant ploy. But if the man was telling the truth about Henry, Catesby knew he was finished. He couldn't take the risk of believing him.

The other man seemed to grow impatient. 'Aren't you going to say anything?'

'I don't believe you. Henry Bone is the name of a former colleague. I'm sure that you could bandy the names of many of my former colleagues – and many of their personal details as well.'

Catesby suddenly became aware that the man next to him was naked.

'I don't want to be rude, William, but you are a fool to keep up this pretence. Your cover has been busted. Your mission is a failure – we need to get you out of here.'

'Who are you working for?' said Catesby.

'Ah, what an interesting question. You want to lead me into *ein Fang*, how do you say ...'

'An entrapment question.'

'If I were to tell you,' said the other man, 'that I was working for British intelligence, you would know that I was lying – because, I am sure, that you would have heard about me. On the other hand, if I were to tell you the truth, you would not believe me.' The man tapped Catesby's shoulder as if it were a secret sign. 'Or if you did believe me, you might find the truth embarrassing. Don't you realise that Henry Bone is one of ours?'

'He isn't.'

'You are such a fool, William. You still believe kindergarten lies because you want teacher to pat you on the head. And when you vote, you always vote for the party that promises to do most for the weak and the degenerate so that you can pat yourself on the head.'

Catesby felt he was being asked to taste a putrid piece of meat covered in maggots.

'And yet, William, I want to help you.' The man lowered his voice. 'And I will give you some advice whether you want it or not. Erich Mielke knows you are an imposter and wants to get you. It won't be long before Mielke sends you on a long ride.'

'He already has.'

'No, William, not a ride like that one. There are a lot of things you don't know about Erich Mielke. He's not just a loyal ally of the Soviet Union, but Mielke is a Soviet agent as well. And because Erich wants to stay friends with his KGB masters, he's going to offer you as a goodwill present. Mielke is going to wrap you up in ribbons and hand you over to the *rezidentura* in Karlhorst.'

Catesby's late-night visitor was pressing all the right buttons. The risk of his being handed over to the Russians was always the nightmare scenario. When compromised Western agents disappeared into the vast KGB compound in East Berlin's Karlhorst quarter, they were never seen again.

'Shall we go now, William, I can get you away? There's a boat train tonight from Berlin to Stockholm via Sassnitz. I could get you on it.'

'No. I'm not a plant. I'm staying here.'

'You're being absolutely tedious. There isn't much time.' The man sighed. 'You think I'm an agent provocateur, don't you?'

'No, you're more than that – and less than that too.' Catesby tried to make out the other man's features in the dark. The room was in total blackness except for a sliver of moonlight that had escaped through a curtain fold and reflected from the oak floor. 'And I understand what you are,' said Catesby, 'but you neither believe nor understand me.'

'When the time comes, you will accept me.' The other man leaned so close that Catesby could feel his breath and their foreheads almost touched.

Catesby remained silent.

'I'm cold,' said the other man, 'can I get in bed with you?'

'No.'

The other man laughed and gave Catesby a hard punch on the shoulder. It pretended to be a playful punch, but had been delivered with full force. Catesby clenched his teeth and tried to hide the pain. He braced himself for a second punch, but the other man spoke instead. His voice was soft and insinuating. 'I'm glad you said no to my joining you in bed. I was only testing you. I wanted to see if you were a degenerate. Many English are.'

'And Germans?'

'Sadly,' whispered the other man, 'there are far too many.' He stood up. 'I must go now, William, but when you need me, I will help you.' He paused. 'And one more thing, if you tell Mischa about this he won't believe you. Mischa tells so many lies that he seldom can see the truth himself – that is why he believes you.'

As the midnight visitor turned to leave, a beam of reflected moonlight played across the base of his back. But Catesby knew already that it would be there. The scar, purple black against the pale smooth skin, was the perfect shape of a butterfly.

When Catesby came downstairs the next morning it was still dark, but Mischa was already in the kitchen making coffee. He wasn't surprised. Most spies are early risers and some, he thought, never sleep at all. There was, however, no sign of Rudolf.

'Good morning,' said Mischa.

'Good morning. Did you hear,' Catesby looked closely at Wolf, 'the stags last night?'

'Yes, they mate this time of year. I had to stay up late last night to meet one of my officers who had just driven from Warsaw.'

There was, Catesby realised, an openness about Mischa Wolf that was totally disarming. He hid things by pretending not to hide anything. Wolf loved to answer questions and loved astonishing you with frank answers that rang perfectly true. The answers sounded true, because many were true. But not *all*. It was a brilliant strategy. One lie poisoned the whole batch.

The coffee smelled freshly ground and the Kachelöfen was lit and throwing out a warm dry heat. The table was laid with wooden plates, a basket of white rolls, cheese, cold meat, honey and jam – but there were only two settings. Catesby wondered if there were separate breakfast arrangements for Rudolf – or if he had already left. Wolf carried the coffee pot over to the table.

'Please sit down,' said Mischa.

Catesby wasn't flattered by Wolf serving him; he knew that he would be expected to leave a big tip. And yet the friendship and warmth seemed genuine.

'Where are we?' said Catesby.

'The Isle of Rügen. You probably didn't notice that you crossed a causeway in the night. We chose it because of its remoteness.'

Catesby knew that Rügen was in the extreme north of the country; a sparsely populated island sticking out into the Baltic Sea. It explained why Rudolf had mentioned the ferry to Sweden.

'And this house?' said Catesby.

'It's called Kartzitz. It was built in the eighteenth century when the ruling class still had some taste.'

'And listened to Bach and realised that the natural world was the only world we had.'

'Are you are an intellectual?' said Wolf.

'I've never had the time. It's always been a world beyond me.'

'I know how you feel,' said Wolf. 'But we need intellectuals. They're more important to the revolution than we are.'

As Catesby spread plum jam on a roll he remembered the Budapest girls who had leapt like dervishes from alleyways to spread jam on the periscope lenses of Soviet tanks. None of that mattered if you were on the wrong side of history. Which side, thought Catesby, am I on?

'Kartzitz,' said Wolf, 'is what we call a *Herrenhaus*, a gentleman's mansion. Contrary to Western propaganda, we haven't abolished gentlemen, but we have confiscated their houses. A fair compromise.'

'What is it used for now?'

'We've turned it into a holiday home for orphans, but we use it for meetings when the children aren't here.' Wolf paused as if he were listening for something. 'At times, I find it unbearably lonely.

Perhaps, it's the lack of children. I think children have spirit familiars who mourn their absence. You have no children of your own?'

'No.'

'Let me pour you some more coffee.'

'Thank you.'

'I hope,' said Mischa, 'that I'm not boring you on the subject of children's familiars. It's not a very Marxist theory – Erich is always accusing me of bourgeois sentimentality.'

Catesby could easily imagine Wolf charming lumpy undergrads in a seminar room at Cambridge. Except that Cambridge dons didn't get up this early. Mischa was warming his hands around his coffee cup and looking out the window at the first rays of dawn.

'An adult's room,' said Wolf, 'never changes – not even when the person isn't there. My KGB counterpart once took me to visit Tolstoy's house at Yasnaya Polyana.'

Catesby noticed that Mischa pronounced KGB the Russian way: *Kay Gay Bear.*

'They let me sit in Tolstoy's study – at his very desk. Everything seemed perfectly normal. There was an inkwell, a chipped enamel mug with pens and pencils, a little bronze dog on a felt base, a chipped piece of white marble – for what purpose God only knows. It was as if Tolstoy had just stepped out to catch the postman with a letter to Bernard Shaw or Mahatma Ghandi. The study was perfectly content without its adult occupant.' Wolf turned and looked at Catesby. 'But step into a child's room when the child is not there – not a child dangerously ill or dead – but a happy healthy child who just happens to be someplace else. You see their things – toys, books, a balled-up sock, a shirt that needs washing, a picture they love – and suddenly the desolation and emptiness grips you to the heart. And you feel fear; a cold nauseous fear – you just *have* to hold them in your arms again.'

Catesby didn't have children of his own, but he knew what Mischa was saying. He suddenly felt a longing for Petra and an untidy world of balled-up socks and soiled shirts.

After breakfast they walked to the lake. The grass was still dusted with frost. Catesby turned to look at the house as the rising sun began to reflect on the red roof tiles. It was certainly a manor house, but one of modest size and graceful proportions. The walls were painted ochre, but the windows and entrance were white. The house seemed as compact and balanced as a Bach cantata. Catesby half expected to hear cello strings on the morning air.

'Come,' said Mischa taking Catesby by the arm, 'let's boat across the lake.'

The lawn sloped down to a small jetty where a white wooden boat was moored. The boat was rectangular and flat-bottomed with benches for eight passengers. 'There aren't any oars,' said Wolf as they clambered on to the deck. 'It's a rope ferry – we have to pull ourselves to the other side like Volga boatmen.'

The shaded parts of the lake were covered with a layer of ice as sharp and clear as window glass. Catesby stood next to Mischa on the deck as they pulled the double cable through fore and aft pulleys to set off across the water. The resident ducks wrecked the morning stillness with a cacophony of warning calls. The duck noise died down as they reached the middle of the lake.

Without warning, Wolf stopped pulling the cable and turned to Catesby. His face was only inches away and the words came with an awful intensity. 'Twenty-eight million Soviet citizens died in the fight against fascist Germany. Why don't the people in the West know that? Why don't they know what that loss does to a nation?'

Catesby remained silent. The answer was too depressing. The West was a loud-speaking culture that only had ears for its own voice.

'But the Russians,' said Wolf, 'will never admit everything that happened. The worst time was the siege of Leningrad. After all the cats and dogs were eaten, they started on rats, mice and crows. Hunger succeeded where the pest controllers had failed. All the vermin were eaten – even the cockroaches.' Mischa's voice dropped to a whisper. 'But there is one truth they will never tell.'

Catesby looked back at the manor house. It was so bright and innocent in the morning sun. So blissfully unaware of the last two hundred years.

'When it first began, the flesh came from people who were already dead. Why not? But then gangs began to hunt live humans for meat. In the end, the commissars had to form a special police unit to fight the cannibals. More than three hundred were caught and executed. But they were victims too. Most of the cannibals were refugees from the Baltic who had fled to Leningrad to escape the Nazi advance. As refugees, they had no ration cards.'

Mischa hauled on the rope; the boat lurched forward.

'There was no running water, sanitation, light or heating. But there were no epidemics either: when it reaches forty degrees below freezing the bugs can't survive. Nearly a million died, but Leningrad survived because of the leadership of the Party and the heroism of her people. This isn't propaganda – it's truth. The starving skeletons of that city dug 700 kilometres of tank traps and 25,000 kilometres of open trenches.' The boat crunched into the opposite bank. 'The Soviet Union survived, but it was a close contest.' Wolf paused. 'And one of the victors, still very much alive today, is Field Marshal Paranoia. And who can blame the Russians for that? It's amazing that they've remained as sane as they have.'

Catesby looked up at the rough grassland where he had seen the deer in the night. A phrase from his childhood began to repeat in his brain: *Dona nobis pacem*. It was from the Mass, but the words were just as beautiful to an atheist. *Yes, that's what we want and we want it now*. Was there a word more beautiful? Love was a good word too, but love sometimes kept dangerous company with jealousy, anger and insane raving. Peace was a better word: it was cool, fruitful and rational. *Dona nobis pacem*. And yet peace was a word that some called treason.

They walked along a path on the edge of the lake. Catesby's inner ear could hear splashing and the echoes of children's voices from summers past. Mischa had described them as orphans. Stunned ragamuffins pulled from the rubble of broken cities. They must be entering their teens now.

'The Soviet Union,' said Wolf, 'must never be forced into a corner. If that happens, Field Marshal Paranoia will take command. If you corner the bear and keep taunting it, there comes a point when the bear will show its claws and attack. As long as the West, or I should say America, has the power to destroy the Soviet Union with one blow, the situation will be critically dangerous. There is a line of thought in the Kremlin that says: "They are poised to kill us; our only hope of survival is to strike first. What can, after all, be worse than what we have already suffered?" Who can fault their logic?'

'Do you still think,' said Catesby, 'that I'm a British intelligence plant?'

'It doesn't matter if you are.' Mischa smiled. 'We're on the same side.'

'Which side is that?'

'Europe's side. If war comes, we are the ones – especially Britain and Germany – who will be annihilated. Our job is to stop our masters in Washington and Moscow from getting into a fight. We're not allies to the great superpowers – we're their expendable buffer zones.' Wolf laughed. 'We all know this, but none of us can say it.'

They walked in silence back to the landing. As they pulled the flat wooden ferry across the water, the ducks were less noisy than before and merely swam in watchful circles. Catesby was struck once again by the beauty of the landscaped gardens and the calm dignity of the manor house. He imagined an eighteenth-century butterfly flapping its wings near the lake. And the gentle disturbance of air builds into a chaos of shock waves that guides the bullet to Franz Ferdinand's jugular and Little Boy to Hiroshima.

As they moored the boat, the quiet stillness was broken by the sound of a helicopter. Catesby shielded his eyes against the sun and searched the sky. He couldn't see it, but the change in sound suggested it was landing in the near distance.

'They're coming from Karlhorst for a meeting,' said Wolf.

'Who?'

'Erich, the Berlin *resident*, two more KGB from the First Directorate. I'm sure there will be others, but I'm not sure who. Sadly, Erich likes surprises – he thinks it keeps people alert.'

'What's the meeting about?'

Mischa looked closely at Catesby. 'Largely, to discuss your future. By the way, I've brought a suit for you to wear.'

The three Russians were wearing dark-blue lounge suits despite having military rank as KGB officers. The only Russian that Catesby recognised was Yevgeny Pitovranov, the KGB *resident*.

Unlike the Russians, Erich Mielke and two other senior MfS officers were dressed in military uniforms. The one sitting next to Mielke was a bespectacled colonel and appeared to be his aide-de-camp. The third uniformed MfS wore the insignia of a major general, but looked oddly young to bear such a senior rank. The major general had a handsome face like a male doll, the sort of face that veers on being pretty. Catesby looked at the blue eyes. He was sure it was him.

Mischa Wolf was the only MfS officer not in uniform. Mischa was wearing a well-cut lounge suit, clearly not an HO product, and looked more like the chairman of a merchant bank than a communist spy chief. There were two other persons present. One was a man in a grey suit wearing the small oval lapel badge of the ruling Socialist Unity Party, clearly an apparatchik of some rank. The other was a woman in her fifties who was wearing a frumpy blue dress with white polka dots. The hem of the dress had started to come undone.

It was a large room that must have been used for banquets in the old days. There was a table of dark polished wood, bulky sideboards and still enough room for a string quartet. Even though it was the middle of the day, the curtains were drawn and the lights in the crystal chandelier were on. Everyone had leather document folders in front of them embossed with the GDR coat of arms. No one was smiling. Mischa was sitting opposite Catesby, next to the grey party apparatchik, but was studiously avoiding eye contact.

The group had already been in conference for nearly an hour before Catesby had been summoned. He had the distinct impression that things had not gone well – for him. The first to speak was Erich Mielke. 'I would, Herr Catesby, like to introduce Frau Frerk from the Ministry of Justice. Before we go any further, Frau Frerk would like to make a statement.'

Frau Frerk reminded Catesby of a duck grooming its feathers as it waddled out of a pond. She spent a long time patting her hair in place and adjusting her glasses before she began. She started her statement by quoting Article 4 of the Constitution of the German Democratic Republic: 'Every citizen is bound in duty to act in accordance with the Constitution and to defend it against its enemies.'

Catesby tried not to smile. When you're a spy sitting in front of the head of an intelligence agency that you're trying to infiltrate and the first thing you hear is a co-opted judge referring to enemies of the state, it is seldom a good sign.

The woman then moved on to Article 5. 'State authority must also act in accordance with international law ...'

Mielke interrupted. 'What, Frau Frerk, would be the status of someone who committed crimes against the state during a time when he had diplomatic immunity and then, subsequently, lost that immunity.'

Frerk adjusted her glasses. 'Such a person could be held responsible for those crimes within the boundaries of the state concerned. But in practice it seldom happens for such persons are advised not to visit the states concerned.'

'But,' said Mielke, 'could such a person be prosecuted under our laws?'

'Yes, certainly.'

'Could such a person be held in indefinite detention without trial?'

Frau Frerk stirred uneasily. 'No, not within any *legal* framework. It would be a violation of both GDR and international law.'

'Would,' said Mielke, 'such a person be subject to deportation?'

'Yes. Any person who commits a crime against the GDR, who is not a citizen of the GDR, can be deported.'

'To where?'

'Usually back to their home country.'

'But not necessarily?' said Mielke.

'They can,' said Frerk, 'be deported to any country that accepts them and is willing to guarantee their rights under international law.'

Mielke turned and smiled at Yevgeny Pitovranov, the KGB *rezident*. Catesby fully realised that the *rezidentura* and the rest of the Soviet compound at Karlhorst enjoyed the same extraterritorial status as the grounds of an embassy. They didn't need to send him all the way to Moscow, at least not yet.

Mielke then looked across the table at Frerk. 'Thank you for enlightening us, Frau Frerk.'

'Would you like me to stay?' She suddenly seemed nervous and uncertain about her role.

'No, Frau Frerk, we won't be needing you at present.'

There was a hushed silence as the woman gathered her papers and her spectacle case. Catesby watched her walk towards the door. Her hem had completely collapsed. As the door closed behind her, Mischa spoke for the first time, 'Thank you for coming, Frau Frerk.' Always the gentleman.

Catesby wasn't certain whether he was being stitched or intimidated. But he was certain that Mielke was the type of plodding bureaucrat who always covered his own back. He might twist the rules, but he always followed them. Mischa was different. He was a creative risk-taker.

Mielke started first. 'Are your reasons for coming to the GDR primarily ideological or personal?'

Catesby knew it wasn't an innocent question. It was meant to trap him. He needed to choose his words carefully. It wasn't enough to sing the praises of the GDR. Any fake defector would do that. He didn't answer the question immediately. He stared at the table thoughtfully and waited for Mielke to prompt him.

'Herr Catesby, we're waiting.'

'I have great respect for the GDR and socialism, but, if I am completely honest, my primary motive in coming here is to be with the woman I love.'

Mielke looked across at the man from the Party then turned back to Catesby, 'Is name of the woman in question Petra Bontjes van Beek?'

'Yes,' said Catesby.

The man from the Party smiled warmly. The heroism of her sister, Cato, was well known.

'Why,' said Mielke, 'didn't you ask Fräulein Bontjes van Beek to come with you to the West? We wouldn't have stopped her.' Mielke shot a glance at Mischa. 'Even though free movement of GDR citizens is damaging our economy.'

Catesby smiled and shook his head. 'I did ask her. Time and time again. Even though I am a socialist, I didn't want to leave my family in England. It was a constant source of argument between Petra and me.'

Mielke's aide-de-camp turned the page of a folder and said, 'I believe that your sister was also an intelligence officer and that she had to leave the service.'

'That is true. I've already been extensively debriefed on the details, but I'll repeat them if you like.'

It was Mischa's turn. 'And how did your sister's situation affect your own career and your own security clearances?'

'Surprisingly little. The British are not a suspicious people, particularly the establishment. The inborn trust of colleagues may explain previous security breaches.' Catesby noticed that the Russians were nodding vigorous agreement.

'And,' said Mielke, 'does this also explain why your bosses were so unconcerned about your affair with a GDR citizen?'

'I think they were concerned, but they indulged me because they knew that I was planning on leaving the service. In any case, Petra is a committed socialist and would never have consented to being the wife of a British intelligence officer.'

'How interesting,' said Mielke, 'would you like to tell us about your new career plans?'

'Those plans were dropped. Petra refused to come with me.'

'But what were the plans at the time?'

'We would have gone back to England and I would probably have got a job teaching languages.'

'And lived in a house with a nice rose garden and joined the Labour Party?'

Catesby smiled. 'I'm still a member.'

Mielke laughed and slapped the table. 'I thought you were a socialist.'

Catesby felt once again he'd stepped through the looking glass into a world of Mad Hatters and March Hares talking on lobster telephones. He was being prodded into a saloon bar argument about the British Labour Party with the head of the East German security service in front of two KGB generals. He half expected Pitovranov to yawn with boredom and say, 'Anyone fancy a game of darts?'

The fug of pub familiarity soon dissolved under Erich Mielke's accusing stare. 'You're asking us to believe that you are not an active British agent sent to penetrate my organisation?'

'I'm not. I'm here to be with the person I love because she refuses to leave the country that she loves. And because I respect Petra's socialist ideals, I want to offer my services to the German Democratic Republic in any way that you find useful.'

Mielke was still looking at Catesby, but speaking to his MfS assistant. 'Colonel Spix, could you ask Fräulein Petra Bontjes van Beek to join us?'

Catesby wasn't completely surprised, but had never discussed the possibility with Petra. He had never asked her to agree a script because it would have been demeaning. He'd used her enough. Catesby genuinely loved her. But he was one of those lesser beings capable of using someone they love.

When Petra came into the room, Catesby saw a side of her that he had never seen before. She was a hero. He had never seen such complete fearlessness. The others saw it too. The man from the Party rose to greet her and kissed her on both cheeks. Petra then settled into a chair directly opposite Erich Mielke.

'We would like, Fräulein,' said Mielke, 'to ask you …'

'Rubbish.'

Catesby looked at Mielke. He had expected to see anger, but Mielke was smiling with avuncular charm. The security chief wasn't a simpleton. He was perceptive and cunning.

'I agree with you, Fräulein,' Mielke was still smiling, 'a lot of my questions are rubbish. I was hoping that you could help me ask some that aren't rubbish.'

'What do you want to know?'

'I was hoping ... hoping that you might tell us something about your boyfriend.' Mielke paused. 'Normally, I detest interfering in the personal and private lives of others, but ...'

'My lover is a British spy.'

There was a shocked hush in the room.

'But,' said Petra, 'I'm sure that you already knew that. Otherwise, you wouldn't have summoned me for three interviews in Normanennstrasse.'

'Has Herr Catesby ever told you that he was a spy?'

'Of course, he bragged about it the very first night to try to get me to go to bed with him.'

Everyone laughed except for Mielke and Mischa.

Pitovranov spoke for the first time. 'Did it work?'

'No, but I did go to bed with him. I was lonely – and I felt sorry for both of us.'

'The relationship you are describing,' said Mielke, 'does not sound like one based on long-term commitment. It sounds like Herr Catesby did most of the running.' Mielke flashed his fond uncle smile again. 'As if Herr Catesby were trying to establish a base in the GDR.'

Petra seemed a little deflated. 'That isn't true. He loves me.'

Mielke sighed and took off his reading glasses. 'I do not like to pry into personal matters. Perhaps, you would prefer to answer in private – or not to answer at all. But, if not, can you give me some examples of why you think he loves you?'

Petra looked at the table. 'Well, first of all, he gave up his career to be with me.' She suddenly smiled. 'But I'm sure that William must have been a terrible spy. He can't keep a secret for five minutes. I'm sure the British will be better off without him.'

Mischa suddenly looked across the table at his boss. 'Erich, you seem to be turning into a romantic. All these questions about love.'

Mielke laughed. 'Sorry, Mischa, you think I'm trespassing on your territory.'

'I would like,' said Wolf, 'to ask an ideological question.' He turned to Petra. 'In your opinion, Comrade Petra, is William Catesby a committed communist?'

'No.' There was an awkward silence and Petra covered her mouth. 'I hope I haven't said the wrong thing ... I'm sure that William would be loyal to the GDR.'

'Why,' said Wolf, 'did you say he wasn't committed?'

'Because ... because he asked me to leave the GDR and come to the West with him.'

'And you refused?'

'Of course,' said Petra, 'I could never live among capitalists and neo-fascists.'

Wolf looked at her with sad heavy eyes. 'When,' he said, 'did your lover suggest you go to the West?'

'At the beginning of our relationship, when things first got serious.'

'And how soon did he want you to go?'

'As soon as it could be arranged.'

Catesby felt his heart pounding. It was too late to intervene. Once again, he had used her. But maybe they would get away with it. So far, she had been brilliant.

Wolf looked at her for a long time, then said, 'There is a suspicion that William Catesby has been sent here by British intelligence as a deep and long-term penetration agent. If what you say is true, then that suspicion is totally unfounded.'

'Totally unfounded,' Petra repeated the words with a smile as bright as the sun, 'complete and utter nonsense.'

Wolf looked over to Mielke again. 'I would like, Erich, to adjourn this meeting for half an hour.'

Mielke nodded his consent and began to gather his papers.

As Catesby was led from the room, he looked at Mischa Wolf in profile. There was something of the Mediterranean in Mischa's face: the weary refined sadness of a scholar prince carrying scrolls to a mad emperor at midnight. Shadows, torchlight and wild thyme growing between the paving stones – then, screams and blood in the darkness. But the sad scholar was still a loyal Roman, because Rome was all there was.

In retrospect, Catesby knew it was going to happen that way. You always do in retrospect. He knew that he was going to be led into a stuffy little room and guarded by the two Polish-speaking MfS who had driven him to Rügen. He knew that he would have to sit on an uncomfortable creaky chair designed for a ten-year-old. And that he would hear the sounds of furniture being moved around and something being set up. And he knew that he would be called back into the meeting by an MfS officer wearing a colonel's uniform.

It was like one of those Greek dramas where you know exactly what's going to happen, but you can't take your eyes off the stage. In retrospect, he knew that Petra would be sitting there, alone, with her hands over her face and tears dropping through her fingers like bitter rain. And he knew that the major general with the pretty face would be setting up the machine in the middle of the table, his nimble fingers threading the tape. And, when pretty face pressed the button, he knew that it would be Petra's voice they would hear first.

'I've got something important to say. Are you listening?'

'Yes.'

'And, William, I really mean what I'm going to say. Listen. I love you more than my country, more than ... I love you more than the socialist future we are trying to build out of these ruins. I will come with you to the West. I will be your English housewife and prune your roses and make your tea. And if you don't want that, I'll be your mistress or your whore ...'

Catesby was aware that Mischa was staring at him while he listened to the tape. What does he want to see? Shame? Self-contempt? Self-hatred? Well, Mishca, you're going to see them all. Catesby wanted the machine to break. He didn't want to hear his own voice. When his voice did come, it was even cheaper, tinnier and more artificial than he remembered.

'I love you too much to ask that of you. I want to stay here with you. We can build socialism together. I don't deserve your love ...'

'Are you serious?'

'Yes.'

'Do you mean you're going to become a defector?'

'Yes, I am becoming a defector. It's because I love you and want to share your life and your ideals. We can't do that in the West.'

Mischa finally ended the farce. He nodded at the major general and said, 'I think, Comrade Ralswiek, that we have heard enough.' Catesby had been right. It was him. As Rudolf turned off the tape recorder, he wore a smug half-smile.

No one said anything. There was nothing to say. Catesby started to get out of his chair. He wanted to hold Petra in his arms, but as soon as he moved he felt a firm hand on his shoulder. One of the guards was standing behind him. The other guard was taking Petra out of the room. She had finally uncovered her face. Her eyes were red and her face was puffy and chafed. She looked once at Catesby.

It was then that tragedy turned to farce. The comedians come on the stage before the last corpses are carried away. Mischa had begun to get up as if he was about to leave, when Mielke said, 'The meeting hasn't closed.'

Mischa frowned and sat back down.

'Nor is the case against Herr Catesby. There's a question of identity that needs to be resolved.'

On cue Mielke's assistant left the room. A few seconds later, he came back with two people. One was Frau Frerk and the other was a dark middle-aged man. The man seemed uncomfortable to be surrounded by such people. He also looked a little blowzy as if he were hung-over or tired from a long journey. But Catesby still recognised him. He remembered the final words that the man had spoken when they last met by the statue of Anonymous-the-writer: *You must, Comrade Colonel, touch his golden pen. It will help you tell better stories.* Catesby wished he had taken Gábor's advice.

Mielke introduced Gábor and then said to the Hungarian, 'During the recent uprising in Budapest, you met a man who was carrying a GDR passport and an MfS ID identifying him as Colonel Walter Telemann. Can you, Major Gábor, identify that person?'

Gábor pointed at Catesby. 'It's him.'

'What,' said Mielke, 'did the so-called Colonel Telemann want to know?'

'He wanted to know about a colleague of mine called Captain André Lajos.'

'What happened to Captain Lajos?'

'He was murdered the next day in the massacre at Köztársaság tér.'

Catesby turned pale. He looked at Rudolf. His face was an innocent blank – like one of Titian's angels.

Mielke stared at Catesby and frowned. Then he turned back to the Hungarian. 'Can you tell us, Major Gábor, what exactly happened at Köztársaság tér?'

'The Headquarters of the Hungarian People's Working Party was besieged by a mob of counter-revolutionaries. The building was being guarded at the time by a uniformed unit of our police when it came under fire from a tank that had sided with the mob. When resistance became futile, our policemen laid down their arms and surrendered. They were then tortured and summarily executed.'

Catesby thought that Gábor's account was basically true, but heavily edited and slanted. Victor's history didn't need to tell blatant lies: it just needed to leave things out and crop the photos.

'Why do you suppose this mob,' continued Mielke, 'became so savage?'

'There are reports that the rioters were incited by agents provocateurs, some of whom were foreign.'

Catesby sat frozen. He now realised that Gábor had been coached. And he also knew why the woman from the Ministry of Justice had been invited back. The stitch-up was so wonderful and thorough that Erich Mielke wanted an audience. If you take the trouble to be 'just, fair and legal', you don't want to do it in a dark room without witnesses. *Illegal* wet jobs were a lot less trouble, but they came back to haunt you.

'Have you any reason to believe,' said Mielke, 'that William Catesby, alias Colonel Telemann, may have been one of those agent provocateurs?'

Gábor opened his briefcase and removed documents. 'I have witness statements certifying that a man of his description, who spoke German but not Hungarian, was present at the scene of the massacre.'

Catesby looked at Rudolf. He had an impulse to leap up, point a finger and shout, *there's your foreign agent provocateur*. But he didn't. For the first time he noticed that Rudolf was looking at him. His eyes were calm, alert and focused – like an animal about to pounce. The look in Rudolf's eyes stirred a survival instinct in Catesby. It made him a watchful animal too – tense, but calm.

When Gábor had finished, Rudolf caught Mielke's eye. 'There is,' said Rudolf, 'one more issue that I would like to bring up.'

'Please do, Comrade General.'

'Several months ago, one of my agents was murdered in London. I have every reason to believe that William Catesby was directly responsible for the death of Tomasz Król.'

Frau Frerk spoke up. 'Was this murder investigated by the British police?'

Catesby tried not to smile.

'Yes,' said Rudolf, 'it was. A post-mortem was carried out and there was a hearing in a coroner's court which gave a verdict of "unlawful death". But all this was carried out in camera with complete secrecy. The British government practises a form of censorship called the D-Notice. The press are forbidden to report on any matter that the government deems to be a matter of national security.'

Catesby wondered if Rudolf's lecture was aimed at him alone or intended to make Frau Frerk feel better about the GDR legal system. In the end it was all about power. The fewer the people who control power; the fewer the people who know the truth.

Catesby looked at Mielke. He was having a chat with the Russians in Russian. His accent was pretty good. Private conversations had broken out around the room and there was the sound of shuffling chairs. The meeting was over. Catesby looked at Rudolf and thought about the accusation he had just made. It suddenly occurred to Catesby that it wasn't part of Mielke's stitch-up. Rudolf really did believe he had killed Tomasz. But if it wasn't Rudolf's gang and it wasn't him, who was it? And did it matter?

There wasn't a prison cell at Kartzitz, so they handcuffed Catesby to an iron bedstead in a cold attic room. He had already begun to practise imaginary conversations in Russian. He was trying to work out survival tactics. He realised that he might never leave Karl-horst. After the *rezident* and his lads had finished interrogating him, Pitovranov would telephone Mielke and say, 'We're finished, would you like him back?' And Mielke would say, 'Do what you like.' And that would be that. Catesby's best chance was to convince his new owners that he had turned into a *real* defector, worth sending to Moscow. Catesby wasn't a hero like Cato and Libertas and the other Red Orchestra martyrs. He didn't want to die. If there was a way he could wriggle out of it, he would.

It was just after dark and bitterly cold when Catesby heard footsteps on the stairs. At least he wasn't going to freeze to death. The door opened. It was Rudolf and the two Poles.

'The helicopter's broken,' said Rudolf unlocking the handcuffs, 'we're going to have to drive you to Karlhorst. I bet you were looking forward to your first helicopter ride.'

Catesby didn't answer.

'In any case, the Russians are happy to stay for a few days. Pitovranov brought his rifle and wants to do some hunting.'

Rudolf had changed into outdoor-type casual clothes, including a thick navy jumper with a roll neck. He looked, thought Catesby, as if he was going hunting himself.

'We're taking Petra with us.' Rudolf then shifted into English so the Poles wouldn't understand. 'She's a fine woman. I just had some fun with her. She …'

Catesby took a deep breath – and tried not to show his anger and revulsion. Rudolf's obscene account of the rape made Catesby shake with rage and turned his stomach sour. But he needed to stay calm and not lash out and be beaten senseless. Rudolf stepped aside so Catesby could go down the stairs in front of him.

The same black GAZ Volga that had driven him to Kartzitz was parked on the white gravel of the circular drive. The car shone in the moonlight. Catesby had been left alone with one of the Poles. Rudolf and the other had gone back to the house for something.

'Did you know Tomasz Król?'

Catesby was surprised to hear the voice. It was the first time the Pole had spoken to him.

'Yes.'

'Tomasz was a good man, but he knew too much. That's why they killed him. They had to.'

Catesby was surprised that the Pole didn't share Rudolf's view. But he couldn't continue the conversation because Rudolf and the other Pole had just come out of the house with a third person. It was Petra.

Rudolf said something in Polish as he came abreast of the car. Catesby wasn't sure, but it sounded like they were taking Petra to an MfS cell in the Normanennstrasse. Petra was handcuffed to the Pole who had gone into the house with Rudolf. There was a brief palaver, also conducted in Polish, about who was sitting where. In the end, it was decided that the Pole, who had talked about Tomasz, would sit in the back between Catesby and Petra handcuffed to both of them. Once they were settled the Pole thought it was funny. When he put his hands up, Catesby and Petra had to raise their hands too. 'It is,' said the Pole raising all three hands again, 'just like a Party meeting.'

The road south of Kartzitz was a single-lane country track. On either side were flat fields without hedges. Catesby imagined acres of cabbages and root vegetables. It was dullest Norfolk again: the fertile European plain that stretched from the Urals to Peterborough. After half an hour of bumps and puddles they came to a T-junction where a two-lane tarmac road was signposted to Ramitz and Gingst. The driver looked set to turn the Ramitz way, when Rudolf said something in Polish. Catesby picked up a few words. He thought that Rudolf was saying that it was faster to turn right towards Gingst because of something or other. The driver gave a reluctant shrug, but followed Rudolf's instructions on to a road that was flat and dead straight. Five minutes later they came to a wood and Rudolf told the driver to stop the car. He then got out and had a piss. When Rudolf came back to the car there was a gun in his hand.

The whole thing took less than ten seconds, probably less than five seconds, but, like the executions on Shingle Street, it seemed to unroll in excruciatingly slow motion. As soon as the driver saw the gun pointing at him, he scrambled to get out the door. He was leaning over tugging at the door handle when Rudolf shot him behind the ear. Meanwhile, the other Pole started to scream and panic, but couldn't move because he was handcuffed to Catesby and Petra. Catesby struggled to open the car door on his side, but his left arm, tethered to the Pole, was being jerked about. Meanwhile, Petra was saying, 'Nein, nein, nein ...' in a surprisingly calm voice. The thing that Catesby remembered most was the way the gun barrel moved about tracing the gyrations of the Pole's head. Finally, Rudolf pulled the trigger and shot him through his right eye. Catesby remembered feeling something liquid spatter on his left cheek and then, for what seemed a long time, the Pole's body convulsing next to him.

The next few minutes descended into slapstick. It began with Rudolf untangling the driver from the steering wheel and dragging him into the passenger seat. The Pole was a big man and Catesby knew how difficult it is to move dead bodies. They seem to resent being dead and won't do anything to help.

When the driver's seat was finally free, Rudolf crawled behind the wheel, started the engine and drove the big Volga off the road on to a forest track. He was driving without lights and the track was lumpy. Petra finally asked, calmly again, 'Are you going to kill us too?'

Rudolf didn't answer. Catesby, meanwhile, was going through the trouser pockets of the dead Pole trying to find the keys to the handcuffs.

When he was about a hundred yards into the wood, Rudolf stopped the car and turned off the engine. The silence was eerie and far from welcome. For a long time Rudolf sat behind the wheel and stared into the darkness. Finally he said, 'Can you check Stefan's pockets to see if he has the handcuff keys?'

Catesby now began going through his jacket pockets too. It somehow felt less awful knowing the dead man's name. Petra was doing the same on Stefan's other side and Rudolf was searching the pockets of the dead driver. It went on for about fifteen minutes – and still no keys. Catesby began to panic. If they didn't find the keys, would Rudolf leave them there tethered to a dead man to starve to death while the corpse bloated and decomposed? That was a stupid thought. Surely, the two of them would manage to drag the body to the main road. He calmed down again. And Rudolf wasn't going to shoot them; otherwise he wouldn't be looking for the keys. Logic, not panic.

'I've found them.' It was Rudolf's voice.

Catesby looked up just as Rudolf's head popped up above the front seat.

'The keys,' said Rudolf, 'were on the floor. They must have fallen out of Stan's pocket when I moved him.' Another name.

Rudolf passed the keys back and Catesby unlocked his own wrist first. He then leaned across Stefan's body, feeling something drip on the back of his hand as he did so, and freed Petra. Meanwhile, Rudolf had got out of the car and was uncovering something in the undergrowth.

Catesby looked across Stefan at Petra. Her head was a black silhouette against the lesser dark of the car window. 'Can you get out your side?' he said.

She made a little sound, like a wounded animal. It was getting to be too much. Catesby reached over and found her cheek with the palm of his hand. It was wet. She needed comfort, but, if they were to survive, they needed the adrenalin to flow. The tears could flow later.

'Let's go,' he said.

As soon as they emerged, Rudolf called out. 'Don't you two go anywhere – we're going for a motorcycle ride.'

In the dim light of tree-filtered moon, Catesby could see the outlines of a motorbike and sidecar.

'Petra can ride pillion,' said Rudolf.

'Where are we going?' said Catesby.

'You ask too many questions. You'll see when we get there.' Rudolf paused. 'And don't try anything funny. Your best chance of survival is to trust me.'

'Why?' said Petra.

'Work out the maths. If you try to overcome me, there's a chance you might succeed. But there's a greater chance that I will shoot you first. And, suppose you do succeed, what would you achieve? A lifetime in prison – or worse. I'm not asking you to like me – I'm asking you to make a rational choice to survive.'

Catesby squeezed Petra's hand; then helped push the motorbike on to the track. It was a pact with the devil. Rudolf drew himself to full height to kick-start the motorcycle. It roared into life the first time. Catesby climbed into the sidecar. The machine was a BMW R75. He had seen a few in France, but they had been used mostly on the Eastern Front. They were good bikes for travelling off road – which was obviously what Rudolf had in mind.

They came out of the wood on to a marshy track that was scarcely wider than a footpath. Rudolf powered through two hundred metres of puddle and sodden grass until they came out on to rough heath. The heath land was firmer, but more difficult to navigate without lights. They had to stop when they came to a drainage ditch that was six feet wide and full of winter run-off.

'We need,' said Rudolf, 'to find the bridge.'

Petra got off the bike and walked along the ditch. Catesby willed her to run into the night, but she stopped and pointed. 'I think there's a bridge down there. I can see gateposts.'

Rudolf kick-started the bike again. When they got to the bridge, the planks looked rotten. Catesby tried it and his foot went through a hole, but some of it looked sound. 'What do you think?' he said.

Rudolf took out his pistol and pointed it at Catesby. 'You and the whore test it. See if it will bear your weight and wait on the other side.'

Catesby took Petra by the hand. He whispered, 'When we get to …'

Rudolf was right behind them. 'Don't conspire. Just point out the rotten planks.' He kept his pistol pointed at them until they were on the other side. Some of the planks were bad, but the supports underneath appeared solid.

Catesby watched Rudolf mount the bike and was poised to grab Petra and run, but at that moment Rudolf gunned the engine and twisted the right handle to full acceleration. The bridge splintered behind him, but the dark machine leapt into the air. As Rudolf flashed by his teeth were bared like a death's head.

They continued their journey across an immense cabbage field. The cabbage heads thumped against the underside of the sidecar like a quick-march drum roll. When the cabbages ended, a ploughed field began. The field was heavy muddy clay. On several occasions, Catesby and Petra had to get off and push. When they finally reached a tarmac road they were exhausted and covered in glutinous mud.

'We haven't,' said Rudolf wiping his face, 'much farther to go.'

They rode less than a hundred yards down the tarmac before they turned on to a farm track. They continued at a good speed until they reached a place where there were willows on either side of the track. The lane became wetter and wetter and more overgrown. Catesby could see that the track hadn't been used for some time. It reminded him of the impenetrable Suffolk marsh lanes he had explored as a child.

Suddenly the engine cut out. They were surrounded by a jungle of reeds and bulrushes. Rudolf had his back turned. For a second, Catesby thought about jumping him. But at the same moment, he heard a sliding sound and a metallic click. Rudolf had just checked the magazine in his automatic.

'We'll have to walk the rest of the way,' said Rudolf. He waved the automatic in Catesby's face. 'Would you like to lead?'

Catesby hesitated.

Rudolf gestured with his pistol. 'I'll cover our rear in case we are being followed. It would be a pity, because we're almost there.'

Catesby took Petra by the hand and led her on to a plank bridge that disappeared into the reeds. As they headed into the marsh they were greeted by the warning calls of ducks. For the first few hundred yards they couldn't see where they were. The causeway of connected planks twisted through a wilderness of reed that was more than head high. Then suddenly the reed beds ended and they were in open marshland. The sky was misting over, but there was still enough moonlight to create a feeling of utter nakedness as they walked in file along the plank bridges. It was then that Catesby heard the lapping wavelets. To their left was a vast expanse of open water. It was like coming home again.

'We are,' said Rudolf, 'by what the locals call the *Hiddensee*.'

For a second Catesby felt exhilarated by their nearness to the sea, but remembered that a Makarov 9mm automatic was pointed at his back.

'Have you,' said Rudolf switching to English, 'done much sailing?'

'A bit.' Once again, Catesby felt his native language strange in his mouth. And once again, he realised, that his native tongue wasn't his mother tongue. *Slaap, kindje, slaap...*

'Good,' said Rudolf, 'because Petra has never sailed – and I need a good crew.'

The plank bridges led to a turf wall that separated the marsh from the arable fields. Catesby scrambled to the top of the wall.

'She's to the left,' said Rudolf.

Catesby continued along the top of the turf wall. It ended where a stream entered a sluice. You would never have found her if you didn't know she was there. The boat was moored in a gully carved out of the mud by the waters from the sluice. Her mast hadn't been stepped and she was painted an ugly black – even the decks were black.

'Do you recognise her type?' said Rudolf.

'She's a clinker built Folkboat.'

'Isn't she a beauty?'

Catesby didn't answer.

'She's one of the earliest ones. I had her built in the middle of the war, but have hardly sailed her at all. Let's go aboard.'

It took an hour to step the heavy wooden mast and to adjust all the stays. Petra quickly got the knack of adjusting rigging screws. Catesby realised she had a gift for just doing things.

'We'll bend the sails,' said Rudolf, 'as we go along.'

'Is there an engine?' said Catesby.

'Yes, but not a very good one.'

Rudolf took a crank handle out of a side locker and lifted a cover. After a half dozen attempts, a sputtering petrol engine came to life.

'We just need it,' said Rudolf, 'to get out of these twisty lagoons.'

Catesby cast off with Rudolf on the tiller. The engine didn't sound healthy at all and the moon had disappeared. It was also freezing cold. Petra had gone down below and found the sails. 'One of these goes on the front?'

'Yes,' said Catesby, 'it's called the jib and those metal clips hank on to the forestay.'

'The what?'

'The wire that goes from the top of the mast to the bow.'

Petra scrambled forward to hank the jib.

'She's a fast learner,' said Rudolf. His face, illuminated by the faint light from the compass binnacle, wore a half-smile of smug possession.

Just, thought Catesby, just give me the chance.

'We have,' said Rudolf speaking his textbook English, 'to find a narrow passage slightly to the north-west. You might have to go forward with a boat hook to test the depth.'

Catesby found the hook on the cabin roof and went forward to where Petra was kneeling down attaching the jib to the forestay. They were approaching a narrow place where a low island almost touched the shore. The passage was about fifty yards wide.

'I think,' called Rudolf from the cockpit, 'the best water is to port.'

Catesby prodded deep with the boathook and touched the bottom. 'No, keep in the middle.'

'Okay.'

As Catesby bent over the bow prodding for deep water, he felt Petra slip something into his pocket.

'More to starboard?' called Rudolf.

'No, we're fine on this track.' Catesby reached into his pocket and felt the blade of a knife. Petra must, he thought, have found it in the galley when she went looking for the sails.

When they were clear of the passage, the lagoon widened out into a great expanse. It was almost like being at sea.

'Come back,' said Rudolf. 'We've got lots of deep water until we get to the entrance.'

As they slid back down into the cockpit, Rudolf said, 'Would you like to take the tiller now? Keep her on south-west by west.'

Catesby took the tiller. He could see a new watchfulness in Rudolf. He never turned his back. He sat facing Catesby while he instructed Petra on how to rig the mainsail. The smug half-smile never left Rudolf's face. As Petra leaned over the boom sliding the main through the sail track, Rudolf ran his hand up the inside of Petra's thigh. 'Good healthy woman,' he said.

'Yes,' said Catesby feeling the knife blade against his thigh.

'I wonder,' said Rudolf, 'if you can work out what we're doing?'

'It looks like we're making an escape by sea.' Catesby smiled. 'Are there any more hoops of the obvious that you would like me to jump through?'

Rudolf paused for a moment, as if working out the words; then said, 'Must you always be ironic?'

'I wasn't being ironic – I was being sarcastic. Shall we speak German again?'

Catesby could see that Rudolf's pride was stung.

'Your German isn't perfect, William, that's why you got caught in that Budapest business.'

'What were you doing in Budapest?' said Catesby.

'I was having fun.'

'What did you enjoy most?'

'I liked seeing children attacking tanks and then getting shot down. I liked the massacre in Köztársaság tér. It's so fine, and so easy, to turn human beings into hate-filled hyenas. And it was good to see the Russian *Untermenschen* dancing in petrol-bomb flames like jigging puppets.'

'Some of us,' said Catesby, 'thought you might be working for the Americans.'

'I don't work for anyone. But Americans are useful because they hate communism so much. They realise that it is a philosophy that stirs up jealousy against the gifted and affluent.' Rudolf smiled. 'And a country that was created by stealing land from inferior races and then enriching that land by slave labour from Africa must have its merits. Unfortunately, many Americans now regret that glorious past and have turned into degenerates – like Kit Fournier.'

'You knew Kit?'

'I knew of him. I know all your secrets.'

Catesby looked closely at Rudolf. His perverse beauty was unearthly in the dim glow of the binnacle lamp. 'Do you want war?' said Catesby.

'Of course I want war. War cleans the world. It gets rid of the weak so we can make something better without the weak whining and getting in the way.'

The moon disappeared behind cloud and they motored on in silence.

It was four o'clock in the morning when they got to the entrance where the *Hiddensee* flowed into the Baltic. The inland sea was protected by a long narrow barrier island that was also called *Hiddensee*.

'The entrance,' said Rudolf, 'is a little tricky. There are sand banks on this side, but there's a passage through them that will save us time. We need to hurry. It will be light in four hours' time. I don't want the *See Polizei* to catch us.'

'Where are we going when we get into the Baltic?'

'Outside territorial waters as quickly as possible.'

Catesby knew that the GDR claimed twelve miles offshore. They'd be very lucky to cover that distance before first light.

'Can you go forward,' said Rudolf, 'to check the depth?'

Catesby took the boathook and went to the bow. A heavy mist had started to roll in from the sea. They were navigating entirely by compass and distance logged. Away from the engine noise, Catesby could hear the faint susurrus of the Baltic Sea breaking on the outer beach. He was lying flat on his stomach as he probed for shallows with the long hook pole. He finally made contact with firm sand. 'Back off,' he shouted.

Rudolf put the engine in reverse, then turned to port and continued along the sand bank at less than walking pace. Rudolf made four more attempts to find a way across the bank before Catesby found deep water. The boat continued for a hundred yards before the hook once again found the bottom. 'It's shoaling again,' said Catesby, 'I don't think we're going to get through.'

'How deep?' called Rudolf.

Catesby looked at the dripping pole. 'A metre and a half at most.'

'We can make it. We only draw a metre.' Rudolf put the engine in gear and the boat went forward at a crawl.

Catesby kept probing and the water kept getting shallower. 'It's getting pretty shallow,' he said.

Rudolf ignored him, and a second later the boat shuddered to a halt.

'We're stuck.' And, thought Catesby, stuck for good. There weren't any tides in the Baltic to float you off. In Suffolk, you just brewed a cup of tea and waited. Catesby looked back towards the cockpit. Rudolf was explaining something to Petra. A second later Petra was perched on the end of the boom. Rudolf then pushed the boom out to one side over the dark water with Petra balanced on the extreme end. He then put the engine into fast forward and repeated the exercise on the other side. The canting and rocking together with the straining engine finally freed the boat and she slid forward into deeper water.

'We've made it,' said Rudolf. 'It's a good thing we got off. There's a *See Polizei* base just south of the entrance. I hope they don't hear us.'

Rudolf steered the boat sharply to starboard. Catesby could smell the fresh tang of the waiting Baltic. The mist was thickening, but he could just make out a low sandy bank that ran parallel to their track. Suddenly the bank disappeared and the smack of larger waves hit the bow. They had made it to the open sea.

'Let's get the sails up,' said Rudolf.

There was very little wind, but it was directly behind them. After the sails were raised it was difficult to keep them in place. The mainsail, which was boomed out to starboard, kept threatening to gybe to the other side. They still needed the engine if they were to get outside GDR waters before first light.

'We need more speed,' said Rudolf. He pushed the throttle all the way forward. 'Bill and the S-boat are expecting us between six and seven.'

'Bill who?' said Catesby.

'You must know,' Rudolf smiled. 'Bill Harvey, your American friend who took you for a drive in his Cadillac.'

The mainsheet block rattled. Catesby watched the mainsail flap lazily. The boom kept threatening to come across. He adjusted the tiller and the sail filled. And then the other thing happened. Catesby had known it was only a matter of time. Getting over the sandbank must have strained her too much. There was a cough, a death rattle and then total silence. The engine was dead. There was a brief whiff of burned oil, the last rites unction of a mechanical soul departing.

'I hope,' said Catesby, 'that Bill Harvey won't mind waiting.'

'Don't worry, he'll wait.' Rudolf turned to Petra. 'Can you use a spirit stove?'

'Of course.'

'Can you make us some black tea?'

Petra looked at Catesby. He nodded. She then disappeared below. Catesby knew the time had come. When Rudolf looked away for a second, Catesby began to edge the knife out of his pocket. He hoped that Petra would serve the tea extra hot so that Rudolf would be distracted and have to shift the burning mug from hand to hand. He would do it then. It couldn't wait.

A few minutes later, Petra emerged from the cabin with two steaming mugs in her gloved hands. Catesby tried to make eye contact, but she was looking at the cups. He wanted her to serve Rudolf first, but she came to the stern instead.

'Thank you,' said Catesby still holding the tiller. 'Put it on the seat beside me.'

Petra then turned towards Rudolf. Her body was between them. Catesby now understood why she had come to him first. Her body completely blocked Rudolf's line of sight. Catesby removed the knife from his pocket.

At first, he didn't understand what had happened. He didn't understand why a black stain had suddenly appeared on the left side of the back of Petra's yellow waterproof. He thought the noise meant the engine had barked into life again. And that the black stain was engine oil that had spat out. Petra dropped Rudolf's tea just before she crumpled. There was the sound of the cup shattering. For a second, Catesby feared that Petra might cut herself on the shards.

The pistol was now aimed at Catesby's face. The rest was reflex. Catesby pushed the tiller hard to starboard with the same hand holding the knife. The boom suddenly gybed and scythed across the cockpit. Rudolf was quick enough to duck, but not quick enough to pull the trigger when he was upright again. Catesby remembered the lesson. He hadn't taken it seriously at the time. He never thought he would have to …

The other chest target is the substernal notch, just below the base of the sternum. Hold the knife firmly and aim straight up, twisting and thrusting at the aortic arch.

The knife went in easily and Catesby kept twisting and thrusting it, but Rudolf wouldn't die. He had dropped his gun and collapsed on to the cockpit seat, but his eyes were open and he was still breathing. Catesby withdrew the knife from Rudolf's chest. It was a small kitchen knife, the blade wasn't long enough to reach the aorta.

Rudolf looked as if he was about to say something. He wasn't smiling now; he was in pain, but the eyes were still trying to take control. Catesby gripped the knife hard and took a deep breath. He plunged the blade straight into Rudolf's right eye. He felt the blade go through the thin bone at the back of the eye socket and into the brain. He twisted it. For two seconds, Rudolf screamed like a banshee. Then he was still. Catesby left the knife where it was.

The rest of the morning was a grey blur. The wind picked up and the mist became denser. The boat was being blown further and further out to sea. But none of it mattered. Catesby let the tiller swing itself. He sat on the floor of the cockpit with Petra in his arms. Her own inner warmth had gone so Catesby wanted to give her his. He kept talking to her. Trying to say all the things he should have said before. He remembered the time he had come back to her. She had been sketching the poster for Langhoff's *King Lear*. Catesby's class had studied the play in the sixth form. He remembered Lear holding the body of dead Cordelia.

> *Why should a dog, a horse, a rat, have life,*
> *And thou no breath at all.*

Catesby whispered the words and sat back numb. The words didn't work for him – just like they didn't work for Lear. There weren't any words. Wounded animals don't use words.

Catesby wasn't surprised when it turned light. He knew that mornings were still going to happen. It was just that they didn't have anything to do with him. The mist was lifting and from time to time the sun broke through. But none of that mattered. There were also some terrible noises about, but Catesby tried to ignore them. There was a gurgling hum from somewhere off the port bow that sounded like the engines of a very powerful boat. And there was another noise coming from the exact opposite direction. It was a loud clattering noise. It seemed to be coming from the sky.

The mist was burning off more quickly as the sun rose. And the noises were getting closer and closer. Catesby saw the S-boat first and remembered that Rudolf had said something about a sea rendezvous with Bill Harvey. The S-boat was one of the long torpedo boats that the West Germans used to patrol the Baltic and to infiltrate agents into the East. It was flying the swallow tail ensign of the new *Bundesmarine*. Someone was bellowing through a loudspeaker in American English. It was Bill Harvey.

'Stay where you are, Rudolf. We're coming alongside.'

The S-boat was more than a hundred yards away, but Catesby could see that Harvey was involved in a shouting match with a German officer. He saw Harvey raise the loudspeaker again, 'Cancel that, Rudolf. We're sending a *rescue* boat over. You're on the wrong side of the border.'

The sound that had been approaching from the other direction was now directly overhead. The prop wash of the helicopter's blades rippled the sea around the yacht and made her sails flap madly. The circling ripples had a proprietary air, as if the helicopter had made the first claim. Catesby looked up. The helicopter was a Soviet Mi-4 Hound, but carried the insignia of the East German People's Army. It was the helicopter's turn to use a loudspeaker. The message was aimed at the S-boat.

'You have entered the territorial waters of the German Democratic Republic. You must leave immediately.'

The S-boat began to back off, but not before launching a high-speed inflatable that was now skimming towards the drifting yacht. Catesby realised that he was present at what the press always referred to as 'a serious confrontation between East and West'. Catesby climbed on the side deck, hung on to the shrouds and looked down into the churning water. The ridiculousness of the situation began to infuriate him.

'This is your final warning,' the helicopter was now hovering over the inflatable, 'if you do not leave sovereign GDR waters we are going to resort to deadly force.'

Catesby looked at the rapidly approaching inflatable and tried to wave it away. But it kept coming. He let go of the shrouds and looked down into the dark water. It seemed so inviting. Catesby didn't know why he jumped into the sea. Maybe he wanted to drown himself. Maybe he wanted to escape the noise. Maybe he wanted to prevent more bloodshed. What did it matter?

The first few seconds, before the cold soaked through, were delicious. Catesby used his feet to kick away from the hull and began to backstroke towards Finland. Then the water soaked through his layers and filled his boots. He began to sink. That wasn't bad either, but the cold was now coming in. He bobbed to the surface once more, just in time for someone to grab the back of his collar. The hands of the boat crew were big and strong. They quickly hauled him over the inflated hull and flopped him on to the plywood deck. Catesby felt like a big North Sea cod that had just been long-lined off Aldeburgh.

'Is there anyone else on board?' The voice spoke German with a slight East Friesland accent, a little like Petra's.

'No,' he said. Catesby never worked out exactly why he lied.

Maybe he wanted to close a door. Maybe it had something to do with an intuitive sense of duty; a desire to get rid of loose ends that could turn septic.

As the inflatable sped back to the S-boat, the helicopter ceased to issue threats, but continued to hover. When Catesby had finished coughing up salt water and bile, he looked up to watch the helicopter as it circled the yacht. Suddenly, it stopped circling and made a strafing run. There must have been a lot of petrol left in the fuel tank for the boat burst into flames.

The helicopter made a second pass at the splintered and listing yacht. This time she rolled on her side and sank. There were no more flames; only broken black planks bobbing on the surface. The helicopter banked and passed close to the inflatable as it headed back to the coast. Catesby looked up. There was a face framed in a window looking down at him. It was Mischa Wolf. Mischa raised his hand. The gesture was slight and almost imperceptible, as if a secret farewell.

'I lied to you. I killed Tomasz Król, I had to.'

Green Park was bathed in milky sunshine. The silky light wove itself around the black bare trees as if it were a tangible fabric. London was slowly rousing itself from its Christmas to New Year languor. The city was like a sleepy woman still in her dressing gown. Catesby stared blankly at the empty park bench opposite theirs.

'Rudolf thought he was playing a clever game. When he took over as Król's control, he passed on my name as well as others, some of whom were completely innocent. Rudolf's next step was to blow Król's cover so that he would be arrested and, almost certainly, reveal our names under interrogation. So, in short, I had to kill your sister's boyfriend before that happened.'

Catesby nodded. Henry's confession didn't surprise him. He always knew that Henry Bone was the 'cuckoo' who Tomasz had referred to on his deathbed.

'Of course, William,' since his return to England Catesby had been elevated to first name status, 'you can always trot over to Five and tell them about my crimes. They might even believe you – they would certainly *like* to believe you. But ...'

'You'll stitch me in return. And your lies will prove more convincing than my truths.'

'That's a very bleak way of looking at it.'

Catesby remembered the Orwell couplet:

Under the spreading chestnut tree
I sold you and you sold me.

'Why don't you just tell me?' said Catesby.

'Tell you what?'

'Who you work for? Mischa or Moscow?'

'I don't work for either of them.' There was a tone in Bone's voice that was both indignant and hurt. He smiled and said, 'It's beautiful here, even in winter.'

Catesby felt the pain come back. He imagined Petra sitting on the bench next to him sketching the winter trees.

'To answer your question,' said Bone, 'I work for the United Kingdom – except I prefer to say England, although that sounds a little old fashioned. Personally, I've always found England a beautiful word – I'm sorry if you find that sentimental.' He murmured as if he were reciting a mantra. *England, England.*

Catesby remembered what the art historian had said about Henry, the one thing that no one must ever doubt: *Henry Bone loves this country.*

'No, William, I don't work for Moscow. But,' Henry paused, 'I have covered and protected those who have. And I'm not the only one who has done so. If our actions amount to treason, the hangman is going to have a very busy day.' He paused. 'Sometimes knowing secrets means making difficult choices.'

'Kursk?' said Catesby.

'Correct. Bletchley knew the German plans for Kursk well in advance of the battle. Bletchley also knew about new tanks and weapons that could have wreaked havoc against the Russians. But our government decided not to share the information. The reason given was that doing so might alert the Germans to the fact that Enigma had been broken. Would,' smiled Bone, 'such information have been withheld from British or American forces for the same reason?'

Catesby wearily shook as head as if he were a schoolboy giving sir the desired response.

'Of course not, and it never was. If a close friend and colleague of mine had not passed on the Enigma intercept to Moscow, the war might have dragged on for years and millions more died. Instead, Kursk was the beginning of the endgame. Hitler was finished.'

'Good.'

'What's wrong, William?'

'Nothing, go on.'

'You know that I was part of the Kursk cover up?'

'I thought so.'

'I protected the man who passed on that information. And yet there are those who point a finger at our former colleague and shout, "Traitor!" Do you know who I'm talking about?'

Catesby said his name.

'That's one of them, but not the one I meant. He was never a traitor, William, but he is the most successful triple agent in espionage history. The Russians trusted him completely because of Kursk – and earlier services rendered.'

'He wasn't your so-called "triple agent". Catesby looked at Bone for the first time. 'Your friend was a double agent who was doubled back under duress.'

'How do you know?'

'I'm guessing.'

'Maybe you're right.' Bone stared across the park at the bare trees. 'Do you remember '48?'

'Berlin blockade?'

'No, just before that. When Stalin had one and a half million troops in place waiting for the order to take West Berlin. Our Berlin garrison was a derisory 20,000 or so. The main topic at JIC meetings wasn't how to fight the Russians in Berlin, but how to evacuate what was left of our troops.'

'And me.'

'And you, William. My dear friend saved your life.'

'How?'

'He passed on false information to his Soviet controller about the size of the American atomic arsenal and Washington's willingness to use it. He grossly exaggerated American strength and caused Stalin to think again – and go for a blockade instead. He later did the same during Korea. Some may call him a traitor, but he did a great deal to win Word War Two and may have prevented World War Three.'

'And the winner of the Oscar is …'

'Your cynicism, William, can be a bit tedious.'

'And your lying is even more tedious.'

Henry tapped the footpath with the tip of his umbrella. 'What's your version of events?'

'If your friend was passing on disinformation to Moscow it was because you and the DG were standing on his testicles. But it was awfully clever.'

'What was clever?'

'Not arresting him – I've even heard he's back on the payroll as a part-timer.' Catesby smiled wanly. 'But the clever thing is the message you're sending to his boss at Moscow Central. Comrade Serov knows that your friend's cover was busted a long time ago. So what do the comrades make of the fact that your friend has never been arrested and still has a job at SIS? Brilliant. Moscow can never be sure of the truth. They'll never know which intelligence is genuine and which is disinfo plant.'

Bone was smiling at the grey sky. 'The truth, William, is a lot more complicated than you realise. And I don't know it all either – but I do know that Bill Harvey is still baying for your blood.'

Catesby shrugged his shoulders.

'But Harvey doesn't believe you killed Rudolf. He thinks you were alone on that yacht.'

'Is that what you want him to think?'

'Yes. Harvey thinks you outed Rudolf to Mischa and then stole his yacht to make a getaway.' Bone leaned forward on his umbrella. 'He thinks you were incapable of killing Rudolf. Bill Harvey is the sort of American who thinks Brits are mincing whores with neither courage nor competence. He's obviously never been in a rugby scrum or faced a fast bowler. They don't understand us.'

'Henry?'

'Yes.'

'Who did out Rudolf to Mischa?'

'I think Mischa knew all along, but couldn't act because he didn't have enough evidence and because Rudolf was too popular with Mielke and the Stalinist knuckle-draggers. So he used you.'

'I don't believe that. It was a stroke of sheer luck that Rudolf didn't kill both of us.'

'Do you think Rudolf would have been stupid enough to leave a sharp object lying around in the boat's galley? I think Mischa gave Petra the knife. And, if that didn't work, the helicopter gun would have done the job. Mischa wanted to get rid of Rudolf one way or the other.'

'And you wanted him dead?'

'Of course. But not just, as your bleak smile suggests, to protect myself or …' Bone paused, 'for revenge. If Rudolf had succeeded in defecting to Washington, he could have wrecked every British insti-tution from the Cats Protection League to the Houses of Parliament. You think I'm exaggerating?'

'Well, are you?'

'No. Rudolf was a collector of names and incriminating facts. He spoke fluent Russian and had access to the KGB archive. He knew the name of every British politician and intelligence officer who had ever flirted with communism – whether as a student fad or afterwards. And ...'

'Go on.'

'Things weren't straightforward during the war. Russia had been our ally. There was moral ambiguity about what some of my colleagues had done. A lot of us protected them afterwards – and Rudolf knew all our names and all the facts.'

'What was in it for him?'

'Rudolf enjoyed hurting people and humiliating them – and, for some reason, he hated the British. He wanted to bring the McCarthy witch hunt to Britain. He wanted to see us at each others' throats. The American right would have loved it – and they would have loved him too. Hollywood would have made a film about him. In some ways, Rudolf was more interested in celebrity than power.'

'What about his master plan?'

'Rudolf wasn't bright enough to have one – other than the usual Nazi tripe.'

'What's your master plan, Henry?'

'Peace. I suppose you find that sentimental?'

'No.'

'The aim of the Americans,' said Bone, 'is to win the Cold War. Our aim is to survive it ... and surviving it and winning it may not be the same thing. If America and Russia fight World War Three they're going to do it on our turf.'

'You sound like Mischa.'

'Do I? What a coincidence.'

'What are our chances?'

'I don't think we are going to make it to the end of the century. But if we do survive, some of us are going to have to walk a tightrope ...'

Catesby remembered what Henry's friend, the art historian, had said. *And that tightrope stretches and sways between loyalty and treason.*

'... and if we fall, that tightrope might end up around our neck.' Henry Bone looked at Catesby. 'Some of us have to do it.'

Catesby looked at Bone's umbrella. He hadn't changed it, but he had wiped the blood off the steel tip. They both knew that individual players were expendable.

'Do you know,' said Bone, 'the current death figures for a nuclear war in Europe?'

'No.'

'Two hundred million.' Bone paused. 'It's taken a long time to build this place. I'm rather fond of it – even the bits that aren't England. I like old buildings, the way wood and stone crafted by hand is smoothed by centuries. I like olive groves and vineyards. And I know, William, that you like those rare languages – Gaelic, Occitan, Basque, Catalan. I remember you once saying, in one of your more poetic turns, that those languages "cling to tongues like the aftertaste of a precious wine".'

Catesby looked away and whispered, '*Slaap kindje slaap, daar buiten loopt een schaap.*'

'The rest of the world won't get off lightly, but a good deal of it will survive. But not Europe. We're no longer a culture and a place, we're a target …'

Catesby saw that Henry had been distracted and was looking at something. He followed his line of sight. Henry was watching a song thrush hopping through the grass foraging for sustenance to see him through the winter.

'There's a poem,' said Bone, 'called "The Darkling Thrush". It's about a lone thrush singing at nightfall on the last day of the century. The poet imagines the thrush possesses a secret that no one else knows:

Some blessed Hope, whereof he knew
And I was unaware.'

Henry turned to look at Catesby. He could see that Catesby was no longer listening. He was deeply lost in his own grief. Henry Bone sat motionless and stared at his umbrella. He hated what he had done, but he didn't regret it. Henry spoke in a low voice that only he himself could hear. It was a voice heavy with sad loneliness. 'I suppose,' he said, 'that I am the darkling spy.'

Henry looked up. The thrush had stopped foraging. It was listening with tense alertness; every nerve was taut and coiled. The policeman was winter dark, his bicycle oiled and silent, but the thrush had flown for deep cover long before he peddled past.

Acknowledgements

First of all, a very belated acknowledgement to those who introduced me to the worlds I have written about in my last two novels.
The first is Professor David Jordan, former US Ambassador to Peru.
I was a student of Professor Jordan in the 1960s. He was an inspiring
teacher who made me aware of the hard realities of international
relations. The second is a man I know only as 'Colonel Peach' who
was one of our lecturers at the JFK Special Warfare Center. On the
other side, so to speak, I would like to thank all my IG Metall trade
union colleagues in 1970s Bremen for teaching me about the realities of working life in Germany.

Moving to the present time, a big thank you is owed to Julia for
discovering a key image which is part of this book. I am also grateful to Julia for far more than can be listed here. Special thanks to
George Szirtes for his kindness in reading and commenting on the
Hungarian section. George's advice was extremely valuable and I
warmly appreciate his generosity in giving it. Roger Elsgood of *Art
and Adventure* deserves a special note of thanks as well. I am sure
that Roger's excellent advice on script writing has also improved my
fiction writing – especially dialogue.

I must, of course, thank Angeline Rothermundt for her invalu-
able efforts as editor and her flawless judgement. And once again
thanks to Gary Pulsifer and Daniela de Groote, my birth publishers,
for their continued support of their offspring.

Finally, I want to acknowledge the following books and sources:

Aldrich, Richard J. *The Hidden Hand: Britain, America and Cold
     War Secret Intelligence.* The Overlook Press, Woodstock and
     New York, 2002.
Colitt, Leslie. *Spymaster.* Da Capo Press, 1995.

Davies, Barry; Gordievsky, Oleg; Tomlinson, Richard. *The Spycraft Manual: The Insider's Guide to Espionage Techniques*. Zenith Press, 2005.

Hamrick, S.J. *Deceiving the Deceivers: Kim Philby, Donald Maclean, and Guy Burgess*. Yale University Press, New Haven, 2004.

Hennessy, Peter. *Having it so Good: Britain in the Fifties*. Penguin Allen Lane, London, 2006.

Herbert, Zbigniew. As quoted in *Unit 32 East European Poets*. The Open University Press, 1976.

Knightley, Phillip. *Philby: KGB Masterspy*. Andre Deutsch Ltd, London, 2003.

Macleod, Murdo. 'Revealed: Secrets Scots Traitor Gave Stalin that Turned the Tide of War'. *NEWS.scotsman.com* 12 April 2005.

Mailer, Norman. *Harlot's Ghost*. Michael Joseph, London, 1991.

Orwell, George. *1984*. Penguin Books, London, 1990.

Third World Traveler. Operation Paperclip Casefile, 8 August 1997.

Wilson, Edward. *The Envoy*. Arcadia Books, London, 2009.

Wright, Peter. *Spy Catcher*. Viking Penguin, New York, 1987.

A number of real historic events are mentioned in this book and real places are mentioned. A few real names are used, but no real people are portrayed. This is a work of fiction. When I have used official titles and positions, I do not suggest that the persons who held those positions in the past are the same persons portrayed in the novel or that they have spoken, thought or behaved in the way I have imagined.